Influence

Influence

Carl Weber

www.urbanbooks.net

Urban Books, LLC
300 Farmingdale Road, NY-Route 109
Farmingdale, NY 11735

Influence Copyright © 2018 Carl Weber

ISBN 13: 978-1-945855-07-8
ISBN 10: 1-945855-07-X

First Hardcover Printing September 2018
Printed in the United States of America

10 9 8 7 6 5 4 3 2 1

This is a work of fiction. Any references or similarities to actual events, real people, living or dead, or to real locales are intended to give the novel a sense of reality. Any similarity in other names, characters, places, and incidents is entirely coincidental.

Distributed by Kensington Publishing Corp.
Submit orders to:
Customer Service
400 Hahn Road
Westminster, MD 21157-4627
Phone: 1-800-733-3000
Fax: 1-800-659-2436

Langston

1

"Yo, we need gas." The traffic was just starting to ease up as I pushed my Audi Q5 over the Verrazano-Narrows Bridge onto the Staten Island Expressway. It had taken a while to round everybody up, but we were finally on our way back to Howard University after spending Easter weekend back home in New York with our families. My mother had surprised me with the new car as an early graduation present. Elaborate gifts were her way of trying to make it up to us for walking out six years ago. "Hey, y'all, seriously, the gas light just came on. Somebody needs to cough up some cash."

You want to make a bunch of college students shut the fuck up? Put free food in front of them or ask them to chip in on gas. Either way, you're going to hear crickets. I held out my palm while trying to keep my eyes on the road, and let out a couple fake coughs, clearing my throat.

"What'd you say?" my frat brother Krush asked from the seat behind me.

"Oh, so now y'all deaf?" I flipped my sun visor down to block the rising sun from blinding me. "Y'all heard me. Don't everybody go reaching in your pockets all at once." Not one of them made a move to retrieve any money. "Y'all keep playing and the next stop is going to be the Port Authority and the Megabus. You got my word on that."

"Man, why you always got to be so damn dramatic and shit?" asked Tony, who was sitting in the passenger's seat. "You acting more and more like your old man every day."

The car erupted in laughter. Everyone got a kick out of his joke except for me. Tony knew I didn't like anyone joking or talking bad about my father. My pops was my hero. Shit, he was probably their hero too.

"You got a problem with that?" I asked.

There was a quiet pause before Tony said, "No, but you the one with the fancy ride and the rich old man. I'm barely getting by on financial aid and student loans. Give a brother a break, frat." He threw up our fraternity sign, and I heard Krush and Kwesi laugh again from the back seat.

"Tony, leave him alone, bro," Krush said, coming to my defense—or at least I thought he was. "His pops probably didn't have a chance to get to the safe after paying eighty grand in cash for this ride, so he only gave him five hundred to get through the week."

Once again, laughter filled the car, so much so that it was pissing me off.

"First of all, my dad isn't paying for this car," I said, shutting the fellas up. "My mom bought it for me," I mumbled under my breath, only making Krush's point.

"Aw, man!" Tony roared in my direction. "You should have just kept your mouth shut, you little spoiled bitch. Ain't nobody giving your rich ass any gas money."

The peanut gallery cosigned from the back.

I glared at Krush and Kwesi through the rearview mirror. "That's a'ight." I nodded knowingly as I put my eyes back on the road. "Next time y'all want a ride to McDonald's late at night, I hope you got your walking shoes, 'cause I ain't getting up. You got my word on that." This time, I threw up our frat sign.

"Damn, it's like that?" Tony asked.

"Yeah, it's like that." I mumbled under my breath, "See if y'all be laughing then."

I felt something lightly rest on my shoulder. I looked to see Kwesi's hand with a fifty-dollar bill in it.

"For you, my brother," Kwesi said in his African accent.

"Thanks." I took the bill out of Kwesi's hand. "At least one of you was raised right," I added sarcastically.

"Dude, we're all struggling college students," Krush chimed in from the back. "What do you expect?"

"Yeah, besides," Tony said, turning to look at Kwesi, "if my granddaddy's face was on the money in my country, I'd be generous too and whip out fifty bucks." He nodded toward Kwesi. "Ol' *Coming to America* mafucka."

This time even I joined in the laughter.

"That was a good one," I said to Tony. "But even if your granddaddy was Bill Gates, you wouldn't chip in a dime, because you're a . . ."

We all turned to Tony and in unison said, "Cheap-ass bastard!"

Tony gave us the finger, just like he always did. He could dish it out, but he couldn't take it worth shit.

"Eff all y'all," Tony said.

"Eff all y'all," Krush mocked in a feminine voice, letting Tony know he was being a baby.

It didn't matter how many times we clowned Tony about being cheap; he always caught an attitude. I would have thought he'd be used to it by now, since for the last four years at school, that's all we ever did was call him out for being so stingy. Tony, Krush, Kwesi, and I always had each other's backs, but whenever it was time to come up off some money, that's where Tony drew the line. I couldn't remember that last time he chipped in on a pizza or paid for a round of beers, but you best believe he was always full and had his thirst quenched before the night was over.

Yeah, he was cheap all right, despite having two part-time jobs, but then again, I tried to remember where he'd come from. Tony was raised by a single mother in Brooklyn's Marcy Projects. He had two brothers who were Bloods gang members, but he busted his ass and made it to Howard, where he was about to graduate with honors in accounting. Cheap or not, I had to admire him. He'd broken the cycle.

Realizing I was going to have to make do with Kwesi's contribution, I turned my focus back to the road. I hadn't even driven for a tenth of a mile before there was a clicking sound, a hiss, and then the car filled with something other than our laughter and music.

I sniffed the air. "Shit! Tell me that's not what the fuck I think it is."

"Depends on what you think it is."

I glanced in my rearview mirror at Krush just in time to see him take a long hit from the blunt he was caressing between his fingers.

"What the hell?" I shouted. "I know you're not smoking that shit in my car!"

"Yo, stop being such a pussy. Ain't nobody gonna harm your precious leather." Krush took another hit of the blunt.

"I'm not worried about the leather. I'm worried about jail," I said.

"Whatever." Krush snapped his head in my direction and gave me a serious look in the rearview mirror. Krush was what you might call a wannabe thug. He got good grades in school, but he dressed and acted like a gangbanger, despite coming from a middle-class Queens home. "It's weed, bro, not heroin. Ain't nobody gonna throw us in jail over a blunt."

"Yeah, don't get your panties in a bunch, Lang," Tony added, reaching his hand back for Krush to hand him the blunt. Once again, the peanut gallery in the back seat thought the wannabe comedian to my right was hysterical.

"Y'all laughing and shit, but I'm serious. We're four black guys riding around in an expensive vehicle, smoking weed. You don't think anything is wrong with that picture?" I couldn't have been the only smart one in a group of four college students. Impossible. "We're a racist cop's dream."

"Man, fuck the po-lice! Ain't nobody scared of them racist bastards!" Krush shouted.

"He does have a point, Lang," Tony said in Krush's defense. "Don't nobody care about weed anymore. Just drive the damn car."

I thought about their argument that marijuana wasn't a big deal. It wasn't like it was heroin or anything. It was a blunt. We all have a blunt now and then. Maybe I was being a little dramatic, as Tony would say. But hell, I was the son of a lawyer and judge and the sibling of two lawyers; being dramatic ran in my blood. On the flip side of things, I'd just been reflecting on how long and hard we'd worked on getting our degrees. Was this even worth the risk?

"I don't know. If you ask me, I think this is stupid," I said, shaking my head. "We are in New York, not Colorado."

"And if you ask me," Tony said, "you need to take a hit of this here." He extended the blunt to me. "After three days with your pops, you need to decompress. That's one intense brother."

"I know that's right." Krush took the liberty of removing the blunt from between Tony's fingers. Through the rearview mirror, I watched him inhale and then extend the blunt to me.

"I don't need that shit. I got something better than drugs." I lifted my phone to my ear. "Siri, call Symone."

"When in doubt, call the pussy." Tony laughed as the car's Bluetooth took over and the phone rang. "You one whipped brother, Lang."

A sudden whooping sound jolted my attention to the rearview mirror, and my heart dropped at the sight of flashing lights behind my car.

"Oh, shit!" I said, my stomach tying up in knots.

Michael

2

I hadn't been there long, but already my dream job at Goldberg, Klein, and Hooper was exceeding my wildest fantasies. This morning, I'd been asked to join some of the firm's top lawyers in the conference room. Sure, I'd dreamed of sitting with the big boys someday, but never expected that it would happen after only a few months on the job. Yet, there I was, along with six other junior associates, around the eight-foot-long conference room table with three partners and three senior associates of one of New York City's most prestigious law firms. We were all facing the door as we waited for the opposing counsel to come in, like a pride of hyenas about to ambush a wounded water buffalo. The aura of power in the room was palpable, and it had my heart pounding with anticipation. My God, it was like having sex for the first time; the only way to describe it was total euphoria.

There were only certain cases that required this type of attention from the firm, and anything to do with The Rockman Group was one of them. They were by far the firm's largest client, and despite the fact that this wasn't a very big or flashy case, our salt-and-pepper senior partner, Walter Klein, had insisted he personally take charge. Walter was the LeBron James of the profession. He was the main reason I'd pursued a job at the firm. I mean, what basketball player wouldn't want to play with LeBron?

"This should be pretty cut and dry," Walter said confidently to Mark Spencer, a senior associate who was bucking for partner. "My guess is we can settle it for half a million."

I watched Mark's uneasy body language. He paused before speaking, probably to make sure he chose his words carefully.

"Well, with all due respect, boss, that might be a little low. The other side does have a pretty good case. And Rockman has authorized us to settle for one point five million, and get it over wi—"

Mark's reiteration of the client's wishes, of which I'm sure our senior partner was aware, was unceremoniously cut off by Walter's icy stare. The entire room became quiet and perhaps even a little cold. It was that type of power that made me want to work for Walter. I wanted the opportunity to be guided and mentored by someone as educated, experienced, admired, respected, and maybe a little bit feared by everyone who came into contact with him.

Despite my stellar grades and the fact that I had passed the Bar on my first attempt, it had been a shot in the dark when I applied to G, K, & H. The firm only hired six new associates each year, and that group had never included more than one African American, if they hired any at all. But somehow, I became one of six hired out of three hundred interviewed, and I was grateful for that fact every single day I came to work and got to watch Walter Klein in action.

"Offer them half a million and they'll be skipping out of here like they won the damn lottery," Walter insisted, pointing at the file in front of him. "I know the firm that's representing the plaintiff. I know them well, and not from having gone against them in the courtroom." He let out a derisive laugh. "They're a bunch of ambulance chasers. Trust me, they'll take this offer."

"How can you be so sure?" asked Dara Grant, a senior associate and the only female in the room.

One of the other senior associates next to her let out a snort. "Haven't you seen those ridiculous commercials they air on cable television?"

"The one with the attorneys mean-mugging the cameras, strutting around and talking about how big and bad they are?" Mark asked.

"Yes." Walter nodded. "The only thing more ridiculous than those stupid commercials is that goofball Steve Robinson who runs the firm. I've had him sitting across from me three times, and all three times his dumb ass has left at least a half a million on the table. Why should this time be any different?"

"You're right. It's best we stay optimistic," Mark conceded, thumbing through the file in front of him. In perfect timing, the conference room phone rang. Mark was quick to hit the intercom button.

"Is that our ten o'clock?" he asked.

"Yes, sir," the receptionist replied.

"Have them take a seat. Someone will be out for them in just a bit," Walter chimed in.

"Will do, sir," the receptionist said then ended the call.

Peter Weisman, one of the junior associates like myself, rose from his seat.

"Where are you going?" Walter barked.

"I was going to get our appointment, sir?" he replied nervously.

"Sit down, Mr. Weisman," Walter ordered.

With a confused look on his face, Peter sat down, curiously eyeballing his colleagues.

"First, you let them stew for a bit." Walter explained his reasoning for not immediately bringing in the opposing party. "Let them wait for you, sit down, get bored with last month's *Sports Illustrated* we have lying out there. Then when you're ready, and only when you're ready, you stick the fork in 'em." We all sat back, delighting in Walter's tactical insight.

Everyone else at the table sat with tablets and pen in hand, ready to take notes when we finally let the opposing counsel in. But not me. I wanted to observe how Walter moved and how he handled this entire meeting from start to finish. He wasn't a senior partner for nothing, and I was blessed with a front row seat to watch and understand why. He was who I aspired to be.

Tony

3

"Roll the windows down! Roll down your fucking window, Tony!" Langston yelled at me frantically.

I opened the window, glancing over my shoulder at the NYPD police cruiser with its lights flashing behind us. Can't say I wasn't nervous, but Langston's ranting and raving was just too over the top.

"Oh God. Oh God. I told you. We're going to jail," Langston continued.

"Lang, man, calm down, bro," Krush said quietly from the back seat.

"How you gonna tell me to calm down, Reem? This is all your fault. You're the one who brought that shit in my car."

"Let's not attack each other. We are supposed to be brothers," Kwesi added, but it had no effect on Lang's continued hysterics.

"Put that thing out, Tony! Put that fucking thing out!" he yelled at me.

"Just chill, bro, seriously. All this yelling and shit ain't helping," I replied, putting out the blunt in the ashtray. I slammed the ashtray closed, trying not to sound as nervous as I really was. "We have to keep levelheaded and act like everything is everything. Now, pull the car over before we have a real problem."

"Yes, those are wise words," Kwesi added. I wondered if he was also trying to hide his nerves, because dude sounded as cool as a cucumber.

I glanced back over at Langston, who was finally pulling the car over.

"Now, everyone try to act normal. You got that?" I looked to Krush and Kwesi, who nodded their understanding. The look on

Lang's face and the beads of sweat on his forehead, on the other hand, were anything but normal. In fact, it screamed of guilt.

"Take a deep breath, frat. We gonna get through this," I said softly.

I looked in the passenger's side mirror at a white NYPD highway cop who was flying solo. We weren't in Brooklyn anymore, that was for sure, because the cops didn't fly solo in my neck of the woods—at least not the ones who wanted to stay alive.

"This is useless," Langston said, now waving his hands around to fan the smell out of his driver's side window. "And the evidence is right there in the ashtray."

"Not anymore it isn't." I opened the ashtray and took the blunt out.

"What are you doing, man?" Langston asked me in panic. "You got the evidence all out in the open now. Oh God, we're definitely going to jail.

"What evidence?" I said before putting the blunt in my mouth and swallowing that shit down. "Now, would you calm down? If your old man could see you now, he'd probably disown you."

Langston stiffened in his seat at the mention of his pops. Meanwhile, I glanced in the side mirror, where I could see the officer headed toward us wearing reflective sunglasses, an eight-point stormtrooper police hat, knee-high boots, and a heavy-ass leather jacket. I turned my face forward as he walked up slowly to the driver's side of the car.

"License, registration, and insurance," was all he said.

"Uh, morning, officer. Beautiful day, isn't it? Supposed to be almost seventy today," Lang stuttered as he reached into the glove compartment for his paperwork.

I didn't know what the fuck he was thinking. This guy wasn't the cashier at Starbucks. He was a damn cop, a white cop at that, and he didn't look like the type who'd be interested in Lang's small talk. I wanted to scream at the top of my lungs, but I couldn't because it felt like the cop was staring directly at me. Damn, we really needed Lang's ass to just chill.

"Where you boys headed today?" the officer asked Langston in a casual yet condescending tone.

"School." Kwesi, Krush, and I all spoke in unison. It went without saying that none of us really wanted Langston to do the talking. He might give the guy our life stories.

"We're, uh, all students, sir," Kwesi said. He was doing the right thing, but I was not sure if his accent was helping. "We were visiting with our parents. We are on our way back to the university."

"Is that so?" the officer asked, his tone now laced with suspicion.

"Yes, sir," I answered.

"What school you fellas attend?" the officer asked.

"We attend Howard University," Kwesi continued.

"That's down there in D.C., isn't?"

"Excuse me, officer, uh . . . I didn't get your name," Langston asked as he handed him the documents.

The cop narrowed his eyes at Langston. "Officer Blake. You want my badge number too?"

"No, thank you, Officer Blake. I can see that just fine from here," Lang replied. I stared at him with my mouth open, and I was sure the guys in the back were doing the same thing. "What I would like to know is why you pulled me over," Lang continued.

What the fuck was he doing? He had taken that comment about his old man a little too seriously for me, and now he was using this condescending, lawyer-like tone that was sure to piss this cop off and put us all in deeper shit.

"Yeah," Krush said boldly. "Was we speeding or something?"

I wanted to reach back there and slap him. With a smirk on his face, the officer bent down and began looking in the back seat at Kwesi and Krush.

Shit, we're in trouble. I squirmed uncomfortably in my seat. Why couldn't these idiots have just kept their mouths shut?

"No, you weren't. As a matter of fact, you were going a little slow to be highway driving. I thought something might have been wrong. But from the smell of things,"—he sniffed the air, moving back to the driver's window—"I think you were just a little distracted."

Langston let out a nervous laugh. "What do you mean by that, Officer?"

Officer Blake slowly rose back up into an erect, standing position. "Come on, now. You mean to tell me you don't smell that?" He let out a taunting chuckle.

This wasn't looking good. We were so busted, but all hope wasn't lost. Regardless of what the officer smelled, I'd made sure there was no evidence. I would probably be shitting green plants for a week.

"Smoke was damn near seeping through the windows," Officer Blake said. "And the way you all were fanning when I was calling in your plates . . ." His face straightened up. "I think you boys were smoking pot in here."

"No," we all said in unison. I shot a side glance at Langston and shook my head.

"We were fanning because I passed gas, officer," I said, waving my hand in my face. "It was really bad. If you smell anything, that's probably what it is."

"Do you boys think I'm some kind of idiot?" Officer Blake asked, sounding quite offended.

"Noooo," we all said, once again in unison. The fact that the scent of weed was filtering through the car, out of the windows, and probably smack into his face didn't help. In short, we were fucked.

"Look, Officer, despite what you may think you smelled, there's no evidence we were smoking or had any marijuana," Langston stated with confidence. I swear I wanted to punch him in his arrogant-ass face. "So, if you're going to give me a ticket, give it to me, because we have a long ride to D.C.," he finished.

"You know what? You're a real smart-ass, aren't you?"

"He didn't mean anything by it, Officer," I said, making a last-ditch effort to smooth things out. Langston blew up that effort in an instant.

"Don't speak for me, Tony," he snapped. "I have my own mouth to speak with. And no, Officer Blake, I'm not a smart-ass, but I do know my rights."

All I could do was lower my head, because Lang was talking with the swagger of his father. His tone was all ego, and I knew there was no turning back for him now that he was channeling his father's personality.

One by one, the cop gave us the once over. His glare was almost menacing. "Okay, everyone out of the car."

"Thanks a lot, Lang," I grumbled as I reached for the door handle.

Bradley

4

"Please have a seat. Someone will be with you momentarily."

Her tone was pleasant enough, but I could see right through the receptionist's fake smile the second she hesitated on the phone. I glanced down at my watch. We were right on time. Certainly, they were all prepared for us and waiting. They had probably met a good fifteen minutes earlier, joking about how easy this win was going to be. The smiley receptionist was just doing her boss's dirty work, but that was okay. That was her job and what she got paid for. Well, her bosses were in for a big surprise when they saw my black face, because while she was paid to be a gatekeeper, we got paid to win cases, big cases. I say "we" as in me and my son, Lamont, my first born and protégé.

I smiled knowingly then looked toward the chairs in the reception area. Turning to walk away, I realized when I reached the chairs that Lamont hadn't budged. He and the receptionist were busy giving each other googly eyes. Had I not known this case was going to be a slam dunk, I probably would have allowed Lamont to use his skills of persuasion to play the young lady to our advantage, but we could tuck that quarter away in his pocket and save it for a rainy day, because this case was over the minute I had agreed to take it. Besides, I couldn't be a hypocrite when it came to Lamont and his overly active libido. That was something I always stayed on him about. The legacy of the Hudson family was that of viciously dangerous, smart lions, not dogs in heat, and I wasn't going to allow him to damage something I had worked decades to create.

"May I, uh, offer you a drink?" the receptionist asked, staring directly at Lamont as she sat up a little straighter so that her ample breasts were front and center on display. "Water? Coffee? Anything?"

"We're good. Thanks." I jumped before Lamont got a chance to rattle off what his choice of "anything" might have been. At least the sound of my voice reminded the two of them that someone else was in the room, as they both shot their attention to me. "Come on, Lamont."

He broke his gaze from the receptionist and settled in to the seat next to me.

I had to give opposing counsel credit for good taste. Their reception area was more comfortable than my office. They showed poor judgement in leaving a hungry shark waiting, but good taste in decor. Clearly, Lamont was impressed as well. He plopped down in a chair, slightly bouncing to test the comfort and durability of his chair.

"Now, see, Pop, this is how we need to model our office to go after the big dollars. Downtown, a view, valet parking . . ."

"We already have big clients, and we are not leaving Harlem. We own the building."

"That doesn't mean we can't have a second office down here."

Watching my son in all of his excitement over the chair, it reminded me of the year he got his first two-wheel bike under the Christmas tree. He had tested out that seat pretty much the same way he was doing now. A slight smile teased my face.

"You've been thinking about this a lot lately, haven't you?"

"I believe we owe it to ourselves to get a slice of the corporate cake, Pop. It's a logical growth area for us, and we've never tapped into it."

I looked around at the flat-screen television with a picture so clear I felt as if Chris Cuomo was sitting in a chair right across from me. The fish tank was large enough for a damn mermaid to live in. I must say that I wouldn't have been mad to have my nameplate attached to one of those heavy cherry wood doors, but that wasn't really my dream. Maybe it was Lamont's, but not mine. I'd always been an uptown guy. For me, the pillar of success was having my adversaries in the courtroom become immediately perturbed at the sight of my name on a court document because they knew I was going to be hard to beat. I took pride in the number of cases that I had won over the years, and although I didn't have the flashy office and wasn't the most well-liked attorney in the state of New York, I had earned the respect of my colleagues and those on the bench. That was my dream, and I'd pretty much lived it for the past twenty-five years.

"I believe we owe it to our client to stay focused on why we're here." I looked straight ahead at the wall.

"But you have to admit that—"

The annoyed look I shot Lamont let him know to dead the conversation and prevented him from finishing his thought. However, it didn't stop him from looking around the office in continued amazement and envy.

"Looks like they're playing right into our hands," Lamont said quietly.

"Yep, it's part of the game, that's all," I said, noticing him anxiously checking his watch. It amused me that now that he was no longer entertained by the receptionist or the exquisite office decor, he was concerned about how long we'd been waiting. "They want us to think they have more important business than what we're here for. They figure we'll sit out here and be impressed by carpets, paintings, and pretty women. Bullshit like that."

"Yeah, but, of course, we know better." He chuckled, and I laughed right along with him. He was still learning, but sooner or later, he'd no longer allow himself to be distracted by the pretty things that opponents would put in his path to try to throw him off his game.

Lamont's phone rang. The volume sounded as if it was on its max.

"Kill that," I said, shooting him an annoyed look.

"All right," he said while checking his caller ID screen. "But it's Dez." He looked at me to see if I would change my position just because his sister was on the line. It didn't, especially since she was supposed to be at this meeting with us.

Just then, I saw a gentleman heading toward us. "I don't have time to listen to her excuses right now. I'll deal with her later. This looks like us."

"Hello," the gentleman approached and greeted. I stood as he extended his hand.

"I'm Peter, one of the associates." We shook hands. "My apologies for the wait. We had some important business to finish up."

Important business, my ass. Lamont and I shot one another a look, a smirk dancing at the corner of my mouth.

"I completely understand, Peter," I said.

"Good. Then why don't you follow me?" He extended his hand toward the large, wood door.

Langston

5

When you're driving down the highway and you see a black or Latino guy sitting on the side of the road while the cops search his car, have you ever wondered what that guy must feel like? Well, now had I firsthand knowledge of it because my frat brothers Kwesi, Krush, Tony, and I were all sitting on the grass in cuffs, watching the cops search my car. It had to be the most humiliating feeling I'd ever experienced.

There were two cops on the scene now, but Officer Blake, the one who pulled us over in the first place, was the one searching the car, while the other cop stood in front of us. I glanced over at the fellas, but none of them would look my way. I couldn't believe they were blaming this on me when it was Krush who had pulled out the blunt and started smoking it.

After about ten minutes, Officer Blake walked over from the car, looking annoyed. He took a deep breath and relaxed his tense shoulders as if trying to regain his professional composure. "Now, I'm going to ask you boys one time whose pot this is." He held up a quarter-ounce bag of weed, slowly walking by each of us. "And if I don't a get satisfactory answer, I'm hauling all your asses in, and we can sort it out in front of the judge."

Fuck! Things had just gone from bad to worse.

Tony, Kwesi, and I shared concerned looks with one another. Of course, we knew who the weed belonged to, but Krush would never fess up. I had already been accepted into law school. No way did I need this on my record.

Dammit, what would Dad do in a situation like this?

I really couldn't be sure what my father would do, but he was never one to back down, so I took my best guess that he would put up a fight. Clearing my throat, I tried to display some of my father's strength as I spoke up.

"Officer Blake," I started, "I didn't give you permission to search my car. You do know you're violating my rights against illegal search and seizure, don't you? You didn't have a search warrant, and I didn't give you permission." I sat up and forced myself to stare at him in an imitation of confidence—though I was scared to death at the moment.

"Lang, will you shut the fuck up?" Tony snapped.

Blake laughed walking over to the other cop. "Maybe these kids need to be taught a lesson. Just because you go to college doesn't mean you know everything."

The other cop nodded, looking directly at me. I had obviously misjudged the situation and was starting to wish I'd just kept my mouth shut.

"For the record, young man, the moment I smelled marijuana, I had probable cause to search your vehicle. So, I didn't need your permission or a search warrant," Blake responded.

There was nothing I could say in response.

"Damn, Lang, to be going to law school next year, you sure are stupid sometimes," Tony added. I didn't respond to him either, because he was right.

"So, what do you want to do?" the other cop asked Blake. "You wanna haul their smart asses in?"

Before Officer Blake could respond, Krush raised his hand, surprising us all. "Officer, that's my weed." From the look on Krush's face, he'd surprised his own damn self. As a matter of fact, he looked like he wanted to change his mind and use that raised hand to point his finger at one of us. Thankfully, it was too late. Officer Blake had already acknowledged his admission of guilt. Krush swallowed hard, no doubt realizing he was now at the point of no return. "These guys had nothing to do with it. In fact, Langston tried to stop me." Krush turned to me with an apologetic look on his face. "I'm really sorry, bro. This is all my fault. I take full responsibility."

I gave Krush a forgiving head nod. I really felt sorry for him, but as heartwarming as this Hallmark moment was, we were certainly not out of the woods yet. I turned my attention to Officer Blake to get a feel for how he was receiving this display of brotherhood. Sure, I was glad Krush had stepped up, but I was now scared to death for him.

Officer Blake stood there for a moment, looking from Krush to me. "Get up." He pointed at me and then Krush, gesturing with his hand for us to stand. I don't know about Krush, but I was so scared that my legs felt like jelly as I struggled to my feet. It was difficult to balance with handcuffs on, and I got no help from either officer.

Officer Blake stood in front of Krush. "I respect your honesty, young man, and your loyalty to your friends," he said to Krush. "Anything else in the car? If I call for a dog, is he going to find anything?"

"No, sir," Krush replied.

"You sure? I'm not going to find anything else in that car, am I?" This time he was speaking to us all.

"Yes, sir, the car's clean. Just our suitcases and some groceries from our moms," Krush answered.

"Okay, I'm going to give you a citation for the marijuana, and your wannabe lawyer friend here a ticket for reckless driving." He placed his hand on Krush's shoulder, firm enough to make Krush squirm uncomfortably. "Leave the pot alone, kid. I'm letting you off because you're in college and I don't want this on your record. Next time, you might not be so lucky."

I swear to God, he sounded like he was delivering a public service announcement, like he'd been rehearsing that line in the mirror for years and finally had the chance to put his skills to work. Krush let out such a huge gust of wind I'm surprised it didn't send Officer Blake stumbling backward.

"Thank you, Officer," Krush said.

"And you," Blake said, directing his comments to me, "next time you run into an officer, keep that jailhouse lawyer shit to yourself." He looked at me with a huge smile of conquest on his face. I did not return the expression. Maybe he wasn't the racist I thought in the beginning, but this experience had not made me a fan of the police.

"Thank you, Officer," I said, forcing myself to deliver the words in a respectful tone. "But there won't be a next time. You can trust me on that."

"Sorry about the cuffs, fellas," Officer Blake said as he and his partner uncuffed us. I felt like a freed captive from a slave ship when Officer Blake removed the cuffs from my hands. "But you all had me outnumbered without backup."

We opened our mouths but looked at one another before anyone dared to speak.

"We understand, sir," I finally replied in a humble tone. Everyone else nodded meekly in agreement.

He pointed at the ground. "Now, grab a seat while I write up these tickets and we'll let you be on your way."

The four of us eyed one another and, in unison, exhaled a sigh of relief. We wiped some of the dust off our clothes and the sweat from our foreheads, then sat back on the grass. I'd never been happy to receive a ticket before, but considering the alternative was being arrested, I was grateful and anxious to get that piece of paper in my hand. I just wanted to get the hell out of there.

Before that could happen, a police K-9 SUV pulled up, and a large, overweight black cop stepped out. He looked stern, like he didn't tolerate any bullshit, as he stared at us sitting on the ground.

I remember thinking, *Shit, I'm glad he wasn't here five minutes ago.*

"Blake, Collins, you a'ight?"

"Yes, sir, Sergeant Lanier," Officer Blake replied.

"What you got here?" Sergeant Lanier asked. He turned his attention toward us.

"Just a bunch of kids smoking pot, Sarg." Officer Blake shooed his hand, brushing the situation off. "Boys being boys. You know." He shrugged. "I'm citing one for the dope and the driver for reckless driving."

"Just a little pot, huh?" Sergeant Lanier's eyes lit up, and he might as well have been drooling. As minor as the situation may have seemed to Officer Blake, from the looks of Sergeant Lanier, the molehill was about to become a mountain.

"Yes, sir," Officer Blake replied nervously. Whoever this Sergeant was, he obviously put some kind of fear in Blake's heart.

Sergeant Lanier let out a *harrumph* as he looked to his comrade. "You run all their names through the system for warrants?"

Sergeant Lanier remained silent for a moment. Mental wheels were turning in his head; it was evident from the expression in his eyes. Sensing a shift in the atmosphere, my frat brothers and I exchanged concerned looks. I could feel the sweat beads pooling on my forehead again.

"No, I uh . . ." Officer Blake started. "I didn't think it was necessary. They're just college kids, Sarg." Once again, he downplayed the scenario.

"Hmmm." Sergeant Lanier stood in front of Krush, staring at him hard.

"Is, uh, there a problem, Sergeant?" Blake asked.

"I don't know. You tell me. This one here looks more like a gang member than a student."

This Lanier person, having only spoken a few words, came across as a . . . an Uncle Tom. And if the use of the N-word wasn't so offensive, I'd be inclined to suggest he was one of those house ones. Neither one could mean us any good right about now.

My friends and I eyeballed one another again. Although none of us spoke a single word, our eyes said the same thing: *What's with this asshole?*

Sergeant Lanier walked over toward Officers Blake and Collins with his hands in his pockets, eyeing us suspiciously. I glanced at my boys. We may as well have been riding the largest rollercoaster in the world as green as everyone's faces looked. I felt like I was about to throw up. There was something about this cop that didn't sit right.

"I say we let my dog search the car," Sergeant Lanier said to Officer Blake. "You know I've got a sixth sense about these kinds of things."

"That you do." Officer Blake let out a nervous chuckle.

Sergeant Lanier was throwing his rank around, and it was obviously intimidating Officer Blake. That was apparent from the hard swallow that rolled across his Adam's apple, not to mention the way his face was splotched with bright red. Officer Collins was so quiet that if he weren't standing in front of me, I would have thought he wasn't even there. This entire scene had me baffled. The tables were turned in the most peculiar way. Officer Blake looked so subservient I swear he was about to start calling Sergeant Lanier *massa*. I'd started out assuming that

Blake was a racist white cop, but it turned out it was a black cop who really had bad intentions for us.

"Why don't we run the dog around the car a few times and see what she finds?" Lanier suggested. He was halfway to his car before Blake could even reply.

"Sure thing, Sarg," Blake replied. He turned to us and shrugged his shoulders, looking almost apologetic.

Lanier opened the rear door of his SUV and let out what looked like a black Labrador Retriever. It was on a leash, and it jumped around excitedly as Sergeant Lanier led it over to my car.

He looked down at the dog and commanded, "Find it, Princess."

Michael

6

Peter left to retrieve the opposing counsel and came back in no time. As the conference room door opened, the smile on Walter's face was sadistically cheery. He turned toward my end of the conference table with a subtle "We got this" nod. This was one of those moments I had been looking forward to all my life, and I could hardly contain my excitement. I leaned back in my chair, wishing I had a bag of popcorn, because this was going to be quite a show—or so I thought. Within a matter of minutes, things took a dramatically unexpected turn, and the show I'd been hoping for turned into a three-ring circus, and we were the ones who looked like clowns.

The first of the morning's surprises was that the two men who followed Peter into the conference room were black men in expensive, tailored suits. One looked to be in his fifties, and the other maybe around thirty, and both of them obviously spent a lot of time and effort to look as good as they did. Walter had described them as ambulance chasers led by a goofball, and I had imagined a couple dudes in baggy suits with bad haircuts. I sure wasn't expecting these brothers, whose suits clearly cost more than I would make in a month as a junior associate.

I turned to look at Walter, and his reaction told me these weren't the guys he had been expecting either. His face dropped, and all the color left his cheeks. He jumped up from his seat as if someone had lit a fire under his ass. I was confused by his reaction, and from the look on my colleagues' faces, so were they. No one seemed to know what to do or say as these two lawyers strolled confidently into the room.

"Hudson? What the hell are you doing here?" Walter asked, with an edge to his voice.

"You don't sound too excited to see me, old friend." The older man gave my boss a casual smile. "It's been a long time."

"Ah, yes, yes, it has. The Klippinger case, if I remember correctly," Walter replied, sounding nervous. It shook me a little, because I'd never seen him this way before, and just five minutes earlier he'd been so damn cocky about how this meeting would go and how he was going to make them his little bitches.

"Still as sharp as ever, aren't you, Walter?" Hudson replied, adjusting the lapel on his suit.

"So, to what do we owe the pleasure?" Walter asked, very obviously trying to regain his composure.

"I'm here for our ten o'clock. We're representing the Cooper family." The way he spoke sounded almost poetic. This guy had a swagger about him like no other lawyer I'd ever seen before.

Walter shot Mark a perplexed look. "I thought you said the Cooper family was represented by—"

"They are—I mean, they were. . . . There must be some mistake." The paper in Mark's hand shook as he looked helplessly at Walter. "It says right here that their attorney is Philip Hall of Dorf, Robinson, and Associates." Mark turned to Dara, another senior associate, attempting to shift the heat to her. "What's going on?"

"I don't know. I spoke with Philip last night," Dara replied as Mark went back to digging through his paperwork.

"There has to be some mistake," Mark said, peering over his glasses.

The black lawyer looked slightly amused by all of this. I wasn't the one in the hot seat, but even I was feeling embarrassed right about now. This guy, whoever he was, had the upper hand for sure, no matter how long we'd kept him in the waiting room.

"There's no mistake. The Coopers were initially represented by Dorf, but we were brought on this morning," Hudson said to Mark in the manner a father might speak to a half-wit son. Then he turned his attention to Walter, who was looking very uncomfortable. "My son, Lamont, and I will be taking over as lead counsel from here—unless, of course, you have an offer."

Mark looked at Walter, who cast his eyes downward and remained silent. The look of defeat on his face was pitiful.

"Well, Walter, do we have an offer?" Hudson asked.

Walter didn't answer.

Mark suddenly found his courage and seized the moment, speaking up. "We're authorized to offer five hundred thousand."

A sudden laugh came from Hudson's son. Hudson, however, wasn't laughing. He looked insulted as he stood glaring at Walter. My boss remained silent, as if he were still trying to comprehend what was happening.

"Of course, we haven't totally familiarized ourselves with this case, but . . ." Hudson looked at his son and extended his hand. The younger man pulled out a file from his briefcase and handed it to him. "We already see strong class action possibilities," Hudson said, opening the file and flipping through it. "But, considering we're old friends"—he closed the folder dramatically—"I'm thinking five million will make everyone happy." He handed the file back to his son.

Mark burst out laughing, then stopped when he realized none of us had joined in.

"You find it funny that we aren't asking for more?" Hudson said to Mark. "I'm sure we easily could, but five million sounds like a fair and reasonable number. Don't you think so, Walter?"

He focused like a laser beam on Walter, who struggled to make eye contact.

I still didn't quite understand how things had gone so wrong so quickly, but I could tell from Walter's behavior that this was bad—real bad. Finally, in a tone that was as stoic as the look on his face, Walter said, "I'll have the paperwork drawn up and a check over to your office first thing in the morning."

"Great." Hudson nodded. "Good to see you again, Walter. Say hello to that lovely wife of yours."

The son had a smirk on his face as he tucked the file back into his briefcase.

"Will do, Hudson." Walter exhaled loudly.

Peter went to stand.

"Oh, no, we appreciate your hospitality, but we can find our way out. I'm sure you have plenty to discuss," Hudson said, then looked at his son. "Ready?"

"Absolutely." He turned to the others in the room. "Have a wonderful day. It was a pleasure."

Hudson led the way out of the conference room, looking back over his shoulder before they exited to say, "By the way, Walter, nice reception area. It's very impressive."

As soon as the door closed behind them, chaos ensued.

"Five million? What was that?" Mark demanded.

"That was Bradley Hudson," Walter said in a defeated voice.

"Wait a minute. *The* Bradley Hudson? The one who took down Russ Oil and TK Shoes, and got TJ Winter off for murdering his wife?" Mark asked.

"One and the same." Walter sighed.

"We studied his Marcus Hall defense in law school," Dara added, clearing her throat to proclaim, "If the witness blacked out, that's reasonable doubt." She was mimicking a male voice.

Peter must've noticed the look of confusion on my face, because he explained, "That was one of his famous lines from that trial."

"I know," I said. "I just can't believe I didn't recognize him." Hell, every black lawyer knew who Bradley Hudson was. He was half the reason I went to law school. I'd studied all of his big cases. I guess in the confusion of this unexpected scene, I hadn't put two and two together.

"He's a legend," Dara added.

"Dammit, Dara, we know who the hell he is, okay?" Walter said.

But she was right; he was a legend, possibly more like an African god. Anyone who had the ability to instill that kind of fear in Walter was at least that.

"Get the hell outta here, all of you!" Walter shouted to the room.

No one else moved at first, but I quickly gathered my things, rushed out of the room, and headed down the hallway. In the distance, I could see Bradley Hudson and his son waiting for the elevator. I doubled my pace and was able to catch them just as they stepped on. The doors were beginning to close, so I held my hand out to stop them. I glanced around, making sure no one saw me before I hopped inside.

"What floor?" Lamont asked me.

"Uh, all the way down," I said.

He looked at the button for the first floor, which was already lit. I knew I had to talk fast, because the chances of us making it all the way to the bottom floor without stopping for more passengers was damn near impossible in our busy building.

"Mr. Hudson, that was very impressive lawyering," I told him.

"Thanks, young man. I appreciate your approval." Hudson smiled at me. "How long have you been here at the firm?" In this small space without the other lawyers around, he seemed much more personable.

"Only a couple of months. I finished Harvard Law this past Spring," I replied proudly.

"Harvard Law, huh? I'm a Howard University man myself. So is my son, but Harvard is a decent school. I'm sure you'll do well. This is one of the top firms in the city."

I could feel the elevator slowing down, and I realized we were about to stop. I had to move quickly. "Thank you, sir, but I have a question."

"Ask away."

I took a deep breath and blurted out, "By any chance, are you hiring?"

He had an amused look on his face. "Don't you already have a job?"

"Yes, sir, I do." I nodded. "But as one black man to another, there is nothing these people can teach me that you can't and more. I'm sure you understand where I'm going with this."

The doors began to open, and the small crowd of people waiting stepped inside with us. Hudson didn't respond. We spent the remaining ride down in silence. When we reached the lobby, everyone stepped off except the three of us.

Hudson turned to his son and said, "Lamont, give him a card. Make sure it's one with my personal cell."

I was so excited I felt my ear jump into overdrive.

Lamont reached inside of his suit jacket and passed me a business card as they stepped off the elevator.

"Give me a call when you're ready, and we'll talk," Hudson said.

"I'll call you this afternoon," I said without hesitation.

"Understand one thing, young man. We aren't all fancy like they are down here. We work for a living." He smiled at me as the elevator doors began to close.

"I can see that, sir, and I'm ready," I replied, watching him walk toward the exit.

Langston

7

Sergeant Lanier and his dog had already searched the front seats of the car, and he was in no way as considerate as Officer Blake, having thrown everything out of my glove compartment and tossing around every item in my center console. I was sweating bullets the entire time. Yeah, I was a little nervous, but I was more pissed. This was bullshit if I ever smelled it. I didn't give a damn if he had a dog or not. If Officer Blake hadn't found anything other Krush's weed, what the hell made this asshole think he would? He was just being a dick—a big, black Uncle Tom dick—and he was just wasting our time looking for something that he wasn't going to find.

"You're not going to find anything, 'cause there's nothing in there!" I shouted. I got the evil eye from Officer Blake and my boys, but at that point, I didn't care. I couldn't wait until Dad ripped these punk-ass cops a new asshole.

"God damn gangbangers," Sergeant Lanier said under his breath as he stood outside the car with his empty hands on his waist. He hadn't found a damn thing, but he wasn't giving up yet. He led the dog to the back seat. "Come on, Princess. Let's find it."

A minute or two later, he was once again assuming the position outside the car with his hands on his hips, shaking his head. It was obvious he was disappointed that he'd come up empty. I thought he would finally give up and agree to let us go, but then he stopped shaking his head and looked toward the trunk of my car. He walked over and pulled on it.

"Open the trunk," he ordered.

For a second, I thought about protesting, because it was within my rights to refuse to let him search the car. But then I realized it wasn't worth it. If I antagonized him, he might just drag us all down to the precinct to spite us. I might as well just let him get the search over with. Then, all we would have to do was clean up the mess he made, and we could be on our way. I aimed the key fob toward my car and clicked the trunk emblem. It immediately popped open. Sergeant Lanier looked as eager as his black Labrador to start searching.

"You're not going to find anything in there either," I said, knocking the smile right off his face.

When the trunk opened, a few bags fell right out onto Lanier's feet. We'd had that trunk stuffed to capacity. Hey, we might have been independent black men, but who doesn't take laundry home to Mama when visiting from college?

"Lang, will you shut up?" Tony snapped.

"Listen to your friend, kid. You're not making this better," Blake whispered as we watched Lanier kick the bags out of his way.

He pulled a Louis Vuitton and a Ralph Lauren bag and dropped them carelessly to the ground. The dog started pacing around the bags.

"What the fuck, man? That's my bag! That shit is worth more than you make in a week." Krush yelled. He was about to stand up, but Blake placed his hand on his holster.

"I'd calm down if I were you, young man."

"But that's my shit," Krush snapped angrily.

"Let the Sergeant complete his search so you boys can get outta here."

"Chill, Reem," I said, looking up at Blake. I could feel the anger in all of us intensifying, but we fell back and let Lanier continue without interruption.

When the trunk was empty, he'd pick up one bag, unzip it, and throw it to the ground so the dog could sniff it. Then they would move on to the next. He looked up at us, laughing as clothes and groceries spilled on the ground.

When he threw one bag, Tony went to make a move, but I held my arm out, halting him. "Don't do it, man. My pops is going to handle this. You best believe that." I said it loud enough for everyone to hear. "This is Staten Island. We don't need another Eric Garner."

"What was that, college boy?" Sergeant Lanier cupped his hand around his ear, daring me to repeat it.

I bit my tongue and tightened my lips, refusing to speak the words again. He was going to get his real soon.

"Thought so." He let out a snicker and then continued digging through the trunk.

I tucked in my bottom lip and bit down to keep myself from crying. I was so heated that tears of anger were starting to form in my eyes. The last thing I wanted was to stand there crying on the side of the road like a little bitch. My boys would never let me live that down. This would all be over in a little bit. I just had to keep my composure and hold on for a while longer.

"Satisfied now?" I asked when he'd gone through all our bags and the trunk was empty. "You gonna put our bags back in the car?"

Sergeant Lanier looked defeated, but not done. "Come on, Princess. Up, girl."

I couldn't believe it, but that fool had his dog jump up in my trunk and start sniffing around. I glanced over at Tony, who was shaking his head, but I shifted my attention back to the car when I heard the dog scratching and barking in my trunk. Lanier turned to us with a satisfied grin as he escorted the dog out of the car and back to his truck. He then walked back to my car and submerged himself in the trunk. After a few tense seconds, he popped back out and strutted over toward Officer Blake, carrying a cloth bag. He said nothing, just simply opened it up wide for Officer Blake to peek into.

The expression on Officer's Blake face did more than concern me. It downright scared me. Something was wrong. That was evident from the way the two cops were ogling the bag.

The fellas and I shot each other questionable looks. Our eyes silently demanded that whoever knew what the two cops had found so interesting should speak up. But no one said a word as Sergeant Lanier placed the bag on the hood of his car. The next thing I knew, he was taking out a rectangular package wrapped in grey duct tape. What the fuck was that? I watched as he used his keys to cut it open. He dipped his index finger into it and tasted the contents of the bag right before a sinister smile took over his face.

"I told you I have a sixth sense about this kind of thing," Lanier bragged to Blake.

"You certainly do, Sarg," Officer Blake replied. The look on his face was a mixture of anger and disappointment. He'd tried to give us a break, and now he had just been humiliated in front of his superior officer.

"Now, would anyone like to 'fess up to this?" Sergeant Lanier asked, holding up the brick of drugs. Nobody said a word. "That's what I thought."

Desiree

8

"Girl, put your records on, play me your favorite song. . . ."

I woke up to loud, off-key singing coming from the bathroom. I rolled over onto my side and blinked my eyes in an effort to focus. Bright sunlight streamed through the blinds and created a prism design on the wall, causing me to realize it was much later than I thought. I glanced over at the clock radio.

Shit. I overslept.

I stood up, taking a moment for my body to get adjusted to shaky legs. Where the fuck were my clothes? I spotted my skirt and blouse laying neatly on the back of a chair in the corner of the room, but I didn't see the lace bra and thong I had worn under them. A flashback of hands slipping the lace from my shoulders, then lips exploring my breasts, filled my head and gave me a hint of where I might find the lingerie. I tossed the duvet and sheets back and ran my hands through them. Bingo! I'd found the bra, but where were my panties?

Think, Des, think. I couldn't believe I had allowed this to happen. I was going to be late again—the third time this week. I grabbed my cell phone off the desk and called my brother. There was no answer. I called again. This time, it rang once and went straight to voicemail.

"Hey, it's me. I know I screwed up, but I need you to cover for me. I'm on my way. I'll just meet you all at Klein's office in half an hour." I ended the call.

"Good morning, sunshine." The bathroom door opened.

"Don't *good morning* me. Why didn't you wake me up? You know I should've gotten up when my alarm went off the first time." I shook my head as I pulled my skirt over my hips without underwear.

"I did wake you up . . . then I put you back to sleep." She laughed. "What's the big deal?"

"The big deal is that I'm gonna get cussed out and maybe fired," I explained, reaching for my blouse.

"You're not gonna get fired over this. That's crazy."

"Okay, you keep thinking that," I snapped, searching the room one last time for my missing underwear. "Where the hell are my panties?"

"That sexy-ass thong you were wearing last night?"

"Yes."

"It's in here," Jerri replied, walking over to her night table. She opened it and pulled out my panties.

"What's it doing there?"

"I wanted a souvenir," she purred in a sultry voice.

I looked at the hands now holding my black Victoria's Secret thong and recalled the feeling of those same fingers as they trailed along my collarbone. I snatched my underwear, ignoring both the seductive smile and the sexual tension in the room.

"You're crazy," I said, more to myself than to her as I slipped on my panties. "I should've never come over here last night."

"Don't be like this. Fine, okay, I'm sorry I didn't wake you up. But you're not going to be fired. You work for your damn daddy, for Christ's sake."

"You just don't get it, do you? I'm a Hudson. I'm not supposed to miss meetings. This is unprofessional no matter who I work for. It may not seem important to you, but—"

"Des, calm the hell down. You're always so uptight. I thought I relaxed your ass last night and this morning." She let out a long, dramatic sigh, like she just couldn't handle me.

"Jerri, I'm serious." I slipped my foot into one of the heels.

"I am too. About you, about us."

Jerri took a step closer to me, and I stepped back, nearly stumbling because I had only one shoe on. She caught me just in time and gave me a smile that I couldn't resist returning. I stared at her as she stood in front of me wrapped in a towel, beads of water dripping from her short, curly hair onto her neck and shoulders. She was so damn sexy. That was one of the main reasons I was with her. I had never been attracted to a woman before, but Jerri was different. She was gorgeous even though she really didn't want to be, so she didn't flaunt it. There was something irresistible about the way she embraced her sexuality, which included her masculinity.

When we met, she'd had no problem letting me know what she wanted and how she wanted it. What she wanted was me, and she wanted me now. I tried explaining to her that I was a straight woman and happily single, but she persisted. As she pursued me, she made me laugh and think, and I began to enjoy her. It was then that I realized there was a mutual attraction, and before I knew it, I found myself doing something I thought I'd never do: date a woman.

"I'm not doing this. I'm getting ready to leave," I said, putting some distance between us before I allowed myself to give in to temptation.

"You're already late, Des. Being later won't matter." She touched my neck seductively.

"No, Jerri," I said, walking past her.

She grabbed me by the arm. "Des, wait."

I turned around to face her and glanced down at her hand. She released her grip as I asked, "What?"

"Are you coming back later?"

"I'll call and let you know once I see how my day goes," I told her.

"What time?"

"I don't know yet."

"I wanted to cook dinner for us. Netflix and chill, and maybe even if you're lucky . . ." She stuck her tongue out playfully.

"Dinner sounds nice, but no promises," I told her. Jerri was an executive chef and an amazing cook. They say that the way to a man's heart is through his stomach, but Jerri's cooking had definitely helped her find her way into mine, that was for sure.

"And you can provide dessert." She gave me a suggestive look. "Lord knows I enjoyed that tasty treat I had last night. Oh, and let's not forget this morning."

"I should've never let you go down on me this morning," I shot back, throwing cold water on her little fantasy. "That's why I'm late now. I'll call you in a little while." I headed out of the bedroom.

"Wait. Does that mean you're going to spend the night?" Jerri was right on my heels as I entered the living room.

"It means I have to go, Jerri, and I'll call you later."

"Can I at least get a good-bye kiss?" she asked.

I turned around, and the simple kiss I planned to give her turned into a minute-long exploration of tongues. That woman could kiss, and I enjoyed it, so much so that I found myself wanting to take off the clothes I had just put on. I ended the kiss, rushed out the door before she could stop me again, and made my way to my Benz that was parked in the visitor space of her parking garage.

In the car, I called my brother Lamont again.

"Yeah," he answered.

"I need you to cover for me. I'm running late for the meeting, but I'll be there in twenty minutes," I said.

"Don't worry about it. The meeting's over. Dad's headed back to the office, and I'm on my way to see a client."

"Dammit, is Daddy pissed?" I asked.

"What do you think? Of course he's pissed," he replied with no sympathy in his voice.

"Guess I'll go take my medicine from the High Bishop Hudson," I said sarcastically and hung up. My mind began working to figure out a lie believable enough for my genius of a father. I prayed for God to send a miracle that would get me out of the mess I would be facing when I arrived at the office.

A call came in from an unfamiliar number, interrupting my brainstorming session. Thinking it was probably one of the pro-bono clients I had taken on, I answered through the car's Bluetooth.

"Hello."

"Des." I recognized the voice but didn't have a clue why my little brother was calling me from some strange number.

"Lang?" I asked.

"Yeah." There was a lot of background noise, but I could still hear the distress in my brother's voice.

"What's wrong? Where are you?"

"I'm in Staten Island." There was an uncomfortable silence, during which I could hear my heart start pounding in my chest. "Des, I've been arrested, and I need your help."

Tony

9

I'd been in this closet of an interrogation room in one of the police precincts in Staten Island for what seemed like forever by the time the two white detectives walked in and sat down. One of them was really skinny, and the other one was fat, but both of them were assholes as far as I was concerned. I had felt like I was in a nightmare from the moment I'd been tossed into the back seat of Officer Blake's car with Krush. Kwesi rode in the back of Lanier's car, and Langston rode in Collins' car. They'd probably separated us so we wouldn't coordinate our stories, and I'm not gonna lie; their tactics were intimidating the shit out of me.

"Anthony, is it, or do you prefer Tony?" the skinny cop asked. I'd heard enough stories from my brothers to understand that these two cops were about to try to play that good cop/bad cop shit on me.

"Tony," I said weakly.

"Okay, then, Tony it is. My name's Detective Cutter, and this is my partner, Detective O'Malley. Can we get you a soda? Something from the snack machine?" Cutter was obviously taking the good cop role today.

"Yeah, I'll take a Pepsi and some chips if they got 'em." My brothers always told me that if you get arrested and the cops offer you shit, always take it, because you never know when you might see it again.

"Sure, thing, Tony." Cutter got up and left the room.

"I see you're wearing your colors proudly. So, when did you get initiated?" Detective O'Malley asked. Maybe I was wrong; maybe he was the good cop. I mean, why else would ask me about my fraternity?

"Spring of 2016. Me and Lang went over the burning sands together," I told him with pride.

He looked a little puzzled as he sat back in his chair. "You and Langston, the kid driving the car?"

"Yeah, that's my LB," I said proudly.

"I'm kind of shocked. He doesn't look the type, I would have thought maybe the kid Krush, but not the other two."

"Please, me and Lang brought them in," I said definitively.

"I see," he replied as his partner walked in the room and took his seat. "I appreciate your honesty. It'll go a long way to get you boys outta here."

"They didn't have Pepsi, so I got you Coke," Cutter said, sliding the can of soda and a bag of Wise potato chips across the table. "So, what did I miss?" He glanced back and forth between his partner and me.

"Well, Tony here just verified that all four of them are members of the Bloods and that he and Langston brought the other two into the gang," O'Malley told his partner.

My mouth dropped open. What the fuck was this guy talking about?

"That true? All of you are Bloods?" Cutter asked.

"Hell, no, that's not true! This fucking guy is a liar. He's trying to entrap me. I ain't no damn Blood," I stood up and yelled.

"You little piece of shit! Don't you call me a liar," Detective O'Malley said, making it clear now he was, indeed, the bad cop. He stood up and pointed at the ceiling in the corner of the room. "You think we're not recording this interview? We got you throwing your little gangbanging buddies under the bus. Now, sit your ass down."

We glared at each other for a few seconds before I said, "I am not a gang member—and I'm definitely not a member of the Bloods. None of us are members of the Bloods."

"Yeah, and neither are your brothers Aaron and Adonis," Detective O'Malley retorted.

I have to admit he'd caught me off guard with that one. How the hell did he know that so fast?

"Man, that's my brothers, not me. I'm not a Blood."

"So, you admit your brothers are both Bloods?" Cutter asked.

"Yeah, it ain't no secret." I exhaled angrily. "But me and my friends aren't."

"What do we look, stupid?" O'Malley shouted as he slammed a file he'd been holding on the table. "Your brothers are two of the highest-ranking Bloods in New York City. They've been charged with drug trafficking and who knows what else. Meanwhile, you're wearing a bright red fucking shirt, driving around with two keys of heroin!" He laughed out loud. "I'm sorry, but that screams you're a fucking Blood to me. You're all fucking Bloods."

This guy was on another planet, so I turned my attention to Cutter. "We are not Bloods. We're members of a fraternity—at a *university*," I added for emphasis, "and crimson and cream just happen to be the fraternity colors. Check with the school."

"Oh, we will," O'Malley snarled.

The two detectives glanced at each other. I wasn't sure about O'Malley, but I think Cutter might have believed me. Damn, at least I hoped he believed me. I'd been trying to run from my brothers' gang affiliation since I was thirteen. If it hadn't been for my mom recognizing my potential and putting her foot down, I'd probably be down with them right now. But she had, and I was not, thank God. Now if I could just get these cops to believe me.

An hour went by, and I found myself nodding my head numbly for the millionth time. At this point, I didn't even know what question O'Malley was asking. The detectives had been drilling me with questions then leaving the room abruptly, during which time I would sweat with anxiety, only to return and drill me with more question. My brain was frazzled. I couldn't make sense of this entire situation.

"So, are your brothers the ones who gave you the heroin, or did you and your buddies get it all by yourselves?" This O'Malley son of a bitch was getting on my nerves even more than Sergeant Lanier, that black bastard.

I threw my hands up in exasperation. "I don't know anything 'bout no fucking heroin from my brothers or any fucking body else, a'ight?" My college vocabulary had gone to visit its cousin in the projects. Stringing my words together properly and using grammatically correct English just wasn't on my list of priorities anymore. "I done told you the drugs ain't mine."

"Okay, then, whose are they?" O'Malley asked.

"I'on't know."

"Yes, you do. Now, did your brothers give them to you? If so, maybe we can arrange for you to go home."

"How many times I gotta tell you? I don't know nothing about no dope, and my brothers ain't give me shit."

I knew what was going on here. They were trying to trip me up. I didn't have to be a rocket scientist to know the oldest trick in the book. I was sure he thought if he asked me the same thing over and over in different ways, it would wear me down. This technique had extracted many confessions from both the innocent and the guilty. I was sticking with my story, though, no matter how many times he asked. Tired, hungry, even if I had to take a piss, my answer would remain the same. My only question was, how many more times was I going to have to repeat my answer, and how many people would I have to repeat it to before someone actually believed me and let me go home?

Krush

10

I guess the Staten Island police didn't pay their gas bills, because it was cold as shit in that little room they had me locked up in while I waited for someone to come tell me what the fuck was going on. I pulled my hoodie over my head and laid my arms on the table as a pillow, but before I could put my head down and get comfortable, I heard the door open. Two cops walked in and sat down.

"Hey, Kirby, my name's Detective Cutter, and this is my partner, Detective O'Malley. Can we get you a soda?"

"Man, fuck you and fuck a soda, my name is Krush. When the fuck do I get my phone call?" I asked as I sat back in my chair and crossed my arms over my chest. It was all an act. I was scared as fuck, but I wasn't gonna let these motherfuckers see me sweat.

"You can make a call in a few minutes, right after we have a little chat," Cutter said all nice and shit.

"What the fuck y'all want?" I huffed.

"We wanna know whose dope that was in the car," the fat cop snapped.

I shook my head. "I don't know, but it ain't mine."

"Look, Krush, Officer Blake already told us that you admitted to the pot. From where I stand, it seems like you're a standup guy. So, why play games? You might as well cop to the heroin and get it over with. Save us all a lot of time. That way we can go to the ADA and tell him you cooperated."

I leaned back in my chair again. "Look, I ain't copping to shit!" I regretted ever having opened my mouth about the weed being mine. Shit, I thought I was doing the right thing at the time, but who would have ever thought it would land me in this kind of trouble? If I had known that, I would have kept my big fucking mouth shut.

"You wanna get your frat brothers all caught up in your mess?" Detective Cutter asked. "Aren't you guys supposed to be tight, like real brothers?"

"We are brothers, and they're not caught in my mess, 'cause I ain't got shit to do with it!"

Who was this Cutter guy kidding? I had no doubt he'd been to each and every one of our interrogation rooms, trying to get us to talk. He'd probably fed the other guys the same bogus line about brothers. I hoped like hell they saw through his bullshit like I did.

He kept pushing. "Well, if it wasn't yours, then whose is it?

"I can't tell you what I don't know." I was trying to remain calm, but these motherfuckers were stressing me the fuck out. If they were getting to me like this, I wondered what they were doing to the other bros. Although Lang had a tendency to run his fucking mouth like he already had a law degree, I was pretty sure that he and Tony could maintain until Langston's pops got here and got us out. It was Kwesi who I was afraid would screw it up for everybody. I didn't know what crazy-ass Sergeant Lanier had said to him on the way over, but Kwesi looked petrified when I saw them bringing him inside. I wanted to tell him to stay strong and keep his mouth shut, but he never even raised his head to acknowledge me. Damn, I sure could've used a blunt right about now.

"Damn it, I swear to God, if you boys don't get to talking—" O'Malley slammed his fist on the table, unable to hide his frustration.

"You'll what?" I asked, fighting like hell to keep from grinning. His outburst told me he wasn't getting anywhere in this interrogation process, not only with me, but with the fellas either.

"I'll throw all your asses in Rikers, and then we'll see how tough you are," he threatened. "Sooner or later, one of you is gonna crack and wanna go home to Mama, and that's the one who's gonna get the deal." He leaned in until we were almost nose to nose. "And if not, all of you are going to prison for a long time."

When I swallowed, it felt like I was trying to force a whole boiled egg down my throat. I'd been trying not to lose my cool in front of these guys, but I didn't want to show them fear either. It sure was getting hard trying to hide it.

"Stay silent all you want," O'Malley said, "but somebody will talk first, and it's the one who talks first who's going to get out of here. Just remember that, kid." On that note, he stood and headed out the door. He was probably on his way to the next interrogation room to try to get the next fella to talk.

Hopefully, none of them would say a word.

Kwesi

11

Never in my wildest dreams had I expected to ever be arrested for drugs. Guilty or not, with something like this on my record, getting accepted into medical school would be no more than a pipe dream. Even worse, what would my family think about the humiliation and embarrassment I was bringing to them? My mother and father had worked so hard to bring us all to this great country, and they wanted nothing more than for me and my brothers and sister to succeed. I could already see the shame on my father's face, and I had not even called him.

The two detectives that had come by earlier walked into the room again. They were nice men and had treated me kindly despite my accident.

"You all cleaned up?" Detective Cutter asked, taking a seat and placing a McDonald's double cheeseburger, fries, and a soda in front of me.

"Yes. Thank you very much for the sweatpants. That was very embarrassing."

"Eat up before it gets cold. These things happen. You're a college student, not a gangbanger," Detective O'Malley replied, taking a seat next to his partner. "Hell, if I was arrested for something I didn't do, I'd probably piss myself too."

I lowered my head in shame. "May I ask you gentlemen a favor, please?"

"Well, that depends on what it is, but we'll see what we can do," Detective O'Malley replied.

"Please, please, do not tell my friends that I relieved myself in such an embarrassing manner. I try to conduct myself around them with dignity and pride."

"Sure, sure," O'Malley replied kindly. "We weren't planning on telling anyone, and as long as you help us, we will definitely help you."

"Thank you," I said humbly. "What do you want from me, Detective?"

When the police took us into custody and were about to separate us, Langston announced that we should not talk to the police until his father arrived. But that was before I met Detectives O'Malley and Cutter. I was sure once Langston found out that they were trying to help us, he would not mind me explaining things.

"I wanna know the truth about those drugs and which one of your buddies they belong to. Because I'm sure they don't belong to you," Cutter said.

"I do not know, Detective. And to be honest with you, I do not think any of my friends would do this."

"You can stop trying to protect them, because when it boils down to it, if you think they are going to protect you, then you are sadly mistaken. I've seen it a million times."

He sounded sincere, but I had to disagree with his assessment of my frat brothers. "They are my friends. They are honest. You'll see. We do not advocate drugs. This is all one big mistake, and things will get figured out."

"They don't advocate drugs, huh? So, why did your friend Krush admit to the pot Officer Blake found in the car?"

He was making a point I could not refute, and what made it worse was that he began laughing like I'd just told a joke.

"I like you, Kwesi, but you really are naïve." He laughed for a while more before he managed to get himself under control. Then, he appeared deadly serious. "That heroin did not magically appear in the trunk of that car. Someone put it there, and you need to be honest with yourself. If you didn't put it there, who did?"

"I don't know."

"Then whoever did is playing you, because if you guys were such brothers, he would just come out and admit it so you wouldn't get in trouble. Isn't that what you would do?"

Once again, he was making a valid point, but where did that leave me? Here, stuck in jail, that's where. I didn't want to believe that Langston, Tony, or Krush would tell lies to save themselves; lies that would land me behind bars for God knows how long. My family would be so disgraced. I'd have nothing.

However, I was not going to give up on my friends, my brothers. "But there has to be another explanation," I said hopefully.

He rolled his eyes and sucked his teeth. "Forget it." He shooed his hand. "I can see right now you are going to be the first one they throw under the bus. I mean, technically, you're not one of them, because you're African and they're American. They are going to stick up for each other first. So, guess who, more than likely, is going to end up doing the time for everybody?" He walked over to me and pointed hard against my chest with each word he spoke. "You are, buddy. And it will be a damn shame because, like I said before, I like you."

The more I sat there and listened to Officer O'Malley, the more I began to question my friendship with my frat brothers, who I'd only known a little under four years. Were they really as loyal and steadfast as I'd convinced myself they were? After all, we'd never been in such dire straits before, so I'd never had to test their commitment. What if Detective O'Malley was right and they would react to the pressure being put upon them? Would my being African suddenly separate me from them, giving them a reason to accuse me? I had no way of knowing for sure. Maybe, just maybe, it was time to start thinking about myself.

James

12

"Okay, what's so important that you dragged me down here?" I walked into the small corridor of rooms that peered into the interrogation rooms through one-way glass, stopping in front of Assistant District Attorney David Wilkins.

"Him." David pointed toward a young black man on the other side of the glass, sitting at a table and looking lost. I walked closer to the glass and studied the boy. He didn't look like much to me, but Dave Wilkins wasn't the type to call me down from the Staten Island DA's office, where I was the assistant district attorney in charge of all criminal cases, over something trivial.

"He doesn't look like a serial killer. What's he here for? Murder?"

"No, drugs," Dave said. "Highway patrol picked him and his three buddies up on the expressway with two kilos of heroin."

"That's some serious weight for a kid his age. Is he talking?"

"Not yet, but he's already pissed himself he's so scared. A day or two in Rikers and he'll crack like an egg," Detective Roger O'Malley replied. O'Malley was a lazy bastard about a year from his retirement. I'd always thought of him as a racist, although he was smart enough to keep his worst thoughts to himself when I was around. He knew I'd beat his ass if he ever pulled that bullshit on me.

I turned back to ADA Wilkins. "Okay, Dave, they found a couple keys of dope in the car of four kids. What's the big deal? This sounds like a no-brainer to me. You could have handled this yourself. Why am I here?"

"I thought it was a no-brainer too, until I found out one of the suspects is the son of Bradley Hudson," Wilkins replied, staring at me as he waited for my reaction to the name.

I could barely believe my ears. "What did you just say?"

"You heard me. One of the suspects is the son of Bradley Hudson." David smiled as if he'd given me a gift. "So, I think that's a good enough reason, don't you?"

"Hell fucking yeah," I said, turning back to the glass with enthusiasm. "It's like my birthday and Christmas all wrapped up into one. So, this kid's the weak link?"

"Pretty much," Dave replied.

"Okay, we have to move fast, 'cause we're not going to be up against some local yahoos from the island. Tell me everything you got on this kid."

O'Malley glanced at a file. "His name's Kwesi Adomako. His parents are college professors at Queens College and SUNY Stony Brook here on work visas. He, along with the other three, attends Howard University."

"So, whose dope is it?"

"We don't know. O'Malley and Cutter don't think it's this kid's, though."

"He's too weak," Cutter said.

"O'Malley, get this kid down to central booking ASAP. I want him in the system and in Rikers before we move the other three out of the building."

O'Malley got up and headed to the door.

"You did good, Dave, really good, and I ain't gonna forget it," I said.

"That's exactly what I was counting on, James," Dave replied with a smile.

David was a terrific prosecutor, probably second only to me in our office, but he had been relegated to the 121st Precinct as a case officer because of questionable relationships with some of the staff. That was no longer tolerated in this "Me Too" era by our liberal female boss who happened to be the district attorney. Dave was looking for a way out, and he knew currying favor by bringing me a case like this might just do it.

"So, what next?" Dave asked.

"I need you to ride over to the courthouse and make sure this kid gets moved through the system fast. Make sure the judge gives him a high bail. I don't want him on the street anytime soon," I explained.

"Piece of cake." Dave sounded confident.

"You sure about this?" Cutter asked. "They're just kids, and this kid especially isn't going to last very long in the system."

I looked through the window at the kid and O'Malley, who had gone back in there. I looked back at Cutter, who was tall and slim, wearing a dusty blue suit. It kind of reminded me of something one of the cops would wear on the old *Barney Miller* sitcom. "Well, then thank God he's not one of our kids."

"Damn, that's cold," Cutter said.

"No, that's life," I replied. "Oh, and Dave, on your way over to the courthouse, make a few off-the-record calls to the press and local networks. Make sure they know Bradley Hudson's son has been arrested for possession with the intent to distribute. Also let them know that it's one of the largest drug seizures in Staten Island history."

"But it's not."

"Well, I guess they'll have to print a redaction at some point." I laughed, and after a brief pause, Dave and Cutter joined in.

"Man, you really are a cold piece of work," Cutter said.

"Yeah, especially when I'm motivated," I whispered.

David slipped out the door while Cutter and I moved down the corridor to the next interrogation viewing room. I stared at the light-skinned young man handcuffed to the table in the adjoining interrogation room. If I didn't know better, I would have sworn he was staring back at me. "That's him, isn't it? That's Hudson's kid."

"Yep. How'd you know?"

"He looks just like his old man thirty years ago," I told him. "Anyone talk to him yet?'

"No, he lawyered up the minute we walked in the room."

"Smart kid." I headed for the exit.

"Where you going?" Cutter asked.

"I'm going to meet the son of the most famous black lawyer in the world and tell him he's going to jail for twenty years," I replied smugly. "Then I'm going to wait for his father to show up, and I'll tell him the same damn thing."

Langston

13

I'd been sitting in that cramped-up, musty-ass room, staring at the one-way glass ever since we'd arrived at the police station. They'd taken my iPhone and my Apple watch, so I had no perception of time, but I knew it was no longer minutes. It had been at least a few hours. Once I told them I wanted my lawyer, no one had even come in the room to see if I was still breathing. So, I sat there anxiously, my knees bouncing up and down as I wondered when the hell my father would arrive and get me out of this mess. I didn't understand why the hell he wasn't there already.

I sure as hell hoped my sister Desiree believed me when I was able to make that quick call to her; otherwise, we were screwed. If the cops hadn't taken my phone, which contained all my contacts, I would have called my father directly. Like an idiot, though, I didn't have my family's numbers memorized. Desiree's was the only one I could dial from memory, so she was my only hope at the moment.

Stay strong, Lang, The calvary is on the way. Stop being paranoid, I told myself just as the door to the interrogation room opened. The sudden motion scared the shit out of me, but I tried to shake it off.

"Langston Hudson." A tall, well-built black man entered the room and announced my name with authority. He was wearing a much better suit than the two detectives I'd seen earlier, so I assumed he was their superior. I'd been hoping someone would eventually come and tell me what the hell was going on; I guessed that someone was him. I watched without saying a word as he crossed the room and sat down in a chair a couple feet away from me.

I nodded, sitting eagerly on the edge of my seat, although I still wasn't answering a damn question without my lawyer present. To my surprise, he wasn't talking either. He just sat there with a frown on his face, not even looking directly at me. After a few seconds, he came to life—not his body, but his eyes. He bent forward and rested his arms on his knees, hands clasped in front of him.

"I just wanted to introduce myself. My name is James Brown. I'm the assistant district attorney in charge of your case."

I couldn't help it; I laughed. I think it's just because I was so nervous. "Seriously, your name is James Brown? Do you sing and dance?" Then did my best James Brown impression. "Jump back and kiss myself! Heeeey!" I thought that was so funny, despite my current situation, that I was damn near crying—until I looked up and saw his agitated face.

"I see you have your father's sense of humor," he said. That shut me up real quick.

"So, you know my father?" I wiped my hand down my face nervously as ADA Brown jotted something in his notebook.

"Yes, we've met." He exhaled loudly. "I suppose you're going to tell me that the drugs aren't yours."

Shit, of course I was going to tell him they weren't mine—because they weren't. I didn't know how the hell those drugs got in my car. Unfortunately, no one in this police station was likely to believe that. Typical cops, they just wanted someone to pin the crime on so they could call it a win. That's why I was planning to stay quiet until my father showed up to help me out of this mess.

"No," I answered. "I'm not going to tell you anything. I'm simply going to ask for my right to counsel, just like I've been asking since I got here. I refuse to speak without my attorney present."

"Yep, you're your father's son all right." ADA Brown sat back in his chair. "But for the record, I wasn't asking you a question, young man. I was making a statement. Just like I'm about to make one now." He looked directly at me for the first time. "You're going to jail, and it's going to be my pleasure to put you there, because I hate drugs."

"They're not mine!" I snapped at him.

The door opened, and I was a little fearful I was about to get a beat down from the fat white detective who walked in.

"Kid's lawyer's here," he said.

"Finally," I stood with a sigh. Needless to say, I was more than ready to go home.

"Don't get too excited. You're not going anywhere," ADA Brown said forcefully. He then turned to the detective. "By all means, show him in, Detective."

Kwesi

14

"Mister uh, Ad . . . Adam . . . Adamko?"

I stared at the man sitting across the table. "Adomako," I corrected him.

"Oh, sorry. Mr. Adomako, I'm Glenn Morris, and I'll be representing you this afternoon when you go before the judge," the man said.

I was a bit confused by the presence of this scrawny white man who looked barely older than me. I'd known Langston for almost four years, and as far as I could recall, he'd never mentioned a white man working at his father's firm. The Hudsons prided themselves on being a black-owned, black-empowering law firm. Based on the cheap suit and the stained tie this man wore, I couldn't imagine Langston's father hiring him even if he were black. Something was very wrong.

"Are you with the Hudson firm?" I asked.

"Huh? Who? No, I'm with legal aid," he said with no further explanation. "Now, you say you don't know anything about the drugs found in the back of the car. Is that correct?"

"Yes, that's correct. I had no knowledge of it. I was just as surprised as everyone else when the police took it out," I said. "I explained that to the officers, and I'm sure my friends did as well."

I was confused about what was happening. I hadn't seen Lang, Tony, or Krush since being brought into the police station. I had been expecting Langston's father or brother to show up and get us out of there, but it had been hours. Now, this frantic stranger was in front of me, asking me questions that I'd already answered.

"Well, what's going to happen is you're going to be brought before the judge, and when he asks how you'd like to plead, then you simply say, 'Not guilty.' Understand?"

"Yes, I understand." I tried not to be offended by his tone. He was speaking to me as if I were a fifth grader about to be sent to the principal's office. I wanted to tell him that I was on the dean's list and a member of Phi Beta Kappa, along with several other academic organizations, in addition to pursuing a double major in biochemistry and physics. I was not dumb by a long shot.

"Where are my friends? Will you be representing them as well?" I asked.

"No, I will only be representing you," he said. "Your friends have their own representation."

"What?" I was now even more confused. Lang had assured all of us that he would make sure we were taken care of and that we would be fine as long as we stuck together. When did the plan change, and where did it leave me? I wondered if they had somehow been released and I hadn't.

"Don't worry about them," the lawyer said as if reading my mind. "Right now, you need to focus on yourself. Now, you've never been in any kind of trouble, so I'm thinking that the judge will be lenient on you. I don't see the district attorney being a problem."

There was a tap at the door, and he stood up. "Okay, I'll see you when we get in court."

"But, wait! I need to speak with my friends and—"

"That's not possible right now. The only thing you need to be worried about is telling the judge that you're not guilty so we can get you out of here." Glenn gathered the papers from the table and tossed them into his briefcase. Before I could say anything else, he was out the door.

I sat alone again in the holding room, just as I'd been doing for most of the past few hours. My mind was racing, and my stomach was in knots. I wondered if I should have just called my parents, instead of depending on Langston to help me. Why, all of a sudden, was I being represented by a legal aid attorney? I couldn't understand why I was even being brought before a judge. I had told the detectives over and over that I had no idea who the drugs belonged to or how they'd gotten into the trunk of the car. Despite their pressuring me to blame one of my boys, I'd refused. I remained loyal to all three of them, but now, I was wondering if they'd done the same thing for me.

About a half hour later, I was escorted into a small courtroom and led to the defense table, where Glenn was waiting for me. He gave me a reassuring nod, but it did nothing to ease the quivering in my stomach. I glanced over at the attorney sitting across the aisle. He looked stern and stoic as we waited for my case to be called.

"Kwesi Adomako." The court reporter read from the docket.

Glenn motioned for me to stand, and I did. My eyes widened and my jaw dropped as the stocky, older woman began reading off the charges like they were menu items at a fast food restaurant.

"Possession of a controlled substance, distribution of narcotics, intent to distribute narcotics . . ." The list went on and on. I couldn't believe how a simple ride home with my fraternity brothers had led to me being arrested and brought up on criminal charges. I felt like I was in the middle of a nightmare and couldn't wake up.

"Mr. Adomako, how would you like to plead?" the judge, a silver-haired white woman asked.

Glenn looked over at me.

"Not guilty," I said, my nervousness causing my voice to crack.

"Bail?" the judge asked the other attorney.

"Your Honor, these are very serious charges, and we're asking that there be no bail and the defendant be remanded. Mr. Adomako had a large amount of heroin in his possession, and we believe this crime is connected to a major drug ring," the district attorney told her.

"What?" I squeaked.

Glenn touched my arm and shook his head at me, then said, "Your Honor, my client is a college student with no criminal record. The drugs weren't even in his possession."

"They were found in the car that he was traveling in, Your Honor," the district attorney responded. Before Glenn could react, he added, "In addition, Mr. Adomako's passport shows that he has made several international trips over the past few months."

I looked at Glenn and rattled off an explanation. "I was visiting my father's family in Ghana and interviewing for internships."

"Shhhh." Glenn put a finger to his lips then addressed the court. "Your Honor, this is ridiculous."

"Bail is set at one million dollars," the judge said quickly without giving me a second look.

"A million dollars?" I began to feel faint.

"I'll speak with the DA and see if I can get him to request that it be lowered. But I'm telling you right now—if you know who that dope belongs to, you may wanna say something, because that may be the only way you're gonna get out of here." Glenn sighed like he was dismissing my concerns as trivial. My freedom was being taken from me, and the man appointed to represent me sounded bored. How the hell had this happened to me?

Desiree

15

It took almost two hours for me to drive from Jerri's house in the Bronx to the 121st Precinct in Staten Island, where Langston had been arrested. I was still totally in the dark because he hadn't given me much information beyond saying he was in trouble and needed my help. I'd made a few calls and tried to pull a few strings on my way over to find out what he'd been charged with, but being out of law school only one year, I didn't have the contacts or the resources that my father, or even my brother Lamont, had. I was tempted to call Cathy, the firm's office manager/keeper of my father's secrets, but I was sure the moment I mentioned Langston's name, she'd be whispering in my father's ear. For a second, I also thought about calling my father directly, but decided against it. If I knew my goody-two-shoes brother, this was probably an arrest for something stupid like a suspended license or a DWI, but to my father, the seriousness of the offense wouldn't matter. He didn't tolerate any kind of screw-ups from his kids.

"I'm looking for my client, Langston Hudson," I said to the desk sergeant when I walked into the precinct. The young white woman dressed in a blue police uniform peered at me over the top of the thick black glasses she wore.

"Hudson?" she repeated and then began typing something into the computer in front of her.

"Yes, ma'am," I replied politely.

A few seconds later, she glanced back up at me and asked, "And you are?"

"I'm his attorney."

She looked unimpressed. "I'll let the detectives know that you're here. You can wait over there." She pointed to the row of hard plastic chairs lined against the wall near the door.

Detectives? I was starting to think this might be a little more serious than a DWI. My phone vibrated in my purse, so I glanced at the Apple Watch I wore on my arm. Seeing Jerri's name on the screen, I sent it to voicemail. *Not now, Jerri, not now.*

"What exactly is he being charged with?" I asked the desk sergeant.

She stopped typing and looked at me. I detected a bit of annoyance from her that I'd interrupted her bookkeeping or whatever.

"I'm sure Detective O'Malley will explain everything to you when he comes out, Miss," she responded. "Do you have some form of ID?"

I reached into my purse and handed her my license and credentials. She barely glanced at them before she handed them back without a word. I walked over to the chairs and took a seat. By the time I got comfortable, my phone was vibrating again, and I had to send it to voicemail again. Why did she not understand that I worked for a living?

After a few minutes, a heavyset white man in a suit walked over and introduced himself. "Ms. Hudson, I'm Detective O'Malley. You can come with me." He knew my name. I guess the sergeant at the desk had read my credentials after all.

He led me down a corridor to a closed door, where he raised his hand for me to wait while he entered the room. A minute later he came out and told me, "You can go in now."

Inside, I found my brother seated at a table with a bald black man in his fifties who did not look happy to see me. Langston, on the other hand, had never looked happier.

"Des!" he said, and I swear I could see the tension leaving his shoulders.

I looked to the man who sat across the table from my brother. "Why are you talking to my client? I'm sure he invoked."

I glanced over at Langston. The worried look on his face let me know that what I originally thought was a simple misdemeanor had to be much more serious. Fortunately, my brother and I grew up with parents in the legal profession. One thing we learned early on was our rights, and what *not* to do if we ever found ourselves in trouble. I was confident that whatever the detectives thought they would get from my brother, they wouldn't. He knew better than to say anything to them.

"Who are you?" the black man asked.

"I'm his attorney," I said forcefully, wishing my dad could see me now. "And I want to know exactly what my client is being charged with, Detective."

"I'm not a detective. I'm Assistant District Attorney Brown, and your client is being charged with possession of a controlled substance with the intent to distribute. He had two kilos of black tar heroin in his car."

"He had *what*?" I snapped, placing my hand on the wall for stability. *Shit*. I was sure the ADA had picked up on my moment of weakness. Suddenly, I knew I was in way over my head. What I really wanted to do was scream at my brother, "What the fuck is wrong with you?"

"It's not mine, Des. I swear to God it's not mine," Langston blurted out.

"Then whose is it?" the ADA asked calmly.

"Shut up, Langston!" Being in the interrogation room of the police precinct was not my forte, but this guy must have thought it was amateur hour. Caught off guard or not, I was still a Hudson, and we knew our shit. I had to get this situation under control in a hurry.

"I'd like to speak with my client," I said.

"Feel free," ADA Brown replied.

I tilted my head to the side but then quickly positioned it upright, straightening my shoulders to display strength and confidence. I was not about to go into sista-girl mode. Too many people in law enforcement already looked at black women in the legal profession as no more than bitter chicks with bad attitudes, so I was always conscious of how I presented myself. I'd worked too damn hard for people to mistake me for Cookie Lyon, when my aim was to be Olivia Pope.

"Privately," I said to both men.

I turned my attention to Langston.

"We can leave," the ADA said, eyeballing the detective, who stood behind me, to determine whether he was in agreement.

"Yeah, then you two can have all the privacy you'd like," the detective said.

"Yeah, right. I want the light turned on in that integration room." I nodded toward the two-way mirror that was taking up the wall behind the table. My asking for privacy was kind of a joke anyway. Langston knew the drill. Whether the officers were inside the room with us or outside of the room drinking coffee and eating donuts, big brother would be watching—and listening—whether they were supposed to or not. We would only be discussing so much while we were in that building, let alone that interrogation room.

"We won't be far," the ADA said as they walked out.

"Des, those aren't my drugs. I swear to God," Langston said when they were gone.

"First of all, are you okay?" I asked. As much as I hated seeing him there, I was glad that he was still alive and his name hadn't become a hashtag like so many other young black men who'd ended up shot and killed as a result of routine traffic stops.

"I'm fine." He nodded. "Where's Dad? Where's Lamont?"

"I didn't call them. I thought you called me because you didn't want them to know."

He dropped his head. "No! Hell no! We're going to need Dad to get us all off."

"What do you mean *all*? Are there other people involved?" I asked, pulling the chair out and sitting down. I made sure he noticed my quick glance toward the mirror behind him, reminding him of the eyes and ears that were on us before he started speaking.

He gave me a slight nod to indicate that he understood, and then he gave me a brief overview of how he and his frat brothers had ended up here.

"Damn it, Langston!" I said when he got to the part about the bricks found in his trunk.

"I swear I didn't know it was back there. You know me, Des. I don't get down like that." He shook his head, looking more like a preppy teenage nerd who should be headed to the library, not a twenty-year-old man who had just been arrested for drug possession. As bad as the circumstances seemed, there had to be some explanation that didn't include Langston's guilt. My brother was more into books than booze and had been on the dean's list consistently since his freshman year. This wasn't him at all.

"I know you don't. This is some bullshit. I'm gonna go to your arraignment and get you bail. Then we go home and tell Dad about this," I said.

"Des, you can't get just me out of here. You have to get all of us out," Langston said.

"What?" I frowned.

"I'm not gonna leave my boys. If I go, we all go," he explained. "We're in this together."

I stared at him, proud of him for his loyalty, but not exactly pleased that he was making my job a hell of a lot harder. "Langston, I know you and your boys are tight, but—"

"Naw, Des. You help one, then you help us all." He sat back and shrugged.

I exhaled loudly, knowing he was not going to change his mind. Standing, I said, "Let me go see what the deal is. You hold tight."

"Does it look like I'm going somewhere?" He tilted his head to the side with a smirk.

"The last thing you need to be giving me is a smart-ass comment," I warned, opening the door and stepping outside into the hallway. I looked from one end to the other, searching for the detective or the ADA. I knew they hadn't gone far.

My phone began ringing. I peeked at my watch and ignored Jerri's call again.

"Finished talking with your client?" ADA Brown strolled over to me. He was now with two more uniformed officers.

"I have. He told me what happened. Listen, I'm not trying to bullshit you by any means, but whatever you found in the back of that car did not belong to him. I can assure you of that. These are four educated young black men, all attending one of the most prestigious colleges in the nation, and they have bright futures ahead of them. Let's come up with a reasonable bail until we can figure this all out," I suggested. "I'm sure there is something we can work out."

"I don't think you're bullshitting me, and I understand everything you're telling me. Trust me, we've pulled the records of all the young men," he said.

"So, what's the problem?" I asked.

ADA Brown leaned his arm against the wall and looked me in the eye. "We're not talking about a simple marijuana charge, Miss Hudson. We're talking about possession with intent to distribute. You want your client out of there, then tell him to tell me which one of his buddies that dope belongs to, because until we find out, the only place any one of them is going is Rikers."

This was not good. On one side, I had a brother who was determined to save his friends; on the other side, I was facing an ADA who was determined to make my brother rat out one of his friends—and neither one looked willing to budge. For a moment, I felt frozen, standing there speechless as I stared at the ADA with the cocky smirk on his face. What the hell was I going to do to convince either one of them?

"Ms. Hudson?" he said when I failed to speak up.

"Yes?"

"When you finish with your client, we're taking him down to central booking to be processed."

I slowly took a step back, then returned to the interrogation room. Langston gave me a look of anticipation. When I shook my head at him, his body deflated.

"Langston, listen to me. This isn't the time for you to prove your loyalty to your friends, your fraternity, or anything else. You've heard Daddy say time and time again that self-preservation is the first law of nature, and this is one of those situations where you need to look out for self," I explained, hoping he would hear me. "That's the only way you're gonna have a chance in hell of getting out of here today."

"But the drugs don't belong to me," he said, his voice full of anger and frustration.

"I know that; you know that; shit, even the cops know that, I think. But they belong to somebody." I walked over and touched his shoulder, leaning down and whispering, "Langston, whose are they?"

Langston pulled away from me, shaking his head. "I swear, I don't know."

Lamont

16

"Lamont Hudson for Felicia Cooper." I announced myself as I entered the reception area of Greene, Parker, and Cooper. The meeting at Klein's office had taken much less time than I expected, and I was actually early for my lunch appointment at the boutique law firm.

"I'll let her know you're here, Mr. Hudson. Can I get you some water or coffee while you wait?" The cute little Latin receptionist directed me to the waiting area.

"No, thank you." I was tempted to get my flirt on, but I was there on a more important mission, and I couldn't afford to get sidetracked.

I had taken a seat on the Italian leather sofa and was admiring the impressive skyline views when I heard the click-clacking of high heels, and then my name being called.

"Mr. Hudson."

I looked up to see some of the finest, shapeliest long legs I'd seen in a long time. Attached to those legs was Felicia Cooper, the beautiful light-eyed, biracial senior partner I was there to meet. Felicia was one of those smart, conservative sisters who was about her business but was so afraid to let down her hair that she came across as arrogant and bitter. But she always looked damn good, no matter how bad her attitude could be.

"Good morning, Ms. Cooper," I said.

"Mr. Hudson, why don't you come on back." Her footsteps clacked against the marble floor as she led me down the corridor into a large corner office. She closed the door behind us and motioned toward the large chairs in front of her mahogany desk. "Please, have a seat."

"Thank you." I waited for her to walk around her desk and sit first. And yes, I was being polite, but I was also checking out her impressive, J Lo–looking ass that could not be hidden by her business-appropriate skirt. Once she took her seat, I sat down, glancing around the room at her office, taking note of the educational accomplishments and various accolades from other organizations and civic leagues hanging on the walls. I was more impressed by her superhero figurine collection and martial arts trophies, along with the 90-inch television hanging on her wall. The damn thing was bigger than the one I had in my media room at my home. Her office would put even some of the best man caves to shame.

After a few moments of silence, I said, "I take it you're a comic book fan?"

"Yes, but I'm more of a super heroine fan. I like strong women. They motivate me," she said in a voice that suddenly made me imagine her as someone's dominatrix.

"I like a strong woman myself. They motivate me as well," I replied with a smile, which she returned. If I wasn't mistaken, we shared a moment, although it didn't last long. She opened the manila folder sitting in front of her and took out a piece of paper.

"I have to admit, I'm surprised. I didn't think you'd take me up on my offer," she said. It would appear she was getting right down to business.

Felicia and I had met about two years ago in a courtroom where I, quite honestly, whipped her ass. She didn't like that, but was impressed by my skills nonetheless, so two days later, she called and offered me a job. I declined, of course, but she'd been pursuing me ever since. We'd bumped into each other a few nights ago at a legal function, and she'd decided that she had to have me, so here we were.

"Well, I haven't decided yet, but I also don't see any harm in taking a meeting and hearing you out."

"You call it a meeting. I like to think of it as an interview." She stared at me as if we were playing poker and she was looking for tells.

"I guess that all depends on who's interviewing who?" I cracked a slight smile, leaning back comfortably in my chair.

"You're an interesting man, Mr. Hudson." She put down the paper, stood up, and slipped her blazer off her shoulders, placing it on the back of the chair. Underneath, she wore a silk camisole, and her lace bra was noticeable. Her eyes met mine, and she gave me a slight smile. "I've often wondered why you've stayed in your father's shadow for so long."

I stared at her intensely as I answered. "You're only in someone's shadow if you don't know your own self-worth, Ms. Cooper. My father's a great lawyer, and so am I, as you well know. He has his strengths, and so do I. Why should we compete with each other, when together we are damn near invincible?"

I think my reply shocked her a little bit. As good as she looked, she probably wasn't used to a man who could contain himself once she'd bared those beautiful, smooth shoulders.

"I can see you're the ultimate team player," she said, not giving up on her pitch just yet. "You definitely have a lot to offer that would be beneficial to me, and I have a lot to offer as well. I'm a strong believer in reciprocity."

She picked up the folder again, then walked to the front of the desk and leaned against it. Her shapely legs crossed at the ankles, and my gaze made its way up her incredible body. She was athletic and toned. I had no doubt she hit the gym on the regular.

"I'm really big on giving and receiving as well. Don't you feel that's important, Ms. Cooper?" I said suggestively as I let my gaze settle around her midsection, where I would have loved to bury my face.

"I do." She removed her glasses and asked, "So, what makes you feel as if you're qualified for the position I'm looking to fill?"

"You've seen my body of work, and I know that I not only have the qualifications needed, but I have the experience. If anything, I'm overqualified," I said with confidence. It might have come across as arrogant, but with a woman like Felicia, you don't back down if you want her to respect you as an equal.

"Well, Mr. Hudson, I would like to stress the importance of . . . flexibility in your job duties. Will that be a problem?" She placed the folder on the desk and then slid up so she was sitting on top of the desk. Her skirt slid up to reveal the sexy black garter that was holding up the sheer black stockings she wore. I allowed my eyes to linger there for a second before I looked back up into her eyes.

"No problem whatsoever, except you keep referring to this job as if it's a forgone conclusion that I'm taking it." I'm not sure if she realized I could see the rise and fall of her chest as she breathed. She could play it cool all she wanted, but I was getting a rise out of this sexy woman. "You have yet to put an offer on the table."

"Well then, Mr. Hudson, when you put it that way, I guess there is no reason to beat around the bush any longer." She raised her skirt all the way, showing off her freshly Brazilian-waxed kitty. "I'd like to officially offer you the position of fuck buddy with full benefits, but I must stress that you take it now, or I'll have to fill the job immediately with someone less qualified."

I admired the view for a second, enjoying the tension I created by making her wait for my answer. "You're rushing me, Ms. Cooper," I teased. "Under normal circumstances, I don't do anything under duress; however, I can see that you are in dire need of my expertise in this area. I accept your offer."

I swear I saw a ripple of anticipation pass over her body, and her thighs trembled ever so slightly. I leaned forward and lowered my head between Felicia's legs, running my tongue along her lips until I found her clit.

"Fuck! I knew you were the man for the job!" Felicia moaned, picking up the remote and turning on the TV so that the rest of her office wouldn't hear her moans.

I licked and sucked her clit until she couldn't take it anymore. She pushed me away after a very intense orgasm.

"Fuck me," she demanded, reaching for her purse to hand me a condom. "I've been waiting to feel you inside me for two years."

I dropped my pants and slipped on the condom. Felicia positioned herself over her desk, ass up. I couldn't wait to get up inside her—until I noticed the picture of my father on the television with the words *Breaking News* flashing beneath it. I stepped away from her, my eyes glued to the screen.

"What are you waiting for, Lamont? Put it in," Felicia snapped at me.

"Hold on a second." I reached for the remote lying on the desk and turned the volume up even higher.

"Are you serious?" She stood up, staring at me—not that I cared.

"This just in: the youngest son of renowned attorney Bradley Hudson, best known for getting actor TJ Winter off for the murder of his wife and in-laws, was arrested today, along with three other men, in one of the largest drug seizures in Staten Island history."

"Oh my God. Is that true, Lamont? Is that your brother?" Felicia came to stand next to me as we watched video of Langston being perp-walked out of a police precinct, handcuffed, for the world to see.

"Looks like him." I felt a giant knot developing in the pit of my stomach because I knew it was, in fact, my little brother. Then I felt my insides lurch, like I might throw up, when I saw my sister on the screen, standing to the side. Desiree was trying to stay in the shadows, but she couldn't hide from me. "Dammit!"

"Is there anything I can do?" Felicia asked.

"You can give me a rain check," I said, reaching for my pants to get my phone. I scrolled through my contacts and dialed.

"Hello," Desiree answered.

"What the fuck is going on? You and Langston are all over the news!" I shouted angrily.

"Oh God," she said. "I was just going to call you."

"Just going to call me? Our little brother just got perp-walked for all of New York to see. You should have called me when you first found out about this, Des! And you should have made them cover his hands to hide the handcuffs, and you should have made him wear his hoodie."

"I didn't think about that," she said. I could hear in her voice she was on the verge of hysteria, and I knew I needed to dial my anger back or she would lose it.

"I can imagine," I said calmly. "That's why you should have called me. Have you spoken to Dad?"

"No, I was hoping you would call him. He's already mad at me."

He hasn't begun to be mad at you, I thought as I stepped into my pants. Felicia zipped me up and buckled my belt.

"Okay, I'll deal with the old man, but you need to hustle down to the Staten Island Courthouse and slow things down until I get there."

"How do I do that?" she asked quietly.

I kept forgetting that she was only one year out of law school. Desiree had a good legal mind, but she was still green when it came to the inner workings of a criminal case. *Shit, a criminal case.* I couldn't believe I was even thinking those words in relation to my brother, the straight-laced college student. I had no idea what the details were, but this was a code red emergency, and Langston was going to need all the help he could get.

"Register with the clerk as Lang's counsel; then leave the courthouse until I get there. They can't arraign him without counsel being present. But whatever you do, Des, don't let him be arraigned. Okay? If you do, he'll get lost in the system for two days."

"Okay. Uh, Lamont?"

"Yeah, sis."

"Is Langston going to be all right?" she whispered.

"Langston is going to be fine. Me and Dad will figure this out. We always do." I said the words, but I wasn't quite sure I believed them myself.

Bradley

17

I texted my driver to bring my car around to the front of the Manhattan Supreme Court the second I got off the phone with Lamont. My son was innocent. Langston might have been capable of many things, but distribution of drugs wasn't one of them. Of this, I was absolutely sure.

There was one thing I had to do before I left the courthouse and headed to Staten Island. It was something I had to do in person, face to face. Of course, I hated the idea of possibly missing Langston's arraignment, but Lamont was more than capable of handling it. Besides, the real lawyering wasn't going to begin until I found out who was prosecuting the case.

"Your Honor, my client had a non-disclosure agreement that forbade him from coming forward with any personal details observed while employed," Richard Engel, the counsel for the defense, stated as I walked into the courtroom of the Honorable Jacqueline Robinson. I'd known Richard for years. He wasn't a great lawyer, but he was a hell of a golfer.

"And your client's sexual harassment of my client makes that agreement null and void," argued Barry Engel, Richard's cousin and the attorney for the other side. I also knew Barry. He wasn't the greatest lawyer either, but he was an even better golfer.

These two particular lawyers had been in a continuous pissing contest ever since they split up their partnership five years ago and went out on their own. I guess Grandma had given more hugs and kisses to one of them. To this day, they acted like they were still competing for good ol' Granny's love.

Barry started, "Your Honor, according to Article—"

"Enough!" Judge Robinson slammed her gavel down.

"But, Your Honor." Richard insisted on getting the last word. "My client is a celebrity. This will have every money-grubbing sycophant filing a lawsuit."

"Especially the ones with three years of evidence," Barry said sarcastically.

"I don't know, gentlemen. This seems like a perfect time to settle," Judge Robinson said in a calm, authoritative voice. She made eye contact with me for the first time since I'd entered the back of her courtroom.

I watched as Barry and Richard shot daggers at one another. My courtroom sixth sense told me that Richard was considering her suggestion. Barry, on the other hand, wasn't convinced a settlement was the right way to go. Just when a flicker of hope sparkled in the Richards's eyes, Barry frowned at him and blew it out.

"We're not settling." Barry could hardly keep the wicked grin from lifting the corners of his mouth.

Richard just about sprang across the aisle, but he caught himself. He cleared his throat and then straightened his tie. I hate to admit it, but I would have loved to see that fight. He shook his head as if clearing it, then looked dead into Barry's eyes. "Then prepare for the first video to go viral on TMZ."

The judge slammed her gavel down again. "No, it won't, Mr. Engel. And if I hear that video is played at so much as a kid's birthday party, I'll lock you up for thirty days and hold you in contempt. Now, I'm sending this case to mediation."

Judge Robinson slammed her gavel down. With business before the court concluded, she locked her eyes on me. It was a cold, hard stare—one I was quite familiar with. She wasn't my biggest fan; but then again, I wasn't exactly in love with her either.

I walked down the center aisle toward the bench. Judge Robinson looked beautiful and youthful despite her fifty-plus years. She seemed ruffled by my appearance in her courtroom, but not intimidated. Unlike most people, she'd never been intimated by me. We continued our stare-down until court officers intercepted me at the little gate that separated her bench and the lawyers' tables from the public seating.

"Can I help you, Mr. Hudson?" she asked me in a no-nonsense tone.

I chuckled. "May I approach, Your Honor?"

She hesitated, releasing a sigh as she glanced at the small crowd of people sitting in her courtroom. Then, finally relenting, she waved me in. The court officer stepped aside, and I made my way to the judge's bench with him lurking behind me.

"Bradley," she whispered between clenched teeth while covering the microphone that sat in front of her. "What are you doing in my courtroom?"

"We need to talk, Jacqueline. It's important."

"You ever heard of a phone?" She could barely contain her disdain for me.

"Of course I have, but you take five days to return my calls. This isn't something that can wait," I replied sternly.

"You are a real piece of work, you know that? What do you want?" She sounded as irritated as she looked.

"Can we go to your chambers?"

"No, we can't go to my chambers. I have cases to try." She shot a quick glance at her court officer. "Now, what do you want to talk about?"

I stared at her for a brief moment, remembering in detail all the reasons we didn't get along. "Okay, I was trying to spare you the embarrassment of finding this out from a colleague, or even worse a reporter, but—"

"Finding out what?" she snapped.

"That your son has been arrested!" I didn't mean to say it so loud, but she had this way of getting under my skin that threw me off my game.

"Oh my God, what has Lamont done?"

"It's not Lamont. It's Langston," I told her.

Her mouth fell open, but my words had stunned her into silence.

Langston

18

Although I had already been photographed and fingerprinted the moment I got out of the paddy wagon and was shuffled into central booking, I was still trying to digest the fact that we'd been arrested. All those reporters and television cameras waiting outside the police precinct when we walked out sure as hell hadn't helped things. My dad had always said that the media was like the opposite sex: you had to embrace them, and they'd fall in love with you. Well, maybe that was true, but so far, I was not feeling the love from those reporters.

Tony, Krush, and I were placed in a holding cell that housed about thirty men. Half of them stank of liquor and were probably there on DUIs, while the other half looked like drug addicts and dope boys. Krush seemed to get along just fine with them. I'd asked the cops several times about Kwesi, but none of them seemed to know where he was. I was worried about my little African buddy. I just hoped he was all right.

"What the fuck? Y'all just got here!" I heard someone yell as my frat brothers and I were summoned by a guard.

"That's what happens when you got a paid lawyer," Krush bragged, bopping over to the gate. "Come on, y'all. I'm ready to get the fuck up outta here," he said to me and Tony.

"Your friends over there hear anything about Kwesi?" I asked Krush as we were led out of the cell.

"Nah, ain't nobody seen him. He may have got his ass caught up in some ICE shit. You know how Trump's boys be fucking with immigrants," Krush said. The way he was talking, you'd think he'd been locked up a million times before, instead of being the suburban college boy he really was. Unfortunately, his comment about Kwesi's immigration status might have been accurate. The way things were going lately, there was a good possibility they were already working on Kwesi's deportation order.

We were escorted from the holding room to the courtroom and guided toward the defense podium, where Lamont and Desiree were standing.

"Wait. Why are your brother and sister here? Where is your dad?" Tony's voice cracked as he whispered to me. I peered back at the packed courtroom, looking for my dad, but he was nowhere to be found. *Jesus, I hope he's not mad.*

"Just chill. Don't worry. We're good. My brother ain't no joke either," I told him, but inside, I was more than a little nervous. I had to remind myself that the people standing next to me bore the Hudson name. We were a family of bad-ass attorneys, and I would one day be joining the ranks. In spite of my fear, I knew that my boys and I would be home in time for an episode of *Empire*.

"Lamont and Desiree Hudson for the defense, Your Honor," Lamont said.

"ADA David Wilkins for the State."

"Langston Hudson, Anthony Baker, and Kirby Wright," the silver-haired judge started in a stern voice after taking a moment to scrutinize each of us. "You are charged with felony possession of a controlled substance, possession with intent to distribute, as well as driving under the influence, in addition to use of a motor vehicle in the commission of a felony . . . the transportation of, and intent to distribute said controlled substance," the judge said all in one breath. "How do you plead?"

We all said, "Not guilty," at the same time.

"Bail recommendations, Mr. Wilkins?" the judge asked.

The ADA looked across the room. I turned to see if he was looking at anyone in particular. That's when I noticed a familiar face. It was ADA James Brown, that slick-ass Uncle Tom who'd been in the interrogation room. He was sitting quietly in the back of the courtroom, observing. Brown gave the other ADA a discreet nod, and Wilkins nodded back.

"Judge, we're going to ask that no bail be set at this time for any of these young men."

Lamont spoke up in protest. "Your Honor, my clients are three college students on the verge of graduating. They have no criminal records, not even a traffic citation outside of the ones received today. They pose no flight risk, and in all actuality, I should expect that they would be released on their own recognizance."

"Your Honor, this wasn't a simple traffic violation like Mr. Hudson is insinuating. The police confiscated several kilos of narcotics from the vehicle. In addition, Anthony Baker has ties to the Bloods street gang," the ADA said matter-of-factly, even though he was twisting the facts.

I was starting to get a bad feeling when the judge glanced at our crimson sweatshirts. I felt even worse when Tony started yelling, "This is some bullshit! I ain't in no gang! And I damn sure ain't no Blood!" Tony took a step toward the ADA.

"Control your clients," Judge Nichols warned Lamont.

"Let me handle this," Lamont whispered harshly to Tony.

"In addition, the young man who was in the vehicle with them during the stop has already been arraigned earlier and given key information." The ADA's announcement felt like a punch in the gut.

"What kind of information?" Lamont asked. That's exactly what I wanted to know. What the hell could Kwesi have said?

"What the fuck are they talking about? What did Kwesi say? This is crazy," Tony and Krush began mumbling simultaneously.

"Your clients, Mr. Hudson."

Lamont turned to me with gritted teeth, his eyes saying what his mouth wouldn't. "Will you keep these two quiet? They're not helping."

"Yo, Tony, chill. Let Lamont handle this," I said.

"Now, on the subject of bail," the judge said. "Bail is set at one million dollars."

"What the fuck!" Even I couldn't control myself this time. I stared at my brother, willing him to do something.

"Your Honor, this is a clear violation of my clients' Eighth Amendment rights!" Lamont interjected.

"Would you like me to take the DA's office recommendation, Mr. Hudson? I can always change it to no bail."

"But, Your Honor, they have no priors." Lamont made his tone more respectful as he tried to reason with the judge.

"No buts. Bail is set at one million dollars." Judge Nichols slammed the gavel down.

I wished I could slap the smirk off the ADA's face as he said, "Thank you, Your Honor."

"Can somebody tell me what the hell just happened?" Krush leaned over and asked. Tony, who always had something to say, just stood there in silent shock.

"You got bail. That's a start," Lamont said. "We're going to make a motion for a bail reduction hearing. We'll get it reduced."

"Easy for you to say," Krush spat, almost on the verge of tears. "You get to go home and sleep safe and sound in your bed and not have to worry about a four-hundred-pound Negro named Bubba crawling up in bed with you."

Desiree turned her attention to me. "Just hang in there, little brother." She looked to the others. "All of you just hang in there, please. I'm not sure what's going on. This is crazy, but I promise we are going to get you out of here. I promise. Daddy's on his way."

I could see the sincerity in Desiree's eyes and believed that she was going to do all that she could for us. For now, though, she could only offer encouragement as we were led back to the lockup.

Krush

19

"A million dollars! They gave us a million dollars bail. That's some bullshit!" I told a couple of the brothers I'd met in the holding cell. Langston had been pulled out of the cell about five minutes ago to speak to his pops, who had finally shown up, and while I talked to the other prisoners, I kept an eye on Tony. He hadn't spoken a word since we left the courtroom.

"Damn, I thought this fifty K they gave me for armed robbery was a lot," one of the brothers replied, "but that shit ain't nothin' compared to you. What the fuck they got you on? A body?"

I wanted to lie and say yeah, because we were going to need all the street cred we could get once we hit Rikers, but I decided against it. The last thing I wanted to do was get caught in a lie, or even worse, have one of my boys bitch up and tell the truth. Besides, the truth wasn't too bad either—if your goal was to impress a cell full of criminals.

"Nah, me and my boys got caught out there with a couple of kilos of that black tar heroin. Motherfucking dog sniffed right through those coffee grounds." I threw the coffee grounds in there for effect. I actually had no idea how the drugs were wrapped.

"Damn, y'all was rolling with some weight. No wonder they hit you with seven figures," another brother said.

I bullshitted with my cell mates for a few more minutes before Langston was escorted into the cell. I jumped up to meet him by the gate.

"What did your pops say?" I tried to read the look on his face, searching for some sign of reassurance, but he barely looked at us. He seemed distracted.

"Is Tony all right?" he asked. The sound of the bars closing and locking behind him echoed loudly as we walked over to the corner where Tony was standing.

"I don't know. I'm starting to think he might be on the verge of losing it," I said.

"Yeah, it's possible. That's why I'm gonna need you to keep an eye on him."

"What exactly do you mean by *me*? You're gonna be keeping an eye on him too, aren't you?"

"Well, not exactly," Lang said. His voice was barely above a whisper, and all kinds of alarms started going off in my mind.

"What the fuck do you mean, not exactly?" I asked sharply.

"I'm getting bailed out, Krush. My pops is putting up the house just to get me out of here." Lang shrugged halfheartedly.

My stomach lurched, and I could feel the bile at the back of my throat. "I keep hearing *me*, but what the fuck happened to *us*, bro?" I pointed at Tony, then myself, and then I flashed the frat sign. "What the fuck, Lang?"

"Krush, man, I promise you I tried to get him to get y'all out too, but . . ." Lang's voice faded.

"What the fuck are we supposed to do, man?" I was shouting now. My emotions had gotten the best of me. I was scared and pissed off at the same time. "What the fuck are we supposed to do?"

Lang blinked stupidly a couple of times, then said, "Bro, you're gonna have to call your parents."

I took a step back, putting some distance between us, and exhaled hard, trying to maintain my composure. "Lang, you know damn well my people's house ain't worth a million dollars. Come on."

"Yeah, I know, but Desiree is trying to get you a bail bondsman. We're gonna get you out." Although Lang sounded sincere, I really didn't give a fuck, because he couldn't make any promises. Desiree *trying* to do something wasn't doing me any good at the moment. He was getting out, and my ass was going to be spending who knows how long at Rikers.

"My peeps ain't got no hundred grand to give no bail bonds-man, and you know Tony's mama ain't got it. She lives in the fucking PJs," I said angrily.

"I'm sorry, man," Lang said.

"Sorry." I sucked my teeth and cut my eyes at my best friend like he was a fucking traitor. "Well, yeah, keep your fucking weak-ass apology."

That was enough to set him off. He dropped the sincerity and stepped up in my face. "Whatever, man. Don't act like I ain't been looking out since we got here. Shit, it was you that got us pulled over with weed in the first place."

"Yeah, but I owned that. It was your ride that they found the got-damn dope in. Not mine, not Tony's, not Kwesi's. Yours, Langton. About time you started owning that, bro."

"You know that dope wasn't mine!"

"Do I?" I asked. "All I know is me and Tony sitting in here about to go to Rikers Island, and your ass is going home to eat steak and lobster with your family. What's wrong with that picture?"

We stared at each other long and hard, and then out of nowhere—*Bam*! Tony's fist connected with Langston's chin. He was knocked backward but maintained his balance.

"Oh, shit!" another inmate in the cell yelled, and suddenly, all eyes were on us.

"Yo!" I jumped between them and put my arms out to keep them apart. "Chill! Now ain't the time for this."

Lang rubbed his chin and turned away. Tony walked in the opposite direction.

A guard approached the cell door. "Break it up!" he yelled at the inmates, then he called out to Langston. "Hudson!"

My heart began pounding. I was pissed at Langston, but I still didn't want to see him punished for the scuffle. Lord knows I'd heard enough stories about racist-ass guards abusing prisoners just because they felt like it.

"Yeah," Lang said, shuffling over toward the guard.

"Let's go." The guard unlocked the door. "You're getting out of here."

Lang eased out of the cell without looking back at us. I glanced over at Tony, who was glaring at him. Then another guard walked up and shocked the hell out of me when he said, "You two fellas can go ahead and get ready too."

"Us?" I asked quickly, hoping that a miracle had happened. "We're leaving too?"

"Yep. I'll be back for you in a few minutes," he said.

"We're going home?" Tony spoke for the first time.

"Nah." The guard shook his head. "Y'all are heading to Rikers."

Suddenly, I was speechless too. Tony and I stared silently at our frat brother as he walked away from the lockup. Lang turned around and said, "I promise I'm gonna get y'all out as soon as I can."

I couldn't respond as I made my way over to a bench to sit down before my legs gave out. Things were going from bad to worse, and I didn't know what we were going to do.

"I can't believe he left us in here," I muttered to myself.

Tony said, "Shit, what was he supposed to do? I know if the roles were reversed, I'd have done the same thing. You would have too. It ain't fucking Chuck E. Cheese they're sending us to. It's jail."

"Wait, so you don't blame him? Why'd you hit him then?" I asked, confused.

"Mostly frustration. But if we're going to jail, he needed to get hit in the mouth." That actually made me chuckle, and I reached out and dapped him up. He continued, "Something ain't right, though. I'm telling you, K."

"What do you mean?"

"Where the fuck is Kwesi, and why didn't he go with us before the judge?"

"Yeah, I been thinking about that too. You think he sold us out?"

"It's possible. He's a weak motherfucker," Tony stated bitterly. "You know how hard it's gonna be to get released without Lang in here with us? Shit is about to get real."

"Hey, we can't give up," I said, struggling to stay positive. "Lang's our brother. He doesn't wanna see us up in here, and he's gonna help get us the fuck out. All we can do is believe in him."

"I hear you, but who's to say he won't go right back to his family and their fuckin' mansion and forget all about us? Right now, the only people we can trust for real is each other," he said.

I looked over at Tony, who looked as defeated as I felt. I prayed that he was wrong and that Langston was going to be true to his word to us, his brothers.

"I hear that," I said. "No matter what happens, we have to stick together."

We gave each other the frat handshake, sealing our bond.

James

20

I stood off to the side, next to a pillar on the Richmond County Courthouse steps, watching Bradley Hudson escort his son Langston out of the building, followed by his two older children. As they were immediately accosted by a swarm of reporters and cameramen, I fought the grin that began spreading across my face.

"Mr. Hudson! Mr. Hudson! Any comment on your son's arrest?" a reporter shouted.

Bradley stopped at the cluster of microphones in front of the courthouse steps. "Yes, I have a comment." He flashed a smile to the cameras and placed his arm around Langston. They'd brought the kid a fresh white collared shirt and a pair of slacks, cleaned him up real nice for this moment in the spotlight. I had to give it to him; the man knew how to play up to the media. "My son is innocent of these *alleged* crimes, and we intend to prove that in a court of law, not in the press. I hope you all respect that he is considered innocent until proven guilty."

"Mr. Hudson, are you representing the other three defendants as well? And if so, when will they be bailed out?" Barry Witten from the *Daily News* shouted. Barry was an old friend, and we'd just had an off-the-record chat before the Hudsons came out. I guess he'd taken our conversation to heart and now wanted some of the same answers I did.

"We haven't been retained by any of them as of yet, and you'd have to ask their families about their bail status. Thank you," Bradley replied then ushered his family toward a silver Rolls Royce before the reporters started asking real questions.

The Hudson shit storm was growing bigger and bigger, and I couldn't have been more pleased. I'd originally come outside the court building to confront Bradley in front of the media and let him know that I would be prosecuting his son's case on behalf of the DA's office; but I decided that could wait, because Mr. Big Shot had his hands full already with the swarm of reporters. No need to fire all your bullets if the first one has hit the target.

"So, that's Bradley Hudson?" O'Malley asked, walking up behind me.

"Yep, that's him, the black messiah of the legal world." I'm sure I sounded a little bitter, and that's because I was. The legend of Bradley Hudson was a fraud, and by the time this case was over, I was going prove it by putting his son behind bars.

"So, how the hell did they post bond so quick? I mean, that was a million dollars bond."

"I suspect he knew there'd be a high bail, so he sent his son and daughter to do the arraignment while he made preparations to bail out his youngest kid," I replied, leaning against the pillar and scanning the crowd. "Probably used one of his houses as collateral."

"Pretty smart," O'Malley said.

"He's not stupid by any means, but neither am I." I turned to look at him. "What about the other three?"

"The African kid is at Rikers being processed, and the other two should be leaving in the next five or ten minutes."

"That's good. Any sign of their parents yet?" I asked.

"Nope, not a peep."

I was scanning the crowd again, mumbling to myself, "Where the fuck are you?"

He stepped forward, following my gaze. "You looking for someone?"

"Yeah, and I think I found her." I watched as the rear door to the Rolls Royce opened and a familiar figure stepped out. Things were becoming more interesting by the minute.

"Who is that?" he asked as we watched the woman hug Langston tightly.

"The Honorable Jacqueline Robinson, Langston's mother and Bradley Hudson's ex-wife."

"Good-looking woman. She a judge?"

"A federal judge—a very powerful federal judge. Some say she was on Obama's short list for the Supreme Court."

"And you wanna fuck with them?" he asked.

Once again, I fought the grin that I could feel spreading on my face. "O'Malley, I been waiting most of my adult life to fuck with them."

Desiree

21

I rode around my block for twenty minutes before I found a parking spot. I loved living in Harlem, but I hated the parking situation with a passion. I'd been thinking for a while about giving up my car and just taking Ubers instead, and every time I had to search for parking like this brought me one step closer to doing it.

I sat inside the car for a few minutes, trying to garner enough energy to get out and walk the half block to my brownstone. To say I was mentally and emotionally drained would be an understatement. I was totally wiped out. I finally motivated myself with the idea of stripping off my clothes and taking a hot shower as soon as I walked through the door. I grabbed my briefcase from the back seat and stepped out. I had just hit the lock button on my car when I looked up and saw Jerri, front and center, standing on the curb, smiling at me. I damn near dropped my briefcase.

"What the hell?" I blinked.

"Surprise!" She walked over and reached out to hug me, but I took a step back.

"Wha—what are . . . how . . . you . . . What are you doing here?" I asked, finally able to articulate a complete sentence. "How did you know where I lived?"

"I was worried about you when I didn't hear from you all day. And I've *been* known where you live for a while." She had an irritated look on her face. "I've been trying to reach you all day."

"I guess you haven't been watching the news. I had an emergency come up and wasn't able to take your calls." I started walking toward my brownstone.

"So much of an emergency that you couldn't answer my calls or call me back? I thought you said you were coming over when you got off work." She had a lot of bass in her voice—enough to piss me off and make me decide that she didn't deserve an explanation.

"I said I would try," I reminded her. I was way too tired for this.

"I cooked dinner. We were supposed to do Netflix and chill, and you left me hanging. That's fucked up, Des," she said, taking big strides to keep up with me.

"I know, and if my fucking brother hadn't gotten arrested, I would have been there," I finally snapped as we arrived in front of my building. "Now, what are you doing here?"

"Oh, baby, I'm sorry." She softened her tone. "I didn't know. Wow, that's horrible. I'm sure your parents are upset, and you. I'm sorry, Des." She stepped closer, and I allowed her to put her arm around my shoulder.

"Now do you understand why I was unavailable and didn't come over?"

"Yeah, and I'm also glad that I'm here for you now. Come on, let's get inside so you can relax. I know just what to do. You need one of my massages." She tried to kiss me, but I moved away, glancing around the block.

"Jerri, not here, okay," I told her.

"What do you mean, not here?" Jerri snapped. "Are you ashamed of me?"

"No, but my parents own this building. Well, technically my mother does, since it was part of her divorce settlement. But I'm not the only one living here, and trust me, people talk."

"So?" She stepped closer. "Why do you care what people think?"

"Because this is new for me, and I'm just getting used to it. I'm not ready to explain myself or us to the world. The last thing I need is someone telling my business." I shrugged. "Especially now that all of this stuff is going on with Langston. It would be . . . a lot."

"I get it . . . I think. So, let's go inside." She reached for my hand and took a step toward the building, but I wouldn't budge.

"No, not tonight. You can't just show up at my place and think it's okay. My house is my safe place, where I get away from the world."

"So, I can't even come in, not even as a friend?" Jerri looked hurt.

I tried to smooth things over as best I could. "Jerri, now you know you wouldn't be coming in as a friend. I'm not crazy, and

you're not either. You know what will happen if you come in."
I gave her a knowing smile and nudged her, and after a few
seconds, she loosened up and grinned.

"But it's times like this that I want to show you that I can be a
friend. It's not just about sex for me," she insisted.

"I know it's not, Jerri, and I appreciate that. I appreciate
everything you do for me: your calls and texts, cooking those
amazing meals, making me laugh, even finding my address and
stalking me," I teased. "But tonight, I just need time to reset,
by myself. And as my real friend, I know you'll understand and
respect that."

"Are you sure?"

"I'm sure. And I promise I'll call you in the morning."

"A'ight. I'll respect your need for some *me time* tonight. I'm
really sorry about what happened to your brother, and you know
if you need me, I'm just a phone call away."

I gave her a brief hug and was relieved when she didn't try to
kiss me. "Thanks, Jerri. I'll talk to you tomorrow."

Jerri waited until I unlocked the door and stepped inside
before she finally left. A few moments later, I opened the door
and peeked out to make sure she was really gone. When I confirmed that she wasn't lurking around in front, I closed the door
and went into my dark and quiet apartment, heading directly
into my bedroom without turning on any lights. I tossed my
briefcase and phone onto my bed then stripped off my clothes,
leaving them in the middle of my bedroom floor. My only goal
was to take a hot shower, decompress, and wash the remnants of
the day from my body.

In the bathroom, I turned on the faucet in the tub, lit the
two oversized candles on the vanity, and poured some laven-
der-scented body wash into the bath. When it was full and steam
started to rise, I stepped into the marble tub and let the hot water
envelop my body. The tension in my back and shoulders began
to subside, and I leaned back to enjoy the sensation, trying to
clear my mind of the events of this horrible day. Afterward, I
went back into my bedroom, feeling better and smelling sweet.
As I began rubbing lotion into my skin, realized that I was a little
turned on.

Maybe I should've let Jerri come inside, I thought, but I knew
that would've been more trouble than it was worth. I'd meant
what I said about my neighbors being nosy, and I hadn't told

anyone that I was seeing someone, let alone a woman. I don't think I would ever be ready to tell anyone, especially when I wasn't sure that the situation I was in with Jerri was really serious, or a temporary experience until I figured out what I truly wanted in a relationship.

I stood and walked over to my dresser, reaching into my underwear drawer and fumbling until I found what I was looking for. Once it was in hand, I closed the drawer and headed out of the bedroom and across the hall. The room was dark and filled with the sound of the TV. I walked over to the bed and slipped under the cool sheets and beside the body lying in the center. As I snuggled closer, still holding my hand tightly so I wouldn't drop the contents grasped inside, I heard a slight moan. I paused and used my free hand to roll the broad shoulders over and eased my body on top so that I was mounted. I could feel my wetness increasing as I anticipated what was about to happen. I leaned over and slowly began kissing from the neck to the chest, playfully biting nipples. Then, I felt the hard flesh against my inner thigh, and I smiled. The closed eyes that I had been staring at since entering the bedroom were now open.

"What the hell are you doing?" he asked, his baritone voice was raspy because of sleep.

"You," I said, moving his hands to my breasts so they now cupped them.

"I thought you said you didn't wanna do this anymore, remember?" He frowned.

"I never said that." I opened my hand so he could see what was inside.

"You're crazy, that's exactly what you said." His thumbs flickered across my hardened nipples, sending a sensation through my body and causing my center to throb even harder.

"No, what I said was I didn't wanna do *us* anymore. I never wanna stop doing this."

I handed him the condom I was holding, and without saying another word, he slipped it on. In one swift motion, he rolled me over and had my legs pinned, causing me to gasp as his swollen erection entered my inviting center, giving me everything I desired and erasing any thoughts I had of Jerri or my promise to call her before I went to bed.

James

22

A light mist fell as a dozen NYPD cruisers, unmarked cars, and SUVs pulled up beside Detectives O'Malley and Cutter's unmarked police car. I was seated in the back of their car, watching as multiple officers exited their vehicles in preparation to enter the building. A few minutes later, there was a squawking over the police radio, and O'Malley turned to me.

"Everyone's in place," he said.

"Okay, let's move in," I told him, picking up the folder from the seat beside me and getting out of the car.

We headed into the building, avoiding the elevator for the stairs and stopping at the second floor. When I entered the corridor, there were officers standing on either side of a door. I glanced down at the paperwork in my hand. *Building 6, Apartment 208*. This was the place. I nodded my approval to Cutter, then handed him the paperwork as one of the uniformed men knocked on the door loudly.

"Who is it?" a woman asked.

"Police!" one of the officers yelled.

We all waited, and a few seconds later, the door slowly opened.

"What do y'all want?" The woman, who appeared to be in her forties, was very attractive in the simple black leggings and T-shirt she wore. Her short hair, a combination of blond and dark brown, was perfectly curled to frame her cute face. Her shape reminded me of Toni Braxton in a hood kind of way. Had I seen her in a social setting, I probably would've made a move on her. She wasn't the marrying type, but she was definitely the fucking type. But, this was business that needed to be taken care of at the moment.

"We have a warrant to search the property," the officer told her, then pushed past her, followed by several others dressed in protective gear with guns drawn. Chances were the full regalia wasn't needed, but you could never tell.

"Clear! Clear! Clear!" I heard an officer yell from inside the home.

"I don't believe this shit!" the woman shouted, staring at the paper that Cutter had handed to her moments before. "Why the hell are y'all here?"

I took her question as my cue, and I proceeded to the front door. "Ms. Baker?"

"Who the hell are you?" She gave me a head-to-toe once-over, and I chose to ignore the look of disdain. I stepped inside the living room, where officers were going through papers and flipping couch cushions. I was surprised, because I'd never seen a home in any project building decorated like hers. She had a brand-new, state-of-the-art kitchen complete with granite countertops and stainless steel appliances, and a living room that looked like a Raymour and Flanigan showroom. I felt like I was taking a tour of an HGTV fantasy home, ghetto edition.

"Are all the apartments in this building like this?" I already knew the answer, but I couldn't help it. I had to ask.

"Who the fuck are you?"

I guess my question had struck a nerve.

"I'm James Brown, and I'm an assistant district attorney," I informed her.

The daggers she shot my way told me that she wasn't a woman I should turn my back on, or else I'd be pulling a knife out of it.

"This is about Tony, isn't it? I don't know why y'all got my son locked up. He's a good kid." She shook her head. "Besides, he don't even live here."

"This is his permanent residence, according to his driver's license," I stated very clearly. "He spent the last four nights here."

"Gun!" an officer yelled from the back of the house.

Ms. Baker's eyes were heavy with concern as O'Malley emerged a few moments later carrying a nine-millimeter handgun.

"Uh-oh . . ." A smile crept up on my face. "What is the housing department going to say when we tell them about this?"

"That's not my gun!" She looked so nervous she began to shake.

"Then whose is it?" I asked, pointing to the sofa. She picked up on the directive and went to sit down.

I nodded toward O'Malley and the other officers, who went into another part of the house to continue their search.

"Where'd the gun come from, Ms. Baker?" I stared at the nervous woman.

"I don't know." She shrugged. "We had a rent party the other day. It could be anybody's."

"Is it Tony's?"

"My son doesn't have a need for a gun. How many times I gotta tell you he's a good kid?" She sounded agitated.

"I'm sure you think your other boys are good kids, too, but we both know they aren't."

"But you ain't here about my other two boys, because you know they don't come around here. You're here about Tony, and he's a good kid." She was not easily intimidated. I was sure this was not her first encounter with the police, but that was no surprise, given the criminal records of her other gang-banging sons.

"You're right. I am here about him. But if the gun doesn't belong to him, then what you're saying is that it belongs to you, right?" I asked.

"No, it's not my—I don't . . . I can't . . ." She struggled to complete a sentence.

"If it's not yours, then I'm gonna have to assume it's Tony's, because the only two people whose names are on your lease are yours and his. Now, you do know Marcy Projects is a city housing unit. You can be evicted because of this gun."

Tears began to form in her eyes. "Listen, that's not my gun, and it's not Tony's. You've gotta believe me. We've both worked so hard these past few years. I know my other sons aren't the best citizens, but that ain't me, and that ain't Tony. Hell, I've battled my own demons in the past, but I'm clean, I'm a hard worker, and so is my baby." She picked up what looked like a middle school graduation photo of Tony and stared at it, a slight smile coming to her face.

I almost felt bad, because I knew she was telling the truth, but I reminded myself again that this was business.

"That's it. We've searched the entire house, Brown," O'Malley walked in and announced. "We didn't find anything other than the one weapon."

"Appreciate it. Go ahead and clear everyone out, but you stay close. I haven't decided if we are going to charge her or not yet," I told him, then turned to Ms. Baker.

"I can help you, and I want to help your son, too. Believe me, I do."

Her eyes met mine, and she searched my face for sincerity, I suppose. I don't know what she saw, but I was surprised by the conclusion she reached. "So, this ain't about Tony, is it, Mr. Brown? This is about his friend Langston and his family."

I didn't answer her question directly. I just said, "I need you to talk to your son and tell him to talk to me."

"What is it that he's supposed to say?" Her question held the wisdom of someone who'd been pressured by the system before. She clearly understood how the game was played.

"You been through this type of thing with your other boys before. I'm sure you and him will figure out something." I got up from my seat and walked toward the door. "But don't wait too long. You're not the only one I'm talking to."

Bradley

23

"Good morning, Mr. Hudson. A late start for you today?" Iris, my housekeeper, asked in heavily-accented English as I sat down to the breakfast table. She filled my cup with coffee, and I reached for the sugar substitute and creamer. Iris was about my age and had been with me since Lamont was a toddler. She was more like family than a housekeeper.

"Yes, Iris, a very late start." I normally came down around six, had my coffee and an English muffin, and watched the cable news shows to see what was going on in my favorite reality show, otherwise known as the White House. But today it was a little after eight by the time I'd showered, dressed, and come downstairs. "I thought I heard Lamont down here."

"You did. Mr. Lamont stepped outside to take a phone call," Iris explained just before Langston walked into the room. "Morning, Mr. Langston," she said.

"Morning, Iris." Langston smiled at her then hesitantly took a seat at the kitchen table. He looked as if he hadn't gotten much sleep, which was understandable. After the events the day before, I hadn't slept much myself; but then again, I barely got five hours of sleep on any given night anyway. "Morning, Dad."

"Morning, son. How're you feeling?" I asked to let him know that my calm demeanor from last night was still intact.

"Like crap," he answered, visibly relaxing now that he knew I wasn't going to be reprimanding him at the breakfast table. "I'm really worried about the guys."

"That's understandable. I just hope they are as worried about you as you are them." It was time to bring Langston into reality.

"Dad, they're in jail. I don't think they have time to be worried about the guy who abandoned them."

I'd never seen him like this. He looked like he was ready to walk over to that jail and turn himself in—and that worried me.

"You didn't abandon them. Your parents came to your rescue and bailed you out," I reminded him. "I'm sure their parents will do the same."

He narrowed his eyes at me as if I were the enemy. "Are you kidding me? Where the hell is Tony's mom going to get the money to bail him out?"

"Coffee, Mr. Langston?" Iris asked. I was sure she was trying to relieve some of the tension in the room. It worked, because Langston took some of the gruffness out of his voice.

"Yes, please," Langston told her, pointing to the carafe of orange juice sitting in the center of the table.

Iris had worked for our family for years and had the tendency to cater to Langston when he was home from school. However, his being here was far from a typical weekend or vacation visit. This was serious. Langston and his friends' mugshots had been plastered all over the news and on the front page of the newspaper. I was certain that Iris had seen it, in addition to her constantly having to answer the phone, which had been ringing nonstop all morning. I had finally turned my own cell phone off for the same reason. I knew that she was making an effort to make things as normal as possible, which I appreciated.

"Give us a minute, will you, Iris?"

"Yes. I'll make you some pancakes, Mr. Langston."

"Thank you, Iris," Langston replied, and she left the room.

"I need to ask you a very serious question, son." I used the word *son* instead of his name because I wanted him to know that it was coming from his father and not his lawyer. "And if you can't be honest with me, I want you to be honest with yourself."

"I don't know who the drugs belong to, Dad," he replied, anticipating my question.

"Well, that was your boy Krush's father." Lamont came in and interrupted our conversation.

Langston sat up in his chair and asked his brother, "Was he asking if you were representing Krush?"

"Yeah, but I think he was more concerned about whether we were going to bail him out than anything else. I told him I was trying to set up a bail reduction hearing, but it was going to take a few days." Lamont sat down and sipped a cup of coffee that was in front of him. "But he's going to be a pain in the ass about us putting up the funds to get his son out." He turned to my father. "Should I just flat out tell this guy it's not happening?"

"What? No! I thought you said you were going to help them. You gotta help get them out. Dad, tell him." Langston turned his attention to me for help, but I had none to offer.

"Langston, we'll do the best we can to help, but—"

He cut me off. "That's not good enough!"

"You little spoiled college brat, do you realize what we had to do to get you out?" Lamont grabbed a bagel from the middle of the table and plopped it onto his plate. "They had to put up this house. Have you lost your fucking mind?"

Langston glanced over at me. "Yes, I know, and I'm grateful, but this isn't the only house we have."

Lamont frowned. "I know you're not suggesting we put up the house in Sag Harbor or L.A. to get your frat brothers out of jail, are you?"

"You make it seem like they're some random guys that I happen to take class with, and you know that's not true. These guys are more than my frat brothers. They're like family, and yeah, I'm asking Dad to look out for them the same way he looked out for me," Langston told him. "Shit, they're your frat brothers too. What if this were John, Kyle, or Wimpy?"

"Hey, man, I can dig it. I love my frat brothers, too. So does Dad. But I love my real brother, my flesh and blood, even more, and he's who I need to be worried about right now. That's my priority," Lamont told him rather eloquently.

"They are my real broth—"

"Langston, listen to me. I know you're worried about Tony, Kwesi, and Krush, but Lamont is right. Right now you need to be worried about yourself. You're in deep trouble, and our main focus is trying to figure out how we're going to handle it," I explained patiently.

"But, Dad—"

"The fact of the matter is I don't know those boys well enough to put my homes on the line," I told him.

"Do *you* even know them well enough, is the question." Lamont spread cream cheese on his bagel and took a bite.

"Yes, I know them well enough," Langston replied indignantly.

"Well, if you do, then can you please tell me which one of them put that heroin in the back of your car?" Lamont asked.

I turned and looked at Langston, waiting for his answer.

He paused for a moment, but it wasn't because he was preparing to give an answer. Finally, he said, "I can't believe this shit! Why can't you just give them the benefit of the doubt?"

"Because I've been a lawyer a long time, and Dad's been one even longer. Now, you don't realize the severity of this situation, but let me make it very clear. You could be going to jail for a long time behind this crap, and it's time you start realizing it." Lamont stared at him intensely.

"But they weren't my drugs!" Langston shouted at him. "How many times do I have to say it?"

"Until a judge throws the case out or a jury acquits you, that's how long," Lamont answered, and I could see the frustration and anger in Langston's face.

"Langston, the drugs were found in your car; a car that you were driving. That makes you the prime suspect out of all four of you. So, all your brother and I care about right now is finding a way to get you out of this. Then we'll worry about your friends," I said, hoping he would understand the practical nature or our dilemma. But I could tell by Langston's face that he just didn't want to hear me.

Lamont exploded. "Fuck those guys! It's time to start thinking about yourself!"

"Your father and brother are right."

We all turned to see Jacqueline standing in the dining room doorway. "One of them put that package in the back of your car. It didn't just get in there by itself."

She entered the room. "Morning Lamont," she said, touching his shoulder.

"Hey, Ma," Lamont said, but he didn't get out of his chair.

"Morning, Ma." Langston stood and gave his mother a hug.

"Hey, sweetie." Jacqueline kissed his cheek then glanced at me and said, "Bradley."

"Jacqueline." I nodded. I hadn't heard the doorbell ring. It wouldn't have been the first time she'd walked in unannounced. We'd been divorced for years, but she seemed to think she was still entitled to the freely roam the house she no longer resided in.

"Just so you know, there are three press trucks outside," she told me.

Lamont stood up and peeked out the window as she turned to Langston. "Honey, why don't you come and stay at my place for a while? This is the last place you need to be."

"I'm fine, Mom," Langston told her. "Simone is on her way here. We're going to drive out to Sag Harbor and spend the day."

I saw the disappointed look on Jacqueline's face and tried not to enjoy it.

"Langston, we have a lot of things to go over to figure out a strategy to get you out of this mess. The last thing you need is Simone distracting you and being in the way," Jacqueline said, her distaste evident in her voice. "I don't know why you even called her over here anyway."

"Because she's my girlfriend," Langston said, "and she's not going to be in the way."

"And because she's welcome here, unlike some people."

For the second time that morning, our attention was drawn to the entryway of the dining room. This time, when we all turned, it was my beautiful wife Carla standing there staring at us. My eyes went from her to Jacqueline, and I slowly let out the air that I had sucked in when I heard her voice. My current wife and my ex got along like oil and water. The problem was that they were both Alpha females with similar personalities. Both women thrived on power, and this morning, they seemed ready for war.

"Good morning, honey." I stood up and greeted my wife.

"Good morning." She smiled at me then turned to Jacqueline. "I wasn't expecting your arrival this early."

"I came to check on my son to make sure he was fine and sit down with *my* family to come up with a plan for him." Jacqueline gave her a fake smile. "I hope you won't feel left out?"

The tension in the dining room was so thick that I could hardly breathe. I could see Jacqueline's nostrils flaring, and Lamont looked like he wanted to get up and run. Everyone was uncomfortable, and no one spoke.

The doorbell rang, and Langston jumped up from the table.

"I never feel left out in my house. The trouble is you keep forgetting that it is my house and not yours. So, if you can't respect it, you can get out. I'm sure things will be a lot more productive without you." Carla gave her a fake smile back. "Isn't that right, Bradley?"

Before I could answer, Jacqueline snapped, "Honey, there's no need for you to feel threatened. I've already been the woman of this house and have no desire to resume that position. It's yours. And for the record, this has nothing to do with Bradley either. It's about my son. So, like it or not, I'm here, and I'm not going anywhere. Now, I'm gonna be here doing any and everything to keep his ass out of jail, whether you like it or not." She pointed at Lamont. "Now, Lamont, call your sister and Perk and tell them to get their asses over here. We got work to do."

Kwesi

24

I stood in the corner of the recreation room of building C74 at Rikers Island, trying my best to remain inconspicuous so that no one would notice the look of terror on my face. I'd watched enough American TV to know that if the wrong person sensed fear, I would become a target, and there was no telling what would happen to me. Hiding my fear was no easy task with my red, swollen eyes. I'd never cried as much as I had the night before.

"Adamack! Adamack!" one of the guards yelled. At first, I ignored him, pretending to be engrossed in the well-worn copy of some book I happened to find in the cell where I'd spent the night. That is, until I realized he was walking toward me.

"Adamack!"

I straightened up and asked politely, "Adomako?"

"What the fuck ever. I'm talking to you. Come on, let's go," he said, standing over me.

"Go where? Am I being released?" A momentary feeling of relief came over me.

"Hell no, you ain't being released, fool. You got a lawyer visitor." He led me out of the room.

Although I wasn't being released yet, I was still hopeful. Maybe it was Langston's father who had come to see me. He would know what to do to get me out of there, unlike the useless Legal Aid lawyer who had represented me at my arraignment.

I was escorted into a small room. As soon as I entered, I was grabbed and pulled into a tight embrace. It scared me, and I initially tried to fight it off, until my mother's voice broke through my disorientation.

"Kwesi, my son. My beloved son, are you all right?"

I wrapped my arms around my mother, who was sobbing into my chest.

"Mother!" I shouted.

"Are you okay?" Her voice was low as she squeezed me tighter.

"Yes, Mother, I'm fine."

She looked up at me and touched my face. "Are you sure? You look like you've been crying. Did anyone hurt you? Oh my God, I cannot believe this."

"No, no one hurt me, Mother. I'm fine, I promise." I refused to tell her how scared I was.

"I could not believe it when they called and said you were in jail. I knew it must be some mistake. My son would never be in jail. Not my Kwesi. He is a good boy!"

"Is she correct? Are you innocent of this crime?" My father's deep voice echoed in the small room. I turned around to see him dressed in a simple black suit and tie, glaring at my mother and me over the wire-rimmed glasses that sat on the edge of his nose. I released my mother and stood in front of him. The look of disappointment that he wore on his face made me feel even more ashamed than I already was.

"Father," I started, but before I could say another word, he held up a palm to stop me.

"Answer me, Kwesi. Are you innocent of transporting these drugs? Or have we been sending you to college to get a degree in stupidity?"

"Akwasi!" My mother stepped beside me.

"Father, I did not do this. There has been a mistake. I should not be here." The words rushed desperately from my mouth.

"This is what happens when you do not concentrate on your studies. I told you that joining this fraternity was beneath you. They are nothing but a bunch of spoiled, lazy students who do not have a sense of honor and pride for their families or this great country we live in. I have warned you time and time again to be careful about the company you keep, and now look at what's happened!" my father yelled. "You have disgraced us all."

"Akwasi! Now is not the time to be critical."

I'd never heard my mother raise her voice to my father like that. My father was also typically mild in nature. Seeing him this emotional caused as much fear in me as the inmates I had just left. I swallowed hard.

"Mr. Adomako."

I looked beyond my father and saw two men sitting at a table that I hadn't noticed before. The one who had called my father's name was a tall black man with a bald head. His skin was just as dark as mine and my father's, but from his accent and the way he carried himself, he seemed American. He stood up and approached us.

"Who are you?" I asked him, hoping he was with the Hudson Group. "Are you my new lawyer?"

"No, my name's James Brown. I'm an assistant district attorney for the City of New York."

"Oh," I said with disappointment. "I don't think I should be talking to you without a lawyer."

"Well, then it's a good thing Mr. Kimba is here." He pointed to the other man, who was now standing by his side.

"Hello, I'm Kenneth Kimba." The man extended his hand to me, and I shook it. It seemed kind of suspicious that these two were so chummy.

I turned back to James Brown and said, "So, you're the prosecutor? Why are you here? I shouldn't be talking with you. I should be talking with him." I turned to the man who was supposed to be my lawyer.

My father interjected, "You don't get to ask questions, young man. And if you must know, he's here to help you."

"Help me how, Father?" I asked.

"He's here to offer you a deal," Mr. Kimba told me.

"A deal for what? I haven't done anything. Why do I need a deal if I'm not guilty?" I turned to my father, my eyes pleading with him to believe me.

"Kwesi, I don't believe you've done anything," ADA Brown said, giving me some small consolation. "But you were in the car where the drugs were found, which makes you guilty by association. I want to help you get out of here, and I can, but you've got to tell me who that heroin belonged to."

I stared at him blankly. "I honestly don't know who it belongs to. I just know it isn't mine. I don't do drugs, nor sell them. As a matter of fact, why don't you give me a polygraph test right now and a drug test?" I suggested.

"I see someone's been watching lots of *Law and Order*," he said with a smirk. "But I'm afraid that's not possible."

"Why not?" I asked.

"Because it's not admissible in court," Mr. Kimba said.

"So, what is it that you want me to do? Lie about one of my friends?"

"Your friends? Where are your friends now?" my father asked angrily. "Why aren't you with them? They have their own attorney and left you with a million-dollar bail to fend for yourself. Your mother and I hired Mr. Kimba to help you get out of this situation. Spent our hard-earned money, and you're worried about your friends?"

His words stung and shocked me at the same time. Had my friends left me high and dry? Had Langston gotten his father to defend everyone else but me? Why was I the only one in Rikers? Had they been released and left me alone?

"It's not about my friends," I protested. "It's about telling the truth. I do not know who the drugs belonged to. I'd never seen them before."

"Let me explain something to you, young man. I was hoping that you'd be a little more cooperative, considering that I'm on your side here. But I'm going to say this: if you don't tell me who the drugs belong to and where they came from, I will have my friends at the state department revoke your family's visas and have ICE pick them up and ship them out on the first thing smoking." ADA Brown's face revealed no emotion.

"No!" My mother gasped and reached for my father's hand.

"You can't do that. You have no right," I said, resisting the urge to punch him.

"Can I speak with you in the hallway for a second, Mr. Brown?" Mr. Kimba said.

"We can chat on my way out." ADA Brown stared at me.

The two of them walked out of the room, leaving me alone with my parents. I sat down in a nearby chair. My father sat in one of the seats beside me.

"Kwesi, listen to me. You must tell that man whatever it is that he wants to hear so that you may leave this horrible place and get back to school. I do not have the resources to bail you out. You have class and finals to prepare for. This is not your fault, and he understands that."

"Father, you want me to lie?" I asked. "Say something I know is not true? Where is the honor in that?"

My father stood and said, "I want you to do whatever you must in order to save yourself and this family, Kwesi." He turned and walked toward the door, then said, "Mamfatou, let's go."

"Kwesi." My mother hugged me.

I hugged her back. "Mother, I'm so sorry."

She pulled my head closer to her and whispered in my ear, "I love you, Kwesi. Be careful and remember your faith. Do you understand? Remember your faith."

I nodded.

"Remember your faith, Kwesi," she repeated again as they exited.

Desiree

25

The twenty-minute drive from my place to my father's felt like forever because of the proverbial elephant in the back seat of the SUV. Perk and I had barely spoken two words this morning, ever since he informed me that we'd been summoned to my father's Riverside Drive estate. Normally, we'd be fighting over what radio station we were going to listen to, or debating politics and social issues, but today, things between us were awkward. He didn't even protest when I reached for the radio and switched from the Breakfast Club to Urban Talk Radio.

"So, we're just not gonna talk?" I finally reached down and turned off the radio.

"What do you wanna talk about, Desiree?" Perk asked, his eyes staring straight ahead and his face looking defiant.

"I don't know. Let's talk about Trump, the weather, or how about my brother's fucking case?" I answered sarcastically. I'd known Perk since my father rescued him from his crack addicted momma and daddy back in junior high school. He was as much a Hudson as any of us, although we never adopted him. Perk had attended Howard University on a football scholarship, although he'd had offers from USC, Penn State, and Florida. After college, he had a short stint in the NFL as a linebacker for the Eagles, until he blew out his knee. That was when Daddy brought him on as the lead investigator for our legal firm.

"You do know he got arrested yesterday, and you haven't said a word about it."

"That's because your father asked me not to."

"Huh? Why?"

"You're asking me what Bradley Hudson is thinking?" He laughed, and I had to chuckle as well. He took his eyes off the road for the first time since we'd left the house, and he stared directly at me. "But if you really wanna talk, let's talk about this little game you played last night."

"Forget it. We don't have to talk," I said, dramatically reaching for the volume button.

Perk and I had always been close, probably closer that we needed to be. I knew it was a bad idea to go into his room the night before, but I would have been tossing and turning all night if I hadn't. Perk was usually an early riser and was almost always out of the house before I even woke up, so the last thing I expected was for us to be sharing a ride to my father's house this morning.

He turned the music back down and said, "Naw, let's chat now."

"I'd rather not." I reached down, but he covered the buttons with his huge hand.

"You're a trip. You know that, right?"

"How?" I turned toward him and waited for his answer.

"Because you are mind-fucking the hell outta me," he said gruffly.

I don't know, maybe it was ego, but I liked the way that sounded. I placed my hand on his thigh. "It wasn't your mind I was fucking, Perk."

"See, that's exactly what I'm talking about." He moved my hand. "You're playing games."

"It takes two to play the game we played last night, and I wasn't the only participant. You could have said no." He remained silent, which amused me. We both knew damn well that no man would say no when he woke up to a naked woman on top of him. "I didn't see you hesitate to put that condom on when I handed it to you."

He deflected with, "You're only doing this because Lena's interested in me."

"You can date who you wanna date, Perk. That ain't my business," I said. Truthfully, the last thing I wanted to hear was Perk talk about Lena, some random hood rat he'd met at Starbucks. They'd been dating about a week. As far as I was concerned, she wasn't a threat to me, because as I'd proved last night, I could have him any time I wanted him.

"Good, because one day you're going to walk in my room, and she's going to be lying there."

This time, it was my turn to be silent, but not for long, "You better not let that bitch in my house, because that's the day I'll catch a case."

"That's my house too—and why she gotta be a bitch, Des?"

"Because I don't like her, and I think you can do better."

"You don't even know her!" he replied.

"I know her type, but if that's who you want, I don't give a shit, as long as it's not in my house." As I sat back in my seat, I realized I should've left well enough alone and endured the ride in silence.

"It's funny how you don't wanna be with me, but when I start dating other people, all of a sudden you wanna start back fucking," he said.

"Perk, why do we keep going through this each and every time?"

My phone rang, and without even looking at it or my watch, I knew who it was. I ignored the call and continued my conversation.

"Because you know I like you, Des. That's why. And I know you're feeling me too, but you got so much shit with you. At least Lena acts like she wants me."

"Perk, we've gone over this enough. Yes, I like you. I enjoy being around you, and yeah, I enjoy fucking you too, but I'm not ready for what you want. I don't want to be in a relationship," I told him.

"Five years of fucking is a relationship," he said matter-of-factly.

"No, it isn't. Why do we need a title? Don't you understand that once you put a title on it, that's when shit gets weird?" I tried to explain. My main reason for not wanting to be in a relationship with Perk was that, although we did work together and live together, my family had no idea we were sleeping together. I knew that if we became involved in a full-fledged relationship and then we were to break up, it would make his working at my father's firm very difficult. I didn't want that for him or me. "Titles put restraints on things."

"Restraints, like not being able to bring people to the house I pay rent on?" He smirked as he made his point.

Again, my phone rang, and I decided to answer, mostly to avoid responding to his question.

"Hello."

"Good morning, beautiful. How are you?" Jerri greeted me.

"Good morning," I said.

"You know I woke up in my feelings because you didn't call me last night like you promised. Then I remembered everything you had going on yesterday and figured you were tired and went straight to bed, so I forgive you," she said. Her sweet tone almost made me feel guilty about the gratifying time I'd spent with Perk instead of calling her.

"I know. I apologize, and I appreciate your understanding."

"Well, you can make it up to me by letting me make you breakfast this morning."

"I can't. I've already left for my dad's house. We have a meeting about my brother's case," I explained, looking at Perk from the corner of my eye to see if he was paying attention to my conversation. He seemed to be more focused on the traffic in front of us.

"Oh, okay then." Jerri's disappointment was obvious. "I guess I'll talk to you later."

"Sounds great. I'll speak with you soon," I said cheerfully.

"Damn, you're sounding quite professional this morning. Is there someone with you?" Jerri asked, picking up on my tone.

"Yes. I'm with Perk, our firm's investigator." Sometimes the truth was the best lie.

"Okay, that I can live with, because that sweet ass belongs to me and me only." Jerri laughed loudly.

Again, I glanced over at Perk to make sure he hadn't heard anything she said. "I'll talk to you later."

"Enjoy your day, beautiful."

I ended the call.

"Can I ask you a question?" Perk asked, causing me to become nervous. Maybe he had been eavesdropping after all.

"What?"

"Are you seeing someone else? Is that what it is?"

I frowned and tried to play dumb. "Huh?"

"Is that what the problem between you and me is?"

"God, no, Perk. That's not it at all. You are way overthinking this." I touched his arm, and he looked at me. I gave him a reassuring smile and told him. "Perk, we're cool."

Fortunately, he dropped the subject, and we spent the remainder of the ride laughing and talking as if things were back to normal.

Several cars were parked outside the house when we arrived, along with a couple of TV vans. This was becoming way bigger than I'd expected. As prominent as my father was, he hated the press when he couldn't control it, and this was probably driving him bananas. Perk ignored them and pulled into the driveway. As soon as he parked the car, he hopped out and headed for the front door.

"You're not gonna open my door?" I called after him.

"You're not my woman, remember? We're cool. Make sure you hit the lock when you get out, buddy," he said. I couldn't tell if he was joking, but I locked the door nonetheless before closing it.

"Hey, everybody!" I said when I walked into the dining room, where the entire family was sitting. I hugged my brother Langston's girlfriend, Simone, and gave a kiss on the cheek to my mother and my brothers. I was headed to greet my father, passing by my stepmother, Carla, who I touched awkwardly on the shoulder. I didn't feel comfortable hugging her, especially with my mother there, but a handshake would've been a little too formal.

"How are you, baby girl?" My dad smiled after our brief embrace. He peeked out the curtains and asked, "Those bastards still camped outside? They didn't bother you, did they?"

"No, they didn't, Daddy," I told him. It had been easy enough to ignore their shouted questions when I headed into the house.

"Well, now that everyone's here, we can get started," my father announced.

"Why don't we go into the study so Iris can clear the table?" My mother stood and suggested. We all followed her lead and were about to walk out when she turned toward Langston's girlfriend and said, "Simone, why don't you stay here with Iris, hun? All this legal talk is just going to go right over your head." Poor Lang just kissed her and began following us. "Oh, and Iris, you might want to wash this tablecloth. It has stains."

I noticed the look Carla gave my mother as she leaned over to my father and whispered loudly, "Does that wench realizes she's no longer the woman of this house?"

"It's fine, sweetheart," my father answered. "She's just trying to be helpful. She knows."

"She better act like it. I'm trying to be tolerant for Langston's sake, Bradley."

Lamont looked over at me, and I could see him trying to contain his laughter as we went into the study.

Michael

26

I stepped into the foyer of the home of Bradley Hudson, and it reminded me of why I'd become a lawyer. His place had to be the grandest home I'd ever been in. I still couldn't believe I was standing there after just having met Bradley Hudson a few days before. Like I'd promised, I called him the afternoon we met, and after a half-hour interview, he hired me with no hesitation. It sure made me feel good, to say the least. This felt like the start of a whole new trajectory for me. As part of the Hudson firm, I knew I was on my way to success. I called my employers this morning to quit, and now here I was, staring at the luxury in amazement as I followed the housekeeper into a large den.

"Mr. Hudson, Mr. Butcher is here," she said, stepping aside so that I could enter.

Bradley Hudson sat in a comfortable chair with half a dozen people around him. His son, Lamont, sat to his left, along with a beautiful young woman who was obviously his daughter based on the resemblance. Next to her was a football-player-sized guy, while off to his right sat two attractive older women and a young man who had to be his youngest son.

"Michael, come on in." Bradley stood, offering his hand, which I shook. "Everyone, this is Michael Butcher, the newest member of our team."

"Hello." I smiled. They all greeted me warmly, and no one looked even slightly upset about a virtual stranger coming into their midst and being introduced as already hired. Bradley was obviously in charge, and I guess they all trusted his judgment without question. I was introduced to everyone by name, and the two older women quickly clarified their positions as the wife and ex-wife as I sat down.

As if I'd been an employee for years, Bradley got right back to the discussion I assumed they'd been having before I entered. "Well, Langston, why don't you tell us everything that happened from the beginning?" he said to his son.

Langston described his recent arrest—which, of course, I knew about from all the news coverage—starting from the moment he was pulled over. He hesitated a little before he admitted they'd been smoking pot in the car, and again when he had to admit he'd mouthed off a little to the cop, but for the most part, he made it through without his parents having a heart attack.

"Sounds like a legal search." Lamont said what I was thinking.

"On the surface, everything seems like it was done by the book," Bradley agreed. "The marijuana gave them cause to search the car. The white officer seemed like he was going to give them a break. They were all Mirandized. There are no loopholes anywhere."

"There's always loopholes," Lamont replied. "Nobody is perfect."

"Exactly my point." Bradley turned to the big guy. "Perk, what do you think? You hear anything in Langston's story that we can use to our advantage?"

It was subtle, but I could see him glance at Langston and then hesitate. "Nah, but I'd like to get a look at those cops' body cams."

"I'll put in a request. See if I can get a copy today or tomorrow," Lamont told Perk, who nodded his approval. "I'm also going to make a motion for a bail reduction hearing for Krush and Tony."

"No, you're not," Bradley informed him.

"Huh?" Lamont looked confused, as if his father was suddenly stepping into his area of expertise. "So, *you're* going to make that motion?"

"No." Bradley looked over at his daughter. "Des, that's what I need you to handle. Lamont's a little opinionated when it comes to these boys. Can you handle it, or should I give the job to Michael?"

I watched Desiree glance from her brother to me, then back to her father. I was surprised to hear my name even mentioned, but a crafty lawyer like Bradley was probably just using me to motivate his daughter and son. And it worked.

"Yeah, I got it, Daddy," she said.

"Good. That leaves you, Michael, to find out everything you can about these cops. Perk will help you, but I want you to do the leg work."

"What about me?" Lamont asked.

Bradley said, "I need you to find Kwesi Adamako and his lawyer, and find out what he's saying to the prosecution. The DA's office is playing some type of game with this kid, and I want to know what it is." He turned in Langston's direction. "Life on the line, is Kwesi friend or foe?"

"Friend," Langston answered without hesitation. "Kwesi wouldn't do anything to hurt me, Dad."

"Langston, we don't know what people will do when they're under the pressure of a long jail sentence. I just want to make sure the story he tells is the same as yours," Bradley explained then turned back to Lamont. "Let's treat him as a friend for now, but I need some answers about this kid today."

"Let me talk to him and—" Langston started.

The ex-wife interrupted. "Honey, let your brother handle this. He's going to do what needs to be done to protect you and your friends, but you have to stay out of the way."

"Your mother's right, Langston." Bradley's words caused the ex-wife to break out in a huge smile, which put a sour look on the face of the new wife. I was figuring out quickly that this was not one big, happy blended family.

"Thank you, darling." The ex-wife stood and placed her hand on Bradley's shoulder. She didn't look in the direction of the new wife, but I could tell she was doing it just to piss her off.

"Perk?" ex-wife said.

The big guy sat up. "Yes, ma'am."

"We need to know where those drugs came from. Two kilos of heroin couldn't have come from some corner boy," she said. "And don't leave any rock unturned. This is my son's life on the line."

Perk nodded. "I'm on it, Jacqueline."

"What do you need me to do?" Langston asked, sounding sincerely eager to help in his own defense. We all turned our attention to Bradley for an answer.

"Uh, well . . . right now, son, we don't need you to do anything other than stay away from the press," Bradley said, sitting up in his chair. "Your girlfriend's in the other room. Go spend some time with her. We'll let you know when we need you."

Langston frowned helplessly. That was our cue that the meeting was over, and we all began to disperse. If this first day was any indication of what it would be like with the Hudsons, then I knew I would never have another boring day at work.

Langston

27

"Your mother hates me, doesn't she?" Simone sighed and rubbed my chest as we lay naked in the middle of the bed. "It doesn't matter what I say or do. The woman just hates me."

"That's not true, boo. She likes you," I said—even if it was stretching the truth—as I nuzzled my chin on the top of her head. Her curly hair smelled like a combination of coconut, flowers, and my sweat.

After hours of explaining the same thing over and over to my family, I'd been thankful when Simone showed up. In spite of my mother's protest, we left and drove out to our summer place in Sag Harbor, where we'd been for the past three days.

"You're a liar, and not a good one at that. I know when someone doesn't like me, and believe me, she doesn't. She never has."

To be quite honest, my mother didn't like Simone, but I wasn't about to say that out loud.

"She does like you. What's not to like? You're smart, funny, beautiful, and you're sexy as hell." My hand slipped around her tiny waist and began easing its way to the soft roundness of her ass.

"I doubt if my sexiness matters to her." Simone removed my hand from her rear. "Seriously, Langston. How are we ever going to get married if your mother doesn't like me?" She turned her body to face me.

"Babe, let's be honest. You did bring this upon yourself," I reminded her.

"Are we really going there again? Is she still pissed because I pledged Delta and not AKA?"

"It sure as hell didn't help, Simone. She did offer to write you a letter."

"Langston, I was not going to pledge that stuck-up-ass sorority. You know how those girls act on campus."

My mother and sister had said the same thing about her sorority, although I didn't want to tell her that and get stuck in the middle of a sorority war.

Simone's phone rang. She rolled over, looked at it and rolled her eyes, and then hit the ignore button.

"Who was that?" I asked.

"It was Kiara again." She shook her head. "I don't have time to be answering fifty million questions about shit I don't have the answers to. She's already feeling some kind of way because you're home and Tony's not."

"I can imagine," I replied. Kiara was Tony's girlfriend and Simone's sorority sister. "You think I should talk to her?"

"No. She's just going to drive you crazy about getting Tony out. Forget her. You have enough to worry about."

"Nah, she's right. I gotta figure out a way to get them out."

"I love your sense of loyalty, but you don't have three million dollars laying around anywhere, do you?" Simone said. "Is there any way your mom could talk to the judge? A million-dollar bond is ridiculous."

"Tell me about it." I sighed as I got up from the bed and walked to the window that overlooked the bay. "She made a few calls to some friends, but people are starting to distance themselves from her and my father now that I'm collateral damage. But it's not the bail I'm worried about."

Simone came up behind me and wrapped her naked arms around my chest. "Then what is it?"

"It's something my family is trying to drill in my head. They want me to believe that one of my friends might be responsible for the drugs." I turned to her and moved my hands around her waist. "I just can't, Simone. For me to believe that would destroy everything I know."

"Langston . . ." I could tell by her expression that she agreed with my family. She hadn't verbalized it yet, but I had known from day one that she thought it was one of the fellas, most likely Krush. "If you ask me, if they were your real friends, whoever put that shit in there would step up and confess. That's what real brothers do. Why should all of y'all take the fall for one?"

"Don't. Okay, Simone? Please just don't say anything else." I gently pushed her away. "I don't need to hear it from you too."

"Well, you're going to," she said adamantly then eased the tone in her voice. "Baby, you have to admit there's a possibility one of them did it."

"I don't have to admit anything. You might not have faith in them, but I do."

"Having faith is great, but acting blindly stupid isn't." She stepped forward and closed the distance between us. "Now, you can lie to me, your parents, and the whole darn world, but you can't lie to yourself, Langston. You say you want to be a lawyer, so what would you say to a client who was in your situation?" I knew Simone was trying to help, but she was doing more harm than good, because she was forcing me to think.

"You've been around them. None of them would do anything to hurt me." I tried to state my case, but I was losing. I didn't want to believe the drugs belonged to one of my friends, but I knew that to anyone else, the question was obvious: if they hadn't come from one of my friends, then where did they come from?

"Not purposely, but one of them put that package in the trunk," she said.

"And how do you know that?" I tried to hold onto a glimmer of hope as she wrapped her arms around me again.

"Because I know you didn't do it, and if you didn't do it, the odds say one of them did." Her words entered my mind like a sledgehammer up against concrete. I refused to allow them to enter my thoughts. I just sat there silently, trying to comprehend the idea that one of my frat brothers would betray my trust.

"Listen," she said, "why don't we take a quick trip so you can clear your head, give you some time to think?" she suggested. "Sun in our face, sand beneath our feet, and me by your side."

"I can't go anywhere. I don't even have my car, and yours barely made it here," I told her.

"Well, we can fly somewhere. We've been talking about learning how to paddleboard all winter. No better time than the present." Simone rubbed my back encouragingly.

"No can do. The judge made me surrender my passport." I sighed and went back to the bed, where I lay down with my hands beneath my head. "Plus, what if they need me in court?"

Simone climbed on top of me. "We can go to Puerto Rico this weekend. They don't have court on the weekends, and you don't need a passport to go there. It's a U.S. territory, despite our president not knowing it."

"Some fun in the sun would be nice," I conceded.

"Of course it will. I'll make all the arrangements. Okay?"

I stared at her dimpled smile and bright eyes. Meeting her and making her my girl was one of the best decisions I'd ever made. A quick weekend getaway with her was sounding better and better. My eyes traveled to her full breasts, and I imagined seeing them in a cute bikini—and all the things I could do to her on a secluded beach.

"Shit, why not? They don't seem to need me around here anyway."

She clapped her hands excitedly. "I'll go online later and find us some cheap flights." Leaning over, she kissed me full on the mouth, then began working her way down. It wasn't long before I forgot all about my boys and the legal troubles we were facing.

Krush

28

"Pleasure doin' business with you, gentlemen," I said sarcastically, scooping up the ten packs of cookies I'd won playing cards. I'd only been in lockup a couple of days, but I was starting to get the hang of this jail shit. I wish I could say the same thing for Tony, who was sitting in a chair by himself, isolated from the rest of the inmates.

I walked over to him and tossed him a pack of cookies. He ripped it open and jammed one in his mouth. I'd been looking out for Tony the best I could, but that sitting in a corner not talking to anyone shit wasn't working, because brothers were starting to size him up.

"Tony, man, you need to wake the fuck up and get out of the corner. Dudes is starting to whisper, and that ain't really safe," I told him.

He stared at me blankly, chewing away on a second cookie.

"Shit, what we need to do is pick out a couple of punk-ass niggas and whip their asses to let everybody know we're not to be fucked with," I suggested, half joking.

He just rolled his eyes, but Tony wasn't gonna be rolling his eyes when they jacked him. Hell, if he wasn't my man, I'd probably jack him too just for being the weirdo in the corner. Tony didn't understand that the key to surviving in jail was all about exuding confidence.

A guard interrupted my little pep talk when he came in and announced, "Wright, you have a visitor."

"A visit?" The only person that would be visiting me was my mom, or maybe this little Zeta chick Cherelle from back at school. "I'll be back, Tony. While I'm gone, man, maybe you could snap the fuck out of your little funk, huh?"

He shrugged and stuffed another cookie in his mouth.

I headed toward the CO's desk, and then I was directed to a big-ass room with a whole bunch of metal tables and chairs. I almost turned right back around when I saw the familiar face at one of the tables. He looked very uncomfortable and way, way out of place. Unfortunately, turning around wasn't an option once my father's gaze found mine.

What the fuck was he doing here? Don't get me wrong; my old man wasn't a bad dude. He wasn't one of those deadbeat dads, wife beaters, or child abusers. He came home every night, and we always had a roof over our heads and food on the table. As far as I knew, he loved my mom and never cheated on her, despite how much of an overbearing pain in the ass she could be. Hell, I loved that woman too, but I don't think I could be married to her for twenty-five years like he'd been. Shit, other than Langston's pops, he was probably the only black man I could truly say I had respect for. But along with that came a healthy dose of fear.

I took in a breath and let it out quickly before heading over to the table where he was sitting alone. Part of me hoped my mother might pop up out of nowhere, but of course, she didn't. When I reached the table, I stood there, and the two of us just stared at each other, me in my jail jumpsuit, and him in his business suit. He usually wore a tie, but the CO must have taken it from him.

Finally, he said, "Sit down, Kirby." I flinched a little, hoping that none of the other inmates had heard him call me by my government name. In here, it would be much better to be known as Krush.

I did as I was told and sat down, leaning back in the uncomfortable metal chair. "I didn't think you'd come," I said softly.

He slowly shook his head, matching my tone when he spoke. "And I didn't think I'd ever see my son in jail."

Coming from him, those words hurt. "This isn't my fault."

"It's never your fault, Kirby."

I raised my voice. "No, but this really isn't my fault, Dad."

"Don't you take that tone with me." He placed his hands flat on the table, probably to stop himself from reaching across it to smack me. "I worked too damn hard to give you everything so you wouldn't have to go to the streets for it. Hell, I even moved into the white neighborhood to keep you out of the streets, but you still found those hooligans hanging out on the corners, smoking weed and selling drugs."

"Dad, that was when I was a minor. They can't hold that against me."

"No, maybe they can't, but I can. Just because you haven't been busted doesn't mean you're innocent, Kirby. You seem to forget I'm the one who found that pound of marijuana in the shoe box under your bed this past summer."

He was right; I'd completely forgotten about that. But shit, he didn't have to go announcing that in front of all the COs in the room, did he?

"What do you want from me, Dad? I'm in school, I get good grades, and I got a job waiting for me when I graduate. What do I have to do to make you happy?"

"You can start by pulling your pants up and wearing a belt." It was the same shit he'd been telling me for ten years—and I'd been giving him the same answer the whole time.

"Dad, it's just a style, part of the hip hop culture I live."

He just shook his head and stared at me disapprovingly. It was no different than usual. My dad had never been one to tell me he was proud of me, even before I started fucking up.

I decided that it was probably best to change the subject. "The Hudsons are going to get my bail reduced, so can you get a bail bondsman to bail me out?"

"A bails bondsman costs fifteen percent of the bond, Kirby. You don't get that money back. Your mother and I don't have that kind of money to be throwing away. We spent all of our money trying to give you a good education."

His answer didn't surprise me. I hadn't really expected him to say yes, so it was time to go to Plan B, which I was sure he'd agree to. My dad might have been on my case most of the time, but deep down, I knew he loved me, and he was the kind of guy who'd do anything for his family.

"A'ight, but if they get my bail lowered, can you put up the house? That ain't gonna cost you nothing. You ain't gotta put up no cash."

He sat there silently for a moment, and I figured he was just making me sweat for a minute. But then he said, "No, Kirby we are not going to put up our house."

What the fuck?

"Come on, Dad. Don't play games. I know this looks bad, but I'm innocent. I wanna go home," I said, fighting to keep the panic out of my voice.

"You're right; it does look bad, and for your sake, Kirby, I hope you're innocent. But, son, your mother and I are tired. We don't have any faith in your innocence, and we're not about to put up the house we've worked thirty years to obtain to find out."

"Dad—"

He shook his head, basically telling me not to bother trying to change his mind.

"You're fucking serious, aren't you? You're going to leave me in here?"

"Yes, that's exactly what I'm going to do. Maybe this will make you understand that life isn't to be taken for granted, and neither is your freedom."

"This is bullshit. I'm calling Mom. She'll get me out. She'll make you get me out!" I was shouting now. A guard shot a look in our direction, warning me to calm down.

"No, she won't. Your mother is tired, Kirby. She told me to handle everything, and she'd back me one hundred percent. That's why she's not here." He got up and smoothed the wrinkles out of his pants.

For the first time since I'd arrived at Rikers Island, I had tears in my eyes. "Dad, don't do this. Dad! Dad!" I watched him walk away. At that moment, I felt nothing but hatred for the one man I loved more than any other in the world.

Lamont

29

The office of Kenneth Kimba and Associates, LLP, was located on Queens Boulevard, above a nail salon, one block away from the Queens County Courthouse. It was much smaller than I expected. Normally a firm with associates has more than a receptionist's desk with a single door behind it. Nevertheless, the place looked decent, and the receptionist was nice. Besides, I didn't really care what the office looked like. My only concern was the matter at hand.

After she seated me and kept me waiting there for more than twenty minutes, I walked over to the receptionist's desk and asked, "Does Mr. Kimba know that I'm here?"

"Yes, he knows. I told him when you first arrived." She was an attractive, albeit pudgy, brown-skinned woman. According to the nameplate on her desk, her name was Meghan.

"Okay, and our meeting was scheduled for two thirty, correct?" I looked at my watch to make sure it was indeed two fifty and I had a right to question her.

"Yes, according to the calendar, it is," she said then went back to typing on the computer in front of her.

"Would you happen to have any water?" I asked.

"No, but there's a vending machine with water and sodas in the hall if you'd like." Finally, Meghan pulled her eyes from the computer screen and looked up at me. "I can give you change if you'd like."

"No, thanks. I'm okay." I heaved a sigh.

The look I gave must have embarrassed her, because then she said, "I'm not trying to be rude, and normally we do have bottled water in the fridge, but I've been kinda swamped the past few weeks and barely have time to go home to get some sleep at night, let alone stop at Costco to buy water for the office."

"I understand. Being a receptionist in a law office isn't an easy task," I told her.

"Especially when you're the receptionist, the paralegal, and sometimes, on occasion, the process server." She laughed, and I took notice of her high cheekbones.

"You're a regular one-woman show," I joked. "I can appreciate a hardworking woman."

"Thank you." She blushed, and then, sufficiently buttered up, she leaned forward and whispered, "To be honest, he's in there trying to clean up. He's a big fan of you and your father."

I chuckled, and she joined right in. I was happy to see that my skills for charming women were as good as ever.

The office door behind her opened, and a tall, dark-skinned man dressed in a sweater vest and bow tie walked out. "Mr. Hudson," he said in a deep bass voice, "sorry to keep you waiting. You can come on back."

I gave Meghan a wink and followed Kenneth Kimba back into his office. Inside was just as basic as the outside. If he'd spent the past twenty minutes straightening up, I would have hated to see what the place looked like before, because it was a mess. There were papers strewn all over his desk, his computer, both chairs, and the bookshelf.

"How are you, Mr. Kimba? Lamont Hudson." I extended my hand, and he shook it.

"Have a seat, Mr. Hudson." He lifted a pile of papers from one of the chairs and dusted it off so I could sit. "It's a pleasure to meet a colleague of your caliber. I was hoping to meet your father as well. I have long admired his work." He walked behind the desk and took a seat.

"I'm sure you'll meet him soon."

"Yes, of course," he said. "Your message said you wanted to talk about my client, Kwesi Adomako."

I nodded. "We represent the other three defendants in the case. I'm here to discuss strategy."

He leaned back in his chair and said, "I agree. I think we should work together, but, Mr. Hudson, I'd be remiss if I didn't make something very clear."

"What's that?"

"My job is to represent Kwesi Adomako. He is my top priority, and I will only do what is in his best interest."

"Of course," I replied, though I was a little concerned. Every lawyer has a duty to put his client's needs first, so why did he feel the need to state that so directly? He continued, and I got my answer.

"So, with that said, you should know that we are considering filing a motion for my client to be tried separately from your three clients."

"What? Why? That makes no sense." I sat on the edge of my seat. I was no longer just concerned; I was very worried.

"It makes all the sense in the world from my client's perspective. Mr. Adomako is innocent." He gave me a shit-eating grin.

"All of them are innocent, Mr. Kimba. Don't you realize how this is going to make the rest of them look? We have a much stronger chance of beating this case if they're tried together and we are united," I explained, trying to maintain my composure.

"No, Mr. Hudson, *your* clients have a much stronger case if we're united." Kimba's smile faded away, and he became serious. "My client may be better served by going it alone. He was not driving; he was in the back seat. He was not smoking any marijuana. He was an innocent bystander who happened to be a passenger. He's just a victim of circumstance, and one, if not all, of your clients are guilty. You know it as well as I."

I had to keep my poker face on for that one. This guy may have been in a tiny office over a nail shop, but he wasn't stupid. Or was he? I decided to call his bluff and see which one it was.

"Sounds like you've been talking to the DA's office, Mr. Kimba. What did they offer you? I hope it's as good as the deal they offered us."

Kimba sat back, looking surprised. In truth, we'd talked to the DA's office and they had made an offer to us, but it was twenty years for each one of our clients. Not a good deal by any stretch of the imagination.

"I am not at liberty to say, but my client has declined the district attorney's offer for now," Kimba said.

"My clients have declined the district attorney's offer as well." I matched his smile from a moment ago. "So, now that we have all our cards on the table, maybe we should talk strategy."

He remained silent for a minute—maybe deciding whether he could trust me, or figuring out how he could take advantage of joining forces with the Hudsons. Either way, I waited quietly for his answer.

Finally, he said, "Mr. Adomako has rejected their offer, but there is one thing that could sway my client to helping the DA's office, Mr. Hudson."

"And what's that?"

"The DA's office has made threats to revoke the visas of my client's parents and siblings. They are hardworking people in this country legally."

Wow, the DA's office was really going all out. It was bad enough they had a great case up until this point, but to go after Kwesi's parents in order to get him to roll over seemed over the top.

"What can I do?" I asked.

"It's common knowledge that your mother is a federal judge in high standing. Perhaps she could intervene on the Adomakos' behalf. Put in a good word with the government to move along their citizenship."

"I'll see what I can do. If not, I'll represent them myself."

My answer seemed to satisfy him. "Thank you. I will tell Mr. Adomako. So, what type of strategy were you thinking?"

"Well, the bail set is astronomical and excessive. My firm is already drafting a bail reduction motion. We'd like to attach your client to it," I told him.

"I've already put things in place to file the motion for my client, Mr. Hudson."

"You have? That's great. I'll put you in touch with the people on our side who are drafting a motion. We can file them simultaneously so all three will be on the docket together." I was relieved that he had already started the process and I wouldn't have to babysit him through it. This whole situation was a mess, and having one less headache would be a relief, as things were bound to get even more complicated than they already were.

Perk

30

"That was my guy over at One P. P. He'll have something for us this afternoon," I said, placing my cell phone back in its holster on the dash of my truck. I didn't hear a response, so I glanced over at Michael, who was gawking at me from the passenger's seat. "What?"

"You have a source over at One P. P. that gives you information? As in One Police Plaza, the NYPD headquarters?"

"Yeah, and?" I replied as if this was common practice. "I'm the lead investigator for Bradley Hudson, one of the most well-known attorneys in the country. I have sources everywhere. Hell, my sources have sources. Otherwise, I don't have a job. You do the math."

"I am . . . I have." He still looked astonished. "You know, Perk, when Bradley first told me to work with you, I thought it was going to be a waste of time. But I've learned more in the past few days working with you than I did the entire time I was at Goldberg, Klein, and Hooper sitting in that cubicle."

"Mike, we haven't even touched the tip of the iceberg. That shit you learned at Harvard Law School and from them folks downtown is fantasy land. We get down and dirty. Coming to work with us is like learning to ride a bike without training wheels: either you gonna learn to ride fast, or you gonna get bruised up like a motherfucker."

Michael nodded his understanding. "Don't worry. I'm a fast learner."

"You seem to be, which is why I'm gonna teach you everything I can before Bradley kicks you over to Carla's team." Once again, he looked bewildered.

"Carla's team? Who is Carla?" Before I could reply, he answered his own question. "Oh, yeah. Carla, the new wife."

"Yeah, the new wife." I couldn't help but laugh out loud. "But I wouldn't let anyone hear you say that other than me. Far as Carla's concerned, she's the only wife. She's been trying to rewrite history for the past five years."

"That sounds like good advice," he whispered. "So, what exactly does Carla do for the firm? Is she a lawyer? I thought she was just his wife."

"Oh, she's more than just his wife. The entire third floor of our office is her domain. She runs all the firm's jury consulting, and she's the best there is at what she does. Trust me."

"I feel like I'm in some type of black version of *The Practice*," Michael said as we pulled into the circular driveway of the Hudsons' summer house in Sag Harbor. He looked around in awe as we got out of the truck. "They own this too?"

"Yup, wait until the summer. The parties we have here are off the charts." Memories of last summer, jumping off the roof and into the pool came to mind. How fucking stupid was I? That was the day I gave up tequila.

It was cold for a late spring day, so I tightened my jacket as we walked toward the house. Before we could ring the bell, the door opened and Langston appeared. "What's up, fellas? Come on in."

"What's up, Lang?" We followed him into the living area of the house, where Simone was laid out across a love seat.

"Hi, Perk." Simone sat up and smiled. Langston settled on the seat next to her.

"How ya doing, Simone?" I leaned over and kissed her cheek. "This is Michael. I don't think you met him at the house the other day."

Michael reached his hand out to shake Simone's. "Nice to meet you."

"Sorry to bother you, bro, but we needed a little information to help move the case along."

"Sure. Whatever I can do to help. It is my ass on the line. Any word on that bail reduction hearing for my boys?"

"Your sister said that it's scheduled for tomorrow," Michael replied.

"Good. What about the case? Any new updates on that?" he asked.

"You should probably talk to your old man about that, but everyone's working hard." I felt bad not having anything else to say about it. "I was kind of hoping you could give me some insight into how things went down."

"Perk, I already told you everything I know. I'm starting to think those cops set me up." He was getting agitated, but Simone placed her hand on his shoulder, and it seemed to calm him down.

"If they did, then we're going to find out. I'll have copies of their body and dash cams tomorrow."

"Good."

"But what I need now is what happened before they arrested you," I explained.

I nudged Michael. I wanted him to ask Lang the first few questions, so I could analyze Lang's answer and hit him with a follow-up. Sometimes hearing other people brought new questions to light.

Michael caught on quick. He looked down at his notes and said, "Your mother said she bought the car on Friday. So, it's safe to assume you were out and about Friday night, showing off your new ride, right?"

"Nah, I stayed home Friday night," Lang answered. "I didn't go anywhere until Saturday morning." He glanced over at Simone for backup.

"Yeah, he FaceTimed me about seven that night, all excited when he brought the car home." Simone laughed. "He was like a kid with a new toy."

"So, you didn't go anywhere?" Michael asked. "I mean, a new ride like that, I would have had to put some miles on that baby."

"I know, right? And I wanted to, but I had this paper I had to finish up and email to my professor. The deadline was ten p.m. Simone and I were going back and forth on it. She was proof reading it."

"Damn, I wish I had a girlfriend like that when I was in school. No wonder you get all A's," I commented, but then sat back to let Michael continue his line of questions.

"You didn't drive the car Friday, so where was the first place you went Saturday?" he asked.

"It wasn't to see his girlfriend, who spent half the night reading his paper," Simone said with an attitude. "He went out to show off his new car to his friends."

"I wasn't driving all the way from New York to B-More, Simone, when I was going back to school the next day," Lang snapped back with just as much attitude. It surprised me, because I'd never seen him be anything but respectful to his woman. "Besides, you were busy. You had plans to go to dinner with your line sisters, remember?"

"You still could've driven down. You could've gone to dinner with us," she said.

"Yeah, right." He laughed, then looked to me and Michael. "Would y'all drive three hours to go to dinner with fifteen women?"

"Sounds like a fun time to me." I shrugged happily. "Where do I sign up?"

Michael nodded enthusiastically. "I'm with Perk. Hand me a pen."

"See!" Simone sat back and folded her arms.

"Whatever," Lang groaned.

"So, where did you go Saturday?" Michael asked as he pulled out a legal pad. "Where was your first stop?"

"I went to Krush's first. We were supposed to go over to the park near his house and ball with some of our frat brothers from City College." He hesitated, glancing over at Simone.

"Supposed to?" I snapped. "Look, Lang, I need you to tell us everything you did from the minute you left the house until that cop pulled you over. Don't be leaving shit out."

He glanced at Simone again before he spoke. "When I got there, he had some chick he'd met at the strip club with him. She had made this big-ass breakfast when I got there."

"What chick? Isn't he seeing that Zeta?" Simone sounded really pissed now.

"I don't know. I don't think so, not anymore." He turned his attention back to me. "Anyway, she was about to call an Uber, but Krush insisted that I let him drive her home."

Simone gasped. "You let him drive some random ho around in your new car?"

"She didn't live that far, Simone, and I was in the middle of eating. It was no big deal." Lang sounded like he was pleading with her to believe him.

"So, you let Krush drive the car?" Michael asked, glancing at me. "How long was he gone?"

"Not long. Maybe twenty, thirty minutes."

"Do you know where this girl lives?" Michael asked.

"No, but like I said, it wasn't far, because he wasn't gone long. I'm sure he remembers."

"Do you even know her name?" Simone asked. Langston reached for her hand, but she pulled it away. "See, that's why I didn't hook Krush up with my friend, Lauryn. Fucking with nasty-ass strippers. That's disgusting."

"Are you sure that's the only place he went?" I asked, trying to keep the conversation focused on Langston's defense, not on their lovers' quarrel.

"As far as I know," he replied with the look of a man in the doghouse.

"Okay, so where did you go next?" I asked.

"We played ball for about three hours; then we went to Kwesi's. His mom made us a bunch of African food, and we watched the playoffs." He kept looking over at Simone, who refused to meet his eyes. "We were there for a while, eating and talking."

"The car didn't move?" Michael asked.

"No. Well, wait. His pops was blocked in the driveway, so his brother moved it, but that was it until I left."

Once again, Michael and I shared a knowing look. Michael was taking detailed notes each time Langston gave him an answer. He was definitely giving us some good information we could use in his defense.

"Okay, then from there, where did you go?" Michael asked.

"We went to Tony's crib and picked him up. We didn't get out the car at all. Then we went to this kickback by the Barclays Center for a sec."

"A sec?" I asked.

"A couple of hours. We were outta there by ten tops."

"A kickback? You didn't tell me you were going to a kickback." Simone rolled her eyes at him.

"It wasn't something that was planned, Simone," he huffed.

"Then why'd you keep it secret?" she shouted. Lang turned to her and gave her the "will you chill?" look.

Michael pressed on. "Where'd you go from there?"

"We drove over to Benny's bar, played some pool, and had a nightcap."

"Who is *we*?" Simone asked suspiciously.

"Me, Tony, Kwesi, and Krush. That's it," he said. "After that, I dropped Kwesi and Tony off at the train around one and took Krush home; then I went home. The next day, I picked them all up, and we hit the road."

"So, the next morning, when you got ready to leave, did you notice anything? Was there anything in the trunk other than your bag?" Michael asked.

"Nope. The trunk was empty far as I could tell." He shrugged.

"And when you picked up your boys, did each of them put their own bags in the trunk?" I asked.

"Yep."

"Did you get out and watch?" Michael asked.

"No, I didn't watch. It was cold. I wasn't getting out the car. We've been riding home together for damn near four years. Nothing changed except I was driving a different car. They're my best friends. I trust them," he said, giving us answers to questions we hadn't even asked. "That's why I let Krush drive my brand-new car. And Kwesi's brother. It's just a car."

"Oh, yeah? Then how come you never let me even drive your old car?" Simone stood up and walked out of the room. She was fuming, and he was definitely going to hear about it after we left.

"So, that's it? Those are the only places and people who were around the car?" Michael asked.

"Uh, yeah." He nodded.

"You sure about that?" I asked. "That's all you gotta say?"

He gave us this innocent look and said, "Yep."

I glared at him for about five seconds, then like a cobra, I grabbed him by the color roughly. Michael looked like he was about to faint as I led Langston to the door. "Will you excuse us for a minute, Michael? Me and Langston have to talk in private for a minute."

"Perk, what the fuck?" Langston tried to struggle free, but he wasn't going anywhere as I dragged his ass out of the house. "Have you lost your mind?"

"Have you?" I growled back, throwing him on the lawn. "Now, I'm going to ask you this one more time. Were those drugs yours?"

"No! Hell no, Perk," he protested, shaking his head furiously. "You know I've never touched that shit! I barely smoke weed."

"Then who put those drugs in the car?" I clenched my fists and stepped to him.

"I don't know. I swear to God I don't—" He flinched, probably sensing that he was about as close to a beatdown as you could get. I didn't care if it cost me my job. I was going to get to the truth. "Don't you think if I knew, I'd tell you?" he asked.

"Then why the fuck are you lying to me?" I was breathing heavy with anger.

"I'm not lying to you!"

I stared him in the eyes as he started to tear up.

"Yes, you are. You started this whole damn conversation off with a lie," I barked. "I was at your house Friday night, working with Carla and your pops. When I left, you weren't there, and neither was your fucking car."

His eyes grew wide like he couldn't believe I'd figured out his lie. After all the years I'd been with the family, his dumb ass should have known I was not the one to lie to.

"Okay, okay, you're right," he finally said. He stared at the house as if he were more scared of it—or, rather, of Simone—than he was of me. "I left right after I sent my professor the paper."

"What the fuck, Lang? I thought we was better than that."

"We are, Perk. I swear we are."

"Then why'd you lie to me, bro? I'm trying to help you."

"I know that, but I couldn't say where I was in front of Simone."

"Why? Where'd you go?" I demanded to know.

He glanced up at the window to make sure Simone wasn't standing up there listening. "I went and got Tony and Krush. We all went to this underground strip club Tony's brothers run."

I wanted to pop him in the mouth right then and there.

"We were there a couple of hours, drinking and getting lap dances and shit."

I sighed. "What the fuck was you thinking? Don't you know those places get raided all the time? That was stupid."

"I wasn't thinking. I was just trying to have a good time with my boys."

"There's a lot of places an aspiring lawyer could have had a good time, but a Bloods hangout shouldn't be one of them."

"I know it looks bad, but Tony's brothers aren't as bad as you may think. They stay on us about being legit," he explained.

"I'm not sure how much faith I have in that, but at least things are finally starting to add up," I said.

"Perk, you can't say shit about this to Ma and Dad," he pleaded. "They'll kill me. And Simone . . . I don't even wanna think about what she'll do."

"I hear you, but I got a job to do. Not only that, but you're like a little brother to me. I know those are your boys, but my concern is keeping your ass out of jail, not them." I really did feel for him. "Look, I can't promise I won't tell your pops, so I suggest you tell him yourself." I sighed, shaking my head in disappointment. I guess I'd given him too much credit before. He was much dumber than I thought. "As far as Simone and your mom are concerned, I work for your father, and this is covered by attorney/client privilege. Man, you shoulda *been* told me this."

"I know. I fucked up."

"You don't know the half of it. Did either of his brothers have access to your car?"

"Well, yeah. They were . . . Fuck! Perk, they were sitting in my car the whole time we were in the club. You don't think—"

"I don't know," I interrupted, "but I'm gonna find out."

I turned around and saw Simone standing in the doorway, arms crossed and a frown on her face. I didn't think she'd heard anything we had said, but judging by the look on her face, this wasn't going to be a good night for Langston. Then again, it hadn't been a good week for him.

"I'll holla at you later. Right now, you better get in there and talk to your girl. Tell Mike I'm in the truck."

Desiree

31

"You sure you don't want me to handle this?" Lamont asked for the twentieth time. I wished he would stop badgering me.

"I got it," I replied, placing my briefcase on the side of the table for the defense.

"Okay, but this isn't one of those family court passion projects you love so much. This is the real deal. How we go forward from here may determine the case," he stated.

I ignored his arrogance as I sat down and glanced at the same white ADA who'd handled Langston's arraignment. For some reason, I'd expected the black guy who tried to act so big and bad at the precinct to be sitting on the other side, but he was nowhere to be found—although I was sure that at some point they'd bring in someone black to sit in one of those chairs. This was too high profile a case, and when it came to my father, every case eventually became related to race.

Speaking of my father, I turned to Lamont and asked, "Where's Daddy?"

"Where do you think? He's outside in front of the cameras," Lamont replied, then changed his tone and grunted, "What the fuck is wrong with that boy?"

The word "Who?" barely escaped my lips before I saw Langston walk into the courtroom and take a seat behind me.

"Will you please deal with him?" Lamont asked as Kwesi's lawyer approached and shook his hand. I had met with Kwesi's lawyer after Lamont's meeting with him, and we came up with a damn good motion. I was fairly certain that we would be able to get the bail reduced for the boys, especially since we weren't appearing in front of the same judge.

I turned around in my chair and said between clenched teeth, "What are you doing here? Didn't we tell you to stay home?"

"I came to make sure everything was straight with my boys," Langston answered.

"You need to leave. We've got this under control. This courthouse is the last place you need to be seen. Didn't Daddy tell you not to go out in public unless it was important?" I stared at my younger brother, dressed in khakis, button-down shirt, and his fraternity tie.

"This is important, Des." Langston glared at me.

"Go home." Lamont finally turned around and joined the conversation.

"No." He folded his arms defiantly.

Lamont looked like he wanted to punch him. I put my hands on Lamont's shoulders and turned him around.

"It's a simple bail reduction hearing, Langston. This isn't a trial. You don't need to be here," I pleaded.

"Yes, I do."

The courtroom door opened, and Tony's mom entered, along with Kwesi's parents.

"Hey, Ms. Rita." Langston hugged Tony's mother, then spoke to Kwesi's parents. There was no sign of Krush's family. "How you doing, Mr. and Mrs. Adomako?"

"Langston." Mr. Adomako nodded; then he and his wife took seats. Talk about throwing shade. Could he have been any more obvious that he blamed this whole thing on Langston?

The side door of the courtroom opened, and Tony, Krush, and finally Kwesi were brought in. Their hands were cuffed, and all three were wearing prison jumpsuits. I had to admit even I was taken aback by their appearance, and poor Langston looked horrified. They'd only been in Rikers a couple of days, but it was clearly taking a toll on them. I prayed that I would be able to get their bail reduced so they could all go home.

"My poor baby," Kwesi's mother gasped and put her hands over her mouth. Her husband put his arm around her to comfort her.

"I am okay, Mother." Kwesi nodded toward her.

"Head up, son," Tony's mother said aloud. He glanced back, and they gave one another a knowing look.

The guys took their seats beside me at the defense table.

Langston leaned forward and told them, "Everything's gonna be cool." None of his friends responded. Instead, they focused their attention on the judge, who had just entered the courtroom.

"Sit back and be quiet, Langston," Lamont snapped at him. Then he turned to Krush and Tony and said, "Just remember what I told y'all when we met earlier, guys. This shouldn't take too long."

"All rise!" The bailiff announced the entrance of the judge, and we stood. I mentally went over everything I had prepared to say.

"Good. Dad's here," Langston whispered.

I looked over my shoulder and saw that my father had slipped into the courtroom, in spite of my suggestion that he not be there. The last thing I needed was his appearance causing a distraction, which it was. It was bad enough that Langston had shown up.

"Your Honor, Anthony Baker, Kwesi Adomako, and Kirby Wright versus the State of New York," the clerk read after we were seated.

"Why are we here, counselors?" Judge Rodrigues asked, peering over his glasses at the defense table. Judge Rodrigues was a Latin man in his late fifties. Carla had checked him out and said he was about as fair a judge as we were going to get in racist Staten Island.

"Your Honor, we believe the bail originally set by the court was excessive. We are requesting a bail reduction for all three of our clients from one million dollars to one hundred thousand."

"Mr. Wilkins, does the State have any objection to this reduction?"

ADA Wilkins stood up and said, "Your Honor, we have serious objections. As I stated at the defendants' arraignment, this is a serious drug trafficking crime and warrants the bail amount that has been set."

"This excessive bail is clearly prejudicial, and a violation of my clients' Eighth Amendment rights. They are all upstanding college students who have no criminal past," I countered.

"These so-called college students had two kilos of pure heroin in their car. Anthony Baker has ties to the Bloods street gang. Kwesi Adomako is a Ghanaian national who poses a major flight risk, and Kirby Wright was found in possession of felony marijuana during the traffic stop."

"Your Honor, these young men are scholars who have been serving their school and the community, and they're well respected by their professors and peers." I added, "I have letters here to attest to their character from several members of the academic staff of Howard University, including the Provost."

I passed the letters that had been sent to me, per my request, from teachers and classmates of all three. I had been thoroughly impressed while reading them, and I was sure it would be a positive reflection for the judge to consider. The bailiff took the papers from me and passed them over the bench.

The judge began flipping through them. Tony and Krush sat up straight in their chairs, trying to look as respectful as possible.

ADA Wilkins started to speak. "Your Honor, as we previously pointed out, Anthony Baker is a resident of Marcy Projects, and—"

"Your Honor!" Lamont stood up to object before I could even get the words out. "What does this young man's place of residence have to do with anything? That's assumptive and racist." I was glad he'd jumped in, because I wouldn't have used such professional language. I couldn't believe opposing counsel had the audacity to even say something of that nature, and part of me wanted to cuss his ass out.

"If I may be allowed to finish." Wilkins glared at us.

"You're on the verge of crossing a line, sir. I would choose my words carefully, counselor," the judge warned.

"Certainly, Your Honor. I was going to say that during a search of his home, a nine-millimeter handgun was found at his residence."

I was surprised that Tony didn't bark out a protest, but he seemed subdued.

Wilkins continued, "We've also found that Mr. Wright has a previous conviction for the sale of a controlled substance within a school."

Unlike Tony, Krush didn't hold back. "What does that have to do with anything? I was fifteen years old. You can't use that against me, I was a minor," he yelled. "It was just a little weed."

"Ms. Hudson, please control your client." The warning from the judge was now directed at me.

I looked over at Krush and frowned. He beckoned for me, and I leaned forward to hear what he had to say.

"That was supposed to be taken off my record and sealed when I became eighteen," he whispered. "They can't do this."

I directed my attention back to the bench. "Your Honor, my client has never been arrested for drugs as an adult, and furthermore, these charges the DA's office is speaking about have been sealed. We are talking about young men who are weeks away from graduation and have a sincere desire to get back to school to complete their degrees. These aren't some rogue gang members aiming to become drug lords as the DA is attempting to make them out to be."

"We are just making them out to be exactly what they are: four men driving in a car with two kilos of heroin," the ADA said flatly. "Can you imagine if every college student did that? We need to send a message, Your Honor, and make sure they don't."

Lamont nudged me, but before I could speak, the judge struck the gavel down. "I think I've heard enough."

I was breathing so hard that I could see my chest rising and falling and felt sweat forming under my arms.

"Gentlemen, please stand," the judge instructed Tony, Kwesi, and Krush, and they rose, looking nervous. "I understand your academic reputations and sincerity in your request; however, you've put yourselves and me in a difficult position here. I am going to reduce your bail, but nowhere near what your attorneys have asked. Bail is set at five hundred thousand dollars cash or bond. The next time I see you gentlemen will be at your arraignment."

The sound of the judge's gavel echoed through the courtroom, and I suddenly felt faint. The hearing had not gone at all like I'd anticipated. I glanced over at my father, who stood up and walked out. I had messed up, and although I did everything I could have possibly done, I had failed.

"What the fuck just happened?" Tony asked.

"We just got fucked," Krush answered. "We ain't getting out. Five hundred thousand might as well be a million. Thanks for nothing."

Two guards came over to escort them back to confinement.

"Wait, this is crazy," Langston said. "Des, you've gotta do something."

"There's nothing I can do right now," I told him as his friends were being led away.

"I need to go and talk to the parents," I said. "I'll be back."

I was headed to the back of the courtroom, searching for Tony's mom, when I stopped in the middle of the aisle. I blinked for a couple of seconds, confused by the woman standing near the back door. I looked through the crowd of people exiting through the doors as I began moving forward, searching for the face again, but she was gone. Maybe I was mistaken, but I could've sworn the woman I saw was Jerri.

Michael

32

"Are you saying the judge didn't reduce the bail because I'm a woman?"

Desiree was yelling at her brother, but it was pretty obvious that her anger was not really directed at Lamont, but more about the result of the bail reduction hearing they'd just returned from. Bradley had stormed in about fifteen minutes before them, heading directly for his office and slamming the door.

"No, that's not what I'm saying at all. I'm just pointing out that had you been a little more aggressive with your retort, then maybe things would've gone differently," Lamont replied.

"What makes you think I wasn't aggressive?" Desiree asked. "I did everything right. I didn't know the police found a gun in one client's home and the other was arrested selling dope in high school, and neither did you. So, don't come at me with your high and mighty shit, 'cause I don't wanna hear it." She looked like she was on the verge of tears. Say whatever she would, Desiree was obviously devasted that she didn't get those boys' bail reduced even more. "How's that for aggression?"

"There's a difference between being aggressive and being emotional. Right now, you're emotional." Lamont looked over at me and said, "Tell her, Mike."

I threw my hands up defensively. "Hey, don't bring me into this. I've got my hands full trying to figure out the skinny on these cops."

Perk laughed. "Good answer."

Lamont was about to say something when the conference room door opened and Bradley walked in, followed by his ex-wife. Lamont moved one seat over, and Bradley took his seat at the head of the table. Jacqueline sat in the other seat next to him. They both wore slate gray pantsuits and crisp white shirts. If the mood in the office weren't so tense, I would've asked if they had planned to dress alike.

"Well, that was a real shit show we put on today," Bradley stated definitively. He didn't look at anyone in particular, but I could see Desiree's eyes start to fill up with tears.

"Daddy, I'm sorr—" Desiree tried to apologize, but Bradley raised his hand to silence her.

"When I'm looking for a sacrificial lamb, Desiree, I know where to find you. But this isn't about one sheep; it's about the entire goddamn flock." He slammed his hand down on the table. "How the fuck did the police issue a search warrant on Tony's home and find a gun and we didn't know about it, Lamont?"

Lamont looked like he was going to shit a pickle. "When I spoke to Tony's mother, she never mentioned it."

"Did you ask her if she had any contact with law enforcement, or were you too busy looking at her ass?" I think everyone cracked a smile on that one, but Perk actually laughed out loud.

"What the fuck are you laughing at, Mr. Investigator?" Bradley turned his attention to Perk, who now looked as uncomfortable as Lamont. "Aren't you the one who did the background on Krush? How the hell did we not know he was caught selling drugs to ninth graders?"

Did Bradley really expect Perk to find out about a sealed juvenile document? I wondered, but I soon received my answer via Perk himself.

"Because I fucked up, Bradley. It won't happen again."

"It better not. I don't wanna visit my son wearing an orange jumpsuit at Sing-Sing," Bradley said. Then it was my turn. "Michael, what do we have on the cops that made the arrest?"

I opened the folder in front of me and glanced through it for appearances. I already knew every word in it. Hell, I had even practiced what I was going to say. "The initial arresting officer, Thomas Blake, is clean as a whistle. Ten years with the Army's military police, over ten years on the NYPD, and not one civilian complaint. I very much doubt that we'll be able to pin any type of racial angle on him."

"Why not? He's a white cop who arrested black college students. We've done more with less," Lamont replied skeptically.

"Considering he's married to a black woman who he has three kids by, and he's an award-winning coach for the PAL's football team that's predominantly black, I think maybe he gets a pass," I said smugly. Lamont leaned back in his seat and let me continue.

"There is, however, a Sergeant Lanier that we should really be focused on. He has several civilian complaints and has been investigated several times by Internal Affairs for improprieties unbecoming an officer. He'd probably be out of a job if it wasn't for the fact that he's a damn good K-9 officer and trainer," I concluded, closing the folder in front of me.

"That's something we can definitely use. I'm sure that racist son of a bitch has a lot more dirt we can dig up," Bradley said. He turned to Jacqueline and asked, "Were you able to take care of that little thing Lamont spoke to you about?"

"Yes. I've got a friend who's fast-tracking the Adomakos' citizenship application as we speak," she replied. "Regardless, you are going to need a speedy trial. These types of things have a way of coming back to bite you in the ass when you least expect them. I don't care about myself, but the last thing we want is for the press to get wind of my involvement before Langston is cleared of these charges."

"They sure do," Bradley replied. "But I've had my rabies shot. I suggest the rest of you do the same."

Jacqueline didn't notice Carla slipping in to take a seat as she turned to Perk and asked, "Where are we with finding out where the hell those drugs came from?"

"Michael and I are still reviewing the cops' body and dash cams, but so far nothing has raised any red flags." He turned his attention to the boss. "Like I told you earlier, Bradley, Lang's moves over that weekend were a lot more involved than we expected." It was very obvious that Perk was choosing his words carefully. "Right now, everything still points to one of the boys being the culprit, but I'm following a couple of promising leads, and we'll see where they go. Eventually I will find out where it came from. You can bet on that."

"We already have," Jacqueline replied. "We're betting our son's life."

"Where the hell is Langston anyway?" Bradley asked.

"He said he wasn't coming, that he wasn't needed around here," Desiree responded.

"What are you talking about? He's the client," Bradley snapped. "He knows that."

"Let him cool off, Bradley. He's upset that his friends aren't getting out. He called after the hearing, begging me to put up my apartment so they could get out," Jacquelyn explained in a way that almost sounded motherly. From what I'd learned about the family, this wasn't typical.

"You're going to put your apartment up?" Desiree sat up in her chair with a look of total surprise.

"Of course not. Don't be preposterous," her mother replied, snapping out of the momentary character change. She was back to business. "I'm a federal judge. Can you imagine what that would do to my reputation?"

"I'm sure that didn't go over well with Langston," Perk replied. I flinched a little, wondering if he'd just overstepped his bounds. After all, he wasn't family, and his comment came pretty close to sounding judgmental.

Jacqueline didn't seem to mind, though, and she even allowed herself to appear vulnerable for a second. "He very eloquently told me how he felt about me as a mother." She eased back in her chair, looking misty. "I'm not that bad a mother, am I?"

The room fell silent until Bradley said, "I'll talk to him, Jackie. He shouldn't have spoken to you that way."

Carla shifted in her seat, and Jacqueline seemed to notice for the first time that she was in the room. The tears in her eyes dried up in a hurry. These women clearly had major issues with each other.

"It's okay. He was just upset about his friends," she said to Bradley after rolling her eyes at Carla.

"He better be glad that we've officially taken on Tony and Krush," Lamont interjected.

"So, that's official now?" Carla asked, writing down some notes.

"Yes," Bradley responded. "We didn't have much of a choice. It was either us or Legal Aid, and we didn't want Legal Aid getting in the way."

"It'd be just our luck those idiots would talk one of those boys into pleading out." Lamont continued the rhetoric.

"Or worse, flipping on Langston," Jacqueline added.

"That brings me to a question I'm sure we've all thought about." Bradley's eyes moved around the room. "What do we do if we find out one of them is guilty of stashing that dope in Langston's car?"

There was no immediate answer, but he was right; I was sure we had all thought about that. I had also thought about something else. What if we found out that Langston was the guilty one and his overwhelming concern for his friends was really concern for his own freedom?

Kwesi

33

My stomach tightened as the corrections bus turned the corner and revealed the large sign that read: RIKERS ISLAND, HOME OF NEW YORK CITY'S BOLDEST. The vehicle, a renovated school bus, struggled to climb the steep bridge that separated the island prison from the rest of New York City. In a few minutes, we'd be back on the island behind bars, struggling for not only our sanity, but for our lives.

"Bye, world!" I heard my fraternity brother Krush shout out from the row next to me as the bus crested over the bridge and the New York City skyscrapers disappeared in the horizon.

I glanced over at my other fraternity brother, Tony, who was sitting four seats in front of me, stone-faced. He'd barely said a word since I first saw him and Krush stepping onto the corrections bus that transported us to the Staten Island Courthouse for our bail reduction hearing early that morning. Tony didn't look good at all. I was starting to think he may have had a psychotic break of some kind. I had tried to talk to him when we arrived at the courthouse and were placed in a holding cell, but he just sat there staring into space. Krush, on the other hand, seemed to be adjusting fine. He was cracking jokes and holding court all day, like being in jail was the most natural thing in the world. If he hadn't damn near cursed Langston's sister out because of the bail reduction hearing results, I wouldn't have even known he cared about getting out.

"Kwesi, you gonna be a'ight?" Krush asked as the bus came to a halt.

"I hope so," I replied nervously. I was trying to be as strong as he was, but deep down, I was terrified.

"Don't worry, man. Just keep your head up. I'll see if I can find someone in your unit to look out for you."

"Thank you, my brother."

He gave me the fraternity sign and smiled as he stood and began walking down the aisle to the bus entrance.

"But who knows?" I continued. "Perhaps my parents will find enough money from friends and family to bail me out like Langston."

"Fuck Langston," he said over his shoulder. "That nigga's probably getting some pussy as we speak." Krush, like me, was jealous of Langston's freedom, but unlike me, he seemed to blame our friend for our current predicament.

We exited the bus and had our cuffs and shackles removed. Krush and Tony were escorted in one line of inmates back to their unit, and I was regrettably brought to another. It had felt good to be around them, even if it was only for a few hours.

"What the fuck you looking at, nigga?" I heard a man scream from the other side of the corridor. He was in a line of inmates going in the opposite direction. I glanced in his direction but tried not to move my head. He was yelling at an inmate about three people ahead of me.

"You, nigga!" the man yelled. "What you gonna do about it?"

Before I could blink, the man on the opposite side of the corridor jumped out of line and ran toward the man in my line. I didn't realize it right away, but he slashed the man's face with a razor blade straight through to the white meat.

"Get on the fucking ground!" A corrections officer shouted, and then a loud alarm went off.

We must have been on the ground for twenty minutes before they moved us on. All I could think was, *Look straight ahead. Just look straight ahead. Do not make eye contact.* Those were the words I kept repeating in my head. I hadn't been in jail a week, but I'd already witnessed what could happen to someone in there if they looked at another man wrong, or for too long, even. I mean, who ever heard of slicing someone's face with a razor simply because they looked at you? I know it may seem hard to believe and quite inhumane, to say at the least, but it was reality—my reality—and I was terrified.

As we were heading back to the compound, I saw another group of inmates heading in the opposite direction. There was something calm and serene about them.

"Where are they going?" I asked the CO.

He looked at his watch and said, "They're heading to evening prayer."

My mother's words echoed in my head, and suddenly, I told him, "I would like to attend evening prayer. What do I have to do?"

"Let me see your ID card."

I handed my card to him.

"Says here your classification is Muslim. You're entitled to go to prayers if you want."

"I'd like that," I replied.

"Hey, Montgomery, this guy's one of yours." He pointed at a woman CO, who waved me on. "Show her your ID. She'll get you where you need to go."

Langston

34

I adjusted my travel bag over my shoulder as I headed down the stairs, stopping halfway down when I heard my father's voice. He was talking to Simone as she waited for me so we could leave. I had hoped that he and Lamont already left for the office by now, but like everything else the past week and a half, my luck was for shit, and now I regretted coming downstairs at all. My pops and I had been avoiding each other since the bail reduction hearing a few days ago—or at least I'd been sidestepping him, because he wouldn't put up the necessary collateral to bail out my friends. Sure, I understood that he was already representing them for free, but I also needed him to understand how important it was for them to be out as well. Every day I was out here and they were in there ripped a larger hole in our fraternal bond.

I shook it off and headed down the stairs. I wasn't going to let any of this ruin my weekend with Simone, especially since she had just started talking to me again after Michael and Perk had me confessing shit in front of her that she was never meant to hear.

"Morning," I said when my father and Simone came into view. My voice was cheerful, and it was fake as hell.

"Good morning, son."

"Morning, baby." Simone came over and kissed me. I guess she was excited about our trip, because it was the first time she'd kissed me since Perk and Michael left the house in Sag Harbor a few days ago. "You ready?"

"Yep." I adjusted my bag again, and she hooked her arm around mine.

"We have a preliminary hearing strategy session at the office on Monday at two. I'd like you to be there." From the tone of my father's voice, I knew this wasn't a suggestion; it was a command.

I acknowledged his words with a nod, walking to the front door without saying another word to him.

"Did you tell him we were going to Puerto Rico?" Simone asked as we stepped outside and the door shut behind us.

"Nah, I figured it was better if I didn't say anything. He probably thinks we're going to Sag Harbor."

"Langston." My father's voice stopped me in my tracks about ten feet from Simone's car. I turned around, and he was standing in the doorway.

"Yeah, Pop."

"I love you, son."

My father, unlike my mother, never had to say that he loved me, because he'd always proven it through his actions. We always knew we were loved by him. Still, to hear those words from him at that moment meant the world to me. I know it wasn't the macho and manly thing to do, but I ran back and hugged him.

"Love you too, Dad." We hadn't hugged like that since the day he left me at college for the first time almost four years ago.

"Lang. Lang. Lang!" Simone repeated.

"What, babe?" I released my father and turned to her.

"You might wanna take a look at this." She pointed toward the entrance of the circular driveway. Two NYPD cruisers and two unmarked cars were coming up on either side.

"What the . . ." I glanced at my father, who looked just as bewildered as me. But he got it together quick. "Dad?"

"Let me handle this. They're probably going to issue a search warrant. Simone, go in the house and get Lamont, please."

I recognized the first cop to get out his car. It was that asshole Detective O'Malley from Staten Island, and he was followed by several uniformed officers.

"What can I do for you, gentlemen?" my father asked.

"You can't do anything—but he can." O'Malley smirked, dangling a pair of handcuffs as if daring me to resist. "Langston Hudson, we are taking you into custody for violating the terms of your bail."

"What the hell are you talking about?" my father barked. "I'm his attorney, and you're not taking him anywhere without showing me some paperwork signed by a judge."

"He figured you'd say that," O'Malley answered.

The biggest question at this point was: who the fuck was "he"?

O'Malley turned and waved at the last car in the procession, and that's when all my questions and probably a few of my father's were answered. The black ADA from Staten Island stepped out of the car, buttoning his jacket as if he were approaching a gaggle of reporters and wanted to look good for the photos.

"James Brown . . ." my father mumbled.

"You know this guy?" I asked.

"We used to work together a long time ago." His tone didn't reveal whether that was a good thing or a bad thing.

"Bradley Hudson," he said to my father when they were close enough to talk. "It's been a long time."

"Yeah, it has. So, James, what's this all about?"

"Your son—or I guess in this instance, your client." He handed my father some papers then looked at O'Malley. "You can go ahead and take him into custody."

"What! What the hell? Dad. Dad. Do something, Dad!" I recoiled as O'Malley and some other officers reached for me.

"Langston, don't resist. That's what they want you to do in front of all these cameras."

I followed his gaze out to the street and realized the ADA had, in fact, been trying to look good for the cameras. There were three times as many members of the media as there had been the day before. Well, I was not going to give them a scene to air on the nightly news. I relented and let them handcuff me.

"James, what's this all about? Did you leak to the press you were coming—"

He cut my dad off, finishing his sentence. "Here to take your son into custody?" He stood there smirking for a second, obviously amused with himself. "Yeah, I guess I did."

"What the hell are you trying to do, set my son up?" my father yelled irately, stepping toward him with his fists balled. Either he'd forgotten about the cameras, or he was mad enough that he didn't give a shit. "This is not a game," he spat. "This is my son's life, you son of a bitch."

"Dad, no!" Out of nowhere, Lamont grabbed him and pulled him back. I'm sure he had saved James Brown from an ass whooping, but the crazy the thing was that the ADA looked like he'd wanted it to happen.

"Still have that hair-thin trigger temper, don't you, Bradley? You're lucky he saved you from taking a trip to Rikers with this one." Brown glared at me.

"Let go of me, Lamont." My father's voice was much calmer now.

"Okay, but you need to relax."

He nodded, and Lamont released him.

"What the hell's going on?" Lamont asked.

"Read the arrest warrant. It's all there in black and white." O'Malley picked up the papers my father had dropped and handed them to Lamont. He began reading then quickly turned his head in my direction.

"This is a bunch of bull." Lamont handed the paperwork back to my father so he could read it.

"Is it? Your client was planning to flee our jurisdiction," Brown stated. "We are here to make sure that doesn't happen, so we're taking him into custody."

"But I didn't do anything!" I yelled.

"Shut up, Lang," Lamont warned, gesturing toward the bustling crowd of reporters.

My father glared at Brown. "James, I don't know what you're trying to pull here, but whatever it is—"

"I'm not pulling anything. Maybe you should talk to your client. He's the one traveling to Guam."

"Langston, what is he talking about?" my father growled.

This was one of those times that you don't want to tell the truth, but you have to.

"I don't know anything about Guam, but Simone and I were going to Puerto Rico for the weekend. Not Guam. I'm not fleeing anyone's jurisdiction. P.R. is a part of the United States."

"Then why did you purchase tickets to Guam?" Brown asked.

Lamont quickly said, "Don't answer that."

"Oh my God," Simone stuttered, stepping forward. "Mr. Hudson, this may all be my fault."

"What are you talking about, Simone?" I was totally confused.

"Langston, I—"

"I don't care whose fault it is. You can settle this with the judge, Bradley. O'Malley, take him away," Brown snapped. The officers began to perp walk me toward their cars, walking nice and slow so the photographers with their long lenses could get plenty of shots.

I turned around and looked at my father. "Dad . . ."

"Don't worry, son. I'm going to take care of this." Unfortunately, his voice didn't have its usual confidence. The look on my brother's face told me that he wasn't feeling confident either. My heart sank as they covered my head and lowered me into the back seat of the police cruiser.

Bradley

35

"I saw a few parking spaces down the block, Mr. Hudson. Just text me when you're ready to be picked up." Ernest, my driver, explained as he opened the rear door of my Bentley.

"No, I'll probably be here for a while. I'll have a car service take me home when I'm ready to leave, Ernie. I'll see you tomorrow morning." It was late, and he'd been at work way before the police showed up to take Langston away, so there was no point in making him stay. Besides, I had no idea when I'd be getting out of there.

"Thank you, sir. You enjoy your evening," Ernest replied appreciatively.

I picked up my briefcase, along with the brown paper bag lying beside it on the seat, and I stepped out.

"And I'm praying everything works out for Langston. He's a good kid, and I hate that this is happening to him. Those cops are really trying to railroad him."

"Not the cops, the District Attorney's office. But now that I know who's trying the case, we'll be all right," I told him, grateful for his show of concern and loyalty to me and my son. Like my housekeeper Iris, Ernie had been with me and my family a long time. In fact, he was the first person I'd ever defended.

"I like the sound of that. If there's anything I can do, don't hesitate to ask. I like to think of myself as an uncle to all your children." He closed the car door and walked around to the driver's side door.

"One of their favorite uncles, I might add," I said.

He gave me an appreciative grin before stepping into the car. I waited for him to pull into the busy Upper East Side traffic, then turned to look up at the high rise building I was about to enter.

"Good evening, Mr. Hudson." The doorman greeted me as I passed him.

"Evening," I said simply, keeping my gaze forward and not making eye contact.

I walked directly to the elevator and pushed the button. When I stepped on, I ignored the once over given to me by an older, white gentleman with a pug dog. He continued to stare at me as I pushed the button for the penthouse and slid my access card into the slot. I would not give him the satisfaction of acknowledging his presence just so he could give me the cold shoulder. We rode up, both pretending to enjoy the sounds of Barry Manilow coming from the speakers, until we arrived at the twelfth floor and he stepped off. I was tempted to say something smart before the doors closed, but I knew it would be pointless. The man lived on the twelfth floor, a basic commoner who would probably never have access to the penthouse, and he knew it.

I stepped off the elevator and went to the first of two doors on this floor. Taking a deep breath to calm my nerves, I paused, then rang the bell and waited.

The door opened, and the first thing out of Jacqueline's mouth when she saw me was, "Is my son home? Did you get my baby out of that place?" She stepped into the hall and looked up and down as if she expected to see him standing there.

"No, but he's all right. Desiree and Perk went to Rikers and saw him about an hour ago."

My words didn't give her any comfort. "I don't care who saw him, Bradley. I want him home. How the fuck did you let this happen to my son?"

I held my breath and took a step back because I was about to lose it.

Lamont and I had spent the entire day scrambling around the Staten Island Courthouse, trying to get the court to issue a stay on Langston's bail being revoked. We were finally issued a hearing on the matter at around 4:30. Unfortunately, Judge Rodriguez was out of town, so we had to be heard by Judge Weinstein, the judge who had signed the forfeiture early that morning. Weinstein was one of those old school judges who needed to retire ten years ago. So, despite what I considered a great argument for reinstatement, the judge flat out denied our request, leaving my son a prisoner on Rikers Island. My reaction to his ruling was more than colorful, and I left the courthouse five thousand dollars lighter but feeling a tad bit better.

"It's been a long, hard day, so I'm going to take into consideration that we're both upset and that you have temporarily forgotten that he's also my son and that I love him as much, if not more than you do, considering you walked out on us six years ago."

She glared at me. Jacqueline hated to be called out on her shit, and although I didn't do it often in order to keep the peace, I was the absolute best at it.

"What happened? It was that little bitch Simone's fault, wasn't it? I'm going to fuck her up when I see her, Bradley."

"You'll do nothing of the sort." I held up the brown paper bag and said, "That's why I'm here, so you don't get information secondhand. Let's sit down and have a drink."

She stared at the bag and said, "That better not be domestic."

"Please. I know you better than that." I laughed, and she took the bottle and let me inside. I noticed her white silk nightgown under the robe she wore, but I knew that even if she had been in bed, she wasn't close to sleep with everything going on with Langston. Jacqueline, for all her cool demeanor and superior intellect, was really a big softy and a major worrier.

Her apartment was massive, almost half the penthouse floor. It was tastefully decorated, and I had no doubt that my ex-wife had spared no expense in making sure it was to her liking. Jacqueline had a love of art, and her collection of paintings and pieces was as exquisite as the price tags that came with them. We'd bought the place during the housing crisis for about three million as an investment, or at least I'd thought that was why we bought it. Then she took the lead on the renovations and made it exactly to her liking, with nothing but the best high-end finishes. Now the damn thing was probably worth twenty million.

She walked behind the bar in the corner of the living room and took out two glasses, placing ice in each. I opened the bottle and poured the 70-year-old cognac. We each picked up a glass, and I followed her over to the sofa.

"Oh my God, this is like heaven." Jacqueline closed her eyes and savored the liquor. "There is only one thing that would make it better."

"You mean something like this?" I reached in my breast pocket and pulled out two Cuban cigars and a cutter. Jacqueline's face lit up. She took a cigar and the cutter from me. Jacqueline was unlike most women I'd ever met, and that included my current wife. She truly enjoyed a good cognac and a superior cigar.

I watched her light the cigar then draw from it. She savored the smoke then let it out with a satisfied smile. "This might get you off the hook, but not that little whore our son seems to be so smitten with. Her, I'm going to kill with my bare hands."

"You're not going to kill anyone. This is Langston's fault just as much as it is hers." I took a sip of my cognac and leaned back on the soft leather cushion. "He knew better than this."

"Don't make excuses for her. I know she bought the tickets."

"It really wasn't her fault, Jackie. Langston gave her his credit card to book a weekend getaway to Puerto Rico. Simone thought she was saving him money by booking their tickets on Skiplagged, some new cheap travel app. She booked them on a flight to Guam that had a layover, because it was cheaper than a direct flight to San Juan. They were just going to get off in San Juan and purposely miss the connecting flight. But to the DA, it looked like they were trying to leave the country."

"They shouldn't have been flying to Puerto Rico anyway. What the fuck were they thinking?"

"They weren't thinking. They're kids. Biggest mistake she made was not booking a return flight because she didn't know when they were going to return."

"You know what? She wasn't thinking because she's dumb as hell, and the only reason he likes her is because she has big tits."

"That's not a bad thing." I motioned toward Jacqueline's own well-endowed chest that was half the reason I'd noticed her when we met years ago. "We Hudsons are breast men."

She quickly folded her arms and smirked. "The apple doesn't fall far from the tree, huh? But I had beauty and brains to go with my boobs. There's a difference." She tossed back the rest of her cognac. "Just when I thought this shit couldn't get any worse. He's out on bail, facing serious criminal charges, and she decides to plan a fucking vacation. She's a dumb broad."

Jacqueline had never been one to hide her true feelings. When she didn't like someone, she made it known. However, I wasn't here to trash Langston's girlfriend. We had much more important things to discuss.

"Lamont and I spent the entire day working on a motion to get his bail reinstated, but that judge wasn't hearing any of it."

"He didn't fall for your charm, huh?"

I frowned, slightly bothered by her statement. "My charm is always backed by sound legal arguments. And you know it." I took a manila folder out of my briefcase and handed it to her. She pulled on her cigar while she read the brief I'd filed earlier.

"I'm biased, of course, but other than a lack of a return ticket, I can't see a reason why he didn't reinstate Langston's bail." She tightened her lip in a gesture of annoyance.

"I can give you one," I replied.

"I'm listening." She exhaled a cloud of smoke.

"The argument of an overzealous prosecutor with an axe to grind. This was personal."

She didn't look surprised. "You've made your share of enemies over the years, that's for sure."

"So have you. I'm not the only one with a closet full of skeletons, my dear."

"What are you saying? This is about me?" she asked.

"Nope, this is about us, Jackie. The DA on this case is our old friend, James Brown."

"Shut up!" Jacqueline nearly dropped her cigar. "Eight-inch afro James Brown?"

"Well, he's bald now, but yes, we're talking about the same guy. Not the singer."

Jacqueline took a moment, looking almost nostalgic. "Damn, it's been so long I'd almost forgotten about James."

"I don't think he's forgotten about you—or me, for that matter." I finished off my drink and poured another glass, then offered Jacqueline a refill as well. She lifted her glass, and I topped her off. "This isn't good, Jacqueline. That man's going to take his hate for us out on our son."

"I can see that." She sighed. "Why the hell is he working for the Staten Island DA's office? Why isn't he in private practice somewhere?"

"I don't know. Once a loser, always a loser, I guess. I have Carla looking into him, but from the smirk on his face this morning, this is personal. Very personal."

"Bradley, I need you to go and talk to him. I don't care what you have to offer him, but get him to call off the dogs and bring my—*our* son home."

"I figured I'd leave that conversation to you." I raised an eyebrow at her.

"No, I think you should go first. Let's see where his head is at."

"Fine. I'll speak with him, but we both know it probably won't help. You're the one he—"

"Just try." Jacqueline leaned over and touched my hand.

"I said I would, Jackie," I assured her.

She kept her hand on mine. "What time do you have to be home?" She gave me an endearing look. I'd seen it before, usually when she was drunk. It was her "she-tiger" look, and it usually meant trouble.

"When I get there," I answered. "But now might be as good a time as any to head home." I reached for my cell phone to summon an Uber.

"It won't matter if it was now or three hours from now. She's still going to think we had sex, you know."

She was probably right, but I wasn't going to justify her with an answer.

"After all, it was the one thing that we were good at as a couple—other than practicing law." She gave me a knowing look, and we stared at one another for a few seconds.

"Yeah, we were definitely good at that," I said.

"I'm fifty-eight years old, and no man has ever been able to do to me what you used to do with your tongue, Bradley Hudson. Your oral skills were the absolute best," she teased.

"Were? Trust me, they still are." I gave her a seductive smile.

"I'll be the judge of that," she said boldly, opening her robe to expose her bare breasts under the sheer nightgown. I must admit I was flirting with her, but I never expected her to react like this. "How about a little reminder for old time's sake? I mean, if you're going to get in trouble for something, you might as well be guilty."

"Not going to happen."

"You sure? Why not?"

"Because, despite being married to a wonderful woman who I love, I actually have feelings for you, Jackie. I always have, and you know it. And every time I do something stupid like this, you always break my heart."

Perk

36

I parked the car on the street on Nostrand Avenue in Brooklyn and headed for the small basement store. I felt kind of bad leaving my new homie Michael behind, but where I was about to go wasn't the type of place a Harvard-educated lawyer needed to be found.

I descended the steps leading to the entrance. The music was blasting so loud I could hear it from outside. A couple of dudes were posted up by the door wearing oversized white T-shirts and skinny jeans with red bandanas. I had expected them to be there and was prepared for what they were about to ask.

"What's up?" the first one asked, blocking the door.

"Here to check out the sights and spend some money," I told him, taking out a wad of cash from my left pocket.

"I ain't never seen you here before."

As he gave me the once over, the other guy said, "How you know what we got up in here?"

I snickered. "Aaron and Adonis told me to come through when I had the chance."

Satisfied with my answer, the first guy said, "It's a twenty-dollar cover."

"Man, that's funny. They told me it was ten." I peeled off a twenty while the other guy patted me down. I hated to do it, but I'd already been advised to leave my piece behind.

He took the money from my hand and said, "They lied."

They opened the door for me, and I was immediately hit by a cloud of smoke. My nostrils filled with the smell of weed. I entered the long corridor where I saw two more guys smoking a blunt. Neither one of them said anything to me. They must've picked up on the vibe that I wasn't to be fucked with.

After I passed, I heard one of them ask, "Who the hell is that big motherfucker?"

"Don't know and don't care," the other one answered.

I went through another door into a dimly lit strip club. Naked women danced on two small tables located in the center of the room, and there were lap dances happening around the room. I went and ordered an overpriced drink from the bar in the corner. At least five women approached me to ask if I wanted a lap dance, and two came right out and asked me if I wanted to fuck. On another day I might have said yes, but I was there to work. I politely declined their offers as I scanned the room until I saw the two people I'd been looking for. Damn, if Tony didn't look just like them.

"You wanna dance, daddy?" a fine-ass brown-skinned girl asked.

I gave her the once over, reaching into my pocket and peeling off a fifty from my roll. I held it out to her. "No, but you can tell those two guys over there that I wanna see them."

She turned in the direction I was looking then turned back to me, surprised. "Aaron and Adonis? You wanna talk to them?" I nodded, and she snatched the fifty out my hand. "Okay, but it's your funeral."

She walked over to talk to them, said a few words, and pointed in my direction. It didn't take long before they were standing in front of me. Now I really regretted not being strapped.

"Who the fuck are you?" Adonis, the older brother, yelled over the music.

"Name's Perk," I yelled back.

Aaron cocked his head to the side, sizing me up. "Yeah, and? What the fuck do you want, Perk?"

"I need to holla at you about your brother Tony," I told them.

"We don't talk to police." He turned to walk away.

"I ain't the fucking police. If I was five-oh, don't you think there'd be a lot more motherfuckers with me?" That was enough to make them stop and listen. Then I added, "I work for Hudson and Associates, your brother's attorneys."

The two of them exchanged a look, then Adonis said, "A'ight, we can chat in the back."

I followed them into a back room that was already occupied by a couple fucking on the couch.

"What the—" the guy yelled. He jumped up with his pants around his ankles.

"Heeeeey!" the woman whined.

"Get the fuck out, Pee Wee!" Adonis yelled. "We got business to handle in here."

Pee Wee pulled his pants up, but the woman had nothing to cover herself with. Obviously, she was on the clock. She gave Adonis a seductive smile as she walked out, and he playfully smacked her perfectly round ass.

"Man, that ass is the absolute phattest." Aaron nodded at his brother.

"And you told me not to hit that," Adonis commented.

"Maybe I have to reevaluate my thinking," Aaron replied. "Damn, I wonder what her momma fed her to get an ass like that."

I couldn't help sneaking a final glimpse just before the door closed. They were right; her ass was amazing.

"How much you want from us?" Adonis asked when the three of us were alone. He reached into his pocket and took out a fat roll of bills. "We ain't got that type of bail money, but I know you lawyers ain't cheap."

"Especially someone like Bradley Hudson," Aaron added, reaching into his pocket too.

"Nah, I ain't here for no money," I told them.

Aaron folded his arms and looked at me suspiciously. "Well, what you here for then?"

"I'm here to talk to you about that dope that was in the car," I answered. "Where did it come from?"

"Aw, hell naw. Yo, let's go." Adonis nudged his brother.

"We don't know nothing about no dope," Aaron said, standing his ground. "And neither do Tony."

"Maybe he did it to impress you," I said. "You know, little brother trying to outdo his big brothers and all that. That was some high-grade stuff. It didn't come from just anywhere."

"We don't make our money in dope. We make it selling ass," Adonis said.

"Is that why you have sixteen drug arrests between the two of you?"

"I thought you said you ain't police?" Aaron shook his head, letting me know I'd pushed too hard. "We ain't got nothing to say. Come on."

"A'ight. Your brother's in jail and y'all are just walking away. Before you leave, though, I think there's somebody you need to talk to." I took out my phone and speed-dialed a number. Luckily, the brothers stayed where they were long enough for the call to connect.

"Aye, cuz," I spoke into the phone. "I'm down here with your people, and they treating me like a three-legged stepchild. They about to walk out on me." I held the phone out for Adonis.

"Who the fuck is that?" he asked me.

"Take the phone and ask him."

He snatched it from my hand and said, "Who dis?"

"Who is it, bruh?" Aaron asked, but Adonis didn't answer him.

"Yeah, uh, okay. A'ight. I understand. Cool." Adonis ended the call and handed me the phone.

"Who the fuck was that?" Aaron asked again. "That Tony?"

"Nah, it was Mandel."

"Get the fuck outta here. For real?" Aaron looked shocked.

Mandel, who was one of the highest-ranking members of the East Coast Bloods, was not only a client but a personal friend of mine. Our relationship was mutually beneficial, and he always let it be known that I was to be given the same respect that he was.

"Yeah." Adonis stared at me.

"You wanna go ahead and tell me about the dope now?" I asked.

"There's nothing to tell, for real. We don't know any more about that dope than you do," Aaron explained, sounding a whole lot more respectful now.

I still wasn't buying it. "Man, don't bullshit me. Everyone knows the two of you run the fucking streets and handle more business than anyone else around here. You mean to tell me your brother—"

"Hold on, man. Let me stop you right there," Adonis snapped, looking truly agitated. "Mandel said to keep it real with you, so that's what we doing. Now, what me and Aaron do out there in the streets ain't got shit to do with our little brother."

"Most of the shit we do is so he don't have to. We've always taken care of him because he was smart and a good kid," Aaron added. "He wasn't raised for this street bullshit, and we never let him get caught up in it. And he ain't caught up now."

Adonis continued where his brother left off. "Tony ain't have to sell dope. We paid for his books and made sure he kept money in his account. He wanted to pledge, we made sure he had everything he needed—spring break trips, mini vacations with his boys, everything. Our little brother ain't miss out on shit. We bust our ass because we believe in him and didn't want him to feel less than when he was around those other bougie fools. We put our lives and freedom on the line so he don't have to. He got more important shit to do with his life, and he understands that. So, I don't care what nobody says. That dope ain't his, and it ain't ours."

"And real talk, if we even thought Tony was out here in the streets, we would fuck him up ourselves. Trust me, our brother is more scared of what we would do to his ass than the threat of jail time. He ain't do this," Aaron finished.

I looked at the two brothers, and something told me they weren't bullshitting. If the dope was Tony's, they sure as hell didn't know about it.

Kwesi

37

I had just returned from evening prayers when the guard told me I had a legal visit. I hadn't spoken to my lawyer since the bail hearing a week ago, so this was a surprise. I hoped he had good news, especially since I'd probably miss chow in the process.

After going through all the jail protocols, I was taken into a smaller cell with a table and chair. Waiting for me was my attorney, Kenneth Kimba. As usual, he was dressed like Carlton Banks from the *Fresh Prince of Bel Air*, and he greeted me with a smile. I was still uneasy about being represented by him because for someone so inexperienced in the courtroom, he had this air of overconfident arrogance about him. He was smart and smooth, I would give him that, but he reminded me of a used car salesman. Men like Kimba had been fleecing people from my country for years, but at this point, what could I do? My parents had already paid him a significant sum.

"Kwesi, how are you doing?" he asked, watching as the guard removed the cuffs from my wrists.

I sat at the table across from him and said, "Considering I'm still in jail, with a five hundred thousand–dollar bail, I am not very happy."

"Understandable, and trust me, I'm working hard to remedy the situation. I'm sure you know that," Kimba told me with another smile that seemed so inappropriate for the situation I was in. He opened the briefcase in front of him and took out a folder.

"Well, work harder," I said, not caring if I sounded rude. "My parents are paying you good money, and we have received very little in results other than seeing you standing next to Bradley Hudson on the news last night."

He didn't even flinch. The man had no shame. "I have spoken with the Hudsons, and they have helped move your parents' and siblings' paperwork for citizenship through the process very quickly," Kimba said. "They should have full citizenship by the time you go to trial."

"That's good news." Hearing that he was working with Bradley Hudson to handle my parents' citizenship, not just to get on camera, brought me great relief. "So, what about my case? You just mentioned a trial."

"Yes, it's more than likely that we're going to have to take this case to trial. However, we do have other options to consider."

I stared at Kimba nervously. "What other options?"

He pulled his chair up closer. "Kwesi, I'm your lawyer. You're the only person involved in this case that I represent. You are the only person I am obligated to."

"What are you trying to say?"

He took in a breath. "That I represent you, not your friends Langston, Tony, or Kirby. Unlike the Hudsons, I have your best interests to protect and no one else's."

"Mr. Kimba, you keep talking, but you're not saying anything."

He shrugged his shoulders and got to the point. "Kwesi, I don't trust the Hudsons, and I think if it comes down to your freedom or Langston's, they are going to choose Langston."

"I don't necessarily disagree with you," I replied in my most forthright voice. "My parents would probably do the same if they were lawyers or had that kind of money. Now, will you please tell me what you are alluding to?"

"I think we should work with the Hudsons, but we should also have more than one plan. Let's call it a Plan B."

He was not very original. It was another sign of his inexperience, I thought.

"And what would that Plan B consist of?"

I turned to see the cell door opening. District Attorney James Brown walked in. He was carrying a manila folder in one hand and had the audacity to be carrying a box of doughnuts in the other, which he placed directly in front of me. The smell of warm vanilla drifted into my nostrils, causing my stomach to growl and my mouth to water. It had been so long since I'd had something decent to eat that I was tempted to snatch the top off the box and tear into one.

"Is this what you call another plan? Selling out my friends?" I said, blinking to bring myself out of the trance I'd been in while staring at the doughnut box. "I've already told you I'm not making a deal. I have nothing to say to you. I hope that's not why you're here."

"You don't have to talk. You can just listen," Brown said, lifting the top and picking up one of the glazed treats with his bare hands. "Would you like one? They're fresh. Krispy Kreme."

I didn't answer, but I couldn't help but stare as he dramatically took a bite. My mouth began to water instantly.

Brown sat down beside my lawyer.

"I'm sure my client has no problem in hearing what you have to say," Kimba told him, speaking for me.

"I should hope not. I'm here as a courtesy and to keep you informed."

"Informed of what?" I asked him, sliding my chair back to avoid the box of temptation still sitting in front of me. "The only thing I need to know is when I'm getting out of here. Are you here to inform me of that?"

"Well, not exactly," Brown said, finishing the rest of the doughnut in one bite. He reached in his pocket and took out a handkerchief to wipe his mouth. Then, he spoke to Kimba as if I were not sitting there in front of them. "I believe he was just an innocent bystander in all of this. Someone who was in the wrong place at the wrong time. I don't think it's fair to be in a position where he's facing multiple federal charges when he did nothing wrong."

I frowned at Brown. "If you know that, then why am I still here?"

Finally, he turned and spoke directly to me. "Because even though you didn't do anything, someone did. Those drugs belong to someone."

"They don't belong to me, and they don't belong to my friends either," I told him.

Brown raised an eyebrow. "Friends? Are you sure about that?"

"Yes, I'm sure. We are college students. We don't sell drugs," I replied.

"I'm not talking about the dope. I'm talking about your so-called friendship," Brown said.

"What is that supposed to mean? What is he talking about?" I directed the second question to Kimba, who looked just as confused as I felt.

"I'm talking about the fact that your 'friend' Langston Hudson attempted to flee the country. He and his girlfriend were captured on their way to the airport for a flight to Guam when we stopped them," Brown said. "Innocent men don't run, Kwesi."

"You're lying," I said.

"I wish I was, son." Brown opened the folder and took out a stack of photos. "These were taken this morning at the Hudson's Riverside Drive home. The handsome guy with the bald head is me."

As I felt my stomach begin to churn, this guy was cracking weak jokes.

"This is some kind of trick to get me to roll over on Lang," I protested. "He would never do anything like that."

Brown passed the photo to Kimba and said, "Langston and his girlfriend Simone were scheduled to leave this morning, and there was no return ticket found."

I looked over at Kimba, who was now flipping through the photos. He passed them to me. "Take a look. These are pretty incriminating," he said.

"Yeah, I got them from a photographer friend of mine. This story should be all over the six o'clock news if you need verification," Brown added.

I looked down at the photos and inhaled sharply. Brown wasn't lying. It appeared Langston really was arrested. For a second, I was hurt, wondering how one of my best friends, who was as close to me as a brother, would skip out on us. What about the oath of our fraternity and the bond that we shared?

"Is that something a friend would—"

"Shut up. Just shut up. I can't believe this. He was just going to leave me, Tony, and Krush? What the hell was he thinking? I don't understand. I, I don't believe you." I shook my head. "No, it can't be true. You're lying. Those pictures could have been photoshopped."

"Mr. Adomako, I don't have a reason to lie to you. As I stated, I came to tell you this as a courtesy. If you don't believe me, I'm sure you can ask him yourself when you see him on the cell block you'll both be housed in," Brown said calmly.

"What is it that you want from my client?" Mr. Kimba asked.

"I just want him to tell me who the drugs belong to, and I'll take it from there," Brown answered.

I stood up and announced, "I have nothing to say."

"Kwesi, wait. Mr. Brown, I need a moment with my client," Kimba said.

"Well, I'll leave you two gentlemen to chat. Call me when you're ready to talk."

I glared at Brown as he walked out.

When he was gone, Kimba said, "Listen, I know you're shocked and upset, but this is your chance to get out of here. I think we should see what he's offeri—"

"You work for me, right?" I spat at Kimba.

"Yes, of course," he replied.

"Good, then continue to work with the Hudsons on my parents' citizenship and this case until I tell you not to. I've got a lot of thinking and praying to do." I reached down in the box and grabbed a doughnut with each hand, stuffing one in my face. It was so good I can't even describe it.

"Guard!" I yelled.

"Kwesi, wait. We need to discuss—"

"There's nothing to discuss. I'll call you when I'm ready to talk," I told him, finishing off one doughnut and starting in on the other.

The guard came to the cell door. "You ready?"

I nodded. "Yes, I am."

As he put the cuffs back around my wrist, I glanced back at the doughnut box and thought about how good they were and how many things I'd taken for granted. Things as small as being able to eat a doughnut. I walked past Kimba with my head held high and headed back to my unit.

Jacqueline

38

Walking into 1551 Lenox Avenue, or Malcolm X Boulevard as they called it now, was like visiting an old friend. The building always gave me comfort, a true feeling of home—perhaps because it was the first one Bradley and I shared. We'd rented the first floor for our budding new law practice when we left the U.S. attorney's office and the second floor to live in, until we purchased the brownstone Desiree and Perk lived in now. Back then, the third and fourth floors weren't even habitable, but over the years, we renovated it little by little, until it was known by damn near everybody in Harlem as the Hudson building.

As I entered the building, I waved at Ernie, Bradley's driver. He was sitting in his usual spot, reading the paper. I ignored the receptionist as I walked past her to the elevator, although I was sure she had already picked up the phone and announced my arrival to Cathy, the office manager on the fourth floor. Cathy, in turn, would text Carla, on the third floor, and Bradley.

I stepped off the elevator onto the fourth floor, and just as I had predicted, Cathy was standing there waiting for me.

"Where is he?" I asked.

"In his office with Perk." She didn't say anything else as I stepped around her, probably because she understood I had no use for her. We'd been through this too many times before to pretend we liked each other, or even really to be cordial. She was loyal to Carla, and that was all I needed to know.

I walked down the hall and entered Bradley's office without knocking. I kissed Perk, who stood up to greet me right away then excused himself, leaving me face to face with the man who had rejected my sexual advances less than a week ago. It was a feat that, when I was honest with myself, only made me want the bastard even more. Between worrying about Langston and thinking about how much I wanted to rip off his father's clothes, I could barely sleep at night. Bradley wasn't the best lover I'd ever had, although his oral skills were off the chart. It was his cocky confidence and never-let-them-see-you-sweat demeanor that made my panties wet. He was like the grown up, successful version of the bad boy that so many young girls chase after, and that swagger was way more appealing than anything he could do with that thing swinging between his legs.

"Hello, Jackie. What can I do for you?" Bradley asked as if I were just any client showing up for an appointment, not his ex-wife barging into his office. I guess this was his way of letting me know that my moves the other night were not appreciated. He knew it drove me crazy when he acted this way. Sometimes I just wanted his attention, but he would only give it on his terms.

I sat down in the chair Perk had vacated. "I'm here to find out how your meeting with James went this morning, and for an update on our son."

"Our son is as well as can be expected under the circumstances. I saw him today, and he's lost a few pounds, but other than that, he's fine. He just wants to come home. You should go see him, Jackie."

"I'm not going to Rikers Island. I'm not sitting in some dingy visiting room, and I'm definitely not going through all that crap you have to do to before you even see someone. I don't understand why I can't just do a legal visit like you and the kids."

"Because we are his attorneys of record, and you're not." He shot me a look that said *Let's be real.* "But, of course, you know that."

I did know it, but that didn't mean I had to like it.

"What I know is that I'm not going in there like some wayward mother. I'm a federal judge. It's beneath me." I folded my arms defiantly.

"This isn't a high school play or a basketball game you are missing, Jackie—although there have been plenty of those. Our son is in jail, and he needs you."

I leaned forward and stated my point emphatically. "I am not going to that jail, Bradley." With that settled, I sat back again and changed the subject. "I'm making other arrangements. Now, how did your meeting with James go?"

He released a frustrated sigh. "The meeting with James was for shit. That bastard offered us fifteen years for Langston because it was his car and he was driving, and ten years apiece for Tony and Krush. I told him to shove it up his ass, literally."

"What about Kwesi?"

"His lawyer never showed up. Lamont's gonna give him a call this afternoon, but I don't like it. It's got James' fingerprints all over it."

"Should I slow my friends down at the State Department? They haven't gotten their citizenship yet," I said with a smirk.

"I'll let you know, but it's best we hold that card until we know for sure. We don't want to piss Kwesi and his parents off unless we need to."

"It looks like James is feeling pretty confident about his case."

"I'd feel confident too if I had his case. He's got four black guys in a car with two kilos of heroin. Somebody's gotta be guilty."

He had a point, but I was not interested in considering that possibility. This was my son we were talking about. I didn't give a shit who the drugs belonged to; Langston was not about to get caught up in the system.

"Did you speak to him about us? About what this is really about?" I asked.

"Yeah, and that's when he told me to shove it up *my* ass."

I nodded my head in understanding. Not only did James have a good case to prosecute, but I knew he would go after it more aggressively because of our history. I felt sick to my stomach.

"If we're going to make any headway with this guy and get him to ease up on Langston, you're going to have to talk to him. You're the only one who can do it," Bradley said.

I exhaled loudly, but I didn't protest, because he was right. Still, I dreaded the thought of having to do it. Although I loved my son, I wasn't quite sure if I could face James Brown.

Carla walked in, followed by Lamont. She paused briefly, glancing at me as if she expected me to get up and give her my seat. I almost laughed out loud. She knew damn well that would never happen.

She rolled her eyes and then said to Bradley, "Sorry for interrupting. We were putting together some rather critical data that I knew you'd want to hear."

"It's fine. What did you gather?" Bradley asked.

Carla went around and stood next to Bradley behind his desk, marking her territory, I suppose. In her hand was a manila folder, which she placed in front of him. "If we are going to acquit these boys, we're going to need a change of venue."

"I'm not sure about that," Bradley said.

Lamont agreed with him. "I'm not even sure we can get a judge to agree to that, and the prosecution will definitely be opposed to it."

"They'll definitely fight it," Carla said. "But that's the only way we'll have a chance of winning this case."

"Why?" I asked. "Why are you so opposed to Staten Island?"

"I'm sure you're aware of what happened to Eric Garner a few years ago. They didn't even file charges against the white police officers, even after the M. E. ruled his death a homicide—and the community didn't even flinch."

"Yes, but with the interviews Bradley's doing and the media coverage we're getting, people are already starting to question if the boys are guilty before we've even tried our case," I said. It wasn't even necessarily that I disagreed with her argument, it was just that she was Bradley's new wife, and I would antagonize her any chance I got. The thing is, she knew this, so she would never back down, either.

"That's the national news." Carla stepped over to the computer keyboard on a side table. Bradley's wall-mounted monitor changed from the Hudson logo to a web browser. She began typing, and the website SIlive.com came on the screen, with Bradley's picture and a caption that read: CELEBRITY ATTORNEY'S SON BRINGS DRUGS AND GANG ACTIVITY TO STATEN ISLAND.

"This is the local news," she said.

"That's preposterous!" Bradley yelled.

"This just ran this morning on TV1/Staten Island." This time, it was a video of Langston being led to a police car in handcuffs, and the caption scrolling at the bottom of the screen read: SON OF RENOWNED ATTORNEY BRADLEY HUDSON REARRESTED FOR ATTEMPTING TO FLEE THE COUNTRY.

"That's just simply not true!" Bradley yelled even louder.

"Maybe, but similar stories have been running in the *Staten Island Press* and other local news sites 24/7. Langston's bail being revoked is killing us locally, and if anywhere in New York City is Trump country, Staten Island is it. The island is sixty-nine percent white and heavily Republican. Less than ten percent of the black and Latino population show up for jury duty. You're talking about four young, black men traveling with a significant amount of drugs in the car. We can't win with that jury pool. I don't care how many exceptions we have."

"She's right," I said, and everyone turned their heads to me with wide eyes.

Sure, Carla and I were mortal enemies. Usually, however, my opposition to her was over trivial family matters. I'd never had to work with her on a legal matter, especially one involving my son. I hated to admit it, but I saw that she was good at what she did, and if agreeing with her was going to help Langston, then dammit, I'd swallow my pride just this once.

"You're actually agreeing with her?" Lamont was stunned.

"I am. There may be some things I flat out don't like about Carla, but one thing I have is a healthy respect for that little cluster of geeks she has working upstairs. She knows her shit, and I think she's right about this. The best thing for us to do is file for a change of venue."

I glanced up and saw a look of pride on Carla's her face. I had to resist the urge to smack it right off.

"Then it's settled," Bradley announced. "We'll file for a change of venue and hope that it works."

"Where are we going to request it be changed to?" Lamont asked.

"They'll never go for Manhattan or Brooklyn. Too much ethnicity," Bradley said. "And we're not going to go for Long Island or Westchester. Too segregated. We might as well stay in Staten Island for that."

Carla looked at me, and we stared at one another briefly before we finally said in unison, "What about Queens?"

Langston

39

I wiped away tears as I walked out of the visitor's room after seeing Simone. Nothing like a forty-five-minute conversation in a prison visiting room to remind you how much you love and appreciate someone. I had mostly kept to myself for the past two weeks, especially since I had yet to run into any of the other guys, other than spotting Kwesi for a brief second when I was first brought in. I figured they were being housed in another building or unit. So after that much time feeling isolated, I can't tell you how good it was to see my girl. We talked about school, friends, and what she'd had for dinner the past three nights, but more importantly, we talked about getting married. We were no longer going to wait until I finished law school to do it. I swear it was the most satisfying conversation I'd had in years. If I didn't think Simone loved me before this, I sure as hell knew now, because my own mother wouldn't get on that bus to see me. Sure, she accepted my collect calls, but she drew the line on coming to see me. So, having Simone come see me was like a fantasy, and all I could picture was her and me chilling on a beach, until the CO ended it. That's when the grey walls, the steel doors, and the bars on the windows came back into view, and I remembered that I was in fucking jail.

As I walked down the corridor to my unit, tears just kept flowing. I didn't give a shit who saw me crying. All I wanted was to go home and be with my girl. I'd tried to be strong, and I'd tried to be patient like my pops had told me to do the other day when he stopped by for a so-called legal visit. I think I would have been all right if it weren't for seeing Simone, but as soon as I got back to my unit, I was going to call my father and plead with him to get me the fuck out of there. I'd been punished enough. I didn't care if he had to break me out; I just wanted to go home.

In the unit, my plan changed, because there were long lines of men waiting to use the phones. They were usually less crowded late at night, so I'd make my call then. Instead, I decided to volunteer to go outside to the yard as part of a work detail one of the friendlier COs had told me about. It was just picking up papers and wrappers, but it got me outside in the fresh air where I was able to think.

I had made it from one side to the other, filling up half a bag of trash, before I looked over and saw Kwesi sitting at a metal picnic table near the fence. He was dressed in the same outfit as the rest of us, but on his head was a small, round hat looked to be made out of white linen.

I rushed over to him. "Kwesi! Oh my God, brother, you are a sight for sore eyes!"

He looked up at me but didn't say anything or show any type of recognition. I tilted my head and asked, "Kwesi? You a'ight, man? It's me, Langston."

"I know who you are," he said, sounding uninterested.

I ignored that, because I was just so damn happy to finally connect with one of my frat brothers. "Man, it's good to see you." I leaned toward him so that we could exchange our fraternity grip, but he leaned back as if I'd invaded his personal space.

"Don't."

I glanced around to see if maybe the guards were watching us and he didn't want to get in any type of trouble, but no one was paying us any attention—except for maybe the other guys at the table. I leaned in again, but Kwesi gave me the same reaction.

"What the hell is wrong with you, Kwesi? You ain't gripping me up? What's up with that?"

"There is nothing wrong with me, Langston. The problem is you." Kwesi was frowning, and his voice was anything but friendly.

"Look, frat, I'm sorry you're in here. I'm sorry we're all in here, but this ain't my fault," I said, starting to get a little pissed off with his attitude.

"You were going to leave us in here to face all these charges alone while you jumped bail." Kwesi's eyes were full of disappointment as he shook his head at me. "You are disloyal, Langston. I can't believe you had the nerve to walk over here and greet me."

Although he hadn't laid a hand on me, I felt as if Kwesi had punched me in the stomach. I exhaled harshly. "No, Kwes, man. I would never do that. I wasn't jumping bail at all. We were going to hang out in Puerto Rico for the weekend—"

"Wow, so you felt that it was okay to go on a weekend vacation with your girlfriend while your brothers were sitting in jail? I don't know which story is worse: the truth or the lie," he said incredulously, making me feel worse than I already felt.

"No, that's not how it was, Kwesi. Let me explain. . . ."

"There's nothing to explain, Langston. You're disloyal and dishonorable, and this entire situation just shows how privileged you truly think you are. We are no longer brothers." He went to walk away from me, but I grabbed him.

"Kwesi, will you stop acting fucking stupid?" I said, tightening my fingers around his jumpsuit and raising my voice.

"Get your hands off of me," he said simply, causing my anger to bloom. Here I was trying to explain, and he was being dismissive.

"No, you're gonna listen to me. None of this shit is my fault, and you know it. Simone booked the tickets through Skiplagged, and the fucking ADA James Brown has some kind of beef with my pops," I said, still holding onto him.

"Here you go again. Normally you're blaming your mother for everything that's going wrong. Now it's your father's fault?" Kwesi snatched away from me. "A little advice: this is not Howard University, and definitely not Riverside Drive. This is jail. Your parents can't rescue you here."

"I don't need your advice!" I was furious at this point, and I pushed my body against Kwesi's with so much force that he stumbled backward. I reached out to grab him so he wouldn't fall, but before I could catch him, I felt myself being pulled back. I turned to see three large dudes, one of whom had me by the collar.

"Is there a problem, brother Kwesi?" one of them asked as two different men helped him up, brushing him off like he was special.

All the men stood and stared at Kwesi as if waiting for instructions from him. I got the sense that if he told them to snap my neck, they would do it.

He glanced over at me before turning his attention back to them. "No, there is no problem. This man and I were just completing some unfinished business, but we're done. Aren't we?"

The big dudes glared at me with contempt. I was sure if I said the wrong thing, they could be my last words. So, I said the only thing I could say. "Yeah, we're done."

As he walked away, the men surrounded him like personal security and followed his lead. I watched them, dumbfounded by everything that had just taken place.

I heard someone say, "Man, what's wrong with you? Don't you know not to mess with them?" I turned and saw another inmate standing nearby, watching me.

"What do you mean, *them*? That used to be one of my best friends," I told him.

"Yeah, well, it don't look like you're best friends to me. Word to the wise: there are certain folks you just don't mess with inside, friend or not. You got the Crips, Bloods, MS13s, what's left of the Latin Kings, and you got them." His gazed in the direction of Kwesi and his entourage walking away. "The Muslims. You don't fuck with none of them, or you'll find yourself in trouble."

"Muslim?" It dawned on me now why Kwesi was wearing the white cap. He had found another brotherhood in here. The question was, did he mean what he said? Did he no longer recognize the bond he had with me, Krush, and Tony? Saying that this could cause trouble would be an understatement.

Jacqueline

40

I stepped out of the hired car and quickly climbed the ten or twelve steps to the brownstone's front door. Glancing around to make sure nobody was watching, I took a moment to catch my breath and get myself together before I finally pushed the small doorbell. It made the same weird buzzing sound it had thirty years ago. I couldn't believe James still lived there after all these years. I mean, who did that? Who stayed in their momma's house their entire adult life?

A few seconds later, I heard movement on the other side of the door. My heart began pounding when I saw the shadow come over the peephole.

"Who is it?" he asked.

I wavered before answering. "It's . . . It's me, James. Jackie."

"Who?" I couldn't tell if he was playing games or seriously didn't know.

"It's Jackie Cooper."

There was a silence long enough that I almost turned to walk away, thinking he wasn't going to open the door. Then the sound of the deadbolt unlocking stopped me in my tracks. Slowly, the door opened.

I swallowed the lump in my throat and managed to squeak out, "Hi, James."

"Hello, Jackie."

He stared at me, and I stared at him. He looked different yet the same. Like most of us, he'd gained some weight over the past thirty years, but he was still in shape for a guy his age.

"Can I come in?"

"Sure, I guess." He held the door open, and I stepped inside.

It was different than I remembered. The décor was updated, but the earth tones said more late nineties than new millennium.

"I like what you've done with the place. Those windows must bring a lot of light in during the daytime," I said awkwardly.

"It could use a new paint job. We renovated in ninety-eight after my mother passed."

"I can't believe you still live here. I thought you would've left Brooklyn. . . ."

"No, Jacqueline. I've always been satisfied living here. I don't need a mansion and a Bentley to be happy. But I wouldn't expect you to understand," he said, walking past me.

I followed him into the living room. "I guess I deserved that."

"That's an understatement," he commented as he flopped down on the sofa. "I would ask why you're here, but that would be a dumb question."

"Well, I called your office and left several messages, but you didn't return any of my calls." I waited for him to offer me a seat, but he didn't.

"So you decided to show up on my doorstep unannounced? That's more Bradley's style than yours." His attitude was cold, but he had let me in, which let me know he was open to having a conversation. I took it upon myself to sit down.

"Maybe, but I needed to talk to you," I told him.

"We have nothing to talk about. As a matter of fact, it's probably best that you leave. I'm sure this is violating some type of ethical line, since I'm prosecuting your son's case." He stood, and I jumped up as well.

I took a deep breath, knowing that it was time for me to have the conversation I'd been avoiding for damn near three decades. There was no way around it.

"Why are you prosecuting my son's case?"

"Because it's my job. I'm the lead prosecutor, and this a high-profile case. That's what they pay me for, to prosecute criminals," he told me with a hint of anger in his tone. "And if they haven't told you yet, your son had two kilos of heroin in his car. That makes him a criminal. Or is that little fact immaterial?"

I stuffed my own anger deep down inside. I couldn't risk blowing up at him the way I wanted to. He held Langston's fate in his hands.

"He's not a criminal until convicted," I said calmly. "But what is material is that you, me, and Bradley have history, and by definition, you should recuse yourself from the case."

"I'll tell you what. If you and your ex-husband think a thirty-year-old spat between colleagues who haven't seen each other in at least that time is relevant, then by all means, have Bradley make a motion to the court to have me removed from this case." He laughed. "I'm sure that will play well on the six o'clock news—but not as well as you showing up at my door after hours trying to sway this case, Ms. Federal Judge."

I swear, if I were a man, I would have punched him. "We just want a fair trial for our son."

"And I'm not going to be fair?" he snapped. "Think back, Jackie, because when we met, I was the fairest, most honorable man you ever met."

"What happened to that man?" I regretted that question as soon as it left my lips.

"You happened!" he shouted. "You and your nice ass and your perfect fucking tits, taking my virginity and making me fall in love like a schoolboy. I didn't deserve what you did to me, Jackie, and you know it."

"I'm sorry," I said quietly.

"It's too late for that."

"I know, and you're right. It is too late, but I still owe you an apology. I was wrong. We were wrong. And I'm sorry."

"Yes, you are. Now, you can go."

"That's it? That's all you're gonna say, James?"

"What else is there to say?"

I stepped closer to him—so close that I could smell the scent of his cologne, mixed with the perspiration that was starting to form on his neck.

"You want me to say that I forgive you for what you did? Because I don't! He was my best friend, and he ruined my life. But the worst part is that you were my fiancée, and you helped him," he said.

"I know that. We were wrong. I was wrong," I repeated. "But, James, I was young and naïve, and he was bold and charismatic. He was driven, and . . ." I tried to find the words to explain the fatal mistake that had been made all those years ago when all three of us were just trying to find our way.

"And I was stupid," he said adamantly.

"No, James, I was the stupid one," I explained.

"Not too stupid. You ended up being a federal judge. I mean, I get it. He was a challenge, and we all know how much you love a challenge."

Even if he was right, he was starting to irritate me. God, how I wished I could have gone another thirty years without talking to James Brown.

"You're right. He was a challenge, and you were neglectful," I retorted, thinking it was time to chop him down a peg. "I could have never fallen in his arms if you weren't pushing me out of yours."

"Pushed you out? My father had just been diagnosed with stage four lung cancer!" he screamed, and suddenly, it all came racing back to me.

I'd just fucked up. I'd completely forgotten about his father. My faux pas made Bradley's and my actions even worse, and my apology worthless. Still, I couldn't give up yet.

"And I tried to help you and be there for you, but you kept pushing me away, and . . ." My bottom lip quivered, and tears formed in my eyes.

James had always been the "close second" when it came to Bradley. Where Bradley was handsome, brilliant, and daring, James was attractive, smart, and likeable. They were both smart as hell, passing the Bar on the first try without studying, but Bradley always seemed smarter. It was probably his confidence, bordering on arrogance, that had convinced me he was superior in every way.

"And he pulled you in," James snapped, confirming my thoughts.

I was going to have to change tactics, because this was not working. I could see the hurt that was still there. It had festered, a pain that had lingered and grown. Pain that deep could only come from one place: love.

He looked away from me, but I took another step toward him and touched the side of his face to turn him back in my direction. To my surprise, he didn't push my hand away. Instead, he touched it. I eased closer and touched his other cheek, then leaned my head against this chin.

"James . . ." I whispered.

He tilted my head up and kissed me full on the lips. Surrounded by the familiarity of the apartment he lived in, I felt warmth and nostalgia in his kiss. His taste, his scent, the fluttering in my chest—it was as if I had been away on a long and eventful vacation and had finally made it home.

I wrapped my arms around his waist, now a little thicker than years ago. He reached up and released my hair, which came tumbling down around my shoulders. Brushing a few strands out of my face, James looked into my eyes, and without saying another word, he grabbed me and led me into his bedroom.

James had always been a tender lover, so I expected him to carefully remove my clothes. He didn't. He snatched them off and wasted no time removing his own, and then he ravished me with a passion that I'd never experienced. The sex was aggressive, hot, and pleasurable, and as I lay there afterward in the same bed I had laid in years before, I realized that, had I not been drawn in by Bradley, I would probably still be married to this man, who truly loved me. The same man who now had the power to save the life of my son.

Perk

41

I'd just pulled into my parking space behind the Hudson offices when I spotted Desiree stepping out of her car. She didn't seem to notice me as she placed a cup of coffee on the roof and retrieved a black blazer from the trunk, then checked her hair in the reflection from her car's rear window. Apparently satisfied with her appearance, she picked up her coffee and headed to the back entrance of the building. As she walked past my truck, I enjoyed the sight of her curved hips in the snug skirt she wore.

"It's not going to work," I said as I stepped out of the truck, slinging my knapsack over my shoulder.

She stopped walking and turned to look at me. "What's not going to work?"

"That blazer. It's not going to work."

"Really? Why?" She looked confused.

"Because every woman in our office is going to notice you're wearing the same clothes you did yesterday, and they'll know you're wearing the blazer to try to change things up."

Desiree wasn't one to show emotion very often, but right then, her face was showing a shitload of embarrassment. "That obvious, huh?" She was so much like her mother sometimes, focused on herself or her self-serving liberal projects. It was obvious she hadn't even realized how this current walk-of-shame situation could pertain to both of us.

"Yep, that and the fact that I'm your roommate. I know you didn't come home last night," I said. Then, as much I hated the fact that I cared, I had to ask: "Are you seeing someone?"

She coughed, nearly dropping the coffee, and I knew the answer before she gave it. I handed her a napkin, and she dabbed at the drops of liquid that had spilled on her blouse as we entered the building.

I followed her into her office, where she finally managed to speak. "You can't be serious right now. Why do you keep asking me that?"

"Like I said, you didn't come home last night, and it wasn't the first time. So, I'm just curious," I said.

"I didn't come home because I stayed at a friend's house." She squinted at me like she was trying to figure out my true motives.

"What's his name?" I tried to keep my face neutral.

"Tuh! I'm not even gonna justify that with an answer. And you know what? I don't have to. You're not my man, Perk," she said, visibly aggravated by the conversation.

I remained as cool as the gentle breeze coming through the vent in her office. "You know what?" I said. "You're absolutely right. I'm not your man. I may wanna be, and even try to be, but I'm not, and that's your choice, not mine." I turned to leave.

"Why are you so damn dramatic, Perk?" she whined.

"I'm not, but one of us has to put an end to this situation, and that person is me. We're done. Our relationship from this point on is strictly professional, and there won't be any further physical contact, because after all, I ain't your man. I'm also moving out, so you might want to find another roommate." I stomped out.

"Perk!" She hollered after me, but I ignored her, stepping onto the elevator before she could catch me.

"Yo, Perk, you got a visitor, man," Michael said when I arrived on the fourth floor. Believe it or not, Desiree had taken the stairs and made it up there at the same time as me.

"A'ight, I'm coming," I told him.

"Who's here to see you? Is it someone about Lang?" Desiree huffed, out of breath, staring at Michael.

"No, I don't think this person is involved with the case." Michael gave her a small smile and then looked at me. "She's waiting in your office."

"She?" Desiree's neck swiveled like she was an around-the-way girl from Brooklyn instead of her Upper Manhattan self.

"Thanks," I said to Michael, bypassing Des and walking down the hall.

When I got to my office, I was pleasantly surprised to see Lena, the girl I'd met at Starbucks, waiting there. She looked cute as hell in a simple black blouse that revealed just enough cleavage, a pair of tight jeans that showed off her round curves, and a pair of thigh-high boots.

"Hey, handsome." She stood up, tossing her long braids over her shoulder and greeting me with a warm smile and a passionate kiss.

"Wow, this is a surprise," I said.

"A good one, I hope." She grinned.

We'd communicated briefly via text a few times since the case started, but I hadn't seen her. Honestly, I hadn't really thought about seeing her because I'd been so busy. And, of course, I'd been sleeping with Des again.

"Oh, it is a good surprise. Believe it or not, you're right on time." Noticing the brown paper shopping bag she carried, I asked, "What's that?"

"This is the reason for my visit." She held the bag out to me. "I wanted to give you this."

"And here I thought you just wanted to see me," I teased, placing the bag on my desk.

"Well, of course, that too."

"Whatever it is, I appreciate the gift and the giver," I said with a smile.

"You can open the bag, Perk," she said.

I peeked inside the bag and then took out its contents: a round Tupperware container with a handle. "You made me a cake?"

"No, silly. It's not a cake." She laughed. "It's a pie."

I lifted the top from the container, and my mouth began to water. Inside was a perfect mass of the most beautiful strawberries with a red glaze, sitting on top of graham cracker crumbs and topped with fresh, homemade whipped cream. I closed my eyes and inhaled the scent.

"Oh my God," I moaned.

"I remember how you said your favorite dessert was strawberry pie from Shoney's. And, well, of course there aren't any Shoney's around here, so I decided to make you one," she told me.

"You made this? For me?" I asked, genuinely touched by her gesture.

"Yeah, what's wrong? Isn't that what you told me? It was strawberry, right?" she asked with a worried look on her face.

"Damn right it's strawberry! I can't believe you did this for me, that's all," I said, staring at the pie. No one had ever made a pie for me before, especially not anyone I hadn't known very long. I was surprised Lena even remembered me telling her. I was downright impressed.

"It's no big deal." She shrugged.

"Yo, I gotta taste it. We have some plates and forks in the breakroom," I said. "Get the door."

She opened the door, and we stepped out.

As we passed by Michael's office, he saw the Tupperware and asked, "What's that?"

"A pie. Lena made it." I nudged my head toward her.

"Homemade?" He smiled at her.

"Yep, strawberry," she said proudly. "Would you like a piece?"

"Damn right!" Michael followed us to the breakroom.

The pie tasted as good as it looked. Michael and I were enjoying it and praising Lena when I looked up and saw Desiree standing in the doorway. I was surprised she'd waited as long as she had to barge in and check out who had come to see me. I eased closer to Lena as I shoved another forkful in my mouth.

"Hey, Des, you gotta try this," Michael said enthusiastically.

"I swear," I said with my mouth full. "This is the best damn pie I've ever tasted. It's better than Shoney's."

"Would you like a piece? There's plenty left," Lena offered.

"This pie is good as hell, Des. And it's homemade. You should try it," Michael said.

"It's just pie, Michael. Damn." Desiree stood there, staring at all three of us like we were vagabonds off the street who had been given a free meal.

"Des, come on in. I want you to meet Lena," I said, loving every minute of this scene.

"Nice to meet you . . . Des, is it?" Lena asked.

"It's Desiree. Hudson. As in the name on the wall, Hudson and Associates." Desiree's voice was cold and unwelcoming.

To my surprise, Lena wasn't intimidated by her demeanor. Instead, she said, "Well, Ms. Hudson, I'm sure these two gentlemen will definitely be working hard for your family's firm this afternoon, because they are full and happy. That's what you sometimes have to do to get a brother to put in work, you know what I mean?"

I couldn't believe it when Lena winked at her.

"No, actually, I don't. My momma didn't cook, and neither do I," Desiree scoffed. The way she was staring Lena down made me think there could be a fight. There was enough estrogen in the room that I worried we might be approaching a danger zone

"Lena, let me walk you out," I said, putting down my plate and wiping my mouth.

"I'll leave the rest of the pie container here until you're finished. You can bring it by tonight. I'll be up pretty late," Lena said suggestively.

As I was hurrying Lena out the door, Michael called out, "Nice to meet you, Lena. Anytime you wanna bring treats, you're always welcome."

Desiree looked like she wanted to stab him in the neck with the fork he was holding. She gave me the same look, amusing me even more than I already was.

"What's the deal with her?" Lena asked when we exited the building.

"She's just stressed about her brother's case, that's all. Everyone around here is on edge, really, including me," I explained.

"Well, I hope I was able to make you feel better," she said with a smile.

I took a good look at her. She was a cute girl, a little younger than I normally dated, but she was nice—and her body was tight as hell, which gave her a plus. But even with all of that, I wasn't sure if I was really feeling her.

"You definitely did," I told her. "I'm glad you came by, and not because of the pie, either."

"I would love for you to come by later . . . if you'd like. Strawberry pie ain't the only thing I have that's sweet and sticky for you to enjoy." She bit her bottom lip seductively and gave me a look to let me know exactly what she was offering.

I pulled her to me and kissed her deeply, letting my tongue explore her mouth.

"Damn, was that a yes?" she asked when we broke the kiss.

"That's a *we'll see*." I gave her a smile to let her down easy.

I called an Uber and waited with her until it pulled up to the curb. When she was gone, as I turned to go back into the building, I felt someone looking at me. I glanced up to the fourth floor window. Desiree was scowling down at me, but when we made eye contact, she disappeared from view.

Back on the fourth floor, I headed to the breakroom to pick up what was left of the pie and bring it to my office. There were too many greedy motherfuckers at Hudson and Associates to leave something like that lying around.

I stepped into the room to find Desiree waiting for me, looking ready to kill. "Don't bring that bitch back here," she snarled.

"She wasn't bothering anybody." I snapped back, trying to keep my voice down. "What the fuck is your problem with her?"

"I don't have a problem with her, my problem is with you," she mumbled. We were both trying to keep our voices down so the rest of the office didn't hear us.

"I don't have time for this,"

I was about to walk away when she said, "I hope you weren't planning on finishing that pie."

That's when I spotted the pie—and the Tupperware—in the garbage can. "You threw my fucking pie away?"

"No, I just threw it. I didn't give a shit where it landed," she said like it was no big deal.

"You're crazy, you know that?"

"No, you're crazy if you think you're just gonna parade some bitch in here like some bakery thot bringing you treats. This is a fucking place of business, and everyone in here should be focused on my brother, who's facing life in prison. Instead, you got everyone around here gushing over your fucking random of the week." Surprisingly, she was on the verge of tears. "So, yeah, I threw the fucking pie away, Perk. Her popping in the office was unprofessional."

I stood, shocked by her reaction. I knew she was jealous, but damn. I'd never seen her act like this.

"Fine, I get it. Won't happen again. From now on, I'll invite her to my new home. But I meant what I said, Desiree. We're done."

James

42

The first thing I noticed when my eyes fluttered open was that the sun was rising. What I thought was going to be a brief post-coital nap had turned into an all-night sleep. I glanced down at Jackie, still asleep, snuggled up next to me. I was still a bit stunned by the events of the night before. Jacqueline had been right; I had ignored the calls and messages she'd made to my office. In my mind, she'd died a long time ago, and I had nothing to say. I knew when I took on this case that eventually we'd cross paths, but having her show up on my doorstep had never crossed my mind. When I saw her through the peephole, I'd been unprepared for the conversation that would take place and the wave of emotions that came with seeing her. She was still beautiful and sexy as hell, and deep down, despite everything, I'd be lying if didn't admit I still loved her.

The sound of her voice speaking my name was still music to my ears, but also pierced my heart. Still, the more she talked and tried to explain, the more I realized I still wanted her. So, I kissed her, I touched her, and I took her to my bed and did something I should have done thirty years ago to keep her from walking out on me for Bradley. I fucked her—hard, fast, and more importantly, memorably. No matter what happened after today, she'd remember last night.

"Good morning," she whispered, draping her arm across my chest.

"Morning," I mumbled.

We lay together silently for a few more minutes before I eased from under her and sat on the side of the bed. My mind was all over the place, and I needed to clear my head.

"You want breakfast?" she asked, sitting up and rubbing my back.

I glanced over my shoulder and nodded. "Sure. Breakfast would be nice. I'm gonna go and take a shower."

Jacqueline got up, and I couldn't help but stare at her body as she walked over to my closet, grabbed one of my button-down shirts, and slipped it on. Even in her late fifties, her breasts were still full and perky, and it made me wonder if she'd had some work done. Her hips were a little wider, but her legs were muscled and toned, along with her arms. She had kept herself up very well, and her physique could compete with any woman in her early forties.

"Still like your eggs over easy?" she asked as she was walking out of the bedroom.

"I do."

When she was gone, I stood and went into the bathroom down the hallway.

"Oh my God, James!" I heard her yell.

"What? What's wrong?" I stuck my head out of the bathroom.

"You still have these yellow pots and pans?" She laughed. "And they look like they're barely used."

"Well, I don't really cook much." I sighed, suddenly embarrassed that I still had the same cookware that she'd given my mother as a Christmas gift many years ago. My mother had been so happy to receive them. She liked Jacqueline a lot, and so did my father. They both made it very clear how much they looked forward to having her as a daughter-in-law. Mom also liked Bradley. She used to say he was like a second son. It had broken her heart almost as much as mine when the news about their involvement surfaced—among other things.

As I stood in the shower, letting the hot water cascade over my bald head, I allowed the memories of that fateful spring to come running back to me. The three of us were the only black lawyers working for the United States Attorney's Office for the Eastern District of New York. The office was exceptionally busy, but the U.S. attorney's attention was focused on the case of Fat Bruce, one of the biggest drug dealers in the city. Fat Bruce was the black version of John Gotti. He'd been arrested nine times on everything from murder to drugs and RICO charges, but each and every time, he was acquitted. Our boss thought he was finally going to put him away for good, when all of a sudden, Fat Bruce's lawyer pulled a rabbit out of his hat and presented a legal precedent and motion to dismiss that threatened to kill the entire case. The powers that be were at a loss, and my boss was getting so many threatening calls from his boss, the Attorney General, that he started packing up his stuff because he was positive he was going to be fired at the end of the trial.

The night before the motion was to be heard by the judge, I was sitting in my father's hospital room, prepping for a case, when a particular piece of case law struck me. The more I read, the more it dawned on me that I could not only turn the case around for my boss, but I could win it—and a lot of other cases for our side. I immediately called Bradley and asked him to meet me at a nearby coffee shop so I could run it by him.

"I don't really know about that," Bradley said when I shared my thoughts about the case. "Bruce's lawyer is pretty savvy."

"There's case law backing us up, Brad. In Hunt v. the United States, the Supreme Court sided with the government. It might be a Prohibition case, but it's still on the books," I explained.

"It's too risky, man." Bradley shook his head. "If you're wrong, the AG's office is going to bounce us out of here right along with Schaefer and his cronies. We're just starting to get our own caseloads. Hell, you have a trial tomorrow."

"Brad, you know I'm not a risk taker, but I'm telling you, it's worth the risk. We pull Schaefer's butt out of this fire and we can write our own ticket around this place."

I could see the idea of having the U.S. attorney beholden to us was appealing to him, but he wasn't a hundred percent on board yet.

"Maybe, but I'd like to do a little research of my own before presenting it to Schaefer. It's possible there are other relevant cases that came up after that ruling."

"I guess," I said, feeling kind of deflated.

"What about Jackie? Did you run this by her?" he asked.

"No, she's at the office, working on some white-collar case for David Nugent. You were the first person I thought of. I mean, Jackie's smart, but she's more of the paper-pushing type," I said.

"You know, James, for someone so smart, you're a lot more naïve than I thought."

"What's that supposed to mean?"

"What makes you think Jackie's a paper pusher? She's a damn good lawyer, and very ambitious. If I ever start my own firm, she's the first person I'd want as my partner."

"Thanks," I said coldly.

"Stop acting like a baby. You already said you don't want to go into private practice. But for the record, I say we bring Jackie in on this."

"No," I refused flatly.

"Why not?"

"If this happens to work, it will propel her career into something I won't be able to control. Once we get married, she's not going to be doing much of this type of work anyway. She'll be taking care of our house and kids."

He shook his head. "Man, you can't control a woman like her."

"Watch me," I said defiantly. "So, are you in? Are we going to talk to Schaefer tomorrow?"

"I think so, but why don't we head on down to the office and do the research?"

"I gotta stick around here and see my old man. He ain't got much time. You take a look and let me know what you think," I said. "If you want to draw up a response, I'll head down to the office and meet you."

"Sure thing. If it bears any fruit, we'll present it to Schaefer together in the morning."

I left that meeting feeling good about our prospects for success on the case, not to mention our prospects for career advancement. Bradley was exceptionally smart, and I valued his opinion. If he looked at the case law and thought it was a dud, I'd leave it alone, but I was pretty sure he'd be calling to tell me I was right.

Well, I never got a call that night. When I arrived at work the next day, I didn't see Bradley, but I figured I would talk to him as soon as I came back from my scheduled court appearance. I got my paperwork together and went to the courthouse, where I won at trial. It wasn't a big case, but it was my first, and it felt good. My day went downhill fast after that.

I went back to the office just in time for everyone to be summoned into a meeting. The speculation was that Schaefer would announce that the Fat Bruce case had been dismissed and he'd been fired. So, we were all surprised when he walked into the room followed by his chief of staff Greg Williamson. Bradley and Jackie came in with them too. They were all wearing smiles.

"Ladies and gentlemen," Schaefer said, "I'm happy to announce that Fat Bruce Farrow's motion to dismiss has been denied, and he has accepted a plea agreement of twenty years in federal prison."

The entire office exploded in cheers—except for me, because I was wondering how this miraculous event happened, and even more so, why my best friend and girlfriend were up there to celebrate with the bosses. Schaefer started speaking again, and I got my answer.

He held up a hand to quiet the room, and said, "Before I take all the credit, let me give some praise to the two individuals that made this happen." Schaefer graciously waved his hand toward my supposed comrades. "Bradley Hudson and Jacqueline Cooper, whose written response to the defendant's motion, based on case law from Hunt v. the United States, was so thorough that we are submitting it to the Law Journal for publication."

I felt like I'd been punched in the gut as I stood there staring in disbelief at Bradley and Jackie. There was applause and whistling for the shit I had shared with Bradley the night before. Everyone began talking about him and Jackie like they were heroes. Meanwhile, Bradley soaked up the praise without a hint of shame. He didn't even glance in my direction.

When I couldn't take it anymore, I went over to pull him aside and discuss it. But Bradley turned his back when he saw me coming, and then Schaefer called him over to a group of more senior lawyers, looking like he was introducing a candidate for mayor. I knew I wouldn't be able to confront him until this impromptu office party was over.

But I did get to Jackie, pulling her out of the room into a small office.

"What the fuck was that? You two just stole my idea and took it to Schaefer?" I was livid.

"Calm down, James," she snapped. "We didn't steal anything

from you. And let's be clear. You didn't write one word of that response. We spent most of the night writing it."

I was confused by her coldness. This was not the woman I thought I knew. "Why didn't that son of a bitch Bradley call me?"

"Because I told him not to," she said with undisguised contempt. "He wanted to, but you wouldn't have wanted me there."

"He told you that?" I asked, trying not to look guilty.

"No, he didn't have to. From the day we met, I've tried to help you in any way possible. Did everything a supportive woman would do for her man. And in return, all you've done is try to hold me back. Well, not anymore you don't." She took off her ring and handed it to me. "Me and you, we are through."

I stared at her for a brief moment as my anger evolved into pure rage. I grabbed her arm and squeezed. "You fucked him, didn't you? You fucked Bradley?"

She didn't hesitate. "Yes," she said, pulling herself free and walking away.

I watched her disappear into the meeting room then glanced down at the engagement ring in my hand. Staring at it for a few moments, I tried unsuccessfully to hold back tears.

Half out of my mind, I ran back into the meeting area and searched for Bradley. I charged at him, knocking Schaefer down in the process. "You son of a bitch!" While he was on the floor, I punched him in the eye, then rained down blows around his head and chest. I wanted to see blood.

"James! James! You're gonna kill him!" I could hear Jackie screaming, but I didn't stop for fear that if I did, I would aim my attack at her.

Bradley tried to block the blows to his body and face, but I was still able to land quite a few. Over and over I hit him, until finally, they pulled me off. Jacqueline's eyes met mine briefly, and then she stepped past me and rushed to Bradley.

I closed my eyes and slumped to the floor, unable to move. And then, security arrived and took me away. I was arrested and charged with assault. Luckily, the charges were dropped, but of course, I lost my job.

Both Bradley and Jackie were thrust into national cases, where they thrived, making headlines and being quickly and frequently promoted. He and Jacqueline married, had children, and began living the life that she and I had planned. They finally left the US attorney's office five years later to open their own very successful law practice. I wound up working Legal Aid for fifteen years before someone finally took a chance and hired me at the Staten Island DA's office. I vowed that one day, karma would arrive and be served to Bradley Hudson on a silver platter. That day had finally arrived.

I finished showering then slipped into my bedroom and got dressed. I could hear Jackie singing, and the smell of eggs and bacon filled my nostrils. When I walked into the kitchen, she frowned.

"You're dressed already? I thought we'd have round two after we ate breakfast."

"I'm not going to have time to eat. And there won't be another round. I'm sorry. I have a huge case I'm working on. I'm sure you know that already."

She froze for a second, and I was satisfied, knowing I'd hit my mark. Then, she pulled herself together and put on a neutral face as she stepped closer to me. "But, James."

I took a step back, out of her reach. "You need to get dressed so you can leave," I said, looking at the stove. She had prepared two perfect plates. Although I was starving, I wasn't going to eat.

"Are you really going to act like this?"

"Act like what?" I asked.

"Like last night didn't happen. I mean, I thought we could at least talk."

"Talk about what? We don't have anything to discuss. I certainly hope you don't think what happened last night would have some type of bearing on your son's case, Jacqueline. You're a sitting judge, for God's sake. You wouldn't dare risk your position—or mine, I hope."

"No, not at all," she quickly said. "But, James, my son's life is in your hands. I'm begging you to consider—"

"I'm considering the evidence that my office has against him. That's all," I told her.

"What am I supposed to do?" Tears formed in her eyes and rolled down her cheeks. I was almost tempted to wipe them away. "I can't have my son go away. It's twenty years, for God's sake."

"Jacqueline, my advice to you is that you need to prepare," I said, stuffing any tenderness I felt for her deep down inside.

"Prepare for what?" she asked.

"Prepare yourself and your son, because he and his friends are going to jail for a very long time." I turned and walked away before I crumbled. I felt bad because, in all honesty, this had nothing to do with her. I had forgiven her. However, Bradley Hudson deserved every bad thing that was getting ready to happen to his family.

Bradley

43

"Mr. Hudson! Mr. Hudson! Do you think anything meaningful will come out of today's hearing?" a lone reporter asked me as Desiree and I ascended the courthouse steps. Usually, they swarmed my car the moment Ernie pulled up to the curb, but other than this reporter and his cameraman, the media was ignoring me.

I stopped and turned to answer the question. "This is just a hearing, but I'm sure there'll be a few surprises today. However, we will make our case in the courtroom, not in the media. Thank you." I turned back toward the courthouse entrance and continued to climb the steps.

"Looks like you have competition, Dad." Desiree pointed to our right at the top of the steps, where James appeared to be giving a press briefing.

"Don't be insulting. That man's never been my competition in anything," I said. It was true that James had never been my equal, but it didn't make me any less agitated as I watched him holding the spotlight over there.

"Well, at least we know where the media went to," she joked.

"Yes, I guess they're sick of talking to me." I pulled out my cell and called my wife. "James Brown is having some type of news conference. It would be nice if I knew what he was talking about before we start this hearing."

"Your wish is my command, my love. Put in your earpiece when you get in the courtroom, and I'll give you a rundown in the next five minutes or so."

"Thanks, babe," I said as Desiree and I entered the building and walked down the hall to the courtroom.

I sat beside Desiree. On the other side of her, already seated, was Kenneth Kimba, Kwesi's attorney. He was looking rather foolish in a sweater vest and colorful bowtie. Lamont, who had written the motion we were about to be heard on, had decided to stay at the office and sulk like a baby because I'd made his sister second chair instead of him. I didn't have the time or the patience for his nonsense, so I just left him behind. Meanwhile, on the other side of the aisle, ADA David Carpenter sat alone, until James Brown final strutted down the aisle and took a seat next to him. He leaned over and whispered something in Carpenter's ear, and the two of them began laughing. I just hoped the joke wasn't on me.

"If we're lucky, this should be wrapped up by lunchtime, don't you think, Daddy?" Desiree whispered.

"We can only hope, dear," I answered, my eyes remaining straight ahead as I put in my wireless two-way earpiece. I loved the damn thing, because judges never question a man of my age with a hearing aid, so I could get real-time information form Carla and her people on the third floor without pissing off the judge.

"Testing one, two, three," I said.

"Hello, my dear." Carla's voice rang in my ear.

"So, what was James up to?" I asked.

"Nothing really. Same old BS about all he wants is justice for the people of Staten Island. The usual."

"That's what I thought. Everything okay at the shop?"

"Other than Lamont moping around like he's lost his best friend, yeah, everything's fine."

"He'll be okay," I said.

"The two of you should talk when you get back. Clear the air. He's smart and has some great ideas."

"I know he's smart—sometimes too smart for his own good— but Lamont has to understand that I'm the managing partner. I know what I'm doing," I said with finality.

"I understand what you're doing with Desiree, but you should explain it to him. After all, you may be the managing partner, but he is a partner."

"Lamont's a big boy, darling. He'll be okay. These are all teaching moments," I said as I watched Kimba get up from his seat. "What is this clown doing?"

"What's going on?" Carla asked.

I drummed my fingers on the table to get Desiree's attention.

"Kwesi's attorney just got up and is headed toward the DA's table," I explained to my wife. I watched as he casually strolled over to the other side and began speaking with David and James.

"Why is he doing that?" Carla asked as Desiree and I exchanged a concerned glance.

"I don't know," I replied to my wife; then I leaned over to Desiree and whispered, "What the hell is that about?"

"I have no clue." The frustration on Desiree's face was evident. "Should I go over and find out?"

"No, let them talk. Mr. Kimba isn't the brightest of legal minds. If there's a play to be made, James will be the one to make it." I raised my hand to my mouth casually, so that no one could read my lips. "Carla, honey, I need you to have someone hack into Mr. Kimba's email. Let's find out what kind of correspondence he and the DA's office are having."

"I'm on it. Let me have someone log into a foreign IP. I'll get back to you on it as soon as I can. Just holler if you need me."

"All rise!" the bailiff announced, and Kimba made his way back to the defense table as the judge walked in. "State of New York versus Langston Hudson, Anthony Baker, Kirby Wright, and Kwesi Adomako, the Honorable Juan Rodriguez presiding," the bailiff read off.

I watched as my son was escorted into the room, along with Tony, Kwesi, and Krush. The formalities and charges were read, and then we all moved to take our seats. Judge Rodriguez held up his hand to indicate that he hadn't finished reading the file he'd begun flipping through once he sat down. He didn't take his eyes off the file, even as he slowly put his hand back down.

"Court, you may be seated," the bailiff finally said.

"James Brown for the State, Your Honor."

"Bradley and Desiree Hudson for the defense."

"Kenneth Kimba, also for the defense, Your Honor."

After a few moments, the judge removed his reading glasses and focused his attention on the courtroom. "Okay, gentlemen, and lady, we are supposed to be choosing a date for trial, but I have read your motion, Mr. Hudson, and it would make sense to at least address it now."

"Thank you, Your Honor," I said.

"So, it appears that you feel a change of venue would more fairly serve your clients." The judge looked at me directly, and I could tell our motion had already been sunk before he'd even taken his seat. "That about sums it up, doesn't it?"

"Well, to be fair, I—"

"It's a simple question, Mr. Hudson." The judge sounded testy as he stared at me over the rim of his glasses. "Save all the dramatics and courtroom antics for the actual trial. I need not be entertained at this point."

I suppressed a weary sigh. I'd seen this kind of judge before. Some of them seemed to hate lawyers, forgetting that once upon a time they'd been lawyers themselves, and technically still were. I'd never understood that mentality.

"Yes, Your Honor. We do feel there are certain factors that weigh heavily against our clients locally." As I spoke, I unbuttoned the jacket of my tailor-made suit. I was getting ready for a fight.

"And you, Mr. Kimba?" He looked at Kwesi's attorney. "Do you join them in this request for change of venue, counsel?"

"We do, Your Honor."

"Gentlemen, I am certain that the fine citizens of Richmond County would have no problem being impartial as they listen to the evidence being brought before them, but—"

I broke in and said passionately, "Your Honor, in light of recent events, such as the Eric Garner case and others involving the Staten Island branch of the NYPD, we are concerned that the trial being held in this jurisdiction will be prejudicial and biased. This case has already been tried in the local media."

"Coverage of which you've been a large part," the judge pointed out.

"Our concern is that our clients receive a fair trial, Your Honor," I replied, refusing to rise to his bait. He wasn't the first one to blast me for talking to the press, and he wouldn't be the last. But hell, my media presence had helped me in the past, no matter how much the judges hated it. "I insist we at least have a hearing to argue the merits of our motion."

The judge sat silently for a moment before he relented. "Okay, Mr. Hudson, I'll hear your argu—"

"Your Honor," James interrupted. "May I be heard on the motion?

"Ah, Mister Brown, I was wondering when you might chime in on this subject." This was the most favorable emotion the judge had shown since walking into the courtroom. I knew I was wasting my breath. No way was prosecution going to allow us a change of venue without putting up a fight.

"Do the people have anything to say regarding the defense's motion for a venue change?"

"Actually, Your Honor, the people have no objection to the defense's motion for a change of venue."

James's statement shocked plenty of people in the room, including me. I had trouble keeping my composure as I turned to stare at him.

"Did he just say what I think he said?" Carla whispered in my ear.

"Yes, he did," I mumbled. I looked at Desiree and saw the look of confusion on her face. Things were not usually this easy.

The look on the faces of Judge Rodriguez and his bailiff revealed that they were equally stunned. This was not the typical response to be expected from the prosecution. To be honest, I wasn't sure how to take this. Having them so willingly support a change of venue was cause for concern.

"Excuse me?" Judge Rodriguez said. I guess he wanted to make sure he'd heard correctly.

"In the interest of justice, we agree to a change of venue," James reiterated. He now stood beside David, presenting what seemed to be a united front. "It's our opinion that we can obtain a conviction in any jurisdiction, and we do not want the case to be overturned for any reason."

"It would appear the DA's office is doing our job for us," Carla stated, but I could hear confusion in her voice.

I had been prepared to rebut any argument that the DA's office presented, so this really threw me for a loop and had me suspicious of their motives. James was too smug, and too at ease. He'd been too quick to side with us, as if it had already been planned out. Something was up.

"Well, alrighty then. I want both sides to submit locations for the change of venue by noon Friday." The judge shook his head like he still couldn't believe this turn of events. "I guess all we need to do now is pick a trial date."

He turned his attention back to the boys. "All right, gentlemen, it's already been noted in the record that all of you have pleaded not guilty." Then he turned toward the prosecution. "Mr. Brown, is the State prepared to proceed with their case?"

"Yes, Your Honor, we are ready for trial."

"How about the defense? Mr. Hudson, Mr. Kimba, are we ready to set a date for trial?"

"Yes, Your Honor. We'd like to request the first available date on the docket," I replied, hoping he'd have some mercy on us. "Our clients are eager to exonerate themselves. We ask for an immediate jury trial."

The judge examined his calendar and said, "How's early September?"

"Any time after the Labor Day holiday, Your Honor," James answered.

I could hear Carla rambling in my ear about how we needed to get date sooner rather than later. The further out we took this, the more chance of something big happening and us losing the news cycle. "Your Honor, if I may, that is almost five months from now. If the prosecution case is prepared, I must insist on a much earlier trial date," I said dramatically. "May I suggest early June?"

"Don't push it, Mr. Hudson. You know darn well four weeks is not going to happen."

"Well, then how about we make it eight weeks?"

"Your Honor, the State has no objections to an eight week start date," James announced.

The judge leaned over to the clerk and murmured something to him, then announced, "All right, gentlemen. How does July seventh sound?"

"July seventh is fine, judge," I agreed, knowing it was the best I was going to get.

"That works fine," James agreed.

"Bradley?" Carla said in my ear.

"Mm-hmm?" I said quietly.

"Why is he being so agreeable to the early date?"

"Don't know." I glanced over at James, who smirked at me.

"Did you say something, Mr. Hudson?" the judge asked.

"No, just making a mental note, Your Honor." I nodded reassuringly.

"Okay then, we will reconvene on July seventh, with jury selection to begin on July eighth." The judge struck his gavel.

"Bradley, honey," Carla spoke in my ear. "I don't like what just happened. Something doesn't smell right."

"I can smell it too," I said, feeling free to speak more clearly now that court had been dismissed. This had certainly gone better than I anticipated, much better, but based on the confidence of James and David, his legal sidekick, something told me this wasn't going to be the only thing that would surprise me with their case. "So, Carla, what is it we don't know?"

"I don't know," she replied, "but I promise you I'm going to find out."

Krush

44

"Shit! Not again." Little Richie tossed his cards down and stood up from the table. He looked like he was ready to fight, but Richie's short ass didn't want none of this.

"Hey, you play the game, you gotta be prepared to pay the price. Now hand over the cell phone and the charger," I told him, holding out my hand.

"Look, I can't just give you this cell phone. My girl's about have this baby any minute. Lemme give you something else."

"Nah, son. You were the one who decided what you wanted to risk. I put up my entire stack." I pointed at my pile of cookies and snacks in front of me. I'd been gambling all afternoon using simple statistics, and I'd been whipping these niggas' asses in craps and cards so bad I must have had thirty honey buns, forty packs of cookies, and fifty packs of Kool-Aid—and that didn't include the shit I had stashed under my bed. "If I hada lost, you woulda took my shit."

"That's true, Richie!" another inmate agreed.

"Yeah, but that shit ain't worth no cell phone, bro."

He was right. A cell phone was worth more than anything I had and more. A cell phone was going to make me a king around this bitch.

I stood up, and although I was skinny at six foot five, I towered over Richie's little ass. "How about an ass whoopin'? Is it worth an ass whoopin' every day until I get the phone?"

Richie looked sick to his stomach, but he handed over the phone.

"Let this be a lesson, though," I told him. "Never put up what you ain't willing to lose. Nice doing business with you." I stashed the phone in my pocket and scooped up my loot before heading back to my bed.

"Yo, Krush, you gonna give me a chance to get my shit back?" the brother asked.

"No doubt, right after chow. But you gonna have to come up with a whole buncha shit in order to get this phone back," I said as I was stashing my shit.

I made my way over to Tony, who was still sitting in that same damn chair after three weeks of being locked up. The shit was just weird as hell. The only time he moved from it was to go to the bathroom, the mess hall, or to sleep. He didn't even go outside to the yard. Some people had given him a nickname: Doctor Strange.

"Come on, T, let's line up," I said to him. "It's time to go to chow, and my man said they serving tacos tonight."

For the most part, jail food wasn't worth a shit, and most of us survived on ramen noodles, cookies, Kool-Aid, and chips from the commissary. These sorry-ass motherfuckers they had cooking couldn't boil water, but for some reason, they could make the hell out of some tacos. Those things put Taco Bell to shame.

We got in line, and after they counted up our unit, we headed down to the mess. Me and Tony were making our way through the makeshift line. The kitchen inmates filled our plates and trays buffet style as we walked by. I was happy as fuck when I saw that my man was right and they were serving tacos.

"Thank you," I mumbled to the brother who placed two tacos on my plate. I moved down to the next item, but when I looked down at Tony's plate, I stopped.

"Hey," I said to the brother who'd just served me. "He got four tacos. Why'd you only give me two?" I probably should have just shut my mouth, but those tacos was good as shit, and I wanted more.

"Be glad I gave you any, nigga. Now keep the line moving."

I was about to say something smart, but Tony gave me a look and shook his head slowly. He barely spoke five words a day, but that look was enough for me.

"Fuck it. Don't nobody want your nasty-ass tacos anyway," I spat, moving to the next food station.

When we got to our seats, Tony picked up a taco and placed it on my plate. I smiled my gratitude as I picked it up and took a bite.

"Yo, T, why'd he give you extra tacos?"

Tony just shrugged and began eating. I didn't say anything else as I finished my first taco, but I did look down at his tray and realize they'd also given him extra dessert and two milks.

From the corner of my eye, I spotted that short bastard Richie talking to a Spanish dude and glancing over at me. Neither one of them looked happy, and my guard went up immediately. They didn't mean nothing good for me. Moments later, they were headed in my direction. I eased up from the table and slowly moved back.

"Yo, motherfucker, he needs his shit back," the Spanish dude told me.

"I ain't got his shit. Everything I got belongs to me," I answered, looking over at Richie.

"The phone you just took from him. He needs it back."

"First of all, I ain't take shit. He lost them to me." I folded my arms.

"Plain and simple, it wasn't his to lose. It belonged to me," the dude said.

"You just said that it was his shit, which means it was his. And if it wasn't his, then he shouldn't have put it up." I looked at Richie, who looked like he wanted to bitch up. "I told you never risk what you can't afford to lose."

The big dude turned to Richie and said something in Spanish. It didn't take a rocket scientist to figure out what was going on. Richie had dark skin, and I thought he was a black dude. Now I understood that he was probably Dominican, which meant when I fucked with him, I was fucking with the Latin dudes. This was bad.

"Man, ain't nobody got time to debate with your ass. Give him his shit so he can give it back to me." The Spanish guy stepped toward me and squared up.

"Hey, fellas, hold up." Another inmate tried to intervene.

"Who the fuck are you, his daddy?" Dude asked him, and the guy just backed away. Then the Spanish guy looked back at me. "Give him his shit back."

"Fuck you. I ain't giving shit b—"

I felt a blow to my stomach, and then my head. Surprisingly, it wasn't the big Spanish dude who hit me. It was little-ass Richie. Unfortunately, dude didn't take long to join in. In a matter of seconds, I was on the floor, getting the shit stomped out of me. I could barely see from the blows, and all I could hear was inmates yelling encouragement to my attackers. This was entertainment for these motherfuckers.

I didn't think it would ever end, but out of nowhere, one of them stopped. He yelled out in pain, and then the other one quickly joined him. By the time I got my head out my ass, I saw Tony on top of the Spanish guy, swinging a bloody sock filled with something. Richie was already on the ground, bleeding more from his head than me.

The alarm went off, and the COs started shouting commands. "Get on the floor! Get down now!"

Out of everybody, I made out the best. Yeah, I had a lot of bumps and bruises and would be sporting a black eye for a while, but for the most part, I was all right and only spent an hour in the infirmary. Richie and the Spanish dude were not so lucky. They were taken away to the infirmary, and word got back that their injuries were severe. Whatever Tony had in that sock—I suspected it was bars of soap—must have been hard as shit, because both of them had broken ribs, and Richie had a facial fracture that would keep him in the infirmary for three or four months. Meanwhile, bad-ass Tony didn't have a scratch on him. As he was being led out of the mess hall for two weeks in the hole, he'd given me the frat sign. He sure as hell was stronger than I'd thought. I wouldn't see him until our next hearing date, but I now knew Tony would be okay. I just wasn't sure about me anymore, because that was the moment I realized I wasn't a fighter, and I really didn't want to be one.

Perk

45

I slowly pulled the car under the bridge and turned off the engine. From where we were parked, I could see the reflection of the city on the Hudson River. It looked peaceful and reminded me of my days before I met Bradley and his family, when I would walk along the riverbank, fishing for snappers and searching for clams and mussels just so I could have something to eat. I had so much fun that summer that I didn't even know how bad I had it until winter came. It was a miracle I was still alive after eating seafood out of that polluted river. But as Bradley always said, I was a survivor.

"Sooooo, what's the deal with you and Desiree?"

"What? Where the hell did that come from?" I frowned and looked over at Michael in the passenger's seat. I had managed to not think about Desiree all day, and here he was bringing her up. Shit!

He shrugged. "Nowhere. I've just been wondering what's up with y'all, so I figured I'd ask. I mean, y'all do live together, don't you?"

"Yeah, we're roommates. But I'm in the process of moving out," I said.

"Are you sure that's all you are?" Michael continued his line of questioning as if I were on the witness stand. I guess that's what happens when you're around lawyers all day.

"What the heck, Mike? Am I on trial here? She's like a sister to me." I searched his face for any signs that he knew I was bullshitting. "What the hell she tell you?" I didn't know why I'd said that. Of course she hadn't said anything. She barely knew Michael, and she'd never revealed anything about us, even to her best friends.

"It ain't what she said. It's what she did," Michael said confidently, like he'd just solved a case. "I saw her hating on your girl Lena for no apparent reason; then I saw her throw that pie in the trash. You don't snap like that over a roommate, bruh. That was some pure jealousy shit."

His observational skills were strong. He would be a great asset to the Hudson firm someday.

"Mike, if I were you, I'd forget I saw all that . . . for your own good," I told him.

Desiree and I hadn't said anything to each other since the incident with Lena, and I had made it a point to avoid her unless it was work related. She had made that easy by not coming home.

"So, there used to be something there? I knew it." He raised an eyebrow at me.

I hesitated for a minute, wondering if I should continue to deny everything, but it was obvious he would see right through my lies. So, I admitted it while still telling him as little as possible. "It was complicated, but it's over. Like I said, I'm moving out." I checked the rearview mirror.

"Too bad. Des is a fine woman," Michael said.

"Heads up. We have company," I told him. A mysterious figure appeared in the side mirror about a hundred feet away and was approaching the back of the car fast. I placed my hand on the waistband of my jeans, where my Glock was located, just in case it wasn't who I was expecting. As the figure got closer, I recognized the face and hit the unlock button. The rear door opened, and he jumped in.

The scrawny white guy, who now sat in the back seat, greeted me. "What's up, Perk?"

"I can't call it, Nate." I turned to my side and said, "This is Mike. He's my new partner. He's a lawyer, but he's learning the legal business from the ground up."

"What's up, Mike?" Nate stretched his hand out, and Michael shook it. "So, Perk, why do we always have to meet in these shadowy places? For once can we meet at a nice restaurant, where I can order steak and you can pick up the tab?"

"No, because I took you to a restaurant one time and it cost me four hundred bucks." I turned toward Michael. "This skinny son of a bitch here is a food-eating champion. I've seen him eat a hundred bratwurst in like five minutes at one event."

"It was a hundred forty, and it was hot dogs, not bratwurst. Bratwurst give me gas," he said with a laugh.

"So, what you got for me, Nate? Bradley is on my ass, and all I keep hearing is bad news. I need something." I reached inside the center console and took out an envelope that I handed to Nate. "Tell me you don't have me out here on some bullshit."

Nate took the envelope and tucked it away without even looking at the contents. "Tony's brother Adonis was arrested last night with a little more than a kilo of black tar heroin, twenty pounds of weed, and a shitload of Oxy in Queens last night."

"Get the fuck outta here!" I shouted.

Michael and I looked at each other briefly before we both turned our bodies toward the back.

"Did you have it tested against the dope that was found in the car?" I asked. This man had just made my dick hard with this information. "Did it come from the same stash?"

"Right now, I'm not sure. It's still being processed, and they're keeping a close eye on it. I'll let you know as soon as I find out something, but it's gonna take some finagling to get a sample from both labs to confirm," Nate said. "Adonis was arrested by the Feds, and you know how they feel about sharing information with locals. So far, nobody has made the connection."

"Nate, I'm gonna need you to work your fucking magic and get those samples as soon as possible. You know I'm gonna take care of you for all your hard work," I assured him.

"I got you, Perk. I'm a little curious myself," he said, looking me right in the eye so I could see he meant it. I'd known Nate long enough to know he wasn't a bullshitter. If he promised to make something happen, he would do everything in his power to do that. If something failed, it damn sure wasn't for lack of trying.

He opened the car door and stepped out. "Listen, I gotta get back to work. I'll reach out in a couple of days."

"Hit me up anytime," I told him then watched him jog away.

"Who the fuck was that? He looks like a pedophile," Michael commented.

"That, my friend, is one of the finest crime scene specialists the NYPD Crime Scene Unit has working for them," I answered casually, as if Nate owned a hot dog stand on the corner.

"That guy's with CSU?"

"Yep, for twenty years."

"What the hell? From what I just saw, it looks like he works for you," Michael said, sounding surprised and a little impressed.

"Sometimes, but his main gig is with CSU." I started the truck engine. "Sure, I give Nate a few bucks here and there, but he'll never compromise his integrity."

"So, what's our next step? I'm sure the boss is going to be happy to find out it was Tony's drugs in the car." Michael nodded.

"No, he's not, because we're not going to tell him just yet," I said. "I'll tell him I'm working on a major lead, but I won't give him any specifics."

"What? Why not? This is the break we've been looking for. Why wouldn't you tell him?"

"It's too early," I explained patiently. He was, after all, just a rookie. "We gotta wait and see what the narcotics analysis determines. They might not have come from the same source, which would fuck up our case. Trust me, you don't want to take anything to Bradley Hudson unless it's concrete evidence. Something like this could blow up in your face."

"Man, what are the odds of that heroin not coming from the same place? You need to tell him. This is the kind of thing that could create reasonable doubt for the other three," Michael said excitedly. Although I appreciated his enthusiasm, my years of experience taught had taught me to proceed with caution.

"Calm down, grasshopper. You're getting ahead of yourself. We're not going to make any premature assumptions, because if you're wrong, you're gonna find yourself out of a job you just started."

He thought about that for a minute then finally said, "Okay, I'm going to follow your lead, but I think we're wasting valuable time." He sat back and relaxed a little in his seat. "So, what about the stripper that Krush was with? Did you follow up on her?"

"Nah, she's good. Everything checked out with her. Her building has a video surveillance system. I watched the tape. She didn't do it," I told him. "She was just a chick that happened to be there that night."

"So, where to now?" Michael asked.

"How about lunch? For some reason, I'm craving hot dogs." I laughed as we pulled off.

James

46

Tap. Tap. Tap.

I looked up and saw Grace Frazier, the district attorney for Richmond County, New York, standing in the doorway of my office. We'd worked together back in my days in the U.S. attorney's office, and she'd been responsible for bringing me to the Staten Island DA's office fifteen years ago. I had to give it to her; she was a formidable colleague and a decent supervisor when she had my job. She'd always been fair, well respected, and approachable, but she was also no nonsense and knowledgeable when it came to the law. Most folks underestimated her because she looked more like a librarian than a powerful attorney, but they quickly learned that she was a force to reckoned with. Her ferocity in the courtroom had once earned her the nickname "Grace Under Fire." But Grace barely entered the courtroom these days, after winning the office of district attorney.

"Since when did you start knocking, boss?" I asked with a friendly smile.

She shrugged and walked in. "I overheard one of the newbies saying something about me barging into her office, so I decided that maybe I should work on my office manners."

"I swear, these millennials complain about every damn thing. I heard one of them complaining that we didn't have two recycle bins in the break room beside the regular trash can, because it should be one for paper and one for plastic to make it easier for people." I shook my head. "So, what's up?"

"Just checking in and seeing how things are going with the Hudson case," Grace said.

"Going fine. I'm going over trial notes now," I told her. "No worries. I'm gonna nail the son of a bitch."

"Trial notes? Isn't that a little presumptive?" Grace took a seat in front of my desk. "Are we really taking this to trial?"

"That's the plan. I'm going to nail these sons of bitches, Grace," I said adamantly.

"Of that I have no doubt, but have you talked to Hudson about a plea?"

I swallowed hard. Truth was, I hadn't talked to Hudson at all, other than to offer his son fifteen years, which I had known they would reject. "I tried to get the defendants to talk, and they wouldn't budge."

"That's not what I asked, James." She picked up the 1986 World Series ball I'd had signed by most of the New York Mets, studying the signatures on it.

"No, I haven't talked to Hudson about a plea, but like I said, I'm prepared to go to trial and win big."

"When is a win not a win, James?"

I didn't know what this was about, so I shrugged my shoulders and played along. "I don't know."

"A win is not a win when I lose, because if I lose, we all lose," she said firmly. "Are you following me?"

"Not exactly."

"James, I don't want this thing to go to trial. We need to make a deal and make this thing go away. I've got the borough president and half his cronies on my ass because you agreed to a change of venue," Grace explained. "A change of venue you did not run by me, I might add. The last thing this office needs is the media frenzy that comes along whenever Bradley Hudson is involved. You were here during the Eric Garner fiasco. You know how the press can be."

"That's why I agreed to the change of venue—to get it off the island, so it wouldn't come back to slap you, Grace."

She shook her head. "You're not hearing me. Do you have any idea how much this change of venue is going to cost the county? And with Bradley Hudson involved, it's going to cost even more."

"You're starting to sound like a politician," I replied.

"James, I am a politician. I didn't get this job because I was the most qualified; I got this job because I got the most votes. I've had the NAACP and the ACLU presidents in my office this week, and Al Sharpton hating on me on TV, and I'm a damn Democrat in a Republican borough! Do you not understand who this man is?" She sighed heavily.

I fought the urge to roll my eyes. I was so sick of everyone acting like Bradley Hudson was the only talented lawyer in the state.

"I sure do. He's a TV lawyer," I said. "I'm a prosecutor with a slam dunk case. I'm not intimidated by Bradley Hudson—or any of the rest of them. I've got justice on my side, and I'm ready." I leaned back in my chair and finished with, "I'm glad he's opposing counsel, and I'm not backing down from his ass."

"This is an open and shut case. If it were anyone else sitting across the aisle, you would've already made a deal just to save the city the cost of a trial." The way she said it let me know that she knew exactly what I was up to. "I'm starting to think this is personal for you. You're trying to grandstand."

"What? That's not true at all," I protested. "But I know Bradley, and I know that he wouldn't accept a plea deal, so I didn't waste my time or his trying to negotiate one."

"Well, I guess we'll find out if he'll take one or not, because he's waiting for us in the conference room right now," Grace said.

"What did you say?"

"You heard me. He's in the conference room. Now, I want you to go in there and offer these boys three to five so we can wrap this thing up."

I felt rage boiling deep inside. I couldn't let her do this to me. I finally had the opportunity to whip Bradley Hudson's ass fair and square in the courtroom, where he deserved to be whipped. It was my one and only chance to completely humiliate him, and she was trying to take it away.

"Three to five? That's preposterous!" I yelled, then got myself under control and lowered the volume. "That means they'll be out in two years. For two kilos of heroin, Grace?"

"These are four college students. You don't even know which ones are guilty. Make the offer," she said with a sigh.

"You do realize that this is my case, right?"

"And you realize that I'm the district attorney and every case in this office is my case, right?" She peered at me, then her eyes softened. "Listen, I get it. I was in the US attorney's office back then. I was a newbie, probably the same age as that young-ass millennial that's complaining about me now. But I remember the rumors about what Bradley and Jacqueline did to you."

"They weren't rumors," I stated flatly.

"I get it. You've been in this office for damn near fifteen years, and you're feeling like you settled. But you're a damn good lawyer, James. You have nothing to prove—to me, Hudson, or anyone else."

"This isn't personal for me, Grace," I lied.

"Maybe it isn't, but I wouldn't blame you if it was." She stood up and gave me a pointed look. "But you had your fun; now it's over."

"So, are you gonna micromanage all of my cases?" I asked, closing the case file and following her out the door.

"Have I ever micromanaged you, James? But this is just as much my case as it is yours, and I want to make sure we're both handling it without bias."

I kept my mouth shut as we walked down the hall and entered the conference room, where Bradley and two of his children were seated across from Kenneth Kimba, who looked like a kid in a candy store.

"Grace, how wonderful to see you again." Bradley wasted no time getting up and greeting her with a hug and a kiss on the cheek. "You're still the most beautiful woman in the DA's office. And the smartest."

Grace laughed. "Bradley, it's great to see you again too, and I'm flattered by your honesty." The two of them were acting like old friends at a class reunion, rather than two lawyers at a meeting about a pending trial.

"This is my son Lamont, and my daughter, Desiree." Bradley introduced them, then turned and added, "And our co-counsel, Mr. Kimba."

"Nice to meet all of you," Grace said warmly.

"Shall we chat?" Bradley asked, standing behind his chair at the head of the table.

It didn't go unnoticed that he hadn't greeted me nor introduced me the same way he'd done Grace.

"Certainly," Grace said as she sat down beside Kimba. "I'm sure you all know James Brown, the ADA handling the case."

"Where are my manners? It's a pleasure seeing you as well, James. I was so caught up in seeing Grace after all these years that I forgot my manners. How have you been?" Bradley extended his hand, and I gave it a firm grip, wanting to crush it.

"Fine," I told him without bothering to return his fake pleasantries. I took the chair at the opposite end of the table.

"Well then, let's get started." Grace nodded toward me. "In light of the seriousness of the charges, our last offer was fifteen years. We are prepared to come down considerably if you are prepared to negotiate."

"To be honest with you, Grace, we are only here as a courtesy. Our clients are innocent, and we plan on proving that in court," Bradley said smugly.

I wished I could laugh out loud. If I had a hundred bucks for every defense lawyer that used that exact line during plea negations, I'd have a down payment on a house in the Hamptons.

"Bradley, as James pointed out to me earlier, we've got a slam dunk case, and you've got four clients that are looking at twenty years. Now, the only reason I'm here is to save the taxpayers of Staten Island a bunch of money on something we can get done now—away from the cameras. So, if you want to play semantics with me, then by all means, take your merry band back to Harlem and we'll see you in court in three days. Otherwise, cut the crap and let's talk," Grace snapped, surprising me—and pleasing me. I guess she had heard that speech before too.

The two of them were locked in a staring contest, sizing each other up for a moment.

Lamont Hudson jumped in to break the silence. "What are you thinking?" he asked.

"Considering that they have no previous criminal history and are college students, we'd like to offer seven years," I told them. "That's half of what we originally offered."

"Did you say seven years?" Bradley barked, taking a step back from his chair as if he were preparing to leave.

"What I believe he meant to say was five years." Grace sighed.

"You are going to have to do better than that, Grace," Bradley challenged.

"How about a three to five?" Grace said flatly. "That's a more than fair offer, Bradley. And with the time your clients have already served, they will most likely only have to do a year."

Bradley eyed her cautiously. "Three to five, huh?"

"Yes," I said, bringing the attention back to me so that he would know that I was the one making the offer, and not Grace.

"That sounds . . ." Kimba opened his mouth to offer his opinion, but Bradley was quick to cut him off.

"That still seems unreasonable, considering that the drugs found in the vehicle didn't belong to my clients. I was thinking that we would lower the charges to a misdemeanor and seek probation. Supervised, of course." Bradley's look went from me, then back to Grace.

"That won't be happening," I said. "We have plenty of evidence that says the drugs did belong to your clients."

"He's right, Bradley. This deal is more than fair, and you'd be wise to take it," Grace advised.

"And they'd get credit for time served?" Kenneth asked, causing his colleagues at the table to stare at him, and not in a good way.

"We'll take it into consideration," Bradley said, effectively ending the negotiation.

"It's a fair deal," Grace reiterated.

"Three to five for a crime they didn't commit doesn't seem very fair," Desiree chimed in.

"Three to five is a gift compared to twenty years for someone found with two kilos of pure heroin, young lady," I said.

Lamont spoke up again. "We'll discuss it with our clients and let you know."

Bradley shot him a look that I couldn't read. *Is the son stepping on his father's toes?* I wondered.

"Then you'd better talk fast, because it's only on the table for twenty-four hours." I stood up and walked out before anyone could say anything else. I was certain that the meeting had been a waste of time, because there was no way Bradley Hudson would take the deal, whether or not it was a good one. We were going to trial, and I was looking forward to it.

Tony

47

I was finally released from the hole and escorted back to my unit two weeks after the incident I had with the guys who jumped Krush. Time had gone by slow, and those two weeks felt like a month. When I wasn't reading or sleeping, I spent most of my time doing pushups and calisthenics. I also spent a lot of time thinking about how we'd ended up in jail, and how the hell we might be able to get out. I was grateful that my brothers had educated me on how to handle it if I ever found myself in this situation, and once I got over the initial shock of being in jail, I'd done a decent job of following their advice of making people think I was a little nuts. It appeared that even in jail nobody messed with crazy people because they were too unpredictable. But at the end of the day, Langston's pops was going to have to do something, because I wasn't built for this shit the way my brothers were.

"Damn, I'm glad to see your ass. You okay?"

I was getting my things together when Krush came rushing over to me. He gave me the fraternity grip and held me tight. He finally released me, and I stared at him. Krush's face looked way more fucked up than the last time I'd seen him.

"I'm fine, but what the fuck happened to you?" I gestured toward the sling that held his arm.

"Nothing. Just a little disagreement over a dice game."

"I hope you gave as good as you got." I walked over to the chair in the corner and sat down. He didn't answer with words, but the way he lowered his head was all the answer I needed.

"What's up, Blood?" Another inmate who was passing by stopped and gave me a nod.

"'Sup, man?" I nodded back at him.

"Doctor Strange, glad to see you come out that hole, Blood!" another guy yelled. "You need anything?"

"Nah, I'm a'ight," I said and turned back to Krush, who was now looking at me strangely.

"So, you a Blood now, bruh?" he asked.

I leaned over and whispered to him, "If that's what they think, then far be it from me to say otherwise. I'm just trying to get outta here in one piece."

"You ain't answer my question."

"Aye, I'm starving. Give me some cookies or some chips or something," I told him, changing the subject.

He looked down at the floor. "Man, I ain't got nothing."

"What the fuck you mean, you ain't got nothing? Don't tell me you gambled away all of that shit you had stockpiled, Krush. That don't make no sense." I shook my head.

"Nah, I ain't gamble it. After the fight, I was in the infirmary for a couple hours, and when I came out, they took my shit," he said. "It's cool. I'm try'na reach my pops to have him put some money on my books so I can buy some snacks and shit."

"Buy? Krush, man, what the fuck is wrong with you? Why didn't you just take your shit back, or at least win it back like you did before?"

Krush glanced nervously around the room, and I realized that his once confident, overly aggressive demeanor was now gone. As a matter of fact, he seemed damn near paranoid.

He eased over to me and said, "I did. I knew exactly who took it, and when I tried to get it back, they said I won't have to worry about nobody kicking my ass. I'd have to worry about someone fucking me in the ass." He grimaced at the thought. "I can't even sleep, man. I gotta get the fuck outta here." I'd never seen him like this before. He'd always been loud and boisterous, even in the worst of situations.

I put my hands on his shoulders to calm him down. "First of all, you need to man the fuck up. The last thing you need is for anyone to think is that you're afraid."

He nodded his understanding. It was kind of ironic that a few weeks ago, he was the one trying to tell me what to do to survive. But being in here had finally gotten the best of him. Now he needed me to be the strong one.

"It's gonna be fine," I told him. "Now, who took your shit?"

He didn't say anything or point to anyone, but he glanced in the general direction, telling me everything I needed to know.

"They got the cell phone too?"

"Nah, I hid that, but I haven't been able to use it."

"A'ight. You stay here." I got up and walked over to the brother who had asked me if I needed anything. "I need a gat."

Dude looked around for COs, then without hesitation, he reached in his mouth and pulled out a razor blade. I took it from him then walked directly over to the people Krush had glanced at. Four guys were playing cards. I just stood there watching their game until one of them noticed the razor blade in my hand. He stepped back, alerting the others.

"Yo, can we help you?" They'd all been there when I got sent to the hole, so they knew who I was.

"That nigga over there—" I gestured toward Krush, who was standing next to my chair. "He was holding my shit while I was in the hole. You niggas took it. I want it back. I'm not gonna ask twice."

Now, if I did this right like my brothers had taught me, nobody was going to get hurt; but if I didn't, all hell was about to break loose. I stood there, silently caressing the razor blade, until each one of them got up and walked toward their beds. I walked back to my chair and sat down, watching as each one brought a pile of snacks over to Krush's bed, leaving them there.

Krush, who was still standing next to my chair, quietly mumbled, "Thanks."

"No problem, frat." I lifted my hand for a fist bump, keeping my eyes straight ahead. "But just so we're clear: half that shit now belongs to me."

I could feel him looking down on me as I stared straight ahead, but he didn't take long to say, "Okay. You want some cookies?"

"Yeah, man, I'm starving."

He headed over to his bunk.

"Krush," I called after him.

He turned around. "Yep."

"I'm gonna need that cell phone too."

Kwesi

48

As soon as morning prayers were over, the guards escorted me into the room where my parents were waiting for me, along with my attorney. My mother made her way over to hug me, touching the black kufi that I wore over my hair, which I had decided to grow out.

"Hello, Mother." I greeted her with a smile.

"You're looking well," she said, her face a mixture of sadness and pride. I could tell she was doing her best not to cry.

"How are you, son?" My father stood and shook my hand before pressing his chest against mine in a brief hug.

"I'm doing well," I said then turned to Mr. Kimba. "Hello."

"How are things, Kwesi? Do you need anything?" he asked.

"Other than to get out of here? No."

"Well, you know that's everyone's goal at this point," Kimba said.

"So, you told us that you had something to discuss," I said, taking a seat. "Has there been some kind of evidence to clear us?" I knew that whatever Kimba wanted to talk about had to be important for my parents to be there.

"No, no new evidence has been found yet," Kimba answered, and I felt my hope deflating. "But we did have a meeting with the DA's office that was quite interesting."

"Interesting how?" my mother asked.

"Well, they offered the boys a deal," Kimba told her. "They plead guilty and will be sentenced to three to five years."

"Three to five years? You want my son to stay in jail for three to five years?" My father's voice was as stern as the look on his face.

"That's unacceptable, especially for something he did not do," my mother added. I appreciated the fact that she never doubted I was innocent.

"No, listen. He will not be in jail for three to five years. With the time that he's already served, he will most likely be out in a year. The remainder of the time, he will be on probation, and I'm sure Kwesi wouldn't do anything during that time that would land him back in jail."

I frowned. "I haven't done anything to be put in jail for now."

My father looked at my mother, then at me. "One year? That is not that much time."

"It really isn't," Kimba said.

I looked at my father in disbelief. "I think you don't understand what he's asking me to do. He wants me to plead guilty and admit to doing something that I didn't do." Shaking my head adamantly, I said, "I'm not doing that. I don't have to."

"Son . . ." My mother reached out and took my hand.

"Mother, I know that Mr. Kimba is my attorney, and I appreciate you hiring him. But don't forget, he's not working by himself. The Hudsons are working on the case also, and Bradley Hudson is one of the best."

"Yes, you're right, Kwesi. The Hudsons are working hard as well, but the fact is that they have yet to come up with anything that will clear you all. They've tried everything, and it's not working. This case is not looking good, and my fear is that if you don't take the plea deal and the trial does not go our way, you are facing twenty years in prison," Kimba said gravely.

My mother gasped and covered her mouth with her hand. "That cannot happen," she cried.

"Son, this may be the only chance for you to gain your freedom soon." My father gave me a hopeful look.

Twenty years, I thought. *In twenty years, I'll be over forty years old*. My parents were both in their fifties. Even though they were in fairly good health, would they live another twenty years? *Should I risk being in jail for twenty years for a crime I didn't even commit?*

"Kwesi, you're a smart young man with a bright future ahead of you," Kimba told me. "Think about it."

"If I plead guilty, that future will no longer be bright," I said, speaking to my parents. "I cannot go to medical school or even practice medicine as a convicted felon. No one would award me a fellowship to pay for school anyway. Pleading guilty will cost me greatly. I'm afraid they would try to deport me if I have a criminal record."

My father's eyes saddened as he realized the reality of what they were asking me to do.

"Maybe not." Kimba put his hand under his chin as if he were deep in thought, then said, "We can request that the DA lower the charges to misdemeanors."

"Can we do that?" I asked.

Kimba nodded.

"Then that's what we will do," my father said firmly. "Kwesi will accept their offer—if the charges are lowered and his record will not be affected."

"Thank you, Mr. Kimba." My mother's smile widened.

"Well, it is Kwesi's decision to make." Kimba turned his attention to me.

Unlike my parents, I wasn't ready to throw a victory party. Something told me that this wasn't going to be as simple as Kimba was making it out to be.

"I will think about it and talk it over with the others," I told him.

"Well, wait a minute, Kwesi," Kimba said. "I don't think you should do that."

"What do you mean?" I peered at him, wondering why he seemed to be withholding things from me.

"There is a possibility—well, a strong chance—that the DA will agree to our terms in exchange for our cooperation."

I frowned at Kimba, who was now fumbling with his colorful bowtie and looking down at the table.

"What does that mean?" my mother asked.

"It means he wants me to testify against my brothers," I told her, and then I asked Kimba, "Is that true? That's what you mean when you say cooperation, isn't it?"

"Uh, yes." Kimba nodded slowly.

"Then, no," I said adamantly.

"Kwesi." My father called my name the same way he always did when I was about to be lectured. But I wasn't a teenager anymore who had forgotten to take out the trash. I was an adult whose freedom was on the line, and I didn't have to listen.

"No, Father," I told him. "They are just as innocent as I am. All of us are."

"My son, how do you know they aren't making the same deal with the DA? Are you certain that they are not agreeing to testify against you?" my mother asked.

I became quiet, because I didn't know the answer to her question. Were my friends considering a plea agreement to save their own necks? They wouldn't betray me like that, would they? A few moments ago, I'd been considering doing whatever it took to be released in a year. Were they doing the same thing?

"This meeting is over," I said, standing up.

"Kwesi . . ."

I looked over at my mother and said, "I cannot make a decision at this time. I will consider it, but I must pray first." I knew they weren't happy that I was ignoring my lawyer's advice, but I hoped it would bring them some comfort to know I was relying on faith to make my decision.

"I will speak with the DA and see what he says, so we will have a full understanding before you decide anything," Kimba offered.

"Thank you." I hugged my parents and then called to be escorted back to my cell.

Later, as evening prayer ended, I spoke with the imam while we were walking into the day room. I explained what was going on with my case and the offer that was being made. His answer surprised me.

"Kwesi, if I were in your predicament, I would be counting down the next three hundred and sixty-five days and thanking Allah."

"Huh? Even if it means betraying my friends?" I stopped in the middle of the hallway. "And admitting to doing something that I did not do?"

"You don't have to admit to doing something you didn't do," he told me.

"I would have to plead guilty."

"You don't have to do that."

Frustrated, I leaned against the wall and shook my head. "I'm so confused. It's like you're talking to me in riddles and—"

"Calm down, Kwesi. I'm not trying to confuse you. I'm trying to help you see all of your options. Let's go over here and sit." He pointed to a table on the opposite side of the day room.

A few of the inmates greeted him and made small talk. He spoke to them, then motioned for me to take a seat. When we were alone, he quietly began talking. "I understand why you're troubled. But there is another option for you."

"What?"

"Have you heard of *nolo contendere*?" he asked.

"No contest," I said, thankful for the year of Latin I'd taken.

"Yes. It's not an admission of guilt. Essentially, it means that you agree to the facts of the case, but not your guilt, and it protects you from the plea being used against you in any future civil or criminal proceedings," he explained.

Hearing this option gave me a little more clarity about taking a plea agreement.

"I could maintain my innocence," I said.

"Indeed."

"But what about having to testify? I am not a snitch."

"That is something you're going to have to figure out. But I will tell you this: twelve years ago, I was offered a plea deal by a DA anxious to put away the dealer that I happened to be working for. All I had to do was testify, and I would be out in less than thirty-six months. I decided that I hadn't done anything wrong, and the evidence they had against me was circumstantial anyway, so I rolled the dice with a trial . . . and I lost. I was sentenced to ten years, and after a couple of other unfortunate circumstances during that time, that ten turned into a few more. If I had it to do all over again, I would've taken those thirty-six months and skipped out of here in less than three years after singing like a canary." He sighed. "Now, there's no telling when I'm getting out."

"I . . . I don't know," I said, feeling the weight of his story.

"What is more important to you? The bond with three men that you've known less than five years, or your freedom and the future medical career that you've dreamed of your entire life?"

Desiree

49

We had less than twenty-four hours until the beginning of my brother's trial. Michael and I had been working nonstop, reviewing case law and preparing questions for character witnesses. We'd been at it since before the sun came up, going over final documents and making sure everything was in order, while my father and Lamont went to Rikers Island to prep our clients and explain the plea-bargain that was offered by the DA. By the time I realized what time it was, we'd missed lunch and dinner, and my eyes had started getting heavy.

"I need coffee. A big pot of black coffee." I leaned back in my chair and stretched my arms over my head.

"And food. Something other than Chinese or deli sandwiches," Michael added, leaning on his elbows as he stared at one of the many files we had piled up. "You want me to make a run?"

"Make a run where?" I asked.

He was already grabbing his jacket from the back of the chair.

"Don't even try it, mister. It's damn near ten o'clock. Where are you going at this time of night to get food other than Chinese or the deli?" I laughed. "You're just looking for an excuse to get out of here."

"Who, me? Why would I want to get out of here?" He dramatically placed his hand over his chest as if he were offended by my accusation.

"Maybe because we've been working fifteen and sixteen-hour days for the past three months?" I answered.

"True." He sat back down. "But believe it or not, I'm enjoying it and learning a lot. This is the greatest experience of my life."

"Yeah, too bad it came at my brother's expense." I sighed.

"I didn't mean . . ." He stopped mid-sentence and frowned. "Hey, look, I can see what type of toll this is taking on your whole family. If there's anything I can—"

"Don't hand me that bull, Dad!" Lamont was in the hallway, yelling so loud that they could probably hear him on the first floor. I jumped up from my seat, thinking I should go remind them to keep their voices down, but it quickly became clear that they were too angry for me to stop them. I stayed in the conference room with Michael as the fight intensified.

"What you did was unethical, immoral, and possibly enough to get you sanctioned by the bar, and you know it!" Lamont bellowed.

"What are you talking about, son? I presented the offer to them, and they turned it down," my father replied. "What's unethical about that?"

"You told them what you wanted them to hear. Hell, I'm a lawyer, and I would've turned down that deal if it was presented to me like that. You're misleading our clients for your own ego, and one of them happens to be my brother. A brother I love, I might add!"

"I love him too," my dad shouted back. "This is not about my ego. It's about your brother and his freedom. I am not going to let him go to prison and ruin his life. Just like I wouldn't let you or your sister or Perk go down like that. You have to trust me on that."

I shot a glance at Michael, and he was hanging on to every word of this fight that Lamont and Daddy should have been having in private.

"Now, so we are clear, I presented them the damn offer, and they didn't take it—end of story. I don't wanna talk about it anymore," my dad said.

"If we lose, this is on your fucking head!" Lamont shouted emotionally. The next thing I heard was the slamming of a door.

"Fine! Act childish! But we have a trial starting tomorrow, so your ass better be prepared."

I had just taken my seat when Daddy walked into the conference room.

"What the hell was that about?" I asked.

He shrugged then sat down across from Michael at the table. "Your brother seems to think that I misrepresented the DA's plea offer. That I don't want the boys to take the deal for personal reasons."

"*Did* you misrepresent it?" I asked cautiously.

"Not you too, Desiree." He exhaled, rubbing his temples. "I'm going to tell you the same thing I told those boys: If you're guilty, then take the deal. If you're innocent, let's fight these motherfuckers, because the only thing worse than going to jail is going to jail for admitting to something you didn't do."

I understood where Lamont was coming from. Daddy had always loved a good courtroom fight, so his own ego *could* have influenced his push for them to turn down the deal. But I couldn't fault my father's logic. Pleading guilty to something you didn't do is a terrible choice to have to make. Maybe they would have turned down the plea deal even without Dad's advice.

"I hear you, Daddy, but how are we going to win this case with no evidence?" I asked.

"There's this thing in law school they teach you called reasonable doubt," he said halfheartedly. "You see, you only need one juror to hold out to stop a conviction. But we are going to pick three jurors. Once we pick them, we're going to make them feel like Langston, Kwesi, Krush, and Tony could be their sons, grandsons, brothers, nephews, or any other young person they've ever loved. We'll make these young men so sympathetic to these jurors that Langston could shoot someone in front of them and they'd still never convict."

I heard "wow" come out of Michael's mouth, and I had to admit that was also how I felt after listening to my father.

"This is why I came to work for you," Michael gushed.

Perk walked into the room, and I tried not to make eye contact. We hadn't spoken more than five words to each other since he moved out a month ago. I'd be lying if I didn't say I missed the big lug. We'd been so close for so long. He was the only person I could really talk to. I damn sure couldn't talk to Jerri, because she was worse than any man I'd ever met when it came to jealousy. But she had this way of making up with me that was neurotic yet sexy at the same damn time, so I just couldn't make myself quit her.

"Where have you been?" Daddy asked Perk.

"Down at Thompson Audi, looking at surveillance video footage."

"Anything come up?" Michael asked.

"Man, that car's been sitting on their lot for six months. All they did was wash it and start it up. It barely moved the whole time, until Jacqueline purchased it."

My father swiveled his chair in Perk's direction. "I need a smoking gun. I need something."

"I told you I'm working on something, but I need a little more time, Bradley."

I noticed Michael giving him a strange look. The look on my father's face said he'd noticed it too. Perk shook his head almost imperceptibly.

"What? What is it?" I asked Michael. Perk shot an annoyed glance in his direction.

"Um, it's . . . I don't . . ." Michael shook his head.

"Someone tell me what the hell is going on and make it quick." Daddy began opening and closing his hands into fists, a habit he had whenever he was angry.

Perk gave Michael an exasperated glare, but he couldn't ignore a direct order from his boss. "Tony's brother Adonis was arrested a couple weeks ago with a substantial amount of heroin. He's in federal custody," he said.

Daddy exploded. "A couple of weeks! Why the fuck didn't you tell me this sooner? This is what we've been waiting on." He stood up and started pacing the room. "What's wrong with you, Perk?"

I was wondering the same thing. Here we had possible evidence that could get Lang out of jail, and he was keeping it a secret? Why? This was something he should've brought to our attention the moment he found out.

"Well, I didn't say anything because I'm still waiting to confirm that the heroin he had came from the same source as the heroin found in Langston's car. Right now, we don't know that," Perk explained, and I begrudgingly admitted to myself that he was right. It wasn't solid evidence yet.

"Bullshit. Tony was riding in the car with Lang, and the cops found heroin in the trunk. Then, his brother gets busted for the same thing? It's obvious where the dope came from," Daddy said.

"No, it's not. Not until we get the report back from my guy, which should be any day now," Perk told him.

"Reasonable doubt, Perk." Daddy was grinning now. "Reasonable doubt. That's all I need to bring Langston home."

"Bradley, this could just as easily backfire on us as help us. And what about poor Tony? Are we just going to drop this at his feet? What if the drugs don't match? He's gonna be holding the bag if we let out that his brother was arrested."

"He's right, honey," Carla said as she entered the room. "Bringing Tony's brothers arrest into this case is a ticking time bomb without proof the drugs are somehow related."

"Carla, what's the chance they aren't?"

"I don't know, but I'm not going to let you paint Tony in a corner. That boy's slept in our house, and I've read his emails and his texts. He's a good kid. They're all good kids from what I can see," she stated without any hesitation. We might all have been a little afraid of Daddy, but she definitely considered herself his equal. "Now, I don't know how those drugs got in that car, but unless you show me something more concrete, we will defend them all equally, until we can't anymore."

"Okay, okay," Daddy said. Unlike his stance with Lamont, he didn't even sound angry at Carla for disagreeing with him. "Perk, I need you to get that fucking report ASAP. I don't give a shit what you gotta do to get it. It may be the key to this whole case."

Perk nodded. I could see that he was frustrated, but he didn't say anything as he turned and walked out of the office.

Suddenly, a thought came to me. "Daddy, do you think the DA's office knows about Tony's brother being arrested?"

He thought about it for a second, but he didn't look worried. "I doubt it. Our case is state, and that one is federal. Usually, the right hand doesn't know what the left is doing. Besides," he added, "I don't think James Brown is looking to pin this on Tony alone. He's looking for a bigger conviction."

I didn't like the sound of that. "You mean he wants all four of them locked up, no matter who did it?" I asked incredulously. This assistant DA was out for blood, it seemed.

"Yeah. Something like that," Daddy said, glancing over at Carla. Then he changed the subject.

"On another note, is everything ready for tomorrow?" Daddy asked.

"Everything's in place," I told him. "We've gone over all the witness statements and evidence to be presented so far."

"The notes you requested for your opening argument are right here." Michael held up a folder that he took from me.

"The final jury selection looks good, along with the alternates," Carla added. "The only thing we're waiting on is the witness list from the DA's office. They still haven't sent it over."

"They will. We'll have it by midnight. James is just fucking with us," Daddy said.

"I don't know, Bradley. I'm a little worried. He seemed kind of excited about that change of venue. That's not like him, based on his prior case files. There's a reason he wanted to get away from Staten Island."

"He wants to get away from Grace, that's all," Daddy replied.

I agreed. "Could be. She was really pushing for him to plead us out."

"Exactly, that's because the press is roasting her ass. Don't worry, we've got this; especially once Perk brings me that evidence. It may just make this a slam dunk case for us." He smiled confidently. "Des, go and see if you can find some food. We're going to be here a while."

"Will do." I was glad to get a little break, even if it was only to find a late-night Chinese takeout spot.

I headed out of the office and pressed the button for the elevator. The doors opened, but I froze in my spot when I saw who was standing there.

"Hey, beautiful." Jerri repeated the words of the text messages she sent me every morning.

"What—"

"I brought you dinner." She held up a large brown paper bag, reminding me of the one Lena had brought that damn strawberry pie in.

"Wow." I tried to smile. "Thanks."

"No, thank you for this morning." She stepped closer to me, running her finger along the side of my face, down my neck, and into my cleavage. I could feel my nipples hardening, as much as I didn't want them to.

"You didn't have to come all the way down here to do that," I said nervously.

"I wanted to." She went to kiss me, but I stopped her.

"Oh, it's like that?" Her smile faded. "I thought we were beyond this."

"We are. I'm just not into public displays," I said. "You know that."

"Whatever." She sighed.

"How did you get past security?"

"The half asleep guy watching porn on his cell? He barely looked up after I told him I had a food delivery for you." She held up the bag again.

I took the bag from her and said, "I appreciate this. I really do."

"So, I guess having dinner in your office is out of the question, huh?" The dejected way she said it made me feel worse than I already did.

"Yeah, it's a little tense around here with the trial starting tomorrow," I told her. "But I think I know how to thank you."

She brightened a little. "Oh, really? How?"

I pushed the elevator button again, and the doors opened. I stepped in then pulled her inside. As soon as the doors closed behind us, I pulled her to me, kissing her full on the mouth. Hands started wandering, and things got so heated that I almost didn't notice when the doors began to open once again. I now realized we'd never moved, never left the fourth floor. As I pushed Jerri away and scrambled to pull down my skirt, I quickly pressed the button to close the doors again. The last thing I saw as the doors shut was the confused look on Michael's face.

Langston

50

I'd been in Rikers a little over three months. I'd missed my birthday, Memorial Day weekend, Fourth of July in Sag Harbor, and more importantly, my graduation from college. With all that being said, I'd reached the most important day of my life. I was finally getting my day in court. The COs shuttled me to the bus right after breakfast. Tony and Krush were already seated. I stopped in the middle of the aisle when I saw Krush's face.

"What the fuck? What happened to you?" He looked like he'd been in a boxing match.

Krush didn't say anything, but surprisingly, Tony did. "They been whipping his ass daily. Not much I can do if he won't fight back, Lang."

I'd known Krush since my first day on the yard at Howard. He'd been my roommate every year since, so I knew he wasn't as hardcore as he tried to portray. Still, I wouldn't consider him a punk. I stared at Krush then took a look at Tony. There was something about both of them that was different. I just couldn't put my finger on it.

"You a'ight?" I asked Krush.

"Yeah." he nodded, but he didn't make eye contact.

"Keep it moving," the CO yelled. I took a seat behind Krush.

The driver got on board with three other COs. He started the engine and closed the door. I kept looking out the window, expecting to see Kwesi coming out, but then the bus started moving.

Kwesi and I were still in the same unit, but I'd avoided him ever since our conversation on the yard. I had, however, been watching him from afar, and he seemed to be very respected by the Muslims. I'd been hoping that without all them around, we might be able to clear the air between us before trial. Now he was nowhere to be found.

Tony noticed too. "Wait, where the hell is Kwesi?" He turned toward me, looking confused.

"Man, I was about to say the same damn thing," I told him.

"Maybe he's on another bus or something," Krush suggested. "Or caught an earlier one and he's already there."

"I doubt they'd have two buses to Staten Island when this one isn't even filled," Tony explained to him, "This ain't the fucking F train. These buses don't leave every twenty minutes."

The look in Krush's eyes said he understood. He shook his head and said, "Something ain't right. His ass should be here."

Krush finally looked at me, and we locked eyes. I could see what he was thinking, but I didn't want to speak on it.

"Nah, he's gonna be there," I insisted.

"We damn sure better pray that he is," Tony said.

I spent the rest of the bus ride in nervous silence.

At the courthouse, we were brought into a room where we changed into suits. Then we were eventually escorted into the courtroom, where there was still no sign of Kwesi. I didn't see his lawyer, either. I scanned the crowd, and my heart began to race. There was my mother, along with Tony's mom, and a few more familiar faces; however, Kwesi's parents, who had been at each and every court hearing, were nowhere to be found.

Krush was right. Something was very, very wrong.

We shuffled over to the defense table where Dad, Lamont, and Desiree were waiting for us.

"Where the hell is he?" Krush whispered.

I turned to my father and asked, "Where's Kwesi?"

Before my father could speak, Lamont snapped, "We don't know."

"What do you mean, you don't know?"

"We haven't been able to get in touch with his lawyer in two days, and this was delivered this morning." He waved a paper at me.

"What's that?"

"It's the prosecution's witness list," my father chimed in unhappily. "They have Kwesi lined up to testify."

I knew he was going to say that, but it didn't stop my stomach from doing flips.

"What exactly does that mean for us, Mr. Hudson?" Tony asked.

"It means that your friend Kwesi took a deal with the prosecution and he's planning on testifying against you," Dad replied.

I slumped down in my chair, knowing that Kwesi's sudden disappearance would make shit way more complicated than it already had been.

Lamont

51

"Right there. Don't stop. Please, don't stop." Felicia moaned softly as she dug into my lower back with her fingernails. I plunged into her; the sensation of her throbbing wetness and her seductive voice was almost enough to make me forget about Langston's case. I say *almost* because I still couldn't believe that son of a bitch Kimba had stabbed us in the back by taking a deal with the DA and not telling us.

"Oh, shit, Lamont. Please, don't stop!"

After court, I would usually have dinner with my dad, Carla, Desiree, and Perk back at the house to discuss strategy. I just couldn't do it today after my old man refused to let up about Kwesi taking a deal. He insisted it was my fault because I was supposed to babysit his lawyer. So instead, I'd called Felicia to see if she would give me a chance to call in that raincheck, after my "interview" with her had been interrupted last time. After dinner, we'd ended up back at her place, just as I'd hoped. A night with her would be the best kind of distraction.

"Lamont, I'm coming." She grabbed my hands and placed them around her throat. I gently tightened my fingers, and she closed her eyes and smiled. Felicia liked to be choked, saying that it heightened her climax.

She began gasping, then finally screamed, "Ahhhhhhhhhhhh, yesssssssss."

Knowing that she was satisfied, I loosened my grip and allowed myself to release into the condom, fighting my own urge to scream. I collapsed on top of her. As usual, the sex was hot, sweaty, and satisfying. Had I been a smoker, I would've needed a cigarette. It was just that damn good. I was exhausted, but in a good way.

"Damn," I finally said. "That was nice."

"You feel better?" She giggled.

"Hell yeah, I feel much better, thanks to you." I rolled off of her.

"Nobody knows what a trial can do to you like I do."

"I'm sure you do." I placed my hand on her stomach and gently massaged.

"So, other than this guy Kimba sandbagging you and your father placing the weight of the world on your shoulders, how did the rest of the day go?"

"Good, actually," I replied. "We picked a hell of a jury. I think we have half of them rooting for us, and the other half are at least impartial."

"Really? In a case like this, that's imperative." I could tell she was surprised by my confidence. "Who are you using as jury consultants?"

"We have our own. Have you ever heard of Carla Crippen?"

"Only by reputation, but she's good. She used to work with Cochran until he passed, didn't she? Then I think she was teaching at Columbia Law, too, until she fell off the face of the earth a few years back."

"Well, not exactly. She married my old man. Works for us exclusively. And you're wrong—she's not good. She's the fucking best," I boasted. "She's like the COO, office shrink, jury consultant, stepmom, and a best friend all wrapped up in one."

"Sounds like quite a lady."

"She is, and if she weren't involved, I would have forced my brother to take that deal the DA offered. I still think it was foolish not to consider it, but with my father's strategy and Carla's help, I think we might've been able to pull this off with at least a hung jury—until Kwesi's defection."

"That's a pretty bold prediction." She stared at me. "Now, I'm not asking for any privileged information, but you yourself said that your case is pretty weak. They found these boys with two kilos of heroin. How do you beat that kind of physical evidence?"

"You don't."

"Huh?"

"If there is one thing my old man did teach me, it's that winning a jury trial is not as much about the law as everyone thinks. It's about the twelve people in that box, because most people don't understand the law; but they do understand the world they live in. Making sure that you and your client connect with them is what wins cases—not the law. Otherwise, you might as well just ask for a bench trial."

She looked about as impressed as a lawyer could be. "And you think you did that today."

"I know we did. You see, my father and I have this thing we do. He questions male jurors, and I question females."

She raised an eyebrow dubiously. "Why do you question the women?"

"Because women have a thing for me. White, black, yellow, or green, they just do. It's my superpower," I joked. "Call it a gift or a curse, but it just works, and I've even learned how to identify when it's working and when it's not."

"Sounds sexist," she replied.

"That's because it is. But what am I supposed to do: ignore it, or use it to the best of my ability to help my clients?"

"Let me think about that one," she said, rolling slightly away from me.

I took the hint and got up. I went into the bathroom, flushed the condom, and washed myself off. I wet another washcloth and brought it to Felicia.

"Thanks. You're so considerate," she said, snuggling beside me and putting her head on my chest. "Look, I get what you were saying earlier. You can't help it if you're attractive, but don't go saying shit like that to a woman you're sleeping with. It kind of takes your sexy away."

We both laughed, and I kissed her.

"By the way, I saw that James Brown is prosecuting your case. Don't underestimate him," she said. "The man's good."

"Tell me about it. It's like he's got our playbook and he's one step ahead of us. Even my dad is becoming frustrated, and I've never seen this happen."

"Sounds personal."

I nodded. "Yeah, it is. He's got some connection to my mother and father, but neither of them will talk about it."

"Well, you want me to see what the problem is? I can find out," she offered. "One of my partners comes from that office."

I thought about it. Felicia was well connected, and utilizing her might be helpful. At this point, I was willing to take any assistance I could get.

"You think you can? Discreetly, of course."

"Of course," she said. "I wouldn't have it any other way."

"I'd appreciate it. I thought I would be able to knock this thing out of the park, but now I'm not sure."

"Lamont, you're one of the most prodigious young defense attorneys in New York. There's no need to start doubting yourself or your abilities." Her fingers caressed my chest.

"Prodigious?" I looked down at her. Was she talking about my talents or the size of my member?

"Prodigious," she repeated, moving her had a little lower. "And I have a confession."

"What's that?"

"I was really looking forward to working with you at our firm. I know ending up like this wasn't anything either one of us anticipated when you were interviewing, but I really think you'd be an asset. I was disappointed when they said you turned down the offer."

"Yeah, it was a great offer, too. But I thought about it, and I knew it wouldn't be right, especially considering us. You know that wouldn't have been good," I told her.

"It may have worked . . . but I understand. Besides, your family needs you right now. That would've really put you in a difficult position if you'd left last month. I'm glad you stayed."

"True, it worked out for now, but I don't know if my staying is going to be a permanent decision."

"Your father is Bradley Hudson. *The* Bradley Hudson. Do you know how lucky you are?"

"He is one of the best," I agreed. "But I want to grow the firm, bring on other great lawyers as partners, and expand into what I know it could be. He's satisfied with us being a small, family business with me, him, Des—and hopefully, one day Langston. We could be so much bigger, and the clients we would attract would be immeasurable." I'd thought about this potential for so long, but Dad always shot me down whenever I brought it up.

"That is true. Have you explained your vision for the family's firm with him?"

"Many times, but he doesn't want to hear it. It's his way or no way," I said with a sigh.

"Maybe's he's afraid of growing too big, too fast. That can be a bad thing," she suggested.

"Well, thanks to Langston, all eyes are on us right now, that's for sure. Winning this case is going to do wonders for us, and we're gonna be in high demand, whether he likes it or not. But if he doesn't want to grow, maybe I've got to think about my own plans."

Tony

52

I glanced back at my mom, who gave me a small wave with her fingers. She was sitting two rows back, next to Langston's mom. We were all waiting as the judge talked to the lawyers in front of his bench. After opening arguments where the prosecution made us sound like a bunch of thugs, and Bradley Hudson made us sound like saints, the trial was in full swing. Although we'd only been in session a couple of days, it felt like a year.

"Man, I'll be glad when this shit is over and done with," I said, loosening my tie.

"I feel you. They've pretty much called the entire NYPD to testify. Some of them weren't even there when we got picked up." Lang shook his head.

"True, but your pops did his thing yesterday. He made that sergeant look like a fool."

"Yeah, my stepmom said we pulled two jurors to our side yesterday," he said.

"That's what I'm talking about. Your people are the bomb." I laughed quietly then looked over at Krush. He'd been quiet since we arrived in court, probably because they'd beaten his ass again last night. "Hey, man, you a'ight?"

"I'm good," he said unconvincingly. "I hope they wrap this shit up soon, for real."

The lawyers returned to the tables, and we turned our attention back to James Brown with his shiny head and his JC Penney suit. I wasn't sure how much his salary was at the DA's office, but I would've though he could afford better suits than the ones he wore, which clearly were off the rack. Bradley and Lamont Hudson wore custom-fitted menswear, which said a lot, and I hoped the jury would notice.

"Are we ready to proceed, Mr. Brown?" the judge asked. He was a middle-aged, skinny Latin guy who always dabbed at his forehead with a handkerchief. I didn't know why, because I never saw any sweat.

"Yes, I'd like to call Steven Barnes to the stand," Brown answered.

Lang leaned over and asked, "Who the hell is that?"

I shrugged. "Probably another cop." The side door to the courtroom opened, and a guy in a prison-issued jumpsuit was escorted in by a guard.

"Oh, shit," Krush mumbled.

"Yo, Krush, ain't that the dude you used to play cards with all the time?" I asked. "What's his name? Meat?"

"Yeah, it looks like him."

"It looks like him? Nigga, that is him," I growled.

"I don't know," he mumbled.

"You better pray it ain't got nothing to do with you."

I felt Mr. Hudson's eyes on me. I sat up, confused as I watched Meat, the guy who'd slept in the bunk next to Krush when we first arrived at Rikers, placing his hand on the Bible and swearing to tell the truth. What the hell was he about to tell? Whatever it was, it couldn't be nothing good. When we first got there, Krush was running his mouth constantly, and he gossiped with this dude like they were a couple of bitches.

"Mr. Barnes, can you tell the court how you know Kirby Wright?" Brown asked.

"Who?" Meat frowned.

"Kirby Wright," Brown said with an attitude, pointing over to our table. "You might know him as Krush."

"Oh, yeah. Krush and me are tight. Our beds was right next to each other."

"And how long have you been in this proximity?" Brown asked.

"Since he got to Rikers a couple months ago," Meat said.

"And uh, did Krush tell you why he was at Rikers or the events that led up to his being there?"

"Yeah, he's pushing weight." Meat shrugged. A couple of people giggled from the audience. "That nigga Krush ain't no joke when it come to that tar."

Brown turned around and faced the jury with a look that said, *I apologize for this illiterate man.* To Meat, he said, "Can you explain what that means for people who don't know?"

I closed my eyes and began praying as I thought about everything Krush might have said while trying to impress this dumb fuck. I glanced over at Krush, who looked like he wanted to die. That's when I knew that whatever Meat was about to say was really bad for our case.

"Yeah, he sells a lotta dope. He told me him and his boys got popped for a couple keys of that good black tar heroin rolling down to DC—but that was light compared to the weight they normally move," Meat announced as casually as if he'd just said Krush delivered pizza for a living.

"Objection!" Bradley rose to his feet. "Hearsay!"

"He's just explaining what he meant by pushing weight," Brown responded.

"I'll allow it for the time being," the judge told him.

"Thank you. Now, Mr. Barnes, as far as you know, are Krush and his co-defendants involved in the sale of narcotics?" Brown asked.

"Your Honor!" Mr. Hudson yelled. "He is not an expert witness on the defendants."

"Mr. Brown, you're skating on thin ice."

"Yes, Your Honor." He turned back to Meat. "You and Krush recently had a falling out. Why was that?"

"Because of the crowd he runs with. Look, I'm just locked up for drug possession. I'm trying to do my little year and get the hell outta here. I don't need the kind of shit Krush and his people be dealing with."

"And what kind of stuff does he deal with?" Brown asked.

"Everyone knows they're connected and protected by the Bloods. His boy Doctor Strange runs our entire unit."

"By Doctor Strange do you mean his co-defendant, Anthony Baker?" Brown pointed directly at me. There was murmuring in the courtroom, and I glared at Krush.

"Yeah, that's Doctor Strange," Meat replied. "Krush is his enforcer."

"Objection, Your Honor," Bradley yelled again.

Before the judge could reply, Brown asked, "And how do you know that he's a Bloods enforcer?"

"Look at all the bruises on his face." He pointed at Krush. "Krush told me he gets in a fight almost every day for them."

Krush turned to me, and I gave him a look that told him exactly what I was going to do to him when we got back to the island. That was when he snapped.

"You lying son of a bitch! I never told you that shit! What the fuck is wrong with you? You trying to get me killed!" Krush screamed, jumping over the table and heading straight for the witness chair. For a dude that couldn't fight, he was running straight into one—except the court bailiffs caught him before he reached Meat.

"Order! Order!" the judge bellowed. "Mr. Hudson, you need to calm your client. Do you hear me?"

But there was no calming Krush.

"Krush, sit down and be quiet!" Bradley barked, trying to get his attention.

"He's lying!" Krush struggled against the guards. "He's a fucking liar!"

"Bailiff, take him out of here and put him in lockup! I don't want to see that man again in my courtroom!" the judge ordered.

The next thing I knew, Krush was being cuffed and hauled out of the courtroom.

Michael

53

I felt like I was in the middle of a three-ring circus. To say the day in court had been crazy would be an understatement. After the damaging testimony from Krush's supposed friend, things seemed to go downhill, and there was no turning back. By the time we all made it back to the office, tempers were at an all-time high. Bradley, who up until now had seemed cool, calm, and collected, was frazzled and unnerved.

"Damn it, can somebody tell me how this fucking career criminal ended up on the stand? I thought you said Steven Barnes was a cop." He paced back and forth at the front of the conference room where we were all seated.

"We did, Daddy. I guess Steven Barnes is a common name. How were we supposed to know? The cops had another Steven Barnes working the same day of the arrest," Desiree said. "We thought it was him testifying."

"You'll get him on cross, honey," Carla said, but it didn't look like that made Bradley feel any better.

"Carla, find whatever the hell you can about that fucking guy, and also find out every fucking thing you can about Kirby's lying ass. And I mean everything!" Bradley snapped.

"We're digging up everything we can on him as we speak," Carla replied.

"It doesn't matter," Lamont replied cynically. "The damage was already done the second Krush leaped over the damn table."

"Maybe so, but it's worth a try." Bradley then turned to Perk. "I thought you were working on that report. What's the hold up?"

"My source is working as fast as he can, Bradley," Perk tried to explain. "He's gotta get a sample out of the Feds' evidence lockup first, and that shit ain't easy."

"I don't care. I need it. This case will be over before you come through," Bradley said.

Perk glared at Bradley as if he wanted to hit him before getting up from his seat and walking out. I was embarrassed for the brother. I looked over at Desiree, who was avoiding everyone's stares by looking down at the center of the table. Come to think of it, she'd been avoiding eye contact a lot lately, ever since that weird moment by the elevators. Between that and whatever she had going on with Perk, that was one chick with a very interesting life.

Carla spoke up. "Bradley, that was uncalled for, and you are way out of line."

"After the day we had in court, I don't have time to sugar coat anything. Perk has a tough skin, and he knows I meant no harm," Bradley told her.

"For the record, we lost six jurors today," Carla said unhappily. "Lamont, you still have jurors two and five drooling, so a wink here and a smile there might help. Jurors number six and seven seem to be sympathetic to Langston."

"That's it? We're down to four jurors on our side?" Jacqueline chimed in.

"Yep, and we haven't even had Kwesi on the stand yet," Carla replied.

"Tell me about it." Bradley pulled out a chair and sat at the head of the table. "I just wish I knew what the hell else James had up his sleeve."

"We just need a break. Damn, something's gotta give," Lamont huffed.

"What if you don't get a break? Then what?" Jacqueline asked.

"Maybe we can meet with ADA Brown again," Desiree suggested. "And see where his head's at."

Lamont chimed in. "See if the deal he offered—"

"We're not doing that." Bradley shook his head.

"What do you mean *again*?" Jacqueline asked.

Bradley glared at Lamont with the same amount of anger that Perk had shown him earlier. He told Jacqueline, "He offered some ridiculous deal that made absolutely no sense for Langston to accept."

"What was the offer?" Jacqueline directed her question to Lamont, rather than Bradley.

"It doesn't matter what the damn offer was, Jackie. We didn't take it. Contrary to what you may think, I am the defense attorney assigned to Langston's case. You aren't. Your being here is a courtesy. You don't get to dictate what happens," Bradley told her. "So, if you think I'm gonna go groveling to James Brown and beg him for a deal, I'm not. Granted, today was a brutal day in court, but we can come back from this."

Jacqueline was still facing Lamont, and she repeated the question as if Bradley had not just delivered his soliloquy. "Lamont, what were the terms of the plea agreement that the DA's office offered?"

The room remained quiet as we waited to see if Lamont would answer his mother. Finally, he said, "The offer was three to five with a guilty plea on the possession, and they would drop the intent to distribute."

"And Langston said no? He would be out in a year and a half, maybe less." Jacqueline sat up straight. This time, her eyes went from Lamont to each person in the room, including me.

"Jackie, Langston is not pleading guilty. We're going to beat this thing, and neither his record nor his future is going to be damaged by this case. He's got the best damn defense team in the world, and I'm going to see to it that he comes home."

"But what if you don't, Bradley? Then what?" Jacqueline yelled.

"I will. Don't you think I know what's in my son's best interest?" Bradley asked.

"And you think I don't?"

"Don't make me answer that, Jackie," Bradley warned.

"Mom, Dad, come on. This isn't the time or the place," Desiree interjected.

"No. By all means, please answer, Bradley. I'd like to hear what you have to say," Jacqueline said icily.

"You wanna waltz in here, giving all kinds of opinions and talking about what you think we should do for your son. Well, guess what? You don't get a say. You've neglected that boy since the day he was born, pissed off because you said he was a mistake that was getting in the way of your career. How do you think he feels knowing you couldn't bring your ass to visit him in jail?" He folded his arms defiantly. "You wanted an answer? There, you got it."

Jacqueline swallowed hard, then she stood and grabbed her purse.

"Mom, wait," Desiree said.

"I may not be the best mother in the world, and I'm not a renowned defense attorney, but as an appointed federal judge, and a good one at that, I know a sinking ship when I see one. And you, Bradley, are the captain of this one. I pray to God that you find a way to save it. If not, you're going to regret it." She walked out with her head held high.

James

54

"So, Mr. Meat, you do realize that this is a high-profile case with a lot of media attention, don't you?" Bradley Hudson asked, leaning up next to the witness stand like he and Steven "Meat" Barnes were best friends.

"Yeah, I know that," Meat said, rocking his head up and down to agree. "That don't bother me. It's your clients on trial, not me."

I raised a hand to my face to hide my smirk. He was a great witness. When I'd first added Meat's name to the witness list, Grace had opposed the idea. She didn't believe he would be able to handle Bradley's questioning. But I'd prepped him well, and I knew his statement would be damaging and help solidify our already strong case. Meat had been so good that he caused Kirby Wright to lose control and be removed from the courtroom yesterday. Lamont Hudson had spent the morning arguing why Kirby should be let back in the courtroom, but the judge disagreed. So now, up against Bradley's cross, Meat was doing just fine and showing no sign that he might crack.

Bradley rambled on. "Nevertheless, I just want you to be prepared, because they've got television cameras, newspaper reporters, bloggers—hell, they even have a sketch artists drawing your picture as we speak." Bradley pointed to the man in the first row, drawing on a pad. "A handsome guy like you, testifying in a high-profile case like this is going to make you Instagram famous by tomorrow. You're going to be the new Kato Kaelin. You won't be able to walk into a restaurant without TMZ sticking a microphone in your face."

I didn't object, because I had no idea where he was going with this.

Meat's eyes lit up. "You think so?"

"I know so." Bradley did everything but pat him on the back. "You're from Forty Projects in Jamaica, Queens, aren't you?"

"No doubt. South side in the house," Meat announced proudly.

"Lot of tough guys come from those projects, if I remember correctly."

"Hardest projects in New York City," Meat bragged. "And I'm born and bred."

"Wow, with all your street cred and this newfound fame, you're going to be a real celebrity back in Forty." When Meat tried to prop himself up even more in his seat, Bradley smiled—not at him, but at me. "Yes, sir, you're going to be the most famous *snitch* Forty Projects has ever seen." Bradley walked over to stand near the juror's box as he waited for Meat's reaction.

And react he did.

"Huh? I'm no snitch!" Meat's voice got loud as he realized what Bradley was insinuating.

"Yes, you are," Bradley replied. "And soon, everyone on the streets is going to know it."

"Objection, Your Honor! He's badgering the witness." I should have risen to my feet sooner, but to be honest, he'd caught me off guard with this dirty tactic. I was too late, because his words set Meat off.

"Fuck that!" Meat bellowed. "I want it on the record! I'm not a fucking snitch. I'm only doing this 'cause they promised I could go home early. I ain't got no beef with Krush and Tony. I'm only doing what they told me so I can go home. I'm not no snitch!"

"Reeeeeeeally?" Bradley asked dramatically for the benefit of the jurors, who were suddenly looking more interested than they'd been all day. "Who told you to do that? Who told you to lie on the stand?"

"Your Honor!" I shouted, feeling desperate.

"I'll allow it," the judge replied.

"Who did you talk to?" Bradley asked again.

Meat turned directly to me. "That guy. The black ADA."

All I could do was sit there in frustration as Bradley dismantled my witness. Meat sat on the stand looking flustered and confused now. This was something I certainly hadn't anticipated, because this wasn't Meat's first rodeo. He'd been jailed fifteen times, ten of which he'd gotten off early by testifying against other inmates. I figured he was a pro at holding strong under pressure, but Bradley had cracked him wide open.

"What did ADA Brown say to you, Meat?"

"He came to me and asked me what Krush said about the drugs. I ain't go to them."

"And what did the DA's office offer when they came to you, Mr. Barnes?"

"They, uh . . ." Meat's eyes went to me, and he hesitated. Now that he'd calmed down a little, he realized he was killing his chance for early release.

Bradley sighed. "Your Honor, can you please instruct the witness to answer the question?"

"Mr. Barnes, we're waiting. Answer the question, sir," the judge instructed.

"Well, they told me and my lawyer that if I cooperated, I'd be home in two months with home monitoring," Meat explained to the judge. "Man, my girl is pregnant, and they talking about giving me at least a year. When they offered two months, I didn't feel like I had a choice."

"So, you lied so you could go home?" Bradley asked.

"Nah, man. I ain't lie. I just didn't say that I knew Krush was talking bullshit to me in that cell. E'rybody knows that Krush is a punk. He ain't pushin' no heavy weight."

"No further questions for this witness, Your Honor." Bradley walked back to the defense table, where Lamont patted him on the back as he took his seat.

Meat was allowed to step down from the stand, and he walked over to the deputy who was waiting to escort him back to Rikers.

"Are there any more witnesses at this time, Mr. Brown?" the judge asked.

I looked down at the paperwork in front of me, and said, "Yes, Your Honor. We do have one more witness, but I'd like to ask for a brief recess."

The judge looked at his watch and said, "Well, it's a little after three. Let's hold off on that witness and resume in the morning. It's already been a long day. Court is adjourned until nine a.m."

I was packing up my briefcase when David walked over to me and said, "Nice work."

"By who?" I asked him.

"Aw, it wasn't that bad. So what if he got a deal? He still told what Kirby said about the drugs. That's all that matters," David said. I wanted to believe him, but of course, it would all depend on which version of Meat's story the jury chose to believe.

David continued, "But, I did want to let you know that Kimberly and I took care of that thing."

I glanced up at him, feeling a little better. "And how'd it go?"

"Went exactly the way we wanted."

"Great. That's what I needed to hear. At least something's going as planned today," I told him.

"Well, I'm gonna head over to the bar down the block and have a couple of drinks later. You wanna join me?" David offered. "You seem like you can use one."

"Naw, I'm good. I'm gonna head on home in a little while and prep for tomorrow."

"Suit yourself. You may change your mind, though," he said.

"Why?" I frowned.

He pointed to the door of the courtroom and said, "Look who's here."

I looked over and saw Grace standing in the back, talking to a couple of people. David swiftly made his exit as I picked up my briefcase. She was headed my way.

"Grace." I nodded to greet her when she approached. "You don't have to say it. You were right."

"I didn't want to be." She gestured for me to follow as she headed for the exit.

We walked out of the courtroom, and there was Bradley, where he was every time court ended: in front of the cameras, basking in the spotlight. A few members of the media headed in my direction when they saw me and Grace, but I put up my hand and said, "No comment," as we passed by.

"I'm surprised you're not having your grandstanding end-of-the-day news conference like you usually do," Grace commented after I closed the door of the private conference room we'd just entered.

"Today wasn't our greatest day in court with Meat's cross, but we're still winning this thing hands down. Let Bradley showboat for the cameras. It'll make our victory even sweeter once his clients—and his son—are found guilty. He won't have anything to gloat about, and he definitely won't wanna be featured on the news."

Grace sat in one of the chairs and crossed her legs.

"Today's Bradley's day, tomorrow and the rest of this trial will be mine."

"I'm sure Russell Jackal will be pleased," she said.

I stared at her, feeling cornered. I had no response.

"Yes, James, I know about you and Russell."

"Grace," I said quietly.

"Don't you *Grace* me, you back-stabbing son of a bitch! I knew all this grandstanding had to be about more than Jacqueline and Bradley. Why else would you take this case off the island?"

"I told you it wasn't personal," I replied calmly, hoping to ease the tension between us.

"Bullshit! Of course it's personal. Just not in the way I thought."

"Grace, this is not going to affect you at all."

"Do I look stupid?" Grace wasn't one to raise her voice for anyone, but she was damn near screaming now. "You fucked me, James, and by bringing Russel Jackal into it, you did it with no fucking lube. I just don't know what I'm going to do about it," she said menacingly.

"What do you mean?"

"I have half a mind to just walk out there and offer Bradley misdemeanors for the lot of them and be done with this," she snapped.

"You can't do that," I protested. Fuck, she was about to ruin everything.

"I sure as hell can," she countered. "But I can't just let two kilos of heroin go entirely unpunished after spending all this money. I'd never get elected again."

"Thank you," I said humbly, although she didn't deserve it. "Grace, I'm really not trying to fuck you on this."

"Save it, okay, James?" she said icily. "And just so we understand each other, you better win this fucking case. 'Cause when you're done, we are done. You're finished in my office."

She stared at me, and I think she was hoping for a reaction. I didn't want to overplay my hand, so I just stared back until we were both distracted by cell phone alerts. We glanced down at our phones and then raised our heads until our eyes met. Neither of us said a word, but it was obvious she'd just received the same tragic news I had.

Krush

55

Four hours earlier

I was up when Tony left for court, not that I had slept very well under the fear of duress and the dripping drain pipe my new bunk was under. Once again, I tried to apologize to him for everything that had happened yesterday with Meat, but he wasn't having it.

"Just stay the fuck away from me," he'd said, balling a fist like he wanted to punch me. I think I would have taken the beat down if I thought it would mend things between us—but I knew it wouldn't. I'd fucked up running my stupid mouth, and now I had to live with consequences.

"Get up, nigga. What you got to eat?" I looked up and saw two dudes that had taken my stuff when Tony went to the hole. Life in Rikers was hard enough, but word was spreading fast that I no longer had Tony watching my back, so it had just gotten harder.

"I got nothin'," I said.

Before I had a chance to move, they were all over me, punching and kicking me like I was an MMA practice dummy. I finally managed to get away, but then they had all my stuff, including my blanket and sneakers.

"Not so tough without Doctor Strange, are you?" the bigger one said as he gave me one last kick.

I went in the bathroom and washed the blood off my face. How much longer was I going to have to deal with this? I was getting to the point where I couldn't take anymore.

I left the bathroom and trudged over to the phone, where I waited my turn for almost an hour. Phone in hand, I dialed one of the few numbers I knew by heart, praying that there would be an answer on the other end.

"State your name," the prerecorded voice instructed me.

"Kru—Um, Kirby."

"Please hold while we attempt to reach your party."

I waited a few seconds, knowing that the chance of her accepting the call was slim to none. I was about to hang up when I heard a voice, barely above a whisper.

"Kirby?"

"Ma?" I wanted to cry.

"Baby, how are you?" She was talking so low that I had to press the phone to my ear to hear her. I'd checked the time to be sure I was calling during a time my father would be at work.

"I'm okay, Ma. Is he there?" I asked.

"Yes, I had to go to the doctor, and he went with me."

"How are you feeling? What did the doctor say?" I asked. My mother wasn't in the best of health. She'd had breast cancer a few years back.

"I'm fine, Kirby. They changed my medicine, but I'm on the mend."

Hearing her say that made me feel a little better. "That's good. Where is he?"

"He's in the den; I'm in the kitchen," she told me, then added, "I heard what happened in court yesterday. Kirby, you can't be doing that type of thing. You must control your temper."

"No, Ma, but he was lying on me. You know how much I've changed, Ma. I'm not a bad person." I leaned against the wall and stared down at the concrete floor, fighting back tears.

"I know you aren't, son, but I've always told you that you have to control your temper. People think the worst of you because you dress like the worst of us." Now, that was a line right out of my father's mouth. "Did you get the money I sent? They said it would take a few days before it was in your account. It's not much, but I put a little something in there."

"Not yet, but whatever it is, I appreciate it." I knew it wasn't easy to do things like that with my father always hovering around.

"You know I'm praying for you. I wish I could get over there to see you, but because I don't drive, it's hard. But I love you, and—"

"Who the hell is that?" I heard my father's voice, and my heart started racing.

"It's no one. I'll call you back, Norma," my mother said. I heard her trying to hang up the phone.

"Hello? Hello? Who the hell is this?" my father yelled into the receiver. "And I know it ain't no fucking Norma!"

"It's me, Dad."

"Didn't I tell you not to accept any calls from him? We don't have anything to say to you. Don't be calling here begging for shit, because we ain't—"

"He didn't call begging," my mother cried out in the background.

"Dad, I didn't ask for anything. I just called to talk to Mom, that's all," I explained respectfully, hoping he would give her back the phone.

"Talk to her about what? About how you're showing your ass in that courtroom and embarrassing this family even more than you already have?" he snapped.

"No, not that." I felt a lump rising in my throat. "Dad, I'm so sorry. Please know that. I love you and Mom. That's all I need for you to know."

"Stop calling my damn house. Your mother has enough going on with these doctors' appointments, and she don't need to be stressed. I won't have you doing that to her. Do us both a favor and stop calling. I mean it!" He hung up the phone.

I stood there, holding the receiver, feeling even worse than I had before making the call. I'd hoped that talking to my mother would make me feel better. Now, I realized that it was a call I should've never made. My life was fucked up, and the more I tried to fix it, the worse it became.

"You finished with that phone call?" one of the inmates walked over and asked.

"Man, you ain't gotta ask him that. Take that phone from his ass if you need it," another guy yelled. "That punk-ass nigga ain't gonna do shit."

Laughter erupted, and the guy gave me a pitiful look. A few months ago, I was one of the most well-respected guys in there, and now I was a laughingstock. I put the phone back on the receiver and walked away.

I walked over to my bunk and took the few toiletries I had left and headed to the shower area. I'd been holding onto something for Tony, and he'd forgotten to take it back. I had a better use for it than he did.

In the bathroom, I turned on the shower as hot as it could get, then stripped down except for my shower shoes. I stepped in and stood there, wanting to wash away all the bullshit and pain of my life. I had nothing and no one. I had sunk to my lowest point and become an embarrassment to my family, my friends, and myself. The only thing I could count on were daily beatings from my fellow inmates. My life was hopeless, and I just wanted to disappear from everyone and everything.

Langston

56

"Man, your pops did his thing in there today," Tony shouted out of nowhere. I'd been half asleep, dreaming of Simone in the seat next to him on the corrections bus when his voice startled me.

"Yeah, he was pretty good," I replied with pride, looking out the window. We were just crossing the bridge from East Elmhurst to Rikers.

"Man, that's putting it lightly. That dude Meat was trying to make me look like I was some sorta kingpin or something. But your old man tore him apart on that witness stand." Tony laughed.

"Did you see the way he was stuttering?" I said, joining his laughter. My father had made me proud today and reminded me why I wanted to be a lawyer and continue our family tradition.

When our laughter died down, I turned to Tony and said, "That lying sack of shit was really out to hurt us."

"Yeah, well, it's a good thing they transferred his ass to PC, because you know what snitches get." The anger I saw in him that morning when he entered the bus was starting to come out again. In the four years I'd known him, I'd never seen him like this. "But me and my people gonna see him, protective custody or not. That nigga's gonna wear a buck fifty."

"What about Krush? You gonna give him a buck fifty too?" I cringed at the thought. Krush was already so bruised and cut up that I didn't know if he could handle another wound that would need stitches.

"I haven't made up my mind yet." Tony eased back in his seat, silently fuming. His demeanor scared me.

"Tony, you know this wasn't Krush's fault, right? You know he would never do anything to hurt you. He just likes to be the big man on campus and run his mouth. He always has."

"This ain't school, Lang." He lifted his hands so I could see his cuffs. "This is fucking jail. You run your mouth, you best be able to back that shit up. And Krush is a punk."

"I know that, T, but can't you give him a pass just this once? You said it yourself: when everyone thought you was losing it, Krush looked out for you."

With Krush being barred from the courtroom and me in a different unit, I didn't get to see him before I got on the bus that morning. As angry as Tony had been after Meat's testimony, I wouldn't be surprised if he had already taken it out on Krush.

"You didn't do anything to him last night, did you?" I asked.

"Nah. For now, I just made him move his bed as far away from me as possible."

I tried not to let it show, but I was relieved.

"I heard he got his ass whipped again last night, but it wasn't from my people," Tony said. "Krush is his own worst enemy. A few days ago, I had to stop this dude from making Krush his bitch."

The thought of that turned my stomach. "So, after today, you and him cool?"

He thought about it for a second, then said, "I wouldn't say we cool, but he don't have nothing to worry about from me. And I'll keep them off his back best I can. I'm just trying to go home, Lang. That's it."

"Me too, bro," I said as the bus came to a halt and we were escorted off.

Tony went to his unit, and I had just arrived at mine when one of the COs announced my name. "Hudson, let's go!" he yelled, walking toward me with a pair of cuffs.

"What? Go where?" I asked. "I just got back here. Where am I going?"

"Shut the hell up and come on," he said. "You don't ask no questions. You do what the hell you're told."

I glared at him as I held my wrists out for him to cuff. All eyes were on me as we walked out of my unit and down a long string of corridors and gates to an area I'd never been in. Finally, I reached a door where we were met by two forty-something-year-old white men. They had badges hooked to their belts, but they weren't from the Department of Corrections or NYPD.

"We got it from here," one of them said, reaching for me.

I began to panic. I didn't know who the hell they were or where they were taking me. I thought about running, but the thought that I would probably be shot before I got ten feet away quickly changed my mind.

"Wait, who are you? And where are we going?" I asked as they led me out of the building toward a black sedan.

"US marshals," one of them finally said as he opened the back door and guided me into the car. I ducked my head as I slid in. What could the Feds possibly want with me? I hoped I wasn't being slapped with federal charges for the heroin. I racked my brain, trying to remember what I'd learned in law school. Could they even do that, switch charges from state to federal in the middle of a trial? And, I wondered, were Krush and Tony being picked up too? I looked around in search of another car, but I didn't see one.

"Where are we going?" I repeated as they got into the car. Neither one said anything as the car pulled off and we headed off to God knows where.

Around forty minutes later, we pulled into the garage of a building in downtown Manhattan. They used their credentials to open the door to the building, and we went inside and got on what looked like a service elevator. Neither one said anything to me, and I still didn't have a clue where I was being taken to. The elevator stopped, and they walked me down a dim hallway, finally bringing me into an empty office. I looked around, feeling even more confused. Then a side door opened, and I turned nervously in that direction.

"Uncuff him," my mother said. The marshals wasted no time removing the cuffs from my wrists.

"Give us a call when you're ready to take him back," one of the men said. They quickly turned and headed out of the room, leaving my mother and me alone.

"What is going on?" I asked, feeling weak in the knees after all that cloak and dagger shit.

"How are you, Langston?" She touched the side of my face then wrapped her arms around me in an awkward embrace. Instead of flinching and groaning like I normally did when she tried to be affectionate, I hugged her back.

"I'm fine, Ma," I told her. "But I still don't know what's happening here. Are you breaking me out of jail?"

"Hell no, boy! Ain't nobody breaking you out." She shook her head and gave me a half smile. I had to admit I was a little disappointed. Had she said yes, I wouldn't have resisted. It would've been a boss-ass move. "I wanted to see you and I didn't want to see my son behind bars. So, I decided to invite you to dinner." She turned and opened the door she had just come through and beckoned for me to follow.

I hesitated. "Dinner?"

"Yes. All the other times I've invited you to dinner, you brought that girl. Now, you don't have a choice, do you?"

"Her name is Simone, Mom."

"Yes, of course, dear."

We stepped into a large conference room. Immediately, the source of the amazing aroma came into view. Spread out on the conference table was a smorgasboard of all my favorite foods: steak, snow crab legs, macaroni and cheese, smothered pork chops, and fried green tomatoes.

"You hungry?" She held a plate out toward me.

"Heck yeah!" I wasted no time taking it from her and piling it high.

My mother laughed happily. "You don't have to put everything on one plate, Langston. You have time for seconds, or thirds, if you like."

She made her own plate, and we sat across from each other at the end of the table. I dug in, enjoying every bite. My mother poured me a glass of iced tea, and I paused long enough to take a gulp.

"I can't believe you did all of this, Ma." I sighed, cutting into my steak.

"Well, I do have some pull with my position," she said coyly. "There are some things your mama can make happen for you."

"You're right about that. I'm lucky." I suddenly realized that while I was indulging in a meal fit for a king, my boys were still in Rikers, eating swill and cookies for dinner. Guilt and sadness came over me.

"Ma, can you make us getting out of jail happen?"

"I wish I could, Langston." She paused for a minute. "But I did want to talk to you about this situation. I have some thoughts." She sat back and became serious.

"What are they?"

"I've looked at this thing, and I really think you should probably do the same thing that Kwesi did and take the deal."

"Deal? What deal?"

"Your father turned down a plea agreement that I feel you should have taken."

"Mom, wait. . . ."

"Langston, I know you want this thing to go to trial, but if you take the plea agreement, you'll probably have to do less than a year."

My mind began racing. My father hadn't mentioned anything to me about a plea agreement, and neither did Lamont. I didn't want my mother to know that, so I decided to act as if I understood. The deal must not have been worth mentioning if they hadn't said anything.

"Mom, I know you're trying to help, but Dad is the best. If he thinks we can win at trial, then we can win at trial," I told her, picking up one of the crab legs and biting it. The sweet juice leaked out and went down my chin. She picked up a napkin and wiped it like I was a toddler.

"Your father is a brilliant attorney. He can deliver a poignant argument, and his knowledge of the law is beyond impressive. I'll give him that. He's won some landmark cases. But, Langston, your mother is a judge, and a damn good one. I see things from a totally different perspective, and I'm telling you, this case isn't as strong as he thinks it is. Trust me on this one."

"Trust you?" I raised an eyebrow at her.

"Fine, I get it. I'm probably the last person who should be talking to you about trust. I admit I made some poor choices when it came to my family, and I chose my career. I'm woman enough to admit it and apologize for it."

"So, this whole dinner with your incarcerated son is your way of making amends? Kinda like the car, huh? This is some kind of penance for your guilt, and now you're trying to throw a monkey wrench between me and Dad?" I frowned, suddenly ready to leave.

"No, that's not it at all," she said, obviously hurt by my words. "Despite the strained relationship that you and I have, Langston, you are my son, and I love you dearly. I don't want you to spend another night in jail, let alone a year. At the end of the day, I don't give a shit about Bradley. My concern is you, and only you. Take the deal, son."

I heard a phone ring with a sinister tone, and she heaved a loud sigh. "Hold on a minute, sweetie. That's your father. He probably found out that you're with me." She took the phone out of her purse and rolled her eyes as she answered. "Hello, Bradley. What can I do for you?"

I began to eat again as my mother put on airs, making dramatic faces while she listened to my father.

"Yes, Bradley, he is with me." My mother was silent for a second, then the attitude dropped off her face. She looked stricken. "You want me to tell him what? . . . I can't tell him that."

"What, what is it, Ma?" I asked. Her demeanor told me it wasn't anything good.

She didn't speak. She just placed the phone on speaker.

"Dad, what's going on? What wrong with Mom?" I asked hurriedly.

I could hear him exhale wearily. "Son, I don't know how to tell you this, but . . . but Krush is dead."

I was sure I hadn't heard him correctly. "Wait. What did you say, Dad?"

Once again, he let out a huff of air. "I said your friend Krush is dead. He slit his wrists with a razor in the shower at Rikers."

Langston

57

I felt like I'd been moving in a dense fog for the past week. Thank God the judge had ordered the trial halted for the rest of the week for bereavement, because without it, I might have had a mental breakdown. I felt like I was about to cry every time I thought about my poor frat brother taking his own life.

On our first day back to court, Tony and I were escorted into a small attorney's room to meet with my father, Desiree, and Lamont after we dressed. When we were alone, Dad hugged us both tight.

"Listen, I know this is hard on you both. I really am sorry about Kirb—I mean Krush. He was a nice young man, and his death shocked us all, but we've gotta get ready for what's about to happen when we go in there today," Dad explained.

"Kwesi," I said.

"Yes, Kwesi." Dad nodded. "Now, we don't know exactly what his testimony will be, but most likely it's going to be exactly what the DA needs it to be. Just like they did with Meat."

"I can't believe Kwesi's doing this." I stared at the table as tears began to well up in my eyes once again. I looked over to Tony, who was dazed and confused.

"Well, he is, and we need to be prepared," Dad said.

"Krush is gone, and Kwesi's turned his back on us. Do we even have a chance to win this, Mr. Hudson?" Tony asked. "Be honest."

Dad glanced at my brother, who spoke up.

"That's the plan, but the best way to make that happen is to change our strategy," Lamont said.

"To what?" I asked.

Lamont looked at my Dad as if waiting for permission to proceed—or like he really didn't want to have to be the one to say it. I immediately felt it in my gut. I knew what their plan was before Lamont even said it out loud.

"We're going to have to put the drugs on Krush." Lamont was unable to make eye contact as he admitted their shameless strategy.

"What? Hell no. Not Krush." I shook my head. "I'm not doing that. I'm not putting this on him."

"You have to. It's the best chance you have of getting out of here," Desiree said.

"No way. Krush was a good dude, not some hardcore street thug like you want to make him into now that he's not here to defend himself. We're not gonna be disloyal to his memory like that," I insisted. "Come up with another strategy."

Dad said, "This isn't about loyalty. It's about reasonable doubt. Do we really know that the drugs didn't belong to him? Maybe that's why he decided to—"

"Don't, Dad! Don't do that," I said, no longer fighting back the tears.

"We wouldn't have to testify that he did it, would we?" Tony asked.

"Lamont and I will insinuate it, and I'll hopefully lead Kwesi down that road," Dad explained. "But eventually, one of you is going to have to testify. Most likely it will be you, Langston, because you were driving, and we don't want the State to bring Tony's brothers' criminal record into this, which they will if he's on the stand."

I stood my ground. "We're not doing this. I know Kwesi. He's not going—"

Tony stopped me. "We don't know what Kwesi is gonna do, Lang. We thought we knew Krush, didn't we? Right now, we need to do whatever we can to get up out of here."

"I hear you," I said to Tony, "but we ain't blaming Krush."

"Then dammit, let's blame Kwesi!" Tony replied.

Lamont looked at Dad and kind of shrugged like it wasn't the worst idea he'd ever heard. "I like blaming the guy who can't rebuke us more, but it could work," he said. "This would still create reasonable doubt."

"Langston?" My father stared at me, waiting for a response.

Finally, I had to admit I was backed into a corner with no way out—at least not one that would allow me to stay loyal to my frat brother. "Okay, but only if he blames us," I said.

Twenty minutes later, we were sitting in the courtroom, listening to the judge address the jury. The atmosphere was somber. Probably everyone was still in a state of shock, including ADA Brown and the judge.

"Ladies and gentlemen of the jury, I'd like to start by thanking you for your cooperation and patience with this situation," the judge started. Then he turned to James Brown and said, "When we recessed, the prosecution stated it had one final witness. Are you ready to proceed?"

My heart began pounding, and I stared at the side where inmates entered the courtroom, knowing that Kwesi was about to enter and try to seal our fate. I thought about the times he and I had shared and the conversations we'd had over the course of our friendship. Out of everyone, Kwesi had been the who stressed the importance of loyalty among us. We knew he would give us his last dime and the shirt off his back if we needed it, and he had expected the same from us. I couldn't believe he was now about to take the stand and testify against us. I swallowed hard as James Brown stood up.

"Your Honor, in light of the overwhelming evidence and testimony in our favor, the State rests its case at this time. We have no further witnesses."

There was a collective gasp in the courtroom.

So, Kwesi was not testifying after all? Unsure of what this meant, I looked over at my father. He seemed just as confused as I was.

"Okay then," the judge said. "Mr. Hudson, is the defense ready to proceed?"

"Yes, Your Honor." My father stood up. "However, we were expecting the State to continue their case, so we are requesting a one-day recess so that we may prepare."

The judge paused for a moment to consider the request. I swear my heart stopped beating while we waited. Finally, he said, "That will be fine. We will resume tomorrow morning when the defense will present its first witness."

As soon as the gavel hit the podium and we stood, I put my arm on Tony's shoulder then looked at my father, feeling pride for my frat. "I told you. I know my brothers. We would never turn our backs on each other."

Bradley

58

The office had been a somber place in the week after Krush's death, and now that we had begun to present our case, the pressure was enormous. The whole team had been working late, and the night wasn't getting any younger when I walked into the conference room. Lamont, Desiree, and Perk were all diligently working on their individual pieces of Langston's case, and nobody even looked up. I took my regular seat, placing a folder on the conference room table.

I silently watched them for a while. They had no idea how much I loved them—even Perk, who was like a son to me. I looked around the room at all the photos of great Harlemites we'd represented and the civic awards Hudson and Associates had received. We'd come a long way since that one-room office in the basement of a brownstone thirty-something years ago. I felt good about what I had built, and I had hoped to see Langston working alongside them at this very table. Now, I was starting to have my doubts about that.

I yawned and stretched my arms out wide, placing my feet up on the conference room table. Working on Langston's case had worn me out, and I was starting to feel my age. I'd handled even more intense cases than this one, but none had taken its toll on me as physically and mentally as this one. Then again, none of the other cases involved one of my children. Something else had also been weighing heavily on my mind lately, and it was becoming quite a distraction. I'd decided it was time to get it off my chest so my head would be clear for Langston's defense.

"So, Lamont," I said. "You've been trying to get my ear for weeks about the future of this firm. Talk to me."

Lamont raised an eyebrow. "Now? I'm working on my notes for Langston's testimony tomorrow."

Lamont was always trying to tell me what I needed to change, or what I was doing wrong. I was impressed that with this serious work in front of him, he was staying focused. That type of dedication would make him a superstar attorney after a few more years of experience. Still, I needed to have this conversation now, so I didn't back down.

"Come on," I pushed.

Desiree lifted her head up from the file it was buried in, looked at Lamont, then returned her attention to the file.

I could see the wheels turning in his head as he gathered his thoughts, mentally assembling his presentation.

"Well, the short answer is . . ." he started.

I gave him an indifferent nod.

"I think we've reached a point where we either grow or die."

Once again, Desiree snapped her head up. She shot me a look as if to suggest she knew where Lamont was about to go with his spiel, and she wanted to redirect.

She looked to Lamont. "That doesn't feel like an exaggeration to you? I mean, last year was our best year yet."

"Let him talk, Des." I wanted to hear what Lamont had to say. For the past ten years, I might have been the public face of Hudson and Associates, but Lamont was the high-performance engine running in the background. I probably didn't say it enough, but he had no idea how much I relied on him. Maybe it was time to let him take the lead on some things.

"There's all sorts of business out there that we could solicit if we're willing to heighten our profile," Lamont said. "If we don't, we have to recognize that outside of criminal defense work, our client base is either dying off or moving away."

"He's got a point," I said to Desiree. "We've lost two church accounts, and Homewood Insurance is almost ninety days late on our last invoice."

Desiree stared at me. She had no answer for that.

"But heighten the profile how, Lamont?" Perk chimed in.

"By moving downtown and going after *corporate* clients," Desiree answered derisively on Lamont's behalf. My daughter was such a progressive liberal. "You know, defend downtown hotels against unionizing, help companies dodge liability, defend wage discrimination, the stuff that really pays. Right, Lamont?"

I could tell these two were about to get started on one of their tangents, as Lamont was ready with a counter.

"If murderers and purse snatchers can be innocent until proven guilty, then what's wrong with applying the same principle to those who can actually afford our services?" Lamont asked.

"Oh, so now we base it all on a person's income?" Desiree fired back.

"No," Lamont said. "But we don't go broke springing tree-huggers on some feel-good pro bono trip either."

Desiree pointed her finger at Lamont. "Well, that Russ Oil tree-hugging lawsuit sure paid us, and—"

"Will y'all please just—You two do this every time, until one of you takes it personal," Perk said, rubbing his temples with his forefingers.

"No, Perk," I said. "I think the time for debate is now."

The three of them looked at me strangely, probably wary of the fact that I was egging them on to continue the fight. Normally I was the first one putting a stop to their battles. Of course, part of me still wished they would shut up, but this was a conversation that needed to be had, especially if I was going to avert the looming crisis.

"Lamont, you really feel strongly about making changes?"

"I do, Dad."

"I guess the only question now is, are you committed to taking *this* firm to that level?"

"Of course I am. I've always been committed to the firm."

I locked eyes with my son and challenged him. "Have you?"

"Are you serious, Dad?" Desiree shouted, fearful that I was buying into Lamont's corporate plans. "You'd really move Hudson and Associates out of Harlem?"

"No, but if my son and partner came and talked to me man to man, explaining how he felt, I might open up a satellite office downtown." I placed my feet on the floor and turned to face Lamont. "Harlem will always be our headquarters, but we practice law all over the world."

"Amen to that," Lamont said.

"Don't go sprinkling holy water on yourself so fast, young man. I started this conversation for a reason—and it all hinges on you."

Lamont smiled confidently. "Why? Because I'd be heading up the office downtown?"

"No, because you can't run our downtown office, or any other office, if you don't work here," I said with finality.

The room fell ominously silent, and all three of them stared at me.

Desiree spoke. "Daddy, what are you saying?"

"I think I just said it."

They all looked surprised, but Lamont appeared to actually be in pain. "Are you firing me?"

I couldn't help myself. I had to laugh. "No, but I probably should. I'm too hurt to do it now. Like your mother, you've broken my heart, Lamont."

"Daddy, what are you talking about? He was just expressing himself. You always encouraged us to speak our minds," Des said.

"Yes, I have, but I don't consider this speaking your mind. I consider this blindsided betrayal." I handed the folder of documents to Desiree. Lamont and I were now staring each other down. He knew exactly what I knew, and his sister and Perk would soon know it too.

When she read the documents and then lifted her head, her facial expression told the story for all of us. She handed it to Perk. "What the fuck, Lamont? When were you going to tell us you were leaving?"

I'd found the documents they were reading in the executive fax machine an hour ago. Lamont had been faxing a copy to another law firm. It was a list of Lamont's clients, and a letter accepting the other firm's offer of partnership.

Lamont

59

I was more concerned about the tension between me, my father, and my sister than I was about the line of questioning I was about to present in court. I knew they were still upset over what they called my betrayal. My old man hadn't said two words to me all morning. If I was honest with myself, I could kind of understand why they felt that way. I'd never mentioned leaving the firm, so Dad felt blindsided, and it didn't help that I'd been sharing client information with the new firm. Things would have gone much smoother if I'd found a way to talk to them about this, instead of Dad finding out the way he did. For a smart guy, I sure as hell was pretty damn stupid to leave those papers in the fax machine.

After my father blew his top, I'd wasted no time leaving the office. I tried calling Desiree, but she ignored my calls. Hopefully, they would cool off soon, because as much as I tried to act like nothing was wrong, the tension was noticeable.

"What's going on?" Langston leaned over and asked.

"Nothing."

"Did something happen? Why is everyone acting so weird?" he whispered.

"No one's acting weird. Just focus on your testimony. We've paraded enough character witness up here the past few days to nominate you for sainthood. All you have to do is be yourself and tell the truth. You're the last witness of this trial, and yours will be the last voice they remember, other than Dad's closing statements."

"Mr. Hudson, are you ready for your next witness?" the judge asked.

I adjusted my jacket as I stood up and said, "Yes, the defense would like to call Langston Hudson to the stand."

Langston walked with his head held high, looking very much like our father. He'd taken my advice and made sure to get a fresh haircut and shave. As he placed his hand on the Bible that the bailiff held out for him, I glanced over at the jury box. Most of them had neutral expressions, and no one looked angry, so that was a good sign.

"Please state your full name," I said.

"Langston Baldwin Hudson." Langston's voice was confident as he answered.

I continued asking him basic questions about school, his major, his GPA, and the extracurricular and community service activities he was involved in. I needed the jury to get a full picture of who he was and what he was all about, and I wanted them to hear it from his mouth. The longer he talked about himself, the more I saw the faces of some jury members softening. He was a good kid, a likeable kid, and they appeared to be getting that impression from his testimony. That was good, because once the discussion turned toward the drugs, I needed them to feel empathy for Lang.

"Mr. Hudson, can you tell us what happened on the morning in question?"

Langston looked directly at the jury as he gave his account of the events leading up to his arrest. He described the traffic stop, including the weed that Krush had been smoking. I'd been able to convince him that it wasn't disloyal to tell the truth about that. The only other choice would have been to leave it out, and then Brown would have painted him as a liar on cross examination. He also made sure to say it was the first time he'd ever been pulled over. He laid it on thick as he described how scary it was, as a young black man, to be pulled over and questioned just for driving back to college. I shot a quick glance at a black woman on the jury, but I couldn't tell by her face how she felt about those comments. I was hoping she would feel sympathy for him.

He concluded with, "And the next thing I knew, they were putting us all in handcuffs."

"And, Mr. Hudson, did the drugs in the car belong to you?"

"No, they did not," Langston said emphatically. "They weren't my drugs, and I don't know how they got into the trunk. I'd never seen them before."

"No further questions. Thank you, Mr. Hudson." I gave Langston a reassuring smile. I wasn't sure how his testimony was received by the jury, but Lang had presented himself as a respectable young college student, and I hoped that impression would last when they went to deliberate.

The courtroom door opened, and I turned around to see Perk walking in. I glanced over at my father and waited for his instructions. He shook his head at me, then tapped the face of his watch.

"Your Honor, we would like to request a brief recess at this time," I said.

"We'll resume in five minutes," the judge said.

As the boys were escorted to the back to use the restroom, Perk made his way over to the defense table.

"What do you have?" Dad asked.

Perk had a solemn look on his face. "The heroin didn't come from the same source. One sample came from Colombia, and the other from Afghanistan. Test just came back about an hour ago."

"Well, at least we don't have to throw Tony under the bus to save Lang," Desiree injected bitterly.

"Yes, but it still doesn't tell us where these damn drugs came from." My father placed his hand on his ear, listening to Carla through the earpiece. "And we've got another problem."

"What's that?" I asked

"Carla just told me that we've lost jurors two and five, Lamont."

"That's impossible," I said, turning to the jury members as they were filing out for their break. The two women I'd been exchanging flirtatious glances with throughout the trial wouldn't even look at me now. *What the fuck?*

We sat in miserable silence until the break ended.

"All rise," the bailiff said as the judge walked in. Perk headed back to the seats behind our table.

"Mr. Hudson, are we ready to proceed?"

"Ah, yes, Your Honor," I said, glancing over at the two women again. They stared straight ahead coldly.

"Your witness, Mr. Brown," the judge called out.

"Thank you." James walked over toward Langston. "Mr. Hudson, you admit that you were driving the car when you were pulled over, correct?"

"Yes, I was the one driving."

"And you're also the owner of the car where the drugs were found, right?"

"Yes."

"And you're the one who put the drugs in the trunk, were you not?" James turned dramatically and faced the people sitting in the courtroom.

"No, I wasn't," Langston said. I could see the confidence he'd had when he first sat on the stand was slowly leaving. I knew it was because James was intimidating him.

"Then where did they come from? It was your car, and you said it was a new car that you'd just gotten, right?"

"Yes, it was, but I don't—"

"So, how did the drugs get there?"

"I don't know, I—"

"Come on, Mr. Hudson. You already admitted that you all were smoking marijuana."

I jumped up and yelled "Objection, Your Honor! He's badgering the witness!"

"I'm just trying to get a straight answer out of him. He keeps hesitating," James exclaimed.

"Sustained. Mr. Brown, have a little more patience." The judge gave James a warning look.

I sat back down and locked eyes with Langston. After I gave him a nod, he took a deep breath, then said, "They weren't my drugs, and I didn't put them there."

"Let me ask you, are you responsible for putting gas in the car?"

"Yes," Lang replied.

"What about oil, the tires, and insurance? Is that all your responsibility?"

"Yes, but my mom gives me the money for the insurance."

A few people in the back laughed, and the judge shot them a warning look.

"Good, so you're responsible for the car. Am I correct?"

"Yeah, if you put it that way, I am."

"Well, if it was your car, Mr. Hudson, and you're responsible for it, then ultimately anything in it is your responsibility, wouldn't you say?"

A confused look came across Langston's face. I could feel the trap closing, and I wanted to scream out to my brother, "Fuck loyalty! Just say it!" All he had to do was open his mouth and say the drugs belonged to Krush, and we would have the jury right where we wanted them. They already liked Langston and feared Krush.

From the corner of my eye, I saw Tony sit up in his seat. I wondered if he was thinking the same thing I was.

Lang inhaled deeply then began his answer in a strong voice. "Being responsible for a vehicle does not make me responsible for the contents that a third party may have placed in it without my knowledge."

He then looked over at the jury and said, "Yes, Krush was smoking weed, and I know that was wrong. But we would never touch heroin or any other narcotic. We volunteer to help young African American boys in the community, and we guide and encourage them to stay away from drugs. We pride ourselves on being role models and living examples of doing the right thing and working hard to become successful in life. Every night, I beat myself up because I'm right where I tell those little kids not to end up, and I'm disappointed because I know I've let them down. That's important to me, and to every one of us that was in that car. That's how I know the drugs didn't belong to any of us."

Damn. I watched Langston dab at the corner of his eye to stop the tears that had formed. I had to do the same thing, and so did several other people in the courtroom. My brother had made a hell of a statement. I was proud of him.

"No further questions," James said.

"Redirect?" the judge asked.

"No, Your Honor," I said.

My father had handed me a note during James Brown's cross examination of Langston, so I knew we had one more angle to try, but we needed time. I didn't know yet if Langston's speech had pulled any jurors back over to our side, but his passionate statement would be the last thing they heard today.

"We have one more witness flying in tomorrow morning, and then we should be ready to rest our case," I said.

"Then court is adjourned until tomorrow morning at nine o'clock." The judge slammed his gavel down, and the day's proceedings had ended.

Tony

60

I was a ball of nerves and felt like I was about to throw up as I watched the final witness for the defense give his testimony. How Bradley Hudson had convinced former Congressman Cozy Thompson, who also happened to be the president of our fraternity, to testify on our behalf was beyond me. Normally, our organization kept a safe distance from situations like the one we'd found ourselves in.

"No further questions for this witness," Bradley said.

"Mr. Brown?" the judge called out.

"We have no questions, Your Honor," James told him.

I knew the Hudsons were relieved. Langston might have met Cozy once, but I sure as heck hadn't. Cozy was vouching for the character of two people he didn't even know, and a few questions from the ADA would have made Cozy's character endorsement worthless to the jury.

"Any other witnesses at this time, Mr. Hudson?" the judge asked.

"No, Your Honor. The defense rests." Bradley's voice was strong and confident.

"Then we will hear closing arguments in the mor—"

James stood up and interrupted. "Your Honor, just one moment, please."

"What is it, counselor?"

"The State would like to call a rebuttal witness at this time."

The judge looked like he didn't appreciate the sudden change of plans. "And what witness is this?"

James turned and faced the defense table as he said calmly, "We'd like to call Anthony Baker at this time."

"What?"

"Objection! You can't do that!" Bradley, Desiree, and Lamont all shouted at once.

"He put Langston Hudson on the stand. I would like to present a rebuttal witness, Your Honor," James Brown replied.

There was confused chattering coming from both the spectators and the jurors. The only two people who seemed to understand what was happening were James Brown and me. I could feel Langston's eyes on me, but I refused to look at him. I was too busy telling myself that I had no other choice but to do what I had agreed to do.

"Tony, what the fuck is going on?" he whispered.

I didn't answer. I just sat there, waiting to be called up to the witness stand.

"Your Honor, he can't call Mr. Baker to the stand. We wish to invoke his Fifth Amendment right at this time," Bradley said.

"Mr. Baker reached out to me this morning through his new attorney and entered a plea agreement," James Brown said, smirking at Bradley as he spoke.

"What? We are the attorney of record. This is some bull—"

"Hudson!" the judge yelled and struck the gavel.

As the two lawyers began going back and forth, I closed my eyes and thought back to the night before. Right after chow, I'd snuck into the bathroom to call some females using the cell phone I'd taken from Krush. Then I called my mom, because she hadn't been in court for the past few days. She'd never missed more than two days in a row before, and I was kind of worried. I dialed the number, but there was no answer. I dialed again, and after making three more attempts, I called my brother Aaron.

"Yo, what's up? I can't reach Ma," I told him.

"Yo, shit is real crazy around here," he said.

"What do you mean? Why?"

"She's locked up. The cops got her on a gun charge, and they trying to say there's a body on it."

"What gun?" I had to stop myself from losing my shit, because I didn't want the guards to come in and find me with the phone.

"That same gun she had back when we was kids."

"Fuck! Are you serious? Where is she now?"

"They got her out there in Staten Island. They ain't even processed her fully yet. This ain't good, bro. Ma ain't gonna last with diabetes and her bad foot. Why the hell they got her out in Staten Island anyway?"

"I know why," I said.

I knew it had something to do with that motherfucker Brown. I ended the call and went to my bunk, not even trying to fight the silent tears that were falling. I was in jail, Adonis was in jail, and now my mother was in jail. My heart ached as I thought about the woman who had raised me and how much I loved her. I would do whatever it took to get her out of there. Before lights out, I had the COs call the DA's office. By midnight, I had a new lawyer and a promise that my momma would go free.

The judge asked the jury to leave the courtroom, then instructed me to take the stand to be sworn in.

"Mr. Baker, when did you notify Mr. Brown of this information?" the judge asked.

"Uh . . . last night."

"And were you offered some sort of plea agreement?"

"Sorta."

"And who approached you about this deal? Did Mr. Brown contact you?" the judge asked.

"No, I contacted him when I found out that my old lawyer didn't properly explain the three to five we were offered." I looked over at the defense table and saw every one of the Hudsons glaring at me. I didn't give a shit, though. My mother was all that mattered.

"Was your attorney present to sign off on this plea?"

"Yeah, my new lawyer was."

"We have a signed waiver of counsel, Your Honor. It's right here. Mr. Baker was reminded of his Miranda Rights, and he understood them." James Brown passed the bailiff the paper I'd signed when he came over to Riker's that morning to meet with me.

"Mr. Baker, you are aware that if I approve this waiver of counsel, then you no longer have a lawyer representing you?" the judge asked.

"Yeah," I answered.

The judge read the paper he'd been handed and then said, "Looks correct to me, Mr. Hudson. I'm going to allow Mr. Baker to testify. Bring the jury back in."

During my testimony, James Brown had me repeat the details of our arrest, starting with Langston being pulled over, and everything that happened up until the search of the trunk. I confirmed everything that the other officers had said during the trial.

"And, Mr. Baker, do you know who the heroin that was found in the trunk of the car belonged to?" James asked.

"Yes." I nodded.

"Can you tell us?"

I looked down and said, "Langston Hudson."

Langston bolted out of his seat. "What? You lying bastard! Why would you get up there and lie?"

"Mr. Hudson, control your client!" the judge yelled.

Lamont grabbed his brother and pulled him down.

"And do you know where Mr. Hudson got the drugs?" James continued.

"He got them from a connect I know through my brothers. We met up with him at this underground strip club, and he offered a sweet deal. Lang said he wanted to bring the heroin back to D.C. so he could triple his money, because the street value is higher."

"You're a goddamn lie, Tony!" Langston yelled.

"Objection! This is all hearsay!" Bradley shouted.

"No, this isn't hearsay if Mr. Baker witnessed the exchange, Your Honor," James said calmly.

"Overruled."

"So, is it your testimony that the drugs in question were bought and paid for by Langston Hudson?"

"Yes. How else do you think they got in the car?" I said, feeling nothing. As soon as I'd agreed to testify against Lang, I forced myself to go numb inside. I couldn't afford to feel guilty. The only thing I could think about was my mother's freedom.

"No further questions."

I guess the ADA had decided to quit while he was ahead. The damage had already been done. I had helped him poke the biggest hole in Hudson's case, and it was deflating fast. Between Meat's testimony, Krush's violent outburst, and now me, it was looking like this case was going to be the major win the bastard had been wanting.

"Cross, Mr. Hudson?" The judge aimed the question at Bradley, who was already headed toward me with a hateful look.

"Your Honor, I request that this entire testimony be thrown out and the jury be instructed to disregard—"

"No can do, Mr. Hudson. Please ask the witness a question."

Bradley looked like he was struggling to hold it together as he turned to question me. "Tony, why are you just now coming forth with this information? Why didn't you say something sooner?"

"Because . . . you were my lawyer. You told me I couldn't testify, that only Langston could, because you didn't want them to ask me any questions," I mumbled, refusing to look up at him.

"Oh, really? Is that the only reason why?"

"Yeah."

"So why now?" I could hear from his tone that he was suspicious. He probably knew that ADA Brown was somehow behind this, but hell, I wasn't gonna help him prove that. If Bradley and James Brown wanted to kill each other, that was none of my fucking business. I just wanted my mother to go home.

"Well, I thought about it, and why should I go to jail for something I didn't do?" I shrugged, not knowing what else to say.

"Tony, what the hell did you do?" Langston yelled out.

I stared at the floor.

"Mr. Hudson, one more outburst from your client and he'll be escorted out and found in contempt," the judge warned.

Bradley walked over to Langston and whispered something in his ear. Then he said to the judge, "I have no more questions for this witness."

I slowly exited the witness stand, my shoulders slumped and my heart empty. I'd done what had to be done to save my mother, and that was the only thing that mattered, even if I had to betray my best friend in the process.

James announced, "The State rests."

Bradley

61

Six hours. It had only taken six hours for the jury to come back. Any first-year law student knew that wasn't a good sign. Taking my seat at the defense table, I glanced over at James, who was laughing and joking with his colleague like he didn't have a care in the world. I wanted to go over and punch him in the throat for his aggressive prosecution of my son. But then Langston walked out the side entrance, and I tried to calm down. He hugged his sister, brother, and then me. It took me quite a while to let him go, because I was swept with an overwhelming feeling of guilt, and they hadn't even read the verdict yet.

The twelve members of jury entered their box, and I placed my earpiece in preparation for the judge's arrival. When he walked in, the tension in the courtroom was through the roof.

"Testing, one, two, three," I whispered.

"Hey, handsome," I heard in my ear.

"Hey," I replied as the judge spoke to the jury.

"You gonna be okay?'

"I hope so," I said.

As the bailiff handed the jury's verdict to the judge, I swept the jury box, searching for any expression that might give me the slightest hint as to what the verdict was. I knew it was only a matter of seconds before I, as well as everyone else in the room, would learn the outcome, but every second felt more like an hour.

I could not believe that after five months of this crap, Langston was facing this verdict alone. Three frat brothers were in that car with him the day he was arrested, and now he'd been abandoned by every one of them. My son didn't deserve this.

James and his team were assembled behind their table, and I swear they looked relaxed. Were they that confident in their performance? I looked over my shoulder and spotted Jacqueline sitting toward the back. We made eye contact, and she gave me a nod, but her eyes revealed just how nervous she was.

"On the charge of possession of a controlled substance," the judge said, "how do you find?"

The jury foreman was standing to recite the verdict. "We find the defendant guilty."

Chatter rippled through the courtroom, and the scratching sound of reporters scribbling notes became louder, but there was a shrill scream that surpassed every other noise. It was a sound that only a mother could make.

"Oh, Jesus!" Jacqueline screamed before realizing she was still in the courtroom. She quickly put her hand over her mouth.

Langston stood frighteningly still, while Desiree and Lamont looked like they wanted to cry. All I could do was drop my head and close my eyes. Thoughts of what I could have done differently ran through my head. Instead of auditioning Desiree and Lamont to see who would better be suited to take over the firm, perhaps I should have handled Langston's case from the start. I'd honestly had no idea things would get this far.

All of a sudden, I heard a low sound, almost like someone was moaning.

"Noooooooooo."

Then it was louder.

"No!"

My eyes popped open, and I lifted my head to see my oldest son yelling out, distraught over the fate of his baby brother. Once again, I had to close my eyes to lock in the tears that threatened to fall. I was Bradley Hudson, founder and senior partner of Hudson and Associates. I would not let the media portray me as weak at this moment, and I sure as hell wouldn't let James Brown see me cry.

"Possession of a controlled substance. Approximately two kilos of heroin." The judge continued on, overlooking the outcry from Lamont the same way he'd overlooked Jacqueline's.

"Guilty, Your Honor." The foreman delivered the last of the verdicts and then took a seat.

I could feel the sting of each verdict that had been read. By now, Langston had buried his face in his hands. I saw his shoulders heave just slightly. Like father, like son. He refused to shed a tear in the courtroom. I'd done my best with closing arguments, but as the song goes, I guess my best wasn't good enough.

"Jurors, thank you for your time. You are dismissed," the judge said.

Guilty. Fucking guilty. I staggered a bit in disbelief then sat in my chair, unable to move, speak, or even think. Everything around me sounded muffled: my wife in my ear, my daughter gasping, my son saying something inaudible, the reactions of everyone else in the courtroom. It felt as if an elephant were sitting on my chest. I closed my eyes and tried to breathe. I told myself I was having a nightmare and tried to wake up, but the elephant on my chest kept getting heavier. I glanced over at Langston, and the last words out of my mouth were, "I'm sorry, son."

James

62

If I'd ever had a better day in my life, I damn sure didn't remember it. I had won my case, and in the process, beaten the legal system's golden boy, Bradley Hudson, and put his son in jail. Now, the icing on the cake was seeing the EMS staff rushing past with Bradley on a stretcher after his pompous ass had collapsed. With any luck, he'd never see the inside of another courtroom. Now, it was my time to shine. It wasn't Bradley the press was waiting to speak to. It was me.

The number of people shaking my hand or patting my shoulder to congratulate me was countless. I had finally made a name for myself. As I approached the crowded press area outside the courtroom, I straightened my tie. Grace was already standing there waiting. I beamed at her with a prideful smile.

"James, congratulations are in order," she said mildly.

"It was a well-deserved victory for our office, don't you think?" I asked.

"You put up a good fight and didn't waver."

Her lack of excitement was disappointing, but it didn't affect my happiness, which only increased when a tall man in a black wool trenchcoat made his way through the crowd.

"Congratulations, counselor." Russell Jackal held his hand out to me.

"Thank you, sir," I said with pride as we shook hands. "That means a lot."

"Well, this was an impressive case, and you did your thing. We've got some great plans for you over in our office. You've proven that you'll be a valuable asset to our staff," he said, then looked over at Grace. "Hello."

"Asshole," was Grace's response.

Russell's smile faded, but the three of us still turned toward the cameras that were pointed at us and pretended to be a united front.

"You would think you'd be in a better mood, Grace. You do realize your ADA just won a huge case that's been in the headlines for the past six months, right?" Russell asked.

"Don't talk to me," Grace said, her teeth clenched into the fakest smile I'd ever seen.

"Well, I was about to say ladies first and allow you to give your remarks," Russell said.

"I have nothing to say at this time," Grace told him. "I'll let the two of you gloat."

"Fine. Time to give the people what they want." Russell patted me on the back. "Go ahead, James. It's your moment. Make it count."

I walked over to the podium and stood in front of the microphone. The crowd quieted down, and I spoke. "As you all know, today the citizens of New York found Langston Hudson guilty on all charges. This was not an easy case, and our office worked tirelessly over the past few months in order to ensure that we would be successful. I would like to thank the NYPD for their hard work and dedication throughout this process, and the County offices. Because of the teamwork demonstrated, we were able to keep two kilos of heroin off the street. I hope that this case serves as proof that Staten Island DA's office is fair, and we are not biased against race, socioeconomic status, or any other background. If you are breaking the law, then we will convict. Thank you."

"ADA Brown, is it true that Bradley Hudson suffered a heart attack inside the courtroom after losing to you?" one of the reporters yelled.

"It's true that Mr. Hudson did have a medical episode and was removed by medical staff. We are hoping he has a speedy recovery," I said with the best look of concern I could manage to fake.

"Will there be a sentencing recommendation?" another reported asked.

"Do you think the judge will be lenient, considering Mr. Hudson is a first-time offender?" another one yelled.

"That's all we have for now. Again, thank you for your time," I said and stepped away from the microphone.

"Great job," Russell told me.

From the corner of my eye, I saw Jacqueline approaching. I was tempted to turn and run, but I couldn't exactly do that in front of all the press. Her eyes were full of anger, and I prayed that she wasn't about to say anything damaging with all those reporters nearby. Even though she was a smart woman who had more to lose than I did if our recent night of passion got out, she was also a pissed off mother whose son was just put away because of me.

"Hello, Jacqueline, I—"

"Stop it. Don't attempt to be polite and pleasant to me, James, because it's bullshit and you know it." She glared at me, then turned toward Russ. "Russell Jackal. I should've known your ass had something to do with all of this."

"Maybe we should go and talk somewhere a little more private," I suggested, noticing a few of the reporters looking at us.

"But you, Grace, I'm totally surprised that you went along with these two bastards. Three young black men are in jail, and one is dead because of something they didn't even do." Jacqueline shook her head.

"Jacqueline, listen, I'm sorry. I offered them a deal, a hell of a deal, and I was open to negotiating."

Jacqueline cut her eyes at me.

Grace took a step closer and said, "I'm truly sorry, Jackie. But if you find anything to prove those boys had nothing to do with that dope, you call me, and I promise, I'll call the judge and get them out."

Jacqueline didn't respond verbally, but I could see her eyes soften at Grace's statement. She turned and walked away. Grace looked at Russell and me and shook her head. "I want all your things out of my office by Monday, James."

"I wouldn't worry about that, Grace. He'll be out of there way before then. He's only moving across the bridge, and we already have a corner office all set up for him," Russell said.

"I'm sure you do, asshole." Grace walked away.

Michael

63

We were huddled in a waiting room at NYU Medical Center while Bradley underwent surgery for several cardiac blockages. The stress of the trial, his unhealthy eating habits, and cigarettes and cigar smoking had been too much for him. Lamont sat in a corner, not really saying much to anyone, while Perk and Desiree sat together on the sofa. At one point, she rested her head on his shoulder while he rubbed her back. Carla made phone calls in between pacing the floor and walking down the hallway to ask for updates. We hadn't even had time to process and deal with the aftermath of the verdict now that Bradley's life was on the line.

"Is he out yet?" Desiree asked when Carla came back from the nurses' station.

"No, they're still working on him," Carla said.

"They said about four hours, and it's been over five." Desiree sat up on the edge of her seat. "Do you think something happened?"

"No, Des, if something happened, they would've come back and told us." Perk put his arm around her shoulder. "Surgeries always take longer than they anticipate."

Desiree seemed to relax a little. "Yeah, that's true. I remember when Langston got his tonsils out. It was only supposed to take like an hour, and it took three. Dad was freaking out and threatening to sue the surgeon, the hospital, the anesthesiologist, and even the nursing assistants."

"I forgot about that." Lamont's laughter surprised all of us. "He had everyone running scared. Lang had *every* flavor of ice cream on his tray when they brought it to him."

"That's probably why they have us in this fancy waiting room," Desiree said. "They remember Dad's rant."

"Wouldn't you? He was loud enough to wake the dead. As if the fact that he was Bradley Hudson wasn't enough to get people shook." Lamont smiled. "Dad's going to be fine."

"I hope so. Did you see that asshole's face when they were bringing him out?" Desiree said, standing up. "I wanted to smack his smug ass."

"You weren't the only one," I agreed.

We all knew who she was talking about—ADA James Brown. He might have thought he was fooling people with his fake concern in front of the cameras, but everyone in this room knew damn well that inside, that motherfucker was thrilled. While everyone else rushed to Bradley's side after he collapsed, James Brown was too busy shaking hands and making friends. I'd already had a bad vibe about that guy, but now I saw how heinous he really was.

A knock on the waiting room door caused all of us to turn. A nice-looking woman walked in, carrying takeout bags. She looked familiar, but I didn't think much of it until Desiree sprang to her feet.

"Jerri?" She greeted her cautiously. "What are you doing here?"

Oh, shit! I thought. *That's the woman from the elevator.*

"I heard about your father," Jerri said. "I figured you guys would be hungry, so I brought some food. I hope it's okay."

"Thanks," Lamont said, looking at his sister for an introduction.

"Uh, this is my friend, Jerri," Desiree said, and her eyes flashed at me. I looked away in a hurry to avoid the awkwardness.

"Nice to meet you, Jerri," Carla said. "And thanks for the food. I'm not hungry, but I'm sure the guys are."

"You got that right," Perk agreed.

Desiree didn't have much to say as she helped Jerri unload the bags and spread the containers on the table. We were all pretty numb at that point, so there was no small talk as everyone helped themselves to plates of food. Desiree talked quietly to Jerri in the corner, looking nervously toward Perk from time to time. She shot a few more glances in my direction, too, but I think she finally realized I wasn't going to say a word about the elevator incident. No way was I getting in the middle of whatever was going on.

The door opened again, and a doctor in surgical scrubs entered the room.

Carla rushed over to him. "How is he? Is everything okay?"

"Everything is fine. He's stable and in recovery. The surgery went very well."

"Thank God!" Carla clapped her hands and looked upward in praise.

"That's great!" Jerri grabbed Desiree's arm.

"Can we see him?" Desiree asked, nonchalantly pulling away from Jerri.

"Not until the morning. He'll be asleep for a while. Honestly, considering how late it is, the best thing is for you all to go home for the night and come back in the morning, when he'll be moved to a room."

"I'm not going anywhere," Desiree said.

"That's your choice." The doctor shrugged. "But really, there's no need for anyone to stay. I'll keep you updated." He walked out of the room.

"I told you he would pull through," Perk said. "Bradley is a fighter. He wasn't going down like that."

"Yeah, you're right," Lamont said.

With everyone able to breathe a little easier, we began packing up the food and throwing away the trash.

"All right. I'm leaving. I need to call Mom and update her, and I need to make sure Langston knows that Dad is okay. I'll be back in the morning," Lamont said. "Carla, can I give you a ride?"

"You can just take me to get my car from the courthouse. You don't have to take me home." Carla grabbed her coat and put it on. "You gonna be okay here, Des?"

"She'll be okay. I'm with her," Jerri said.

Desiree gave her a weak smile.

That left Perk and me there with Desiree and Jerri. We were cleaning up the rest of the food when Desiree told us, "You guys don't have to stay. You can leave." She looked at Perk and said, "I'm sure Lena is waiting on you."

Perk shook his head. He was about to say something, but his phone rang.

He checked the screen and answered the call. "Nate. What up? Sure, I'll be right down."

Ending the call, he told me, "We gotta go down to the lobby. Nate's waiting for us."

I looked over my shoulder at Desiree as Perk and I left for the lobby. She seemed relieved to see us go.

In the lobby, Nate was waiting for us near the entry.

"Hey, sorry to bother you at a time like this," he said, "but something's been on my mind ever since I gave you that report the other day. I know the verdict was a heavy blow for the Hudsons."

"Okay, talk to me," Perk said.

"I didn't do the report. A friend of mine with the Feds did it down in Quantico," he said.

"Was there something wrong with it?" I asked.

"No, no, the report was fine. The drugs weren't a match."

"So, what's the problem then?" Perk asked, sounding impatient.

"They did match another case the DEA did a few years back. Drugs belonged to a guy by the name of Diego Gonzales."

"Name doesn't ring a bell. You got anything on him?"

"No, just a name. Thought it might help." He shrugged.

"Who knows? It just might," Perk said, then reached into his pocket and handed Nate some money.

Perk

64

I kept thinking about what Nate had said about the heroin they'd found in Langston's car being connected to an old drug case. None of it made sense. There had to be something we were missing. Times like this, I would usually find Bradley in the office and talk it through, but with him in the ICU fighting for his life, I couldn't. Still, I was determined to figure this out, not only for Langston, but for Bradley. I decided to go back to the office and reexamine everything in my files from start to finish.

As I walked down the dark hallway toward my office, I noticed a light coming from under Bradley's door. I stopped, lowering my hand down to my piece, and opened the door without knocking.

"Perk." It was Carla, and she was balled up under a blanket on the leather sofa in Bradley's office. She'd obviously been crying, because her mascara was all over her face. "You damn near scared me to death."

"I didn't think anyone would be here," I said as I stepped inside. "What are you doing here? I thought you'd be at home."

"I couldn't stay in that house without him, Perk, so I came here, to the one place he loved more than the courtroom." She sat up on the sofa, folding the blanket. "I can't tell you how many times I fell asleep on this couch when he worked late."

"I remember," I replied.

"So, why are you tiptoeing in here this late?" She tried to smile, but the poor woman looked heartbroken.

"Couldn't sleep, so I decided to come in for a bit," I said, sitting in one of Bradley's office chairs. "Got some things on my mind about Langston's case that've been bothering me, and I thought coming here might help me to think it through."

"My God, I hate to admit it, but with everything going on with Bradley, I almost forgot about poor Langston," she said with a weary sigh.

"We're missing something, Carla. I can feel it. These boys have been adamant about the drugs not belonging to them. Every last one of them swears they didn't even know they were in the trunk," I said. "Even Tony until today."

"So, maybe one of them is lying. We've all thought that, to be honest."

"Or maybe they're telling the truth. And if that's the case, then those drugs must've already been in the car," I told her. "My source told me tonight those drugs match up with a bust from a few years back, Carla."

"Langston only had the car for two days, and you said it sat on the lot almost six months. We've gone over the previous owners and found nothing. We pulled the VIN report." She got up and stretched, gesturing for me to follow her. "But it does sound like we're missing something."

We walked to the end of the hall and down a flight of stairs, until we reached a door with a keypad lock. The room lit up the moment we came through the door. It looked like something out of NASA with all the computers and big screens on the wall. We walked to her office, which had another keypad lock, and then she sat down behind her sleek, modern desk.

She reached into a tall stack of folders piled at the edge of her desk and took one out. "Previous owner was Leonard Gazda. We ran a background check on him. He's clean. Married, two kids, works as a marketing director for a furniture company in Hartford, Connecticut."

"Leonard Gazda. Are you sure he's clean?" I asked, taking the folder from her and flipping through it. There was a full background check, with all his information, including his driver's license. I had the exact same paperwork in my own file, so I knew she was right.

She began typing on her computer. "The guy's a Scout leader with no record. Hell, he's never even gotten a parking ticket, and you know that's damn near impossible."

"Have you ever been to Hartford? It's possible," I joked, in a failed attempt to lighten the mood. "You said he's married. What about his wife? Did we check her out?"

"His wife Delia is just as clean as he is. She works as a church administrator and has no criminal background either," Carla said.

"Does he have any family ties to the Mob or organized crime, maybe?" I suggested.

"None. We've gone over them with a fine-tooth comb. They had the car for two years, regular maintenance with the records to prove it when the car was traded in. Routine oil changes, tire rotations, and tune-ups. Car was in pristine condition and sat in the back of the dealership. You've seen the car lot surveillance. The car was never moved until Jacqueline purchased it. To be honest, she got a hell of a deal," Carla said. "And we got a dead end."

I told her, "There's one thing Jaqueline has been on me about since day one: she said, 'Find the source of the drugs and you solve the case.' So, my guy just told me the drugs match a federal bust of a guy named Diego Gonzales."

She typed the name into her computer. "A Diego Gonzales was arrested in Trenton, New Jersey in 2014, along with three other men: Manny Gonzales, Pedro Gonzales, and Dominic Gonzales. He's presently serving a twenty-five-year sentence in Petersburg, Virginia for RICO charges, among other things." Carla looked up at me. "Perk, I think this guy is the key."

"Yeah, so do I. I think I'm going to pick up Michael and head to Virginia in the morning. It'll be easier to see him if I have a lawyer with me." I massaged my tired eyes. "Dammit, why couldn't we have gotten this break a month ago?"

"I was just thinking the same thing. But, Perk, this could also turn out to be nothing. I mean, who knows what this Diego Gonzales is going to say. He's been in jail almost four and a half years."

I sat back and processed everything Carla was saying. Then, I sat up in my seat, flipping through the folder again. "Wait, you said this Leonard Gazda cat had the car for two years, right?"

"Yeah." Carla nodded.

"But the car was three years old," I said.

"Gazda purchased it after it came off a lease. It wasn't new."

"Who had the car before that?" I asked. "Did you do a background?"

"We did, and the original owner of the car was Sky Baronet. She was just as clean as Leonard Gazda. So's her family."

"You checked her credit history? Seems like she leased the car for an unusually short time."

"She only had it for about six months," Carla said.

"Any idea why she turned it in so fast?"

Carla shook her head, looking kind of embarrassed to admit, "I didn't even think to look into that."

"Don't feel bad," I told her. "I didn't even realize before now that Gazda wasn't the first owner. Once I saw that the car hadn't moved from the lot, I kind of moved on to other angles and didn't even think about the car again."

We shared a look of regret.

"Can't hurt to check into her again," she said, clicking her mouse to navigate through a few screens. Then she began typing faster. A new page popped up, and after she read it, she looked confused.

"What is it?" I leaned closer to the screen.

"The car was returned to the dealership after only six months," Carla said.

"You already knew that. So, she can't handle money. That doesn't help us," I said.

Carla shook her head. "But it says here her credit history is fine. No blemishes, no repossession."

This was confusing. Why would she turn in a car after only six months if it wasn't about money? "Can you run a check, see if there are any connections between her and Diego Gonzalez?"

Carla entered some more info and clicked through a few more screens.

"Oh my fucking God!" she yelled.

"What? What?"

"Sky Baronet was never arrested, but she did call the cops once on her boyfriend, Manny Gonzales."

I felt my heartbeat quicken. We were onto something. "The same Manny Gonzalez who was arrested with Diego Gonzalez?"

"Looks like it."

"What did they seize after the Gonzalez bust?" I asked, and she began typing.

"They seized four cars, a house, and confiscated sixty-eight kilos of heroin."

I locked eyes with her, almost afraid to believe we'd finally found the evidence we'd been looking for all along.

"Carla, the drugs in Langston's car match the drugs seized from Gonzalez. Can you verify that the car Jacqueline bought was one of the cars seized after his arrest?"

"I can't do that. I can't hack the Feds."

"Huh? Why? I seen you hack all kinds of stuff."

"Yeah, state and local stuff," she said. "But we hack the Feds and get caught, they will shut us down. The last thing we need is for my ex-husband to have a reason to be on our ass."

"Yeah, Russell Jackal ain't no joke," I agreed. "But if you can't do it, I know someone who can." I reached for my cell and dialed a number.

"Hello?" I could tell by her tone she was pissed I'd called so late.

"Jacqueline, if you want Langston out of jail, I'm gonna need your help."

Langston

65

It had been less than forty-eight hours since I was convicted on all charges by a supposed jury of my peers. I was still in a state of disbelief about that and my father's heart attack. I was starting to understand why Krush had killed himself. Sometimes life just wasn't worth living.

I'd decided to venture outside for some yard time. Summer was in full effect, although the sea air was much cooler than I'd anticipated. I looked around the yard, rubbing my hands together to warm them a bit as I began walking. Over in the corner, I saw a group of men clustered together, all wearing the familiar kufis. Among them was Kwesi, whose eyes caught mine. I quickly looked away, remembering the last interaction that had taken place between us. I began walking in the opposite direction.

"Langston," he called out.

I turned to see Kwesi headed toward me. My first reaction was to ignore him, but for some reason, I couldn't. Despite how he'd treated me and everything that had happened, I still felt some small tug of loyalty to someone I once considered a brother. I would at least hear him out.

"What's up?" I said, my voice void of any emotion.

"Just seeing how you're holding up. I heard about the verdict and your father. I hope he's okay. He's a good man," he told me.

"Yeah, he is, but I'm good." I turned to walk away, but he put a hand on my arm to stop me.

"Lang, I . . . we . . . man, I'm sorry." He sighed. "I hate that this happened, and—"

"Yeah, we all are," I told him.

"They transferred Tony to the barge in the Bronx this morning."

"I heard." Knowing that Tony wouldn't be anywhere near me made me feel better. It meant that I wouldn't run the risk of crossing paths and putting my hands on his ass. I wasn't a fighter

by nature, but the level of anger and hurt that I still harbored for
him guaranteed I would fuck him up on sight.

"It's just crazy. A couple of months ago, you were planning
graduation, and I was going to be chapter president and finish
up my senior year. And now, Krush is dead, and the three of us
are serving time for something we didn't even do." Kwesi shook
his head. "Damn, I can't believe Krush is gone."

"Me neither," I said, feeling that old pull of brotherhood. No
matter how things had turned out, his death had been a significant loss for all of us.

"I think it would've made more sense to people if I had done
that instead of him," Kwesi said.

I'd thought something similar on more than one occasion.
Krush had always appeared to be a strong dude who could hold
his own, whereas Kwesi seemed to be the softest one of our bunch.

"Nah, you're stronger than everyone thinks, Kwesi. I learned
that while we were pledging. If you weren't strong, you definitely
wouldn't have made it across those sands, and you know it." I
gave him a halfhearted smile.

"They could have allowed us to go to the funeral though, Lang. I
would have liked to have paid my respects and said a final goodbye."

"Man, his parents wasn't having none of that. They weren't
gonna let us anywhere near that service. Hell, they ain't even
let my parents come, and they offered to help pay for the
arrangements," I said. "But, I guess it's understandable. It's a
messed-up situation all the way around."

"And now, here we are." Kwesi's smile faded a bit.

"Let me ask you a question."

"Go ahead." Kwesi shrugged.

"You think that it really was Krush's dope? Maybe that's why
he took himself out; because he was guilty?" I stared at Kwesi
and waited for his answer. Out of all of us, Kwesi had been the
most level-headed and honest.

He was quiet for a few seconds and then said, "No, I don't
believe they were. It's no secret that Krush kept weed. He couldn't
keep quiet about anything he did. If that was really his dope, we
would've known. I think the pressure of being in here and the lack
of support from his family, especially his pops, really got to him.
He started crumbling, especially after that fight."

"You're right. Then after that guy Meat testified against him
that day in court, I guess it got to be too much. I wish . . . man, I
don't know." I sighed.

"It would be more plausible for that dope to have been Tony's," Kwesi suggested.

I frowned. "You think? Nah, not Tony."

"I mean, he did plead guilty, and then he flipped it and put it on you."

"Come on, Kwesi. You did the same damn thing." I tensed up a bit, wondering how Kwesi, who was the first one to take the deal, was calling Tony out.

"It was Tony who snitched, Lang, not me. I was never going to testify against you. And I didn't plead guilty to anything," he said.

"What do you mean you didn't plead guilty? Your ass is in here with me." I was confused.

"I pleaded no contest, and my charges were reduced as part of that plea. They wanted me to talk and make up a story, but I refused. There is a thing called loyalty to your brothers."

"Damn." For a second, I felt as if I'd been punched right in the stomach. The entire time, I had thought that Kwesi turned State's witness, but he hadn't.

"I did what I had to do," he said. "And so did you, I guess."

"But we were innocent, and we should've stuck together. The verdict might've been different," I said, afraid to admit to myself that maybe I should have taken the deal just like he had.

"Might? I couldn't take a chance on might, Langston. You took a chance on might, and you're here facing twenty years. I'm about to get out in less than one."

The reality of his statement was sobering. Had I not been so hell bent on proving my innocence, things could have turned out differently.

"You're right," I said sadly. Then I asked, "Do you think we'll ever find out where the hell that dope came from?"

Kwesi shrugged. "Probably not. But at this point, does it even matter?"

"I guess not. But, Kwesi, just so you know, I wasn't trying to jump bail and leave you guys hanging. I'd never do that. It was stupid of me to even go along with Simone's idea to get away for the weekend. I wanna say I'm—"

"No need for all of that. We're good, Lang." Kwesi reached over, and we exchanged the fraternity grip he had denied the last time we were face to face. My life was much different now, but some things were still the same, and for that, I was grateful.

"I do have something to ask you, bro," Kwesi said.

"What's that?"

"There's a rumor going around here that you snuck outta here one night to go have a lobster dinner with your moms. Is it true?"

I thought about that night my mother arranged and the trouble she could get into if I confirmed the story. I hated having to lie to my fraternity brother, especially since we had just resolved our issues, but I didn't have a choice.

"Kwesi, my mother may have some influence, but do you think she could pull that off?"

He raised an eyebrow as if to say, "Yeah, I do."

"Nah, it ain't true. I ain't have no lobster dinner with my mom."

As we stood laughing, I realized that it wasn't a lie after all. My mom and I had feasted on a lot of things that night, but lobster wasn't one of them.

"Hudson, Adomako!" A CO called our names, and we walked over to him. "Come with me."

"Where are we going?" I asked as he placed cuffs on us.

"To hell, if you don't pray," he shot back. "Now, stop asking so many damn questions and do what I tell you."

I shook my head and kept my mouth shut. This was my new reality, and I would have to learn to deal with this disrespect daily.

He led us inside, then down quite a few corridors and through some gates before I realized we were headed to the same location where I had been turned over to the marshals that night. Maybe Mom had set up another feast to cheer me up.

Once through the final gate, I almost fainted from surprise. It wasn't marshals who were there to greet me. It was my mother, with Perk, Desiree, Lamont, Carla, and Simone. Kwesi's parents were there too.

"What's going on?" I asked as Mom came up and gave me a hug.

"You're being released on your own recognizance, pending a hearing tomorrow, when the judge will set aside your verdict."

My head was swimming. I couldn't even process this news. "Released? Set aside my verdict? How? Why?"

My mother glanced over at the others. "Perk and Carla. It was more their doing than mine, with a little help from District Attorney Grace Frazier."

"I don't understand," I said.

"Come on. We'll explain it to you in the car. Let's get you to the hospital. Your father wants to see you."

I didn't argue. I just lifted my hands so the CO could remove the cuffs, and Kwesi did the same. We gave each other one last frat grip before we were surrounded by our loved ones.